THE ART OF MURDER
IN THE MUSEUM
OF MAN

ALFRED ALCORN

COLRAIN PRESS

For Jack Estes

The following account of the events that transpired at the Museum of Man, Wainscott University and the city of Seaboard in the aftermath of the financial crisis of 2008 has been drawn from contemporaneous media reporting, my own vivid memories, and other reliable sources. I am particularly indebted to Lieutenant Richard Tracy of the Seaboard Police Department for granting me access to the various case files, some of which contained significant addenda drawn from the state police and, however severely redacted, from the Federal Bureau of Investigation. Along the way invaluable assistance was rendered by my friend and adoptee Alphus de Ratour and by my ever patient wife Diantha Winslow. Where deemed necessary, several names have been changed to protect the publisher from litigation. Any missteps are those of the author.

Norman de Ratour

1

The shot slammed against the stone wall inches from my nose. For several seconds I did not know what had happened. My straw hat fell off and I stood stunned, the loud crack of a gun reverberating like an aural hallucination. Blood began to ooze down either side of my face from my forehead, lacerated by a fragment of rock or bullet. That damn Donny Blanchard, I cursed to myself with familiar irritation. Up on the ridge, blasting away with one of his damn rifles.

When I turned to shout in the direction of the shooter, a second round whistled close by my face and again cracked against the old foundation wall where I was tending the apple trees espaliered there. With incredulous shock I realized that someone was shooting at me.

No movie director needed to tell me to duck and run. I moved spontaneously as a third shot went humming by my head. In a scampering crouch I reached the back door of the cottage. Locked! I ducked and ran to safety behind the oak at the side of the driveway. I paused to catch my breath which was escaping in heaving puffs. Only a few feet of exposure remained between where I estimated the sniper to be shooting from and the sanctuary of the porch and front door. I ducked and ran again. I made it unscathed into the cottage, my heart pumping madly. I tasted my own blood and amazement afresh: Someone was trying to kill me!

I find that words trip over one another as I attempt to describe the progression of emotions that rattled me those first few moments of the attack. Panic, of course, that crippling mix of fear and helplessness and confusion. But also the exhilaration of rage I had experienced the day I shot the mobster Freddie Bain at point-blank range. As then, I wanted to shoot back.

At the same time, like any other law-abiding citizen in those circumstances, I would have picked up the phone and called the police. But we had terminated the land line the year before and all I had was an unreliable pocket phone. But where was it? I had used it that morning to attend to some business at the museum. I tore around the place, looking in all the usual places. No phone. Again, an incipient panic began to make my knees inadequate and my stomach queasy because...

Because circumstances made it impossible for me to make a run for it. My wife Diantha, our two children, and their nanny were en route from Seaboard and I could not intercept them as there was more than one way to reach the cottage. They could come directly, meaning they would arrive from the north on our small road. Or they could go by the village should they need anything at Abe's Seed and Supplies, an old-fashioned general store, meaning they would arrive from the south. Moreover, my assailant would be able to reposition himself for a good shot if I stood in the road and flagged them down or if I tried to get in my old Renault and drive away.

I had no recourse but the Smith & Wesson I keep locked and unloaded in a drawer in the bedroom. I went up the stairs in bounds with an energy that only fear and danger to loved ones can engender. My fingers shook as I picked out the brass-jacketed bullets and inserted them into their snug chambers. I put the rest of the box into the pocket of the windbreaker I was wearing over my plaid work shirt. The heavy, fitted feel of the revolver in my hand had a calming effect. It gave focus to my anger.

Still, it was an enterprise sicklied o'er with the pale cast of second thoughts. Surely the shooter, anticipating the imminent arrival of the authorities -- he didn't know I could not find my phone -- would be tearing away from the scene of his crime. But if not, what was a handgun against a rifle, one probably fitted with a scope? I would be a sizable sitting duck even as I ran. I wouldn't know what hit me.

On the other hand... The gunman had missed me twice while I was relatively stationary. Something didn't tally. Not that I was very good at this kind of addition. Indeed, as I thought about it, the surreality of what was happening struck me anew. Then the reality. Anger again rose with the acridity of bile. How dare someone shoot at me! How dare he threaten me and my family! I would hunt him down and shoot him like a dog! Like I had shot Freddie Bain.

With anger cooling to resolve, I checked myself in the mirror near the front door. I looked a mess. Trickles of blood from my slashed brow, now drying, etched both sides of my long face and made lines between my pale eyes and around my thin, prominent nose. Was this, I wondered in that speculating part of the brain that never shuts up, the origin of war paint?

War is what it felt like as I went out the front door in a running crouch, my revolver in hand, pointed down and out, the way they do in movies. Except for another brief stretch, I had cover behind a hedge of arborvitae that needed trimming as I made my way along one side of the driveway to the road. There I dithered as an inner voice all but shouted at me to go back to the cottage. Ransack the place. Find the phone. Call Diantha. Call the sheriff.

But I had no choice. I inhaled deeply. I ran across the road, nearly fell into a weed-clogged ditch I had forgotten about, and found myself in the glade of hardwood saplings that bordered the lake beyond our frontage. I moved along the edge of the trees, hiding as best I could until I came to the old logging road that follows behind the ridge. The ridge, I should explain, is a pine-covered esker, a formation left behind by the melt water of glaciers. About twenty feet high and ten feet across, it snakes around the back of the garden and ends in an overgrown gravel pit near the main road. I darted across to the where an old logging road opened and, using what cover I had, made my way along the base of the ridge toward where the shots came from. Fresh tire tracks showed on the spongy, leaf-littered surface, which smelled pleasantly of moss and rot.

I edged along the side of this vague road, keeping out of sight until, with shock and surprise, I saw a vehicle in my path. He was still around! Waiting for me no doubt, my face already in the crosshairs of his scope. My adrenaline, nearly at full pump, notched up and I stopped again to catch my breath. Think, I told myself, think, as I moved back into better cover and tried to calm down. It was then that I realized that my apparent fearlessness hinged on the expectation that the miscreant had fled the scene.

I moved closer to get a better view of the vehicle, one of those boxy, off-road things. I committed its license plate to memory. But again, I wavered. Was it not the height of folly to confront someone with a high-powered rifle? I could still retreat and warn Diantha. If I could intercept her. But how? Stand in the road in front of the cottage waving a red flag?

Again my anger stoked itself. Some lowlife was trying to murder me. I knew how to handle my weapon. And if he had the advantage at a distance, I had the edge close in. And I was close in. My calculations had a snarling bravado to them that made me wonder if, in the darker reaches of my being, I relished this confrontation, because I wanted, man-to-man and mano-a-mano, to wreak my vengeance at close range.

Cautiously, moving from tree to tree, my gun up and cocked, I crept nearer the jeep-like thing. I peered quickly through the windows. It was empty except for some haphazard stuff and an open rifle case lying across the backseat. He was still around! My stomach heaved. Anger and fantasies of revenge do not sustain action. But the courage that comes with fear for one's loved ones does. Keeping near the logging road but well out of sight, I crept like an Indian brave toward the ridge. I climbed as noiselessly as I could on the pine needled ground. I stopped again, this time behind the trunk of a tree.

It was then that I sensed something amiss. It didn't add up. The sniper must have known that he had bungled the job and that I had, at the very least, summoned the authorities. Unless, of course, that wasn't his car. Or that he had fled on foot. But why?

Trying not to make a sound, I moved through the gloom of the woods toward the spot from where I estimated the shots to have come. Splinters of light showed through the pines near the top of the ridge. I stopped and peered around carefully. Nothing. Except... There was movement in a tree close to the rounded top of the ridge. With my heart thumping and my hand firmly grasping the revolver, I slid to my right and drew closer. Closer still. Until...

Until, there he was, up in a noble pine, the bottoms of his boots a good fifteen feet off the ground, a heavy man of middle years with black hair and a pudgy, rough, reddish face. He wore coveralls of camouflaged material, the back strap of which had apparently snagged on the end of one of the short, dead branches that stud the trunks of forest evergreens. A light-weight, telescoping aluminum ladder leaned propped against the trunk just to one side of where he hung. He squirmed mightily as on a hook, backlit against the sky, holding his scoped rifle in one hand and trying to extend the other to grasp the ladder. It was just out of reach and there were no tree limbs handy on which he could brace his feet to prop himself up and off.

Now what? It's one thing to find the culprit, even in such a disadvantageous position, but it's quite another, as the police will tell you, to apprehend him. I moved closer and positioned myself just off to one side, no more than forty feet from the tree onto which he was stuck.

I knelt and pondered. Would I have enough time to hurry back and find the phone? Surely, if he got out of the tree without breaking a leg, he would beat a hasty retreat. On the other hand, if, while I drove to a neighbor in search of a phone, Diantha and the children arrived...

That would have been the sensible thing to do. But I was no longer sensible. I wanted to kill my attacker or, at the very least, to humiliate him, to make him crawl -- by using bullets if words did not suffice. The gun felt like part of my hand, my arm, my seething heart. Bang! You're dead.

Instead, without revealing myself, I called loudly, "I think you had better drop that rifle."

He looked around wildly, his face contorting with frustration. He lifted the rifle and had his finger on the trigger. He was one of those people who look naturally belligerent, the small eyes slightly protuberant, alert, and baleful. He appeared to have little or no neck as his head pivoted around like a ball in a socket.

When he paused in his casting about, I called again, "Drop the rifle or I'll shoot you." And cursed the lack of conviction in my voice.

He looked in my direction without seeing me. He gave a loud snarl ending with, "Who the fuck are you?"

"I could ask you the same question."

"Yeah, you could." He kept peering in my direction. "Listen, pal, you don't know who you're messing with." He spoke in a townie Boston accent.

Given the distance, we were not so much calling as speaking with the volume up. I said, "Then please tell me with whom I am messing."

"I ain't telling you jack shit." And with that he aimed the rifle with a quick if awkward motion in my direction and fired. The gun made a sharp crack amidst the trees.

I crouched, took aim, and fired back at a spot just above his head. I was, I told myself, being polite.

"You bastard!" he shouted as bits of bark showered down on him. Then, with the rifle still in an awkward position, he chambered another shell, aimed it in my direction and fired again. It whizzed by very close to my head.

You can imagine my surprise. I had him dead to rights and he was not following the script. I felt like I had walked into one of those absurdist plays prevalent in France some years back. Had Jean Paul Sartre written something titled *L'impasse dans la forêt*? I certainly hadn't counted on this. I'm not sure what I expected. Certainly not the sinister crack of the guns, which lent a fearful aspect to the whole business. My better self neither wanted to wound or kill him nor be wounded or killed myself. But my better self had receded and the ur-Viking in me, antecedents of my Norman forebears, had begun to emerge. The blood I tasted was my own.

At least, I thought, he knows I have a gun. If he gets himself out of the tree, he will no doubt get in his vehicle and drive off. I watched as he took bullets out of a side pocket and carefully insert them into the magazine of the rifle. He worked the bolt. This time his bullet slapped close again into a nearby tree.

I fired back, aiming even closer and moved again. It was then, with the blood throbbing through me, that I realized with a jolt of surprise that I was enjoying myself. It was not, to be sure, the enjoyment of a splendid meal or of some well-timed witticism amid good company. It was something more visceral, perhaps the pleasure of a game with the highest possible stakes, a game seasoned with anger, thirst for vengeance, and fear. "Drop the rifle or I'll keep shooting until I hit you," I yelled.

"You don't have the balls."

I fired again, aiming up between his swinging legs.

"Neither will you," I said as he twisted around violently, almost reaching the ladder. His face had flamed red with rage and frustration. I took a deep breath. I moved up closer but kept out of sight. I asked as civilly as I could, "Just who the hell are you?"

"None of your fucking business."

"I beg to differ... "

"You beg what? Christ, who the hell *are* you?"

"I'm Norman de Ratour. Perhaps you have the wrong party... "

"Ratour. Nah, that sounds about right. And that's your place down there?"

"It is."

"Ratour. You're the guy."

As he again worked the bolt of his rifle, I moved into deeper cover where I could see him but he couldn't see me. The game, the ultimate game, was on in earnest. But in fact, he had seen me. He brought the rifle up and, aiming through the scope, he fired. The bullet clipped the brush just over my head.

At one level, as they say, it felt as though I had been tele-transported by a dream machine to an alternate universe, a nightmare or a daymare too real not to be real and at the same time utterly unreal. These sorts of things happen in movies or novels. But I knew it was real as I could hear the squawk of a nuthatch. I could smell the rich decay of fungus around me. I could see the blue sky and a wisp of cloud. Then it was back to my unreal reality. I would try to disable him with my next shot. Or kill him.

I moved quickly back behind the trunk of a pine. I yelled, "How do you know I haven't called the police and they're on their way as we speak?"

"Because I don't hear any sirens and you woulda told me right off if they were on their way. Face it, pal, you're going to have to kill me."

"No, I don't," I said, contradicting him with words instead of bullets. "I just need to wound you."

"Yeah, you do that and I'll sue your ass off."

"This is my property and I'm defending myself."

"Sure. Try telling that to the judge. Either way, man, you're in deep shit."

"At least I'm still alive."

"Not for long."

I took a deep breath. I said, "Listen, whoever you are, if I have to kill you, I will." And found I meant it.

"As I said, pal, you don't have the balls."

With that I crawled to a mushroom-festooned log lying along the ground amidst a tangle of shrub-sized hemlocks, took careful aim and fired again. This time I made the bark of the tree just under his crotch explode with wood and bark.

"Hey, watch where you're shooting!"

I moved quickly out of the line of fire to one side. I could see him clearly, his face in profile. I watched as he chambered another round.

We remained silent for several minutes. Then, trying to stay sane, I said, loudly but calmly, "We have to talk."

"Yeah. About what? The Red Sox?"

"Our situation."

"So go ahead and talk."

I said, "Do you mind if I ask why are you trying to kill me?"

"Do you mind if I ask," he repeated in mincing tones, mocking me. "Man, you are a piece of work." He leaned his head back and gave an audible sigh. Presently, he said, "It's just a job."

"Just a job?"

"Just a job."

"And that doesn't bother you?"

"Why should it bother me?"

"I'm an innocent man."

"Yeah, sure."

"Seriously."

He thought for a moment. "Okay, the way I figure it, the government hires and trains guys to go out and kill people. And they give them the best equipment and all kinds of medals if they kill a lot of people."

"But those are our enemies."

"Yeah, and you're somebody's enemy."

"But whose?"

"Beats me, pal."

I thought for a moment. "So you kill people for money?"

"Damn right. Only weirdoes do it for nothing."

"Have you killed many people?"

"Quite a few. Yeah, quite a few. All over the country. This one time, down in the Everglades, you know, in Florida, there was this Cuban honcho... But I shouldn't be talking about it. I mean they could make a movie about what I've done. Maybe do a television series. You know, like CSI."

I didn't know, but I asked, "Did you take notes?"

"Nah, but I've got a good memory. I need one of those people who... "

"A ghost writer."

"Yeah, a ghost writer."

I had calmed down. I said, "Look, whoever you are, I don't want to get hurt and I don't want you to get hurt."

"Boy, you really are an a-hole. What are you, some kind of professor?"

"No, I'm the director of the Museum of Man in Seaboard." Voicing that gave me an unexpected pang of pride and confidence.

"Really?"

"Really. But it's no reason to kill me."

"Yeah. You'd be surprised at the reasons people get whacked."

"Well, for what reason I am getting whacked?"

"Beats me. Maybe because of the way you talk."

That irked me. But I resisted shooting at him again. Instead, I said quite loudly, "That may be, sir, but to defend myself and my family I will not hesitate to shoot at you until you are nothing but a bleeding corpse."

He pondered for a moment, his brows knit in a parody of apparent thought. "Okay, maybe I could make an exception. Maybe we could make a deal. First, though, you really don't know who you're messing with. I've got deep, deep cover."

"Do you work for the government?"

"I wouldn't go that far."

"How far would you go?"

"Let's just say if anything happens to me, you'll be in a lot of trouble."

"You mean they might send someone out to finish the job?"

"I ain't saying."

"So it looks like I'm in deep trouble either way."

"Yeah, you could say that."

"So I have nothing to lose by killing you or maiming you in some unspeakable way."

"Unspeakable, huh?" But it gave him pause. I watched as he reached into a pocket with his free hand and take out a pack of cigarettes. He managed to shake one loose, but it dropped to the ground. "Damn," he cursed.

I said, "I'd really appreciate it if you didn't smoke."

"Yeah, I'm trying to quit."

"I mean, it's been fairly dry and if a fire got started, it will be your goose that gets…"

He thought for a moment. "Yeah, you got something there." After a silence, he said, "This your place?"

"Actually, it's my wife's."

"Many acres?"

"About a hundred."

"Nice. Lake frontage?"

"Enough to keep it private."

"Yeah, I noticed."

"So what's your name?"

He thought for a moment. "Call me Sweeney."

"So tell me, Mr. Sweeney…"

"Just Sweeney."

"Okay, Sweeney, who hired you to shoot at me."

"You want the truth, I don't know. A guy shows up. We meet in South Station, but back-to-back in the waiting area. He gives me your name and where I can find you and ten grand in fifties."

"That's all it costs?"

"Nah, I get another ten grand once the job's done. And the job always gets done. I'm the best in the business."

"If you're so good, how come you missed me?"

He hesitated. "Probably the scope." He positioned the gun in front of him and looked along the barrel. "I think it needs to be realigned."

It didn't sound convincing somehow. I asked, "So how would I get in touch with you about a job?"

"Why? You want someone whacked?"

"Not at the moment."

"Okay. You gotta know people who know people."

"And how do you get to know people who know people?"

"Go to Southie… "

"Southie?"

"South Boston."

"I see."

"And ask for the Birdman."

"The Birdman?"

"Yeah, that should do it."

"But you don't know who hired you and you don't know me?"

"Nope. And don't want to."

"Doesn't that bother you?"

"What?"

"Killing someone you don't know."

"It's the other way around. I don't kill people I know. Unless it's necessary. And then I usually charge extra. Hey, look, it's a job. I provide a service."

"So, you're in the service industry?" I was being sardonic, but he went on in all reasonableness.

"Exactly. You want bookkeeping done, you call an accountant. You want to sell your house, you call a realtor. You want someone whacked, you come to me. Face it, somebody's gotta do it." He paused as though thinking about what he had said. "The way I figure it, the mark doesn't know what hit him. He's here and then he ain't here. I mean, compare that to sitting on death row for ten years staring at the walls knowing that someday, maybe soon, your lousy luck is going to run out and they're going to strap you to a table, swab your arm, that's so you don't get an infection, ha, ha, and then stick you with the big needle. Besides, it's mostly bad guys who hire me to whack other bad guys. It's business."

"But I'm not a bad guy."

"Yeah, somebody thinks you're a bad guy."

Out to the blue, the cerulean blue of the waking dream in which I found myself, I asked him, "Do you enjoy killing people?"

He managed a hanging shrug. Then, "Yeah, sometimes. I'm a pro. I take pride in my work. I'm considered the best. I'm the Tom Brady of hitmen."

"You're an artist."

"I don't paint pictures, but you could say that. Yeah, there's a nice jolt when you see the mark drop and you know he ain't gonna get up. I mean wouldn't you if you had my job?"

I thought for a moment. We had in this curious interlude created a sphere of complete freedom in which I could say anything I wanted to. I said, "I've already done it."

"Yeah, sure. When did you ever pop someone?"

"I shot and killed Freddie Bain. And I took pleasure in it. He was threatening the woman I love the same way you are right now."

"You're the guy that capped Freddie?"

"I'm the guy that capped Freddie."

"I don't believe it."

"Right, and you won't be able to when I do the same to you." A version of myself I usually keep locked in the basement of my psyche was emerging. "So drop the rifle or I'll put a bullet in your heart or between your eyes."

"Hey, listen…"

"No more listening. You forfeited your life the moment you climbed that tree and aimed your weapon at me."

"It wasn't like that. I wasn't going to kill you."

"I don't believe you."

A chickadee landed on a branch not far from the rifleman and chirped at him as though he were a fellow bird. Sweeney looked around for me and said, obviously changing the subject, "How come you didn't call the cops when you made it into the house?"

"I couldn't find my cellphone. And it doesn't work that well out here anyway."

"Yeah, those things are overrated, I don't care what they say. And I'll bet there ain't much for cops out here, anyway."

"True. The local sheriff… But the state police know what they're doing."

"Too true."

The chickadee flew away. Into a gathering silence, I said, "Well, we've got a choice."

He was suddenly alert. "What do you mean?"

"I mean we can continue to shoot at each other until one of us gets hit. In either case, Sweeney, you'll still be up in a tree. And, to tell you the truth, I could maim you badly or even kill you if, say, I hit you in the heart."

"Yeah, so what are the other choices?"

"First, you have to give up your weapon."

"No way, José."

"Okay, then, what do you suggest?"

He thought for a few minutes. A shrewd look crossed his face. "Okay, here's the deal. You move the ladder under where my feet can reach it. You walk away. I get down out of here, and I walk away. We call it even."

"But how do I know you won't shoot me the minute I have the ladder in place?"

"You have to trust me."

"Then we have a problem."

"Yeah, but look at it from my side. How do I know you won't take my rifle and go call the cops?"

"You have to trust me."

"Then we still have a problem."

Awkwardly, holding the rifle with one hand, Sweeny reached into his pocket with the other and extracted the cigarette pack again. "Yeah, yeah, I know, no smoking, but I gotta think."

His nonchalance irked me. "Listen, Sweeny, I don't care if you barbecue yourself, but I greatly value these woods and the cottage."

"Yeah, and why don't you go fuck yourself."

It wasn't so much the language as the arrogance behind his words that lit a fuse of anger inside of me. I drew a bead on his heart using the crude sight at the tip of the revolver's barrel. I cocked the revolver. "I mean it, no matches."

"I mean it, no matches," he mocked. "Yeah, and a guy like you took out Freddie Bain." He shook the pack and managed to get another cigarette out far enough to take between his lips. Trying to put the pack back in his shirt pocket, he dropped it. "Damn!"

I waited and watched, my finger against the trigger. "Don't light it," I said loudly, "or I'll shoot."

He ignored me and with studied patience, fumbled a book of matches out of the breast pocket of his coveralls. I wanted to shoot the man. I wanted to kill him at that instant as a quiet rage went seething through me. And I might have had I not been seized by a curiosity as to how he might light a match. So I watched, revolver cocked and ready as he cradled the rifle in the crook of one arm and used both hands to open the matchbook, tear out a match and strike it. Which he did, the flare coming at the same instant that the rifle slipped from its precarious perch and dropped straight down, stock first.

I'm afraid again that mere words are not adequate to catch the absence of time it took for the weapon's impact with the ground followed by the jarring noise and the flash of sound instantaneous with the bullet catching him under the chin and jerking his head back simultaneous with a bursting blister of bone, blood, and brains as it exited the top of his skull. His ruined mouth, open as though in surprise, filled with blood that spilled out in a gush. He slumped forward away from the trunk of the pine and hung there, dripping gore, a grotesque effigy.

I stood abruptly and then knelt on the forest floor, my own brain a confusion of thoughts and emotions taking turns as I tried to assimilate what had just happened. Shock, of course, but also relief, disbelief, and, curiously, disappointment. Had I really wanted to shoot him myself?

I would examine my scruples or lack of them later. I got up and went to make sure the lit match had not survived to start a fire. I found nothing. Flies had already begun to buzz around the body hanging on the tree. With a crown of blood and with arms down and away it looked like a backwoods crucifixion. Not that there was anything remotely Christ-like about this man who had made his living by murdering.

Such thoughts and impressions crowded the sensory overload that came in waves of questions and a bafflement as to what had happened. At the same time, I grew preternaturally aware of the day and of the life around me. It being early September, a hectic note rang in the call of the jays that carried with piercing clarity in the cool air. The carpet of pine needles underfoot had the pungency of long ago. And, with summer's lease giving way to chill, cricket-loud nights, I could see that the lowlands near the pond, where the cold air gathers, were already painted with swaths of red and orange.

The slam of a car door brought me out of my stupor.

I walked to the top of the ridge. From there, as though at a remove seen through binoculars, Diantha, the children, and Bella Martinez, their nanny, had emerged from the SUV. It was parked behind my dusty Renault like a great glossy bug with its wing coverlets spread.

Still shaky, I knelt in dappled light and watched as they unloaded weekend luggage and several bags of groceries. I watched as Diantha went into the cottage and came out again, stepping around to the garden and casting about. Her voice, calling my name reached me distinctly through the pristine air and jarred me awake as from a living dream. I took several deep breaths. I looked around. I would leave everything exactly as it was -- the rifle, the vehicle, the body propped on the tree still dripping blood. I put the revolver in my belt and started back down.

In a state of persisting incredulity, I was walking past the off-road thing on the logging road, when the cellphone, which had been in my shirt pocket the whole time, began to vibrate. I ignored it and kept going.

Diantha, peering at the small screen of her own do-everything device, glanced up just as I turned from the road into the driveway. "Norman. Norman! Good God! What happened?"

"You're not going to believe this… "

"Your face… Bella, watch the kids for a minute." She took me by the hand and led me into the kitchen. She made me sit down while she went into the bathroom. I could hear the tap running. She emerged with a warm, wet facecloth.

"Do you want a drink?" she asked, carefully wiping away the stubborn blood, tutting at me, full of love and care.

"Just water," I said, "a glass of water."

2

"The man who shot at you is the late Dennis 'Blackie' Burker of Boston. He was variously known as 'Sweeney,' 'Sure Shot,' and 'Birdman.'"

The state police detective, Edmund Lupien, was lean, dark, and handsome and possessed the brown black eyes and apparent impassivity of a Native American. At the same time, he spoke with a Bert-and-I Down East drawl as he checked his notes, which were in one of those small notebooks I use myself.

He went on, "Preliminary matches from the state crime lab on the ballistics of the rifle indicate that it was used in any number of gangland hits over the past few years."

"Why 'Birdman'?" I asked.

"Apparently he liked to pick off his victims from up in a tree or some other elevated place."

The news did not afford me any of that "lucky to be alive" relief. Knowledge that a professional killer had been sent to dispatch me deepened the dread in which I had suffered from the instant that second bullet went whizzing by my head. It was a Monday, a sunny September morning a week following the incident, and we were meeting in the fifth floor corner office that I occupy as director of the museum.

The officer went on. "The Boston Police Department, the Massachusetts State Police and the FBI have known about Burker for some time, but they were never able to... " He trailed off and turned to Lieutenant Richard Tracy of the Seaboard Police Department as though for corroboration.

The lieutenant, a friend of long standing, hesitated for a moment. Then he said, "Burker was using an early version of an army-issue M24 sniper rifle. He had the whole kit -- scope, case, bipod, wind meter. Bolt action. Pure gun. You're lucky to be alive, Norman."

Detective Lupien leaned back and his hands. "Our work's done. It's interstate. Federal. The FBI's going to be all over this thing. We'll be off the case." He gave the city detective a slow smile. "You're not officially on the case, anyway, Lieutenant."

"True. But Chief Murphy's a fan of Norman's. He wants me to spend as much time helping out as I can spare. Unofficially, of course."

I sensed from the way they exchanged glances that the two men were holding back. Perhaps intuiting my fears, Lupien said, "It will be the Feebs' case, anyway. The problem, Mr. de Ratour… Well, let's put it this way, the Seaboard office of the FBI is not staffed with their best and brightest."

The lieutenant, now graying just a bit around the edges of his dark hair, looked directly at me with his iceberg eyes. "It's a little more complicated than that… "

Detective Lupien said, "The fact is, Mr. de Ratour, there's been a good deal of surmise that Burker had protection inside the Boston office."

"Of the FBI?" I asked.

The two men nodded.

"Protection? What exactly does that mean?"

"He was an informant," the lieutenant said. "He was what is very loosely called 'an asset.'"

"Who went around killing people?"

Detective Lupien's nod and wry look at the lieutenant bespoke a shared embarrassment. "It's happened before."

"But killing people?"

"Yeah, that seems to have been part of the deal. As long as he only knocked off bad guys."

"Hard to believe. And I'm not a bad guy."

"Maybe he didn't vet you with the powers that be."

The two officers again glanced at each other. The lieutenant said, "It looks like you slipped through the cracks."

I glanced in wonder at the things decorating my office. The sickle-bladed Congo beheading sword with its elaborate handle. The war masks. The two shrunken heads of European missionaries. And other artful objets of man's gruesome legacy. It occurred to me that we are not only a species given to murdering our own kind, but one that has made killing each other into an art form, not to mention an entertainment. Our love of murder mysteries. Our practice of and fascination with genocide and democide. The crowds that used to gather at public executions. The undying fame of serial killers. Few of us are exempt from the allure, including myself. The excitement of my shoot-out with Blackie Burker came back to me with a vivid pulse of pleasure I tried in vain to ignore. It is my dirty little secret.

Indeed, since that memorable day, I have wrestled with recurring moral qualms. To wit: I would have been justified, given the circumstances, in shooting and even killing the man. But what I could not justify was taking pleasure in fantasizing that I had done it and, especially, in regretting that I had not done it. And yet I could not get the regret out of my heart nor could I dispel the daydream of having pulled the trigger and making the gun speak death to the man. Were I a Catholic, I suppose I would find a sympathetic priest and confess my dark reveries and ignoble regrets as mortal sins. Followed by forgiveness and penance. Or, if I believed in psycho-therapy, I would have taken the talking cure and indulged in the illusion of closure. But I remain, alas, a secular Calvinist who cannot conceive of any plausible God who believes in humankind much less cares whether or not we enjoy the thought of murdering one of our own.

"We'll both keep a hand in," the lieutenant was saying, bringing me out of my musings.

Detective Lupien agreed. "If I get a chance, I'll send a team out to the crime scene. If I get a chance. The county sheriff's office went over the place, but they're not… " He picked up a copy of the statement I had made regarding the shooting and glanced over it. "The obvious question, Mr. de Ratour," he said, looking at me with sudden intensity, "is why anyone might want to have you murdered?"

"And if not murdered, then scared off," the lieutenant added.

Detective Lupien frowned his skepticism. "Right. Frankly we're puzzled that Burker took three shots and missed you. He wasn't called 'Sure Shot' for nothing. But whether he was trying to kill you or scare you, the question remains why."

I tried to think, but my head was empty. I had grown momentarily distracted by the state police officer's string tie of rawhide and its oval turquoise slide worked in silver. It was of a piece with his conservatively cut suede jacket, which gave him the appearance of a scholarly naturalist. I said, "I have been involved with Lieutenant Tracy on a very public basis in solving some murders here at the museum."

The state police detective pursed his lips. "That's well known. You also helped take down Freddie Bain and his organization."

"True."

"Well, we have information to the effect that Victor Karnivossky plans to move some of his operations into the Seaboard area."

When I looked puzzled, Lieutenant Tracy explained, "Karnivossky is the New York mobster who forced Bain out of Brooklyn. Which is why he, Bain, ended up around Seaboard."

"Of course, of course." I felt obtuse. "But what does that have to do with me?"

"Perhaps he wanted to send you a message."

"But I have no interest in anything he might be involved in."

Detective Lupien regarded me intently, his dark eyes scanning mine as though for clues. He said, "Sure. But he may not know that. He maybe figures you knocked off Freddie Bain because you wanted a piece of the action. Which isn't good."

"What on earth would I do with a 'piece of the action'?"

He looked at me with mild incredulity.

Lieutenant Tracy smiled dimly as though at the notion. He said, "If Karnivossky was trying to send you a message, the ultimate message, and you end up taking out the messenger, he would take that as a message."

"But I didn't."

"Let's hope he understands that. And maybe he does. But he's not the kind of guy you can just call up and explain things to. I'll have some contacts in New York ask around."

The detective asked, "In your exchange with Mr. Burker, did he indicate in any way who might have hired him?"

I shook my head. "I have almost total recall. What we said is down on paper."

The lieutenant leaned across my desk. "What about the museum, Norman? Anyone here or at the university who might be trying to... communicate with you?" He leaned back in his chair. The Seaboard detective, with whom I had worked on several cases, wore a slightly jazzy tie with his white shirt and charcoal gray suit.

I resisted another shrug. In cases like these, I knew that every detail weighed. But I had a dismissive tone in my voice when I said, "Well, there's Wainscott." I explained at some length for the benefit of Detective Lupien the history of the acrimonious relations between the two institutions. How the university claimed the museum as its own. How I had proved an effective obstacle to these claims.

"The conflict has grown particularly acute with the economic downturn," I went on, looking back into the patient, watchful eyes of the detective. "Against the advice of older and wiser counsel, the university, under the leadership of its current president Malachy Morin, moved a considerable part of its endowment into something called warranted indemnifiable securitized products and other highly leveraged investments. You can imagine how they did in the collapse. So, given their financial woes, they need all the help they can get."

My interlocutors waited for me to continue. I debated with myself whether or not to suggest that Morin, a personal nemesis for some years now, might be capable of having me whacked, as the argot has it. But I doubted it. His name has been linked to an ad hoc, activist alumni organization made up of former Wainscott football players. And even though the man, who weighs over four hundred pounds and stands or slumps six feet eight or thereabouts, is a certifiable slob, a canny self-promoter, and a poor example of the human race, I doubt very much he would become involved in deliberate murder. But you never know.

"Anything more specific than that?" the state police detective asked.

"Well," I said, picking up the loose thread of my thoughts, "there are researchers in the Genetics Lab who may be on the verge of what could be a very lucrative development." I explained how the team, comprised of Wainscott scientists, had reached a critical juncture in the development of an anti-aging therapy based on a genetically modified version of ashwagandha, the Indian herb.

"When you say therapy... ?" Detective Lupien began.

"A pharmaceutical." I paused to choose my words carefully. "Their project has hit a snag that may be relevant." Another pause. Again, they waited. "To be frank, I am the snag. I have not signed off on the authorization to proceed to the next step."

Detective Lupien said, "Is this a big deal? I mean is money involved?"

"Lots. Potentially. And reputations. A firm named Rechronnex has made an offer for a joint venture."

"Why haven't you signed off?" the lieutenant asked.

"I don't think the ethical implications have been fully explored."

"Do you think there's anyone on the research team who might be motivated enough to hire Burker to kill you?"

"Or try to intimidate you?"

I shook my head. "It's not plausible. But, On the other hand..."

Detective Lupien said, "Could you get me a list of the researchers and any affiliations they might have with companies and other institutions?"

"That won't be a problem."

We chatted for a while longer about precautions I should take. Most of them were commonsensical and relevant to the point of dramatizing my predicament and making me even more miserable. Try to avoid routines. Don't stand in windows. Don't wander alone in isolated places. When I remarked that I often rode a bicycle to work in an attempt to stay fit, the state police detective nodded. "But remember, you're especially vulnerable on a bike. Mix it up. Take the bus. Drive in. Walk if it's close enough."

I mentioned that I was planning to attend a theatrical production.

"When?"

"Next week. I was just wondering if that would be a smart thing to do."

Lieutenant Tracy shrugged. "Depends. Has it been highly publicized?"

"Not really. My wife has a part in one of the plays."

"Does she use your name?"

"No. Her stage name is Winslow. Diantha Winslow."

"What's the venue?"

"The Little Theater."

"Down on the wharves?"

"Used to be. They've moved to the old Rialto on Water Street."

The lieutenant grimaced. "Use your judgment. Any sign of funny business, get out of there."

"Do you think my family is at risk?"

"Hard to say. I doubt it. But if you're worried, you might want to get a private security firm to keep an eye on them."

"Any suggestions?"

He gave me the names of several firms.

"Have you considered taking an extended vacation with your family?" Detective Lupien asked.

I shook my head. "I really don't have time."

"Getting murdered will take care of that, Norman," said my friend the lieutenant.

Too true I nodded ruefully and looked at the blank computer screen on my desk. In the silence that followed, I reviewed my current anxieties, being murdered -- my mind a blank screen forever -- heading the list. There was an upcoming meeting of the university's Oversight Committee, a collection of captious busybodies -- with a few important exceptions. I attend gatherings of this august body in an *ex officio* capacity, mostly for purposes of my own. It is to convene shortly to discuss the Byles affair, an unfortunate encounter between the Seaboard police and an eminent professor that has grown into a nasty little dispute.

The committee also wants to stick its pointy nose into my business, namely the impasse between the museum and the team at the Genetics Lab researching the anti-aging drug therapy I mentioned to the officers. In the name of fairness I will begrudge the committee some legitimate interest in the matter as many of the researchers are professors at Wainscott.

Then there's Felix Skinnerman, the museum's general counsel. He has been pressing me with phone calls and e-mails to set up a meeting with the Augusteins, a wealthy couple from Boston. He described them, with a touch of awe in his voice, as *the* parking-garage Augusteins, who, he claims, are potentially big donors to the museum.

Then there is to be that night at the theater. On the bill are two one-act plays. The first is titled *Hitler and Stalin in Hell*, while the second, the one in which Diantha has a significant part, is called *Triad in Silence*. And while she is shocked at what happened to me, Diantha is determined to stay in Seaboard and play her part.

I am also busy with the press. The attempt on my life has generated considerable media attention, local, even national. I have little taste for the limelight. To quote my friend Izzy Landes, I would rather be great than famous and will no doubt be neither. What I have seen of fame and especially of celebrity, makes me believe that snobbery has its place. The bad taste of the Philistines can indeed be exhilarating, but in small doses.

Speaking of things Philistine, *The Seaboard Bugle* played the story on its front page and bungled a lot of details. But then, journalism at all levels has shrunk to an inadvertent parody of what it once was, becoming long on opinion and short on news as it withers to irrelevance.

More to the point, in my statements to the press, I have been careful to avoid any appearance of gloating. Indeed, more than once I voiced regret at Mr. Burker's demise. I am not being high-minded in this matter; I do not want to goad my would-be assassins to keep trying. As I told the eager faces of various interviewers with whom I spoke, I want, above all things, to be left alone.

To the two officers sitting across from me, I said, "I can't leave the museum at this juncture for any appreciable length of time. Aside from a stack of work, I have become knee-deep in efforts to have the MOM join in the renaissance among museums in this country and around the world."

They nodded, but skeptically.

"Not only that, but we're putting on a Friends of the MOM open house in a few weeks. It's become an annual event for the museum's membership. Each of the departments opens its doors and gives guided tours behind the scenes."

I paused and then spoke in language I knew they would understand. "What I really want, gentlemen, is my revolver. I know the state crime lab needs it for tests, but I feel naked without it."

The lieutenant smiled. Out of his briefcase, he produced a short-barreled automatic pistol and three ammunition clips. He placed them on my desk like an exhibit.

"A Glock Nineteen," Detective Lupien said, taking the gun and admiring it before sliding it across the desk to me.

I picked it up and was surprised and not altogether reassured by its lack of heft.

"On loan," said the lieutenant. Compliments of Chief Murphy. There's a belt holster and you can get more rounds at Chandler's."

The state police detective nodded his approval. "That was a brave thing you did confronting Blackie Burker."

I smiled back. "I didn't know it at the time."

"Know what?"

"That it was a brave thing. Besides, he both treed himself and shot himself."

"But you got him to drop the rifle. How many other men would do what you did?"

"I'm afraid he dropped the rifle while trying to light a ciga-rette. Besides, I was defending myself and my family." I paused to change direction. "What about police protection?" I asked at the risk of sounding ungrateful for the pistol.

The two officers looked at each other. Detective Lupien nodded doubtfully. "You could talk to the county people, but I'm afraid in a jurisdictional sense, you fall between the cracks. If you can afford it, you might want to hire one of those private security firms Richard mentioned. Maybe the museum could cover you while you're at work. It can get expensive. Given what's happened, they may not bother you again. It's not every day that a hired pro like Burker goes after someone and ends up eating his own bullet."

"I think we can arrange a cruiser for the next few days," the lieutenant put in. "Like I said, Norman, whatever you do, take precautions. Use common sense."

The state police detective got up to leave. He cast around my well-decorated office. "I like your museum very much, Mr. de Ratour. You do very well by the native peoples around here."

"Thank you." I was more pleased than he might have im-agined. "What is your tribe?"

"Micmac," he said as we shook hands. "But for how long I don't know."

"Really?"

"Yeah. Try teaching kids *Mi'kmaq* in an age of twittering and rap."

3

If only I could, like a prophet of old, walk through the valley of the shadow of death and fear no evil. Alas, I am but a contemporary mortal, one that wakes each morning with a sword hanging over his exposed neck. It is akin to having one of those diseases that can kill you in an instant with no warning. Though I'm not sure I want to be warned. The difference being, of course, is that diseases don't mean anything personal. They are just doing what diseases do. When someone out there is arranging to have you murdered, it feels very personal.

I am varying my routes and routines as advised. Easier said than done, particularly when one is a creature of habit, a subspecies to which I belong. For an example, I am loathe to give up my bicycle as a means of conveyance to and from the office. I do it for exercise and as an exercise in environmental virtue. I had the old black thing I used at Oxford refurbished at considerable expense. I also wear an equestrian helmet, which goes so much better with a tweed jacket than those flashy aerodynamic things.

In a manner of speaking, my rod and my staff do comfort me. Thanks to the SPD, I have the automatic pistol to hand and a police car that parks outside the house or cruises by at frequent, irregular intervals. As for my staff, old Mort, now chief of security at the museum, has assured me that his people are on special alert. (But I did turn down his request for metal detectors at the admissions desk.) My part-time secretary Doreen would not hear of staying at home even though she has a small child. No counseling sessions for that fine young woman, unlike a few of the delicate types on the museum staff who are being counseled for associational traumatic something or other.

In all of this there has been a significant and disquieting development. A day after the visit to the museum by the two police officers, I received via the Post Office a letter in a plain envelope. Inside, on a piece of eight and half by eleven paper and typed in large block letters was the following message:

MR. RATOUR: YOUR WIFE AND CHILDREN ARE IN NO DANGER. ONLY YOU MUST DIE.

Using a pair of latex gloves I keep in my desk, I put the communication in a large manila envelope and sealed it. But to whom to send it? As it stands, the Farland County sheriff's office, the state police, the FBI, and, on an informal basis, the SPD are all involved in the investigation. After some thought, I addressed it to Detective Lupien at the state police and called a courier service to deliver it.

I should mention as well that my misfortune has brought out the best in my friends and others whom I cherish. It is a bright spot amid the shadows. Diantha, so preoccupied of late with her renewed acting career, is once again a doting, loving wife. There are those odd moments when she glances at me in relieved surprise, as though glad to see I am still here. It may be the shock, which continues to reverberate, along with the renewed realization that someone was and perhaps still is trying my quietus to make.

Diantha is afraid for me, of course, and for herself, but far more for our children, for the mute, precocious Elsbeth who, not yet five, has made signing into an art of meaningful gesture and for eighteen-month-old Norman, Jr. who swaggers about using signage and spoken words as he contests the wills of his sister and his parents.

For an entire day and well into the night in the immediate aftermath of the shooting, we huddled in our comfortable home in Seaboard, fearful despite the police cruiser parked out front. We had pondered packing up and going elsewhere. But where? And for how long? When Diantha mentioned the witness protection program, I wondered what it was that I had witnessed. Besides, as I explained to the police, we are both too busy to flee.

Our friends Israel Landes and his wife Lotte came by with a bottle of excellent Malbec and some pointed, practical solicitude: they offered to let us stay "as long as we wanted," at their weekend house, which is just up the coast.

I was also much buoyed by a visit from Alphus de Ratour and his good friend and part-time "keeper" Boyd Ridley. As much of the world knows by now, Alphus, who has taken my surname, is a chimpanzee that some years back underwent a procedure that widened his carotid artery to increase the flow of blood to his brain. Already very intelligent -- far more than the famous Washoe who could communicate by signing -- he became, after the operation, sagacious even by human standards.

Alphus is one of those people (and to me he is a person) whose reality upon first encounter requires a suspension of incredulity. But not for long. His signing is done with an understated elegance making for a kind of visual eloquence, his fine if hairy phalanges serving as long and articulate semaphores. His expressive range goes from *sotto voce*, in which his hand movements are minimal and guarded, to veritable shouting, his arms wind milling for effect.

He also has a convincing if goofy smile and a toothy grimace when expressing doubt. He's very conscious of his looks, denigrating what he calls his "mouth pouch" and wondering aloud, so to speak, whether he should have an "ear job."

Given his chimp voice, he eschews vocalizations and tries to keep his teeth covered even though he's had his formidable canines reduced to human proportions. He has retained the beginning of a typical chimp "pant-hoot" as his version of a laugh, which sounds sardonic if not dismissive.

The production of his intellect is also quite impressive. To date he has not only dictated a memoir that was on the *New York Times* bestseller list (and was subsequently made into a film in which he plays himself), but he has in progress a work titled *A Voice of Nature*. From the little I have seen of it, the book is unsparing about what humankind is doing to the natural world from the point of view of an endangered species.

We are continuing efforts to have him declared a fully fledged person with all the rights that pertain thereto. Alas, there are no precedents in Common Law or under the American Constitution that accommodate such a request. The poor creature, for all his accomplishments, has no more rights than a pet rat.

Upon entering the house, Alphus gave me one of his strong, hirsute hugs and looked for several seconds deep into my eyes with his soulful stare. We have something in common in that my daughter Elsbeth is afflicted with an inexplicable mutism and, like Alphus communicates by means of sign language. It is a manner of discourse in which I have acquired some competence. So that, in meeting each other at the door, we indulged in a hand dance of greeting that included pats on the shoulder. He had brought along a bottle of fine scotch, to which he remains partial, and I joined him in a thoughtful tasting.

Blond, wealthy and southern, his friend Boyd Ridley is studying mathematics and is engaged to Lucille Austral, a winsome young woman who happens to be a graduate student in primatology and a disciple of Jane Goodall. Ridley now spends a good deal of time in her company, which has created something of a problem as Alphus, who, after several disturbing incidents, does not like to be at large by himself. It's a matter we are both working on.

Suffering as he does from a big-cat phobia, Alphus lives in a virtual treehouse close to Thornton Arboretum. When he invited us to stay with him in this time of trouble, I demurred with heartfelt thanks. It's not the three flights of outside stairs to his unique domicile and it's not that I am trying to put on a brave front: it's simply that I would be miserable in hiding or in disguise. As it is, we are taking or planning to take any number of irksome precautions.

An attempt to reassure me in quite another form came from Felix Skinnerman, counsel both for the museum and for me on occasion -- a tricky balancing act he handles most adroitly. "The good news, Norman," he said, during a visit to my office, pacing to the north-facing windows and gazing out of them, his pocked face beamish with mischief, "is that you have been honored in a rare way."

"What are you talking about?"

"I mean think of all the poor *schlubs* walking around out there who are not worth shooting."

"You mean I'm worth shooting?"

"Apparently. And the services of someone like Blackie Burker do not come cheap." He stood in front of the desk, his hands on the back of a chair. "It's like my friend who had her paintings stolen from a gallery on the waterfront. I told her that someone considered her art so highly he was willing to risk jail to possess it. I said it was the highest form of appreciation."

"Did that assuage her?"

"Not really."

I took the opportunity to remind him that the FBI had strongly recommended I bring an attorney to the "interview" they had set up for the following day.

"Don't worry about it," he told me, folding his tall figure into the chair. "The local cops don't call them 'Feebs' for nothing." He then got down to the real business of his visit -- to remonstrate with me yet again for not signing the necessary papers to allow the museum to form a joint venture with Rechronnex to develop the anti-aging cure under development in the Genetics Lab. The pharmaceutical already has a provisional trade name -- Juvenistol.

"What is it, Norman? Are you in favor of senility? Can't wait to wear a diaper again? You think dying is fun? Looking forward to your funeral? Been checking out used coffins on Craigslist? Norman, listen, people really think you're wacko on this one."

"I have my reasons," I murmured.

"Seriously, Norman, money is something you need to worry about. I mean times are tough. As we speak, there are guys walking around Wall Street who don't know where their next billion's coming from."

I gestured a laugh.

"And, just to remind you, I'm going to try to set something up with the Augusteins. They'll be up here around mid-October. They're coming on his yacht. From what I've heard, the thing's as big as a cruise ship."

"I can't wait."

He tried to get serious. "Norman, I know you regard the filthy rich as a kind of refined human slime..."

"Not always that refined..."

"But, Norm, baby, your little museum needs money, lots and lots of money. You want to take back the Primate Pavilion for curatorial space. If you're not going to sign off on the anti-aging deal and let the Genetics Lab make us untold millions, then you are going to have to kiss some ass."

"Thanks for reminding me."

He got up to go. "That's my job. Besides, this place needs to be financially sound if it's going to pay my retainer."

An intense and disturbing response to the attempt on my life came from the actor, playwright, and impresario Ivor Pavonine. The man has become something of a hovering nuisance in the de Ratour household since arriving in Seaboard as Writer in Residence at the Little Theater some weeks back. Diantha met him at an actors' workshop she attended in Boston this past spring and it was through her good offices that he is now ensconced for several months in an apartment at the China Wharf Suites. He's apparently covering his own expenses as the Little Theater no longer enjoys the sizable endowment it had before all the bubbles burst.

Not long after Burker's assault on me, Pavonine dropped by the house uninvited -- as is his wont -- and cornered me immediately with unseemly excitement. "What was your reaction, Norman? What did you feel when you realized that someone was shooting at you?"

"What do you think?" I said, taking in his strange eyes. "I was angry. I wanted to hit back. How else would I feel?" Right then I wanted to attend to some paper work from the office I had scattered on the glass-topped coffee table in the living room.

"And fear?"

"Of course. But my fear was mostly for Diantha and the children. They were on their way out to the cottage for the day." I parried his importuning questions as best I could. Had I taken him seriously, I might have told him that the threat to my life felt like a disease that could strike me dead at any time. But I didn't want to encourage him. When he persisted, I said with evident annoyance, "What is this, twenty questions?"

"Norman, Norman, more like forty questions." His eyes bored in with evident glee. "Perhaps I should change the title of my little play to *Chronicle of a Murder Foretold*. If fact… "

"Is someone murdered in your… play?"

"Not in this version. But then, all living art remains a work in progress."

"So someone might, eventually, be murdered?"

"Of course. But artistically, execution, in all its meanings, is of the essence."

His reference was to a play he is writing for Diantha, something he's titled *Triad in Silence*. The "vehicle," as he calls the thing, is about a playwright who is writing a play for the young wife of an older academic. The play within the play is about a playwright writing a play for the young wife an older academic, *ad infinitum* or *ad nauseam*, according to taste. Upon hearing about it, Izzy Landes said it perhaps ought to be titled *Triage in Silence with Voice*.

Now the man bore in, his face all avid eyes, his words like barbed hooks to catch, hold, and take bits and pieces of one's mind. "Come, Norman, tell me, has life taken on another dimension of reality? I mean when you live in such a state that your next breath, your next heartbeat, your next thought, might be your last?"

"I am merely more conscious of a condition that every living creature must live with."

"Yes, yes. I love that. Please, tell me more."

How this creature slithered into our life I have not been able to fathom. It began with a solicitation to Diantha from a newly formed theater workshop in Boston "open to actors at a point in their careers when they need to hone their skill set, extend their range, and network with leading figures in the worlds of film and stage." The letter stated that they were interested in Diantha's participation as a "player-coach," and in that role offered her a generous stipend to cover much of her expenses. It was to be an intensive, two-week "immersive experience" culminating in the production of something titled "Walk-on Parts." Devised and acted by the participants, the play was to meld together "life as art and art as life." This one-off drama was to be orchestrated by Ivor Pavonine, "a rising star of stage and screen, an *auteur extraordinaire* whose cinematic vision blurs the lines between the real and the surreal."

I wondered at the offer to Diantha to attend the workshop. She is not exactly a household name in any sense of the phrase. She has appeared in several Little Theatre productions, mostly in supporting roles, and in television ads set against our scenic coast. I did not smell a rat at first, but something of stale fish began to taint the air. But then the entertainment industry is filled with start-ups and upstarts, con and conned men and women, and a great deal of bluster and fluster. And, of course, the word "networking."

As such, Ivor Pavonine was expected in the course of things to apply for and receive the honor of Writer in Residence at Seaboard's Little Theater. The drama of all this played out as a kind of background noise to my busy life running the Museum of Man and contending with the gathering forces in the Genetics Lab and their quest for life eternal in the development of Juvenistol.

I confess that I was concerned that Diantha would be seduced into more than acting in going to Boston, but I forebore to voice any misgivings. I like to think I am a man of the world, however big or small that world might be, and I also like to think that jealousy, which I associate with humiliation, is decidedly *infra dig* in my case.

Besides, what could I have done? Tell my young wife that she cannot aspire to anything beyond what she has? I listened with patience when she explained her lack of opportunity in the limited thespian realm around Seaboard. But I told myself that she has two beautiful children, two comfortable homes, a position in the community, a take-anywhere job that is quite remunerative. And she has me. What more could any woman want? At which point my reservations ceased. Of course she craves a larger world for herself. Most of us do. A larger world is more interesting, more challenging, more satisfying. Usually.

The charming, disarming thing is this: Diantha has real acting talent. She possesses a limited range, it is true, and needs to work on her voice. But at certain frequencies she is more than plausible. She can keep a forbidding silence and her eyes speak volumes. She moves with grace and has a reserve that draws the audience in. All quite aside from a beauty that has grown serene and assured with children and age. In short, I am far from being an indulgent husband solicitous of his wife's happiness at the expense of delusion.

As Diantha explained to me, she needed a break given the late blossoming of her art. And that opening through the high wall to success in a world as Darwinian as acting, is what Ivor Pavonine may provide.

Though I resist jealousy, I remain wary. Ambition can exert an aphrodisiac pull. And Diantha remains young, vital and ever more attractive, what with her mother's dark eyes, dark, glossy hair, full figure, and unblemished skin. While I, though still erect and vigorous, am beginning to show the years.

As for Mr. Pavonine, I recall with more clarity than I like my first encounter with and my first impressions of what was to become an elaborate thorn in the bosom of my family. We were out at the cottage on a sunny midsummer day when he arrived in his sporty car, top down, a bouquet of flowers to hand. I remember how, with elastic ease, he sprung out of his vehicle without resort to the door.

I disliked him from the start. I felt a subtle threat from this creature in his mid-thirties of medium dimensions with a large head and sharply defined nose and chin. I remarked a feral glint in his gooseberry green eyes and a nervous agility of movement. His face, conventionally good-looking, had an eagerness of expression you find in people of unbridled enthusiasm. As mentioned, he drives a late-model sports car, a Porsche, I think, and in clement weather wears a light-colored sweater like a shawl -- the sleeves crossing in a loose knot under his muscular throat.

At the same time, he is, intellectually, anything but a lightweight. He is literate, articulate, and even original, but comes across as one of those people who never got a handle on their talent, never learned to focus or channel it to good effect. And, I would say, he likes too well the sound of his own voice.

"Well, well, well, Norman de Ratour, *the* Norman de Ratour," he said when we first met, taking my hand in both of his as though he might possess me. "Diantha has told me so much about you."

"Likewise," I returned, dissembling my antipathy. Diantha's own welcome in that instance had been warm but guarded, no doubt out of consideration for me.

"But no new murders lately," he had said on that occasion, half in jest. Originally from somewhere, he spoke with a kind of jocular precision rinsed of any regional overtones, as though he had done well with elocution lessons.

Diantha had in fact told me a good deal about the man, who had been giving a class in directing at the workshop in Boston. Ivor Pavonine -- "the Ivor Pavonine" she had gushed -- had been an early proponent and practitioner of "Flash Mob," whatever that is. He had also worked for a television series variously praised as "fresh," "serious," "cutting edge." I had refrained from observing that words like "fresh" had grown a bit stale over time.

I might have suffered from the other green-eyed monster had I not noticed that, for all his attentions to Diantha, I.P., as she called him, appeared more interested in me than in her. "To tell you the truth, Norman dear," she said at one point, "I think he engineered my acceptance into the workshop just to get close to you."

"How did I deserve that?"

"Norman, people know about you. I.P. said to me, 'I know, he's the guy that took down Manfred Bannerhoff, AKA Freddie Bain.'"

"When I told him that I had been there and watched it happen,' he said, 'I know, I know. Incredible.' Anyway, he's a fan of yours. Big time. In fact, he's been trying to get the movie rights to the account of the whole thing that you published."

"He makes movies?"

"Only one so far. He did an erotic adaptation of *Mansfield Park*. I think it was called *Fanny*. It didn't do very well. I.P. says it fell between the cracks, you know, half way between Masterpiece Theater and retro porn."

"Retro porn," I mused. "I suppose depictions of sex, like anything else, can get old-fashioned."

4

In the cracked mirror attached to the handlebar of my old bicycle, I noticed that one of those huge Hummer things had slowed and taken up station about fifteen feet behind me. It was big and black and ominous as a hearse with its darkly tinted windows and yawning, toothy grill. I was on Belmont Avenue early in the afternoon with traffic and people all around me. They, whoever *they* were, surely wouldn't try to attack me in broad daylight in front of witnesses. I was also on my way to an appointment at the local office of the FBI, which for some reason gave me a sense of security, however unwarranted.

Trapped in the inside lane by vehicles streaming by on its left, the monster came up on me and then backed away, its engine growling. When the light on its windshield, shifted, I could see the driver, a squinting man of between thirty and forty wearing a baseball cap. That he had a cellphone to his ear gave me a fleeting moment of relief. He may well had slowed and switched to the slower lane behind me to talk on the phone. Unless… Unless he was checking with someone to ascertain that I was the target. I am not being melodramatic. Given what had happened to me at the cottage, I had become susceptible to sudden, crippling fear in situations like this.

Nor did I have an escape route in sight. Two lines of traffic were moving in the regular lanes. To my right a solid row of parked cars blocked access to the sidewalk that ran alongside Thornton Arboretum, in whose leafy paths I might lose my vehicular stalker. I considered weaving out into the traffic and taking my chances. But the speed and closeness of the vehicles made that all but suicidal. I sped up instead, lowering my head and crouching like I was racing in the Tour de France. No luck. The malign presence behind me kept close, then closer. I entered the realm of nightmare.

And sudden, enabling rage. I slowed down and, steering one-handed, reached under my jacket for the Glock. An instant later, just ahead of me, a car swung out of a parking place. Holding the gun up and in sight, I braked and swerved into the spot, pulling up on my front wheel, but not in time to avoid hitting the curb with enough force to send me and the bike sprawling. Hyper alert through the whole thing, I had the presence of mind to roll before slamming up against the low, wrought-iron fence that encloses the arboretum. I came up in a crouch, my gun ready. I heard a screech of tires, the ugly noise of metal on plastic, and the sound of an engine accelerating.

But I was not collected enough to get any of the numbers or letters of the license plate as the offending vehicle sped away. I of course resisted an urge to fire at it. There were too many people and cars around, and bullets have a way of going astray. One of the pedestrians who had jumped out of my way came forth, braving my drawn gun, to ask, "Are you all right?"

I brushed myself off and nodded, adding a "thank you," as I holstered the Glock. Others who had stepped over the low fence returned. "That guy nearly ran you over," one of them said. "Yeah, crazy," another put in.

"Did anyone get his license?" I asked, my voice remarkably calm considering how shaken I was.

"There was a four and maybe a two but it could have been an S," said a bystander with thick-lensed glasses and a puzzled expression.

I took it down mentally and thanked them again. I patted with a handkerchief an ugly abrasion on my left hand. I could tell that my shoulder would shortly hurt more than it did then. Taking out the up-to-date pocket phone Lieutenant Tracy had urged me to carry and which Diantha had procured for me, I called the number of Detective Lupien.

I recounted into his voice mail what had happened, giving a description of the vehicle and its driver and what I could of the license plate. I also requested that he report the same to the Seaboard Police as, quite aside from a possible assault on me, there had been a hit-and-run accident or, at the least, a scrape-and-run incident.

After fixing the clip on my right lower trouser leg, I proceeded on my way, just a bit shakily.

Located in one of those modern, indistinguishable city buildings, the FBI offices contained a windowless, featureless room that served, I would have guessed, for low-level interrogation. There Felix and I were shown to chairs on one side of a wooden table of institutional sturdiness and asked if we would like coffee or water.

We declined and waited. I took the time to tell Felix what had happened to me on the way over.

"You shouldn't be going around on a bike."

"They said to vary my routines."

"Yeah, but there are routines and there are routines."

The two FBI agents that eventually came in might have been character actors out of Central Casting. Agent DeVille Atkins was black and Agent Earnest Willard was white. They both appeared to be clean cut and respectable in non-descript business suits. We began amicably enough with introductions and dry handshakes. They pulled up chairs and sat across from us at the aforementioned table.

In the wake of the assault out at the cottage, it had surprised me when the official-looking summons by the Federal Bureau of Investigation informed me it would be advisable to have an attorney present for what they termed "an initial interview." Lieutenant Tracy reassured me it was standard operating procedure when a suspicious death was involved. When I reminded him there was nothing suspicious about Mr. Burker's death, he nodded and intimated that I was not to expect very much from the federal police.

Agent Atkins, a terse, thin voice belying his large blackness, said "we would like your consent to officially record this interview." And, with his handsome if heavy face in something of a scowl, proffered a one-page document.

Felix took the paper and glanced over it. "As possible evidence?" he asked.

"Of course."

"Of what?"

"That's what we're here to find out," said Agent Willard in a bass baritone that belied his small whiteness.

Felix handed the document back. "Absolutely not."

Eyebrows went up. "Really?"

"Really. Not unless you're willing to charge Mr. de Ratour with a crime."

Agent Willard nodded and with a frown said, "We're not there yet," as though "there" was somewhere we were going.

From their pauses, their lifted chins, and their studied glances, I got the eerie feeling not merely that we were being filmed, but that we were part of a movie or at least an episode in a television drama.

Agent Atkins, straightening his back and inflating his chest, said "We have a considerable file on you, Mr. de Ratour."

Felix said, "Could we see that file, please."

The agents looked at each other. Agent Willard said, "Not at this point."

Agent Atkins continued. "A weapon owned by you, Mr. de Ratour, was involved in the death of one Heinrich von Grumh."

Felix said, "One Heinrich von Grumh committed suicide with Mr. de Ratour's revolver. It's on tape."

"We know all about that," Agent Atkins said.

"Are you suggesting that my client had Mr. von Grumh fake his own suicide and then shot him?"

"Is that what happened?"

"I'm afraid Mr. de Ratour is talented, but not that talented."

"Why don't you let us be the judge of that?"

"For obvious reasons."

They didn't catch it. Agent Atkins merely frowned again and, with considerable flourish, pushed back his chair, stood in all his wide tallness, turned, walked away, pivoted and came back. Giving me a meaningful stare, he said, "Mr. de Ratour, are you now and have you been involved with organized crime?"

The question astonished me. But perhaps it was routine, something on a check list. I said, "Of course not. I'm the director of the Museum of Man, it's more than…" I was going to say more than enough to keep me busy, but such commonsense seemed out of place in that situation.

Agent Willard also gave me a meaningful stare with his oblong face and then bore in as his colleague resumed his chair: "How do we know that isn't just a cover-up for your other activities?"

"The question," Felix said, "is how you guys know anything."

Agent Atkins leaned his bulk forward and said, "Freddie Bain didn't commit suicide, did he? You took him out, didn't you, Mr. de Ratour?"

"And with the same gun," his partner added. They joined in giving me another meaningful stare.

"And saved the police a lot of bother," Felix put in.

Agent Willard glanced down at his papers. "Mr. de Ratour, did you know or have you ever been associated with Mr. Burker before the incident on September 13?"

"No. I had never heard of the man before."

Agent Atkins lowered his voice and asked, "Mr. de Ratour, were you directed by any government agency either officially or unofficially to terminate Mr. Burker?"

When, after a moment of bemused incredulity, I began to reply, Felix put his hand on my arm. "Could you explain that question?" he asked.

"Why does the question need explaining?"

"Because it presumes, first, that my client could have 'terminated' Mr. Burker, to use your terminology. And second, that he worked as a hired killer for a government agency, both assumptions being patently absurd."

It was like talking to a wall. A stupid wall. The expressions of the two agents remained stony. Until Agent Willard cleared his throat and looked at the paper on the table in front of him. "Let me be frank, Mr. de Ratour…"

"Please do," I said, interrupting him.

"Your statement is suspiciously detailed, particularly the conversation you recount having with the deceased just before he was shot."

"Mr. de Ratour has nearly perfect recall," Felix said.

"Can you prove that?" Agent Atkins asked.

"If we have to, but I doubt we will."

"And why is that?"

"Because I doubt any prosecutor or grand jury will let even the FBI look this stupid."

Again, no observable response to the insult. Instead: "You say in your statement that you were in your garden when you thought that a party or parties unknown to you began shooting at you."

Felix again put his hand on my arm, but I would not be restrained. "I did not say in my statement that I thought I was being shot at, I know I was being shot at and that is what I stated in my statement."

Agent Willard nodded as though in agreement. "Tell us, Mr. de Ratour, do you have any idea of who might have hired Mr. Burker to visit you at your cottage."

"No."

"Is the name Victor Karnivossky familiar to you?"

"Yes."

"What can you tell us about him?"

"Not a whole lot. I believe he is an organized criminal of Russian extraction."

Agent Atkins said, "Are you aware that Victor Karnivossky is now in possession through a known associate of a place called the Eigermount?"

Agent Willard added, "A place that was once the headquarters of the Freddie Bain operation?"

"No."

"How might that be relevant?" Felix asked in a neutral tone.

The two agents looked at one another again. "We have information," Agent Willard said, "that Victor Karnivossky is attempting to take over what was left of the Freddie Bain operation..."

"Yes," I said, "Detective Lupien of the state police informed me of the same. He also suggested the possibility that Mr. Karnivossky was trying to send me a message."

"And was he?"

"Why don't you ask him?"

They nodded together as though the possibility might be worth considering. Then Agent Atkins shifted the papers around in front of him. He glanced up and said, "You say in your statement that there is a conflict in your place of work involving your lack of cooperation on an important research project."

I shook my head. "I explained all that in the statement I gave to the state police."

"We know. But we'd like to hear about it directly from you."

Patiently, I reiterated my reluctance to proceed with the research until there had been more consideration given to the social, ethical, and moral issues involved. "As it stands, I have refused to sign a release that would allow the research team to form a joint venture with a company called Rechronnex, a joint venture that would, presumably, take the project to the next stage."

"Which would be?"

"Well, among other things, they would begin using animals larger than small rodents for testing."

Atkins nodded. "You're talking about human beings, aren't you?"

I ignored his assumption and went on to explain that there were people involved, especially among the researchers, who stood to gain wealth and fame should the therapy prove successful. "But, frankly," I added, "I doubt very much any of them would go to the lengths of hiring someone to shoot at me."

"You are also at odds with Wainscott University," Agent Willard said after glancing over the contents of his folder. "At least according to press reports."

I replied that while it would be in the interests of the university to have me out of the way, I doubted very much anyone there would hire a gunman to achieve that result.

"Let's get back to the scene of the crime and what happened on that day out at your cottage." Agent Willard spoke portentously.

"That's all spelled out in Mr. de Ratour's statement to the state police," Felix said.

"We understand that," Agent Atkins replied with what might have been official sympathy. "We'd like to go over a couple of details. Mr. de Ratour, why don't you take us through the events of that day, tell us exactly how it happened."

So I went over it yet again, starting with the garden, the shots, fleeing into the cottage. How I couldn't find the cellphone, and how my wife and children were on their way out. I recounted the sequence in which I used my revolver and what was left of my wits to keep my would-be assassin at bay.

"And you want us to believe that Burker, a hardened professional killer, dropped his weapon while trying to light a cigarette?" Agent Atkins sounded like some of our jibes had begun to register.

I looked from one to the other with a meaningful stare of my own. Irked, I said, "I actually don't give a damn what either of you believe."

Agent Willard nodded in a fake sort of way and asked, in a deceptively neutral manner, "How do we know that you didn't get him to drop his rifle and then pick it up and shoot him with it?"

Felix put his hand on my arm as I began to answer. He said, "It's been more than a week since the incident. Surely you've been able to determine that the fingerprints on the rifle are those of Mr. Burker and not of my client."

Agent Atkins made a shrugging motion. "Let's say for the sake of argument that's what we found. It doesn't mean…"

Felix smiled. "Are you suggesting that Mr. de Ratour made the perpetrator drop his rifle? Then picked it up and shot him with it?"

Agent Willard said, "It's not out of the range of possibility."

Felix nodded. "I see. And then Mr. de Ratour climbed up the tree with the rifle to where Mr. Burker was snagged and maneuvered the dead man's hands over the rifle in such a way as to leave his fingerprints on it?"

"Is that what happened?" asked Agent Atkins, bringing his face around, as though to the camera.

Felix clapped a hand to his forehead. "No. I merely went through the scenario to show you how stupid and improbable it is."

Agent Willard nodded knowingly. "There were no witnesses."

Felix said in a deadpan expression, "Norman, you should have arranged to have witnesses present."

We were interrupted by a knock on the door. A pert young woman in a pants suit came in and handed Agent Atkins what looked like an old-fashioned telegram. He exchanged a significant glance with her and she turned briskly and left. The agent read over the communication. He handed it to Agent Willard. Agent Willard read it as well. He put it on the table in front of him. He said, "It seems, Mr. de Ratour, that you were just involved in a hit-and-run accident."

I turned to Felix, pointedly ignoring the agents. He said, "Sure, go ahead."

I said, "I was not involved in it. On the way over on my bicycle, I witnessed a car, a Humvee, apparently scrape another car and speed away. I called Detective Lupien of the state police and left all the relevant information there."

"Why did you call the state police?" one of them asked.

"I thought it might be another attempt to kill me."

"And why did you think that?"

"The vehicle crept up behind me and acted suspiciously."

Agent Atkins frowned. "In the future, please report all such incidents to this office..."

"And to this office alone," Agent Willard put in.

"That will be at the discretion of my client," Felix said.

Agent Atkins, ignoring him, asked, "Why didn't you stay until local law-enforcement showed up."

"I didn't want to be late for this appointment. I was under the impression it was going to be helpful."

"That will depend on you, Mr. de Ratour," Agent Willard said.

Felix, who is young and handsome despite a pocking of his face from childhood acne, leaned forward into their table space and in his street-lawyer voice said, "My client has been assaulted. An attempt has been made on his life. He is more than likely still in real danger. I suggest you ask questions that elicit information useful for the apprehension of whoever it was that hired Mr. Burker to shoot at Mr. de Ratour."

The expressions of the two agents remained inscrutable in what seemed a practiced way. "How do you know he was hired?" asked Agent Atkins in a voice intimating that deeper, darker truths were at stake.

Felix sighed. "Since it's common knowledge that law enforcement agencies, including your own, have suspected or even known that Mr. Burker was a hired hitperson, it makes sense to draw that conclusion. Otherwise we have to assume he was acting on his own. Or indulging in some recreational murder. Or maybe just getting in some target practice." Then he flared in a way I had not seen before. "Christ, do you people have to take a test to see if you're dumb enough to be FBI agents? No wonder it was such a walk through for the Nine Eleven squads and the retard with a bomb in his crotch. No wonder Robert Hanssen was able to give the Russians top secret stuff for twenty years right under your noses. And the way you protected Whitey Bulger... I can't believe this..."

When we left a few minutes later, Felix remained irked. "Those guys watch too many cop shows," he said as we stood on the sunny sidewalk. "And they were too dumb to know they had been insulted."

"Or considered themselves above insult," I said. "Or, they may have been trying to muddy things deliberately."

Felix gave me a sharp glance. "Why?"

"Detective Lupien mentioned that Burker worked as an informer for someone in the FBI's Boston office. That he was protected."

"Jesus, Norman, you've got to tell me these things."

"Would that have changed anything?" I unlocked my bike and was fastening the chinstrap on my helmet.

"Naw. They're idiots. Hey, you know, you shouldn't be pedaling around on that thing. Why don't you leave it here. I'll give you a lift."

"I'm fine," I said. "I'm going to take it home and use my car."

He shook my hand. "I'd like to avoid going to your funeral, at least for a while."

Little did I know then that on the following morning, I would be deprived of even this paltry and bumbling effort on the part of our federal police to find who hired Blackie Burker to take shots at me.

5

It is strange the way you hear about the news before you hear the news. Reuters reports... We interrupt our regularly scheduled program to bring you... We have a breaking story... Details are still sketchy... Or, sometimes, it's just the tone in the voices of the news people, that note of unrehearsed urgency.

There was I, sitting in easy silence with bright-eyed Elsie, tapping the top of a five-minute egg, the first of two, and perusing the *Bugle*, when a news flash came over the local radio station I had tuned to national news. Something about a Wall Street banker, a corporate lawyer and a U.S. Senator.

It didn't quite register. I had become distracted by my egg and by a highly biased article in the *Bungle*, as we call it, regarding Wainscott's fiscal woes. (All was going to be fine, despite the fact the university had lost half of its endowment.) When I heard the name of our own fair city, I lowered the paper and began to pay a bit more attention while still half reading. I heard the names along with the salient facts: The three individuals involved had apparently been kidnapped by persons unknown from an exclusive resort a few miles up the coast from Seaboard. Police have cordoned off the area and set up roadblocks. The voices of the local reporters were eager. A big story. Their big story.

Diantha came into the kitchen. "Have you heard the news!"

"About the kidnapping?"

"Yes. It's right up at Hooker's Point!"

She picked up the remote and clicked on the small kitchen television. Jack Cogger of the Channel Five All-News Team stood in the murk of a thick sea fog in front of the Gehry-rigged facade of the Sheltering Arms Lodge. He was saying something about how the Coast Guard had secured the area, and that FBI agents were on scene along with the director of Homeland Security. And yes, details were sketchy.

Then it was back to you, Baretta. A comely young woman, Baretta repeated the sketchy details.

Diantha left to get Norman, Jr., who was still upstairs.

On the television there was the requisite solemnity -- given the occasion -- as the local station switched to its affiliated network. No less than the anchor sat ready. He was, naturally enough, one of those people of telegenic authority, though, truth be told, he looked a bit like he had been dragging along the bottom that morning.

He straightened some papers at this desk *cum* podium, looked into the camera and told us eyes-to-eyes that sources inside the White House had confirmed the kidnapping and that state and local police along with the FBI, the Coast Guard, and other agencies had launched a massive search for the three men.

The anchor went back and forth between the reporters live in Washington, Seaboard, and Hooker's Point reiterating pretty much what had already been reported.

There followed a commercial break with ads for car insurance and a medication for erectile dysfunction. All of the people involved lived in nice places and had nice smiles.

Mr. Anchor came back just in time to tell us to stand by for a statement from Janet Fousset, Director of Homeland Security. A moment later, the coverage cut to a helicopter landing platform outside the local Coast Guard station. Director Fousset, looking just a bit ridiculous in combat fatigues, stood behind a make-shift dais and read a prepared statement. With the mist swirling around her dramatically and flanked by various grim-faced officials, she read the following statement:

"At approximately zero three hundred hours, three o'clock this morning, two motorized rubber boats each carrying four individuals came ashore at the Sheltering Cove Resort on Hooker's Point just north of Seaboard. The eight intruders, all armed, quickly overcame the private security detail present at the resort and abducted at gunpoint Wall Street banker Jimmy Daws, Attorney Floyd Blank, and U.S. Senator David Schall.

"Given the nature of the attack and the importance of the persons involved, the President was alerted at the White House. He immediately ordered me, as Director of Homeland Security, to form a rescue and recovery task force comprising elite elements of the FBI, CIA, DEA, NSA, ICE, ATF and AFISRA along with state and local police. We have placed additional law enforcement agencies in a stand-by mode.

"The team has been tasked with finding the abducted men and apprehending those responsible by all means possible. Given that the rubber boats used in the crime have limited range and relatively low speed, we are confident that the victims will be recovered shortly. The system is working."

The director looked at her watch. "We can take some questions, but our time is limited. We have to get back to work."

The clamor started. I refilled my coffee cup and told Elsie what had happened. I had to spell out the word *kidnapping* for her.

She nodded gravely, then signed, "Kidnapping is when you steal people."

"Exactly right," I said aloud, marveling not for the first time at her verbal acumen.

At the same time, I kept an eye and an ear on the television. A reporter asked what the initials AFISRA stood for.

The director frowned and turned to the phalanx of assistants behind her to confer. "That's the Air Force Intelligence, Surveillance, and Reconnaissance Agency."

Another reporter asked how the private security detail, from a firm called Deepwater, had been overpowered.

Director Fousset responded that it appears that most of the security personnel had been drugged. She turned again to confer off-mike to a colleague beside her, then said, "The video coverage shows the guards either acting dazed or passed out."

"An inside job?" someone else asked.

"We're investigating that possibility."

"When will the videos be available?"

"We don't know yet."

A young reporter spoke through his wispy beard asking, "Did the President explain why two rich men and their bought-and-paid for senator are more important than three ordinary citizens?"

Nonplused, the director said, "Next question, please."

"Director Fousset, we have heard reports that authorities have already received a ransom note. Could you comment on that?"

The director turned to a stern-faced man in a windbreaker next to her. "Agent Mack…"

Agent Mack took the podium. "The abductors left a communication behind them that we have determined to be authentic. That document as we speak is on its way to the FBI's forensic lab in Washington…" He was handed a piece of paper. "The contents of the communication read as follows: 'Mr. Blank, Mr. Daws, and Senator Schall have been taken to a secure location. They will be adequately supplied with water and kept from freezing. Each will be provided with a hunting knife with a ten-inch blade. They will have each other for food.' Signed, 'The Ad Hoc Committee for Economic Justice Now.'"

I was digesting this bit of news along with my breakfast when Diantha, with Norman, Jr. grumbling behind her, came back into the kitchen, a horrified look distorting her attractive face. "Norman, did you hear that!"

"Gruesome," I said, not finding a better word suitable to the situation.

She put Norman, Jr. in his high chair and gave him a bowl of cereal. She said, "Hooker's Point is only a few miles from here. And we're rich, too."

"Good God, Diantha, we're not rich. We may be comfortable, but by the standards of those men, dear girl, we are paupers."

"Really?"

"I've never had an annual bonus in my life, much less one of tens of millions of dollars."

"Then why are people shooting at you?"

"I doubt very much there's any connection between the two crimes." I got up and put my arms around her gingerly and tried to comfort her. My shoulder still hurt from the Humvee incident.

"I'm really frightened. For the first time. It's horrible. Horrible! Really, Norman, why would anyone do such a thing?"

"*Peut-être pour décourager les autres,*" I murmured as though to myself.

"What do you mean?"

"Well, I imagine they want to send a message to the other bankers who are rolling dice with the nation's future. The way it's going, to quote Izzy, bankers are beginning to make lawyers look respectable."

"Norman, it's not funny."

"I wasn't trying to be funny."

Like Diantha, I was appalled by the fate of these three men. But that was only in what might be called the proper part of my character, my Sunday-morning best self. In the darker reaches of my soul, I was tempted to acquiesce to this vigilante justice. These men had a lot to answer for. What I had to resist, delving deeper, was the temptation to sadistic glee about what had befallen them.

Norman Jr., on the point of crying, was pushing away his bowl of cereal and demanding to have eggs just like his daddy.

Diantha got up to boil her son an egg and pour herself a cup of coffee. She said something about rehearsals. I was trying to catch the press briefing. A uniformed state policeman was outlining the steps they were taking to cast and close a net around the area. I caught the words, "all available resources."

As I made my way to the front of the house to look out the window, the phone rang. I picked up the hallway extension just as I glanced outside to see that the police cruiser was gone.

Lieutenant Tracy said, "You've probably heard the news. We've got roadblocks and checkpoints set up all around the city. We're going door-to-door. We had to pull the unit we had covering your house. You might want to call a private firm." He gave me some suggestions along with a name and a number and rang off, quite obviously busy with a crisis.

I was on the phone and had just arranged some private security with the person whose name the lieutenant had given me when I noticed Ivor Pavonine purring out of the fog in his sporty little sports car. At least, I thought to myself, he'll distract Diantha from her fears. As I was explaining to her how a private firm was taking over from the SPD, Ivor came through the backdoor into the kitchen with his usual flourish.

"Isn't it fantastic!" he said as a way of greeting. I had never seen him so maniacally gleeful. "I can't believe this. I can't believe this," he repeated, seating himself on a kitchen chair. "Talk about inadvertent theater. Set that stage. *Triad with Blood.* Can't you just see those three guys, reassuring each other and hanging onto their knives…"

"But, Ivor," Diantha protested, handing him a cup of coffee, "they're people. They have wives, children, loved ones… "

"Yes, that's the beauty of the thing. I mean the off-stage scenes, the spousal support groups, crying on one another's shoulders all the while wondering who's eating whom. I mean, talk about *noir.* It doesn't get any darker than this."

I watched Diantha watching him as he spewed forth, hoping she might see him then for what he was. A shade of skepticism had crept into her usually admiring glance.

He was blathering on, oblivious. "Life is art is life. And now we can say, life is art is death. Norman, Diantha, this is a whole new dimension!"

"But Ivor…"

"I mean, *mes petites*, think about it… Theatrical rights. A book. A movie deal. God, I hope someone takes notes. This is big. Huge. Two of the guys are rich, rich, rich. The other one is powerful. With only themselves to eat! All three reduced literally, *literally*, to the dog-eat-dog world they live in. It's brilliant! Brilliant!"

Again, I did not want to examine my own conscience too closely. If I shared a sliver of his manic glee, it was because the three victims were despicable, especially in the ways they had put their obvious intelligence at the service of their greed. That greed and the pandering to that greed by politicians had created a recession that put millions of people out of work, seemingly forever. These unfortunates lost their jobs, their houses, their dreams, even their families. So that there was a certain justice in what had befallen the three men. At the same time, I hoped that it was no more than a malicious prank, and that, after several days and sleepless nights of soul-searching, they would be set free.

My reaction was in part selfish. While I didn't believe there was any connection between the kidnapping and the apparent attempt on my life, I felt the insecurity in which I was living deepen. With the police pre-occupied by the kidnapping, there would be far fewer resources available to protect me and my family and, eventually, to solve the case.

6

I wanted to stay home the rest of that day, hunkered down with the Glock within reach, but in fact I had a meeting in the afternoon with Felix Skinnerman and Maurice Augustein, the parking garage magnate. I did wait until a tank-like Humvee showed up and a young man in combat fatigues bristling with gear did a "perimeter recon" and left me more or less reassured that our house would be safe.

The fact is, like everyone else in America today who is running a large institution, I devote more and more of my time to fundraising, especially in these difficult economic times. It is not something I am good at, though God knows I hold my inner nose for lots of the other things I must do.

Maurice Augustein proved to be one of those boors who are fascinating in their boorishness.

"You have a remarkable place here, Mr. de Ratour," he said with fulsome insincerity after we had shaken hands and he and Felix had settled themselves in front of my desk. "I do not know about these sorts of things. I am a businessman. I buy, built, and operate parking garages all over the world."

"I see," I said, remarking to myself his accent, mittal European but also American.

"Do you know that I started with exactly thirty-four parking spaces in downtown Detroit?"

"Actually, I didn't."

"They all said I was crazy."

"I see."

Despite an impulse to duck, that is, to let some cardboard impersonation of myself go through the motions, I found myself drawn to the man. An expensive, tailored dark blue suit did not do much for his figure, which was on the short and stoutish side. But he had a remarkable head with abundant reddish hair going grey, small eager blue eyes widely spaced above the kind of long, sloping nose you see in Renaissance paintings of churchmen. His mouth looked ready to laugh.

"But I knew what I was doing. I noticed things. I saw all the private garages that there are in America and what they are. Garages are little houses for cars. A lot of them are heated. Some are air-conditioned. They are part of the love and care we bestow on our vehicles. My covered lots provide a home away from home for them."

"I see," I said.

"Do you realize, there are over seven hundred million cars in the world today. And that number is expected to double in the next decade. Seven hundred million. And each and every one of them needs a parking space when it's not on the road or in its own little house. It needs a place to be."

He smiled. "I will be frank with you, Mr. de Ratour..." He paused to laugh, a sharp, almost private bark that went with a sudden glistening of his eyes. "No, I will be Maurice with you."

"And I will be Norman with you."

"*Touché, touché*, most excellent." He turned to Felix. "Your friend is no fool." Then, serious, "The point, Norman, is that I have interests other than parking garages. I have built a very successful retirement complex in Fort Myers. I want to do the same up here. To that end, I have purchased Big Hog Island here in Shag Bay. Shag Bay, wonderful name. It sounds like a place where the British go to fornicate. Ha ha."

Felix grimaced, and then, like me, managed a smile.

"It will be a northern counterpart to my Florida operation. Many of the same retirees who go there for the winter will come here for the warmer months"

"I see," I said, wondering where I fit into all this.

His face crinkled in an understanding smile. "In this endeavor, I would very much like to lean on you for advice and perhaps some help... down the line. Or going forward, as Americans like to say. It is in that context that we would discuss any help I might be able to render your wonderful museum."

"We'd appreciate that," Felix put in when I hesitated.

The garage mogul glanced at his expensive watch. "I do not expect you to endorse anything you have not seen. To this end, I will be sailing up here on my yacht within the next two weeks. I invite you and Felix to join me in a tour of the property and my plans for it. And now I have a plane to catch. It's my own plane, of course, ha ha, but we must keep to schedules."

7

I experienced two distinct kinds of trepidation as I prepared for our night at the theater. One was trivial, an anxiety that Diantha should do well, well enough at any rate not to make herself a laughing stock. The other was downright existential, if fearing for one's life warrants that abused word.

"Break a leg," I said with feigned heartiness as Diantha left for the evening with Ivor Pavonine, who had come by to pick her up. Break your neck, I kept myself from saying to him. I did not like the possessive way in which he squired Diantha through the door. She was now, quite literally, under his protection, which did not reassure me.

Not long after they left, I reluctantly bade good-bye to Elsie and to Norman, Jr. I instructed Bella to call if anything unusual in the least happened. "We fine, Mr. Norman," she told me, her gentle, wise eyes lending me something like courage.

Not so the crewcut, twenty-something security guard sitting in what might have been an armored personnel carrier out in front of the house. Unaware of my approach, he assiduously thumbed words onto a tiny screen he held in both hands.

"All clear, sir," he snapped when he noticed me standing there, the *sir* exaggerated, his posture straightening as though coming to attention while seated, eyes straight ahead. "Just capped visual recon, sir. All signs negative, sir."

I sighed. The story of our times. Life imitating bad art. People do watch too much television.

I nearly decided not to go to the plays. But the Glock in the holster on my belt weighed like a commitment. I touched it for good luck, got in the Renault, and drove towards the old theater where in my tender youth I had watched good guys and bad guys going at it larger than life in black and white.

It was not until I arrived at what had been the Rialto, its marquee no longer bubbling with lights, and went into the lobby where the faint feculence of buttered popcorn used to permeate, that I felt the first intimations of fear. I kept up a brave front, taking a program from a smiling usher, saying hello to a few friends, checking to see where the exit signs glowed red. I went through the swinging, padded doors into the theater proper all the while sensing that my life was in danger. The perfect setting for a murder, I thought, casting about for the best place to sit. Certainly not near the front, which was filling up in any event. Nor in the balcony where lovers used to neck. Nor in the projection booth from whence in those bygone days a cone of talcum light carried the images to the screen through a fug of cigarette smoke. I settled finally in the back row of the main floor up against the paneled wall in an aisle seat next to the padded doors.

There, as the lights dimmed, I sat in a state of low-grade febrile dread, imagining with cinematic vividness someone brushing by me and ending my days with an expertly wielded bodkin. Or some innocuous looking assassin, gun in gloved hand, pressing the muzzle of a silencer against the side of my skull and dispatching me forever with a "splat" sound.

Only slowly and reluctantly did I relax. Indeed I found the light from the stage reassuring as the curtain rose on *Hitler and Stalin in Hell*. The eponymous pair sat in armchairs facing the audience. Above and in front of them and out of our direct view was a large flat television screen. However, because of an enormous sectioned mirror arranged behind the set just below plaster masks of Tragedy and Comedy affixed to the inner arch, we could see the backs of the two characters, the screen they were watching, and, in the shadows beyond, ourselves. A rearview mirror on history, so to speak.

There was a round of polite applause, one assumes for the actors and not for the characters they were portraying. These two turn slightly towards one another after sitting down and gaze up at the screen. Hitler has the remote. He begins by clicking on snippets of old newsreels of his early victories. The occupation of the Rhineland. *Anschluss.* The rape of Czechoslovakia. The appeasement at Munich. The Wehrmacht ravaging Poland to the scream of diving Stukas. The Panzers rolling through France. His triumphant visit to Paris. Then a series of *der Fuhrer* with his entourage at Berghof in Obersalzberg. He says in a stage German accent, "Ah, there's Blondi. I do miss my dogs."

A moment later, Stalin takes the remote. He clicks on footage showing the opening stages of Operation Barbarossa, during which nearly four million German troops and their allies invaded Russia on the dawn of June 22, 1941.

"Monstrous," cries Stalin in a stage-Russian accent, rising and pacing. He stops and points an accusing finger at Hitler. "We were allies, Adolf. Britain was on her knees. We could have crushed her and then America. Together we could have ruled the world. We had already divided up Poland and the Baltic states. What possessed you…?"

Hitler shrugs. "Ours was an alliance of convenience, Comrade Stalin. You still don't realize. The German volk needed *Lebensraum…*"

"You fool, you could have had half the world as living space."

"Yes, but the east, the lands of the Slavic *untermensch*, that was our destiny."

My heart gave a painful lurch as the double doors next to me swung open and a man entered. He stood there, less than a foot away. It wasn't just the way he glanced around, like a predator seeking its prey, but the way he looked like a bad guy out of an old movie -- squat, swarthy, and bald above a fringe of dark hair. And fear does revive buried prejudice. I noiselessly slumped lower in my seat and quietly removed the Glock from its holster to the side pocket of my jacket. Any sudden move on this man's part would have been met with a slug of lead weighing exactly 124 grains.

I watched as he moved slowly down the aisle and take a seat twelve rows (I counted them) ahead of me. At least, I thought, calming, I can keep an eye on him.

On stage Stalin takes what looks like a pool stick and points to the screen, which has changed to an illuminated map showing German and Russian troop dispositions early in the Barbarossa campaign. Stalin raps the screen. "You understand, dear Adolf, that if you had not hesitated on the road to Moscow, if you had massed your forces and kept going, you would have won."

Hitler shakes his head. "The Reich needed the oilfields and granaries to the south. It was part of a larger strategy you would not understand. My generals did not grasp it either. My generals let me down. The German people let me down."

Stalin stands and come center stage to address the audience. He frowns and speaks with lowered tones. "Moscow was the nerve center of our war effort. We were all preparing to evacuate. In that eventuality, I would not have survived the scheming vermin that surrounded me at every turn."

Hitler stands, twitches, and also comes forward stage. "You do not comprehend. I needed the resources."

Stalin smiles under his mustache. He returns to stand in front of his chair. With the pointer he touches the screen. "But here, on July 19, not a month into your attack, dear Adolf, you issued Fuhrer Directive 33 ordering Army Group Centre's two Panzer armies north and south. You then dithered for a month before resuming the drive toward Moscow."

He moves to stand over Hitler, who has retaken his seat. "Your generals begged you to continue straight into Moscow, didn't they? But you lost your nerve, dear Adolf. At the most critical juncture of the war, you blinked and General Winter took over."

"You don't understand..."

"Come, come, *mein liebchen*, remember the terms of our damnation. We must henceforth be honest in all matters. The fact is, you were haunted by history. You were haunted by what happened to Napoleon after he took Smolensk."

Hitler scowls. "And now it is I who haunts history."

"Come, come, *Mein Fuhrer*, admit that you failed as a strategist. Do you not know that the Allies had no plan to assassinate you? Do you not know that because of your arrogance and incompetence, we considered you an asset? It was your own people, your own generals, that tried to murder you!"

"You were no great strategist yourself."

"Yes, but I was smart enough to listen to my generals."

"The few you hadn't murdered."

Stalin settles back into his armchair with a cagey look. "That is true. Don't you find it ironic, dear Adolf, that your attempt to destroy the Jews ended in the foundation of Israel?"

"I do not recognize irony."

"But is it not true, *Mein*... dear Adolf, when they say no Hitler, no Holocaust, no Holocaust, no Israel?"

"The Zionists would dispute that. There was the Balfour Declaration."

"Ah, yes, but how many Jews, after millennia amid the fleshpots of green Europe, would have left to fight the Arabs over a patch of windblown desert? Unless you had driven the survivors to it."

"No, never..."

They are interrupted by an unearthly sound issuing from a nearby barred door. Hitler checks his watch.

Stalin addresses the audience directly. "It is his nine o'clock session. He must go and meet his victims. It's taking forever." He produces a plain black kippah for Hitler to put on. Hitler bridles, shaking his head.

"I can't."

"Think of it as a yarmulke, which is of Turkic origin after all. Skull caps are worn all over the world. The Pope wears one."

Hitler bows his head and lets Stalin put the kippah on him. Then, stiffly, as though afraid, he approaches the door. It creaks open. He enters into a sphere of light. The door partly closes. Curses, lamentations, and accusing voices are heard in Yiddish, Polish, Russian, German, French, Hungarian, Greek, and Hebrew. The lights on the larger stage dim as the voices grow in intensity and rage.

The lights in the theater continue to dim. The whole place darkens. The voices continue in the darkness. The voices stop. For a minute, then a minute more, there is nothing but sightless silence. Not a whisper, not a cough can be heard from the audience. Until, faintly, slowly, the lights come back up.

I was moved, of course, my own fear arousing a visceral empathy with those millions of innocent people -- those countless mothers and fathers, toddlers, newly-weds, old women, little girls. Little girls, for God's sake! I might have wept had I not been anxious to know where my stalker was. Because, as the lights brightened, however dimly, I saw with a surge of fear throbbing in my temples, that the man was gone. I reached into my pocket again and grasped the Glock as I looked over the audience. I could see several other pates shining under what light there was, but none that looked like his. To where had he disappeared? I was reduced to gut-loosening terror, to utter misery. I was not only scared and angry, but, curiously enough, embarrassed. I did not want to be the center of a scene in front of strangers. I did not want to be murdered in plain view. Death should be a private affair. Family and friends only. Certainly not the spectacle of a public execution, however adroitly managed.

In my abject misery, I looked at the stage and thought, so this is what it was like for tens of millions of people living and dying under Hitler and Stalin. Numbing, helpless, endless terror. Hitler and Stalin in Hell? No! No! I nearly shouted. I wanted to stand and march up to the stage and proclaim, Hitler and Stalin are not in hell, you fools. Hitler and Stalin created hell!

Instead, as quietly as I was able, hand in my jacket pocket, fingers still encircling the Glock by its grip, trigger finger on the trigger, I left my seat and pushed through the padded doors into the lobby. It was deserted except for an innocuous-looking couple -- a pimply youth with facial rings wooing with whispers a young woman who had her pierced bellybutton on display along with her upper and nether cleavages.

At which point I staggered under a fresh spasm of fear. Where was my stalker? In the men's room? Killers also answer the call of nature. Setting up for the perfect shot? I wouldn't feel it. I wouldn't even hear it. In an instant, I would go from a moving, sentient being to something in need of dignified disposal. I clutched the Glock. I swear, had I seen anyone acting suspiciously coming toward me, I would have emptied its magazine of fifteen nine-millimeter bullets into his body.

It was then that I experienced an epiphany of which heretofore I had only intimations: Everything that has ever happened remains as real, as fresh, as vivid as what is happening now. The eternal present is real, the pain and joy go on forever. The relief of death is an illusion. And if this is not true, then life is meaningless, a monstrous joke in which nothing matters because everything simply happens and then is no more.

The moment passed. Life resumed its petty pace much the way words follow one another in the sentences of a long novel. Warily, Glock in hand, hand in pocket, I went through the padded doors on the other side of the theater and took a seat against the back wall.

On stage, the lights have returned to their normal luminescence. Stalin is dozing. Hitler reappears through the door from where the light dies. He looks stooped and older. He holds his hands, shaking as they did towards the end, behind his back. He sits down and takes off the skull cap. He says, "The only thing worse than Jews are the ghosts of Jews."

Stalin yawns.

Hitler buries his face in his hands. He speaks through his fingers. "It's always the same. They call me the monster of history. They want me to apologize. Worse than that, they want me to admit that I was wrong."

"But you were, dear Adolf, you were. You could have scape-goated the Jews without destroying them. You could have used them the way I used them. Kaganovich was more than a match for Himmler when it came to eliminating those who stood in the way. My friend, you could have had your cake and eaten it."

"And where are the ghosts of all the people you murdered, Comrade Stalin?"

Stalin laughs. "I wonder about that myself. There are so many of them. Even more than you, dear Adolf. But no one cares about them. Besides, to mention my victims is taken as an anti-Communist slur. Red-baiting, it's called, and such views are not fashionable among the moral elites of the west."

Then, his expression somber, he says, "So dear Adolf, why don't you apologize? Admit everything. They might leave you alone."

"I cannot. Remember, we are sworn to honesty."

"Ah, that is your tragedy."

"And what is your tragedy?"

Stalin smiles his smile. "I do not believe in tragedy." Still amused, he says, "But if I did, my tragedy would be that, like Alexander, I have no more worlds to conquer, no more people to purge."

He uses the remote to click on newsreels of the founding of Israel, the Six Day war, the Yom Kippur war. He says, "There is your legacy, my dear Adolf. You provided the crucible for Jewish rebirth. Because, Adolf, the Jews prevailed. They have their own mighty little nation. They thumb their noses at the world, even at the United States of America. You gave them six million justifications. And here is the crowning joke, dear Adolf: it is the Palestinians and not the Germans who are paying for your murders."

Hitler scowls again. "It's my turn with the remote."

Stalin hands it over with a smile.

Hitler clicks on newscasts from the late twentieth century. The Berlin Wall comes down. The Iron Curtain folds up. The Soviet Union dissolves. Eastern Europe is liberated. Also, the Baltic states, the Ukraine, the various Stans.

Hitler smiles. "See, Comrade Stalin, what has happened to your Communist empire. Poland is a member of NATO! Soon Russia will be a colony of China with your dying, sick, alcoholic population. Capitalism won. Russia is ruled by an oligarchy as it was under the Romanovs. But face it, today's Russian oligarchs have no class, no culture, no past, no future, no… "

Stalin scowls. "But your thousand year Reich is over run with dark strangers."

Hitler nods. "They need me to come back and clean out the Moslem trash."

Stalin agrees emphatically. "And Russia needs me again. I would make them have babies, lots of babies." He laughs. "I mean, my dear Adolf, without babies, in time there would be no one left to liquidate."

In the background, a Viennese waltz starts up. The two men stand and face each other. Stalin says, "We did our best, dear Adolf."

Hitler nods. "We made a difference in the lives of others."

The waltz grows louder. Hitler and Stalin clasp each other in the position of dancers. Hitler says, "It's my turn to lead." To swelling music, they twirl off together around the front of the stage.

The lights dim and the curtain falls to long applause, especially for Herman Klossmann, the German playwright who had been last year's writer in residence. He took several bows and then extended a hand for the two actors.

My apprehension grew. Was this when my killer would strike? Out in the lobby, among the knots of people helping themselves to plastic glasses of wine and cubed pieces of cheese? As I checked around me, I noticed a tall man in his mid-thirties, blue-eyed and black-haired, regarding me intently. Nor did he look away for several meaningful seconds when I returned his stare. Christ, I cursed to myself, was there a team of them?

I moved to where Izzy and Lotte Landes were chatting with the Reverend Alfie Lopes, Father S. J. O'Gould, S.J., Corny Chard and his wife Jocelyn, as well as Joanna Beck, one of the Seaboard Players fund-raisers. Off to one side I saw the food critic Chuck Saignant and his friend Merwin. I waved to the rare coin dealer Max Shofar and his beautiful, now quite pregnant wife, Merissa Bonne.

Izzy was just saying, "It's hard to imagine what the American entertainment industry would do without the Nazis and the Mafia." Then, "Norman, good to see you made it. Come join us."

Which I did with alacrity, as though camaraderie might protect me.

Frank Fogarty, the *Bugle's* theater critic, a long scarf wrapped dramatically around his neck, joined us. He was asked what he thought of the play.

He made a moue of distaste. "I mean really, having Hitler wear a yarmulke was in the worst possible taste… "

"But isn't art supposed to *épater le bourgeois?*" asked Father O'Gould with a smile.

Fogarty sniffed at that and then said he found it a stretch to place Hitler and Stalin on an equal footing, "morally speaking, that is."

"Really?" said Izzy, "I thought the juxtaposition most apposite."

Fogarty quaffed some of the red wine and grimaced. "Well, I think there's no question that Stalin distorted Communism... to his own ends, but..."

Izzy snorted. "That's like saying Hitler gave anti-Semitism a bad name."

The other rolled his eyes. "You don't really believe that."

"I most assuredly do. Good God, man, the Communists murdered millions of innocent people and destroyed civilized life everywhere they came to power. Mao in China, Pol Pot in Cambodia. Stalin in Russia. Of course, people who get their history from Hollywood are ignorant of this. They're ignorant period. But mostly, they don't want to know it. It is the left's version of Holocaust denial."

The critic lifted his nose in incredulity, and the conversation turned to the kidnapping at Hooker's Point. It was the Reverend Lopes who sounded the pervasive note on this topic: "However much we may be tempted to acquiesce inwardly at the fate of those three men, we must, even at the expense of hypocrisy, deplore such vigilante actions. We all know what happens to society when death squads get going."

He glanced sympathetically in my direction. I acknowledged with a nod and turned away. I was again wondering where the swarthy assassin had gotten to when there he was, standing right in front of me, his face quizzical, his voice low. "Mr. de Ratour?"

"Yes," I admitted, such was my social conditioning even as I reached into my pocket.

"I'm Sam Bennington, Seaboard Police undercover unit... "

"Really?"

"I was told that you would be here. I was assigned to keep an eye on you."

I could have laughed. I could have cried. I could have fallen on my knees in gratitude such was my relief. Instead, I said, "That's wonderful. I wish you had told me earlier."

"I couldn't find you."

Though my relief was great, I did not pass the remainder of the evening in unalloyed aesthetic bliss. Upon re-entering the auditorium, I again took a seat in the back row -- just in case. After the audience, noticeably thinned, had settled in and before the lights dimmed, I was concerned not to be able to find Officer Bennington among us. But then, I reasoned, he was an undercover operative.

The lights lowered, the curtain went up, and, despite my best efforts, I found myself in that most untenable of positions -- having to applaud what I deplored. By the latter I mean most of "experimental" music, painting, and drama, which I view as hoaxes in which mediocrities and charlatans, subsidized by well-intentioned people of wealth, foist their concoctions on a gullible and dwindling public in the name of "advancing the form."

With a splattering of applause, the curtain rises and *Triad in Silence* starts. Arturo, the husband, an older academic attired in a maroon velvet smoking jacket, cream colored shirt and paisley cravat, enters first and sits facing the audience in one of three wooden chairs set center stage. Nothing happens for just long enough for the audience to start getting restive.

Then Gwen, Diantha's character, enters from stage left and pauses. She is wearing a diaphanous, skin-tight leotard that doesn't leave much to the imagination. Her beauty and its display was such that I found myself in that male predicament of a prideful "That's all mine" and fearful lest, as on stage, it would tempt a younger rival.

Gwen notices Arturo, starts towards him and stops. Starts again and stops. She approaches the front of the stage and opens her hands as though in a quandary. She takes the chair that leaves her sitting in profile on the left.

The two characters sit there seemingly oblivious of each other. Again, the timing is exquisitely irritating. Just when you are parched for something, anything, to happen, the third character,

Lans, the young playwright, enters stage right. He is played by Ivor Pavonine and is also dressed in a virtually transparent leotard, his virilia or some enhanced facsimile thereof on display. (Talk about props! It made me wonder if Chekov's dictum -- if you bring out a gun on stage, you have to use it -- applied to the male member as well.) He pauses for a moment taking in the other two. Then, with great and bogus deliberation, he takes the chair facing Gwen thus forming the title's triad. The older man in the cuckold's seat and the woman look past one another. The expressions on the faces of the actors are meant to supply the dialogue.

I should explain for my patient reader, who must endure this if only second hand, that the chairs formed a rough isosceles triangle with the base longer than the sides. That placed two chairs in which Gwen and Lans sit at the corners of the base farther from each other than the distance between them and the chair at the apex. I have no idea why this is important except that the program notes mention something about the "geometry of desire and fate." Euclid meets Euripides, I guess.

Again, nothing happens until the yawns and coughing in the audience start up. Then the actors look intently at each other, the older man in the direction of the woman, the woman toward the playwright, and the playwright toward the older man. What Pavonine means to establish is what he calls "the flow of attraction." (I saw the script.) After another annoying delay, the academic rises and approaches the woman. She keeps her attention on the younger man. Thus, with exasperating slowness, is the "flow of attraction" established. The Arturo character approaches center stage, hesitates, turns, and returns to his chair.

After a time, Gwen stands and moves back from the seated pair. She turns to one and then the other. She moves towards one and then the other. Finally, as if choosing, she positions herself in front of Lans. Arturo starts to rise, as though in protest. Gwen turns and retreats to her chair.

Nothing happens for perhaps three minutes. Several of the audience get out of their seats and exit into the lobby, a kind of spontaneous theater when you think about it.

Then Lans rises and positions himself in front of Arturo. After a moment he falls to his knees and bends forward in apparent obeisance. Another interval of time. Gwen, rising, stands over the prostrate Lans who slowly rises, looks at her, and resumes his seat.

Several more in the audience make an exit. I did not join them for obvious reasons. But in truth, I found the whole thing annoying in the way of street mimes who accost people with their clownish antics in the name of spontaneous art. The production also reminded me of the kind of minimalism of Beckett's work, the kind that leaves you craving for any morsel of meaning beyond the profundities of emptiness.

Such that right then I hankered for a triple martini, up with olives, and someone like Izzy to complain to. But I could not even close my eyes. It was Diantha up there and I count marital loyalty among my virtues. Besides, I had to stay alert to stay alive.

But I tuned out, as they say. I caught bits and pieces of the musical chairs happening on stage as they all get up and walk around the outside of the triangle, taking each others seats for a moment. Finally they sit in their seats. Time passes. Lans gets up finally, stands in front of Gwen and takes her hand for a moment. Then he moves behind Arturo and holds his clenched hands above his head as though holding a knife. The tension, if you could call it that, breaks when Gwen rises and leads him back to his chair.

Variations of this get played out with a monotony hard to describe much less endure. As I watched, it irked me no end that Pavonine could have been trying with his little skit -- it scarcely qualified as a play -- to dramatize the situation in the de Ratour household as he sees it. Could they be involved? Sexually, perhaps, but surely not emotionally. Because there was no there there. Or was there? I wouldn't have been the first man or woman to misjudge in such matters. Our appreciation of other human beings, especially in matters of the heart, involves a labyrinth worthy of Daedalus. How many times have we heard, what does she see in him? What indeed? I wondered were I, in the present situation, little more than a pale Othello and Pavonine an Iago, twisting his love and hate of me into some malignant brew he hides behind a steady state of high and low facetiousness? Meaning is he trying to get at me through Diantha? And why me? In the scale of world fame, I scarcely exist. My brief bursts of notoriety have been just that, brief. The outward sign of my legacy will be, at best, a plaque at the entrance to Neanderthal Hall stating that the exhibit has been named in my honor for perpetuity.

Another long interval during which more of the audience quietly and politely vote with their feet.

Arturo now stands as though hearing a call. He regards the other two for a moment and exits left. Another pause and then Gwen and Lans rise, meet in front of the stage and then exit right.

There was what might politely be called "polite applause" except for a young man a few rows down from me, evidently a shill, standing and stamping his feet and yelling, "Bravo, bravo, bravo!"

Complaining, if done right, is a legitimate form of literary expression. Shakespeare is full of eloquent bitching, if you'll allow the vulgarism, as is Dickens and others. Indeed, it reaches its apotheosis in Nabokov, who renders it as dark, malicious comedy. In this sense, I cannot do Pavonine's production justice not only because I lack the verbal flamethrower it deserves, but because, as my astute reader has already grasped, it was Diantha, my life and my love, who was up on the stage. And how can I dismiss or disparage what she holds dear and what to her is art, high art?

The moment of truth came during the drive home in her all-wheel-drive vehicle, a veritable tank, with the rain starting and Diantha besides me full of suffused, contained elation. "So what did you think?" Impatient for my applause.

"You were all very good," I said, coward that I am.

"But did you get it?" she persisted.

"I'm not sure. It's very deep." Digging myself deeper. Nor was it the kind of situation in which one can change the subject without changing the subject becoming the subject. I said lamely, "I'm an old-fashioned crisis-and-catharsis kind of guy."

Silence and swish of windshield wipers.

"And I'm not sure it meets the art is life, life is art requirements."

"Oh, but it does. It's what happens in life to people."

"You mean it's happening to us? I'm the older man and you and the Pavo man are the younger couple?"

Silence again. The metronome of the wipers back and forth. Life as bad art. Then...

"You're just jealous."

"My dear," I said at length, "I may be jealous because you are attracted to that... person. Or, because you may even be having an affair with him, but..." And I paused, as though affected by the pace of the thing we had just witnessed. "But I am in no way envious of the man's dramaturgy, which I find long on the turgid and short on the drama, if you'll allow me a pun."

"Oh, Norman, why do you have to be so small!"

"I am only trying to be honest. Isn't honesty the bedrock of any marriage?"

"Bed of rocks is more like it."

8

Thank God Doreen is still with me. Even part-time she is worth any number of assistants with weighty titles. Among other things, she is proficient at scheduling and has taught me how to use, with something like efficiency, my new computer and its calendar which, I notice, is getting all blocked in. Tomorrow night I must introduce Corny Chard at a lecture sponsored by The Friends of the MOM. The title of his lecture is "Cannibalism in the Modern World."

I'm told the event is fully booked. Corny, Professor of Ethnology at Wainscott, has become something of a celebrity in the wake of *A Leg to Stand On*, the documentary film of his amputational adventures among a cannibal tribe in the Amazon. It's a tribe that kills and ceremoniously cooks and eats loggers and others who trespass on and despoil their lands. (While drastic, the environmentalist in me finds this kind of justice gruesomely poetic.)

According to Doreen, Corny had just been on one of those morning news shows being interviewed about the fate of the three men kidnapped at Hooker's Point. She took the trouble to make a copy of it for my delectation.

I also have a call in to Lieutenant Tracy. He left a message inviting me to, of all things, a poetry reading at the Center for Criminal Justice. It seems that a well-known veteran of Scotland Yard will be reading from a recently published book of his verse. Wonders never cease. More to the point, according to the lieutenant, the Scotland Yarder has evinced an interest in my case. And right now my case can use all the help it can get given the preoccupation by everyone, including, I swear, the Boy Scouts, in the recent kidnappings.

Even in a state of siege, life goes on. There's talk of the Seaboard Players taking the two one-act plays on the road. There's a reminder about the upcoming Oversight Committee meeting on the Byles affair. There's…

I am not complaining. Frankly, I find my chockablock calendar a great if somewhat spurious relief. That is, it allows me the comfortable illusion that I am too busy to be murdered. I think that is why a lot of older people plan trips. If it's December and you are scheduled in April to be in, say, Sardinia, then you simply won't be able to die in the meantime, even if you already have a proverbial foot in the grave.

I was in the midst of getting my disorderly ducks in order for the meeting with the members of the Juvenistol Project when Felix Skinnerman showed up. Matters have come to such a pass with the research team that I thought it advisable to have Felix along for support. Though in fact he thinks I should sign off on the offer by Rechronnex to form a joint venture with the Genetics Lab.

He stopped at the door to my office and peered around. "You know, Norman, I've always loved your office. I think of it as a part of the museum and you as its chief adornment."

"A priceless antique."

"Exactly." He took a chair. "I've been in touch with a honcho at The Augustein Foundation."

"The Augustein Foundation?"

"None other. And here's the deal. If we play ball, there are several options."

"I'm all ears."

"Okay, we can get their foundation to fund an underground lot where we try to park now. It is an issue. Maybe we can go in with the Center for Criminal Justice. Or, we can just keep what we've got there and, for, say, five million or a bit more, we name it after them."

"And what would the naming entail exactly?"

He shrugged. "We might dress up the lot a little, you know a few trees, a little landscaping. Then a sign. The Simone and Maurice Augustein Museum of Man Parking Facility."

"In perpetuity?"

"Yeah, why not? And that wouldn't be the only source of revenue."

"Really?"

"Sure. You could have sections of the lot named after other donors."

"More signs?"

"Yeah. No big deal. 'You are entering the John Doe Parking Area.' Hey, it's money and money is the magic wand of life. And that, my friend, isn't all."

"Please continue."

"Okay, for a tidy sum, we could get individual sponsors for the parking spaces themselves."

"Named parking spaces?"

"Exactly. Each space, with neat parallel striping of course, would have a brass plaque imbedded in the asphalt with the name of the donor inscribed on it."

"The lettering incised or raised."

"Probably incised."

"I suppose we could do the windows next."

"The windows… of the museum? Named windows?"

"Why not?"

"Norman, that's brilliant."

"Then the roof."

"Really?"

"It's slate. We could have named slates. There's a lot of them."

"Okay."

"Then the stairs."

"The stairs?"

"The treads."

The expression on Felix's face grew doubtful. "The stair treads?"

"Yes, but not the risers. The plaques would have to be accordingly small." I allowed myself a small laugh.

"Norman, you joke, but this place could go under, you know. And then Mr. Malachy Morin and the university will come swooping in and gobble it up."

"With what? They're broke."

"It matters not. They would lease it to an entertainment company. Disney or Six Flags. I've heard rumors to that effect."

"Is that why you are being solicitous?"

"I am your solicitor. But also, you're a good account. The Museum of Man looks good on our books when the audits start."

"All right. When you say 'play ball,' what exactly do you mean?"

"I mean the Augusteins who bought the old Hobbes place up the coast. They want to develop it. They'll be coming up next week. We'll go over together. You know, listen to their dreams, grip and grin, wine and dine. He might want to use your good name. Look, the guy isn't even my cup of tea, and his wife is another pot of lobsters altogether."

"I suppose it can't hurt," I allowed. The fact is I would do almost anything to keep the museum independent and thriving.

"Can't hurt for sure. By the way, did you catch Corny on the Tomorrow Show?"

"No, but I heard about it. Doreen saved it for me."

He came around to my side of the desk. "You have to see this." He clicked on a few icons on the screen and there it was, clear as life.

The interlocutor, a supercilious smirk scarcely in check on his glistening face, introduced Corny as "... a researcher in one of the darker realms of human life. Professor Cornelius Chard has not only tasted human flesh himself, but has had a leg eaten by cannibals." Then, turning directly to Corny with abrupt challenge, he asked, "How likely is it that one of the three men kidnapped last week will be cannibalized as real hunger sets in?"

Bristly of chin beneath a red countenance and short-cropped hair, Corny responded with deadpan effect. "Oh, very likely. The historical accounts are numerous and authentic."

"How would it happen?"

"Well, according to British naval tradition if not law, they should draw straws. But usually one of them will weaken and be unable to defend himself."

"And the other two gang up on him?"

"Or perhaps the hungrier of those two."

"And how do you visualize that happening?" The interviewer turned his face to the camera and gave the expressional equivalent of a wink.

Corny said, "Well, the actual slaughter could take many forms. Knife attack. Strangulation. Blunt instrument."

"And then... ?"

"Well, if they knew what they were doing and they had the necessaries available, they would string the victim up by the ankles, slit his throat, drain and save his blood." Corny proceeded with relish into the gory details of butchering a human carcass, the removal of the viscera and organs, muscle meat, and the like.

"I see." The interviewer had the look of someone who has bitten off more than he might want to chew. He glanced down at his notes. Then, still going for the jocular if not the jugular, he asked, "What about preparation... cooking?"

"Well, that would depend on whether or not they have cooking facilities. If they don't... In terms of tenderness it would depend on how much the person exercised. An older, well-conditioned athlete would be tougher than a younger, overweight non-athlete. As Richard Wrangham has pointed out in his book on cooking and human evolution, even meat needs to be stewed, steamed or roasted to obtain optimum nutrient value. And we are meat."

"And how long, would you say, that one of them, as food, would last the other two?"

"Hard to say. It would depend on the weight of the cadaver, how well they butcher and preserve the meat, and how much they ration themselves. The one advantage is that there is, relatively speaking, more edible meat on, say, a 160-pound human than on a deer of comparable weight..."

"Really?"

"Well, yes. On an average American male, even a hairy one, you would be able to eat much of the skin as well as most of the muscle, tendons, fat, and gristle. Not in every case. Remember what the gravedigger told Hamlet about a tanner's hide. At the same time, the hands and feet would be available. In fact, the survivors of that Andean air crash reported that the extremities were regarded as delicacies."

The interviewer, his face growing pale beneath the make-up, appeared to be listening to prompts on his earpiece. "Yes, yes,

Professor Chard, thank you very much. And now, for your local weather, we return you to..."

"Good old Chard," Felix said, resuming his seat in front of the desk.

I shuffled papers. I said, "About this upcoming meeting with the Genetics people..." A premonitory dread had already crept over me.

Felix has a long-suffering pout in his repertory of faces, one he now wore to go with a confiding, convincing voice. "Norman, listen, do us all a favor. Sign the damn thing. It will be win, win, win all the way to the bank. You wouldn't have to mess with the Augusteins. You could... "

"I'm very seriously considering it," I said. And pondered for a moment whether to show Felix the documentation justifying my delay in signing off on the deal. But I knew he would try, probably successfully, to talk me out of using them until he had had a chance to go over them. One was an e-mail I had received that morning from Worried regarding some irregularities in the management of the test mice the team had been using in their research. The second, far more substantial, had to do with an on-going investigation of fraud on the part of Rechronnex.

The fact is, the pleasures of power are vastly overrated. Perhaps it takes a certain kind of personality to enjoy wielding that most real and nebulous of entities. I experienced its discomfits first hand when we assembled later with the principles of the research team in the Twitchell Room. Felix and I got there early. I stood around nervously as Doreen arranged coffee and pastries.

Before I go any further in this account of what turned into a very acrimonious encounter, I would like to state in all conscience that I have nothing but respect, admiration, and not a little envy for members of what might be called the academic class -- the professors, the researchers, and the legion of specialists who assist them, including the diligent curators that report to me. I like to think that earlier on, had I not been an emotional wreck as the result of unrequited love, I might have joined the ranks of the outdoor intellectuals, by whom I mean the archaeologists, anthropologists, geologists and other naturalists -- the intrepid men and women who study the book of man and nature. They are the ones who discover, research, and conjure, in the form of verified data and theoretical constructs, what we know about the world and its life.

Thus my anxiety in having to confront the development team and explain to them my reluctance to allow a joint venture with a private firm specializing in technology transfer in the pharmaceutical industry. To say that there have been rumblings about my obstinacy in this matter is to put it mildly. No less a personage than Robert Remick of the museum's governing board sent me a note saying he had heard "disturbing reports" about my lack of vision.

I will not go so far as to say that the attempt on my life is related to my stance regarding this matter. But I sometimes feel it wouldn't be that far-fetched. Careers, prestige, and large sums of money are at stake. Were I to depart the scene... But I cannot believe that a serious scientist such as Carmina Fortese or one of her colleagues would hire the likes of Blackie Burker to climb a tree and shoot at me.

Winston Maroun, director of the lab and a good and trusted friend, sat to my right at the meeting. Felix was to my immediate left. Across from him was Dr. Fortese, who is a petite, sharp-eyed, sharp-tongued and very attractive molecular biologist with Nobel Prize written all over her. She is also director of the project and will reap much if it succeeds.

Next to her, his laptop open in front of him, sat Ari Cohen, a large, reddish man with a Falstaffian aspect that belies his meticulous approach to all kinds of problems, including how to deal with recalcitrant bureaucrats. Speaking of which, a dark-suited man named Tatum Smith from the Wainscott Office of Technology Transfer joined the meeting at the behest of Dr. Fortese. Finally, Henry Chu bustled in late, bow-tied and bowing, apologizing and smiling before joining the others in their collective, intense and frankly hostile gaze in my direction. Not that I entirely blamed them for their contained animosity. After all the work and paperwork, after all the reports and filings, and after the thousands of hours of research, all they needed was my signature to take their effort to the final and lucrative stage.

Perhaps some background would help to put the matter in perspective for the reader. About two years ago, this same team, building like all good scientists on the work of others, came up with a breakthrough on the cellular mechanisms of aging. The implications of the advance were apparent to anyone who keeps up with this kind of news: if the causes of aging have been deciphered, then a treatment or tidings of such a treatment would inevitably follow.

All of which is predicated, of course, on the notion that aging is very similar to if not in fact a disease. I think it's a subject that requires some intense and intelligent thought. Is youth to be served and served and served? Is our approach to aging culturally wrong? (In considering which, how to avoid the expected witless generalizations about the way America treats its elderly -- as though old people in the tribal areas of, say, Tashkent or the upper reaches of the Congo, get treated with unbounded love and care.) The fact remains that aging in any culture is associated with disease, decrepitude, and death. And, given a choice, who wants to grow old and die?

I mention this to give some idea of the cultural and social momentum -- not to mention the personal and professional ambitions of those assembled -- that constituted the pressure for me to sign the form that would allow the project to go forward.

It didn't take long -- after some brief and minimal courtesies -- for the meeting to descend to verbal venom. Within a few minutes, Dr. Fortese was saying to me, "Exactly what gives you the right to impede our work? It has nothing to do with you and your responsibilities here." She might have murdered me with her eyes as she sat glowering from across the table.

To my left Felix coughed. He said, "The Rules of Governance were amended in the early sixties when the Genetics Lab was established. The relevant section states and I quote, "any significant steps in the development of medical treatments, devices, or therapies, including the transfer of research results at the Genetics Laboratories, and including the sale or licensing of the fruits of research conducted at the lab, will require the written consent and documented signature of the Director of the Museum, as heretofore defined and constituted."

"Nonsense," said Dr. Fortese, "pure bureaucratic fluff."

Felix shook his head. "The Rules are actually quite specific. They go on to repeat that the director's signature is a legal necessity when there are significant financial considerations involved."

That, of course, was the crux of the issue. The offer by Rechronnex involved amounts ranging well into the tens of millions, with substantial royalties if and when the therapy went to market. Given the museum's precarious financial position, it was something I also had a keen interest in, as our portion would be quite generous.

Other members of the team weighed in, but with somewhat less ferocity than Dr. Fortese. Ari Cohen stated with restrained animus that the next stage includes a testing protocol involving animals larger than small rodents. That is to say, primates, including human beings. "Tell me, Norman, is the lab willing to provide the subjects for this part of the research?"

"Surely that work can be contracted out," I suggested mildly, despite the fact that we still have several chimpanzees resident at the museum in comfortable quarters. Among these is a female to whom Alphus makes "conjugal" visits when she comes into estrous.

"At great expense," Dr. Chu put in. "And our funding is starting to run out. But I believe you already know that."

In a reasonable if somewhat incredulous manner, Professor Cohen, whom I know socially, mostly through Winston Maroun, asked, "What, precisely, Norman, are your objections?"

I cleared my throat and glanced around the table as calmly as I could manage. I opened a manila folder. I began, "As some of you already know, Rechronnex is under investigation by the Securities and Exchange Commission for allegations of fraud." With that I handed around copies of a report with attachments that I had made regarding the case.

Felix whispered. "Christ, Norman, you should have shown me this."

I shrugged. He was probably right. Still, in my opinion, the report could stand on its own.

To summarize what they all were reading with that page-snapping decisiveness of busy, important people, I had summarized the investigation of Rechronnex by the Securities and Exchange Commission. The case involved a research project with parallels to our own. That is, a small research lab loosely affiliated with a university had come up with what seemed a genetically based cure for male pattern baldness.

Rechronnex bought the project for a hefty sum and started up a company. Its prospectus, one section of which was titled "Vanity Sells," made extravagant claims for a product to be labeled Hirsutinal. The claims were all in the subjunctive mode, that is, couched in lawyerly phraseology that committed the start-up to little more than dreams. It didn't matter. Venture capitalists, sovereign funds, oil-soaked sheiks, and pension plans all got in line for a piece of the action.

The SEC investigators found indications that the treatment was tested on a strain of genetically glabrous mice designed to grow hair when treated with Hirsutinal.

Professor Cohen, glaring at me, said, when he had the table's attention, "This means nothing. The SEC is investigating half of the companies listed on the Dow."

Professor Chu laughed his infectious laugh. "Good God, Norman, the SEC should be investigating the SEC."

Winston Maroun audibly sighed. "It's an investigation, not a trial. There have been no indictments. And the research on those test subjects had all been included in the filings."

I replied that even a hint of tampering with the research would put the reputation, perhaps even the existence, of the lab in jeopardy.

Mr. Tatum Smith, clearing his throat in an authoritative manner, declared that sufficient legal safeguards could be included to protect against that eventuality.

But I still had an arrow left in my quiver. The email from Worried, like most of his emails, had left me worried. Worried, an unknown friend and accomplice who works in the nether reaches of the museum, keeps me informed from time to time about what's going on behind the scenes.

With some reluctance, I opened the manila folder again and handed around copies of his missive. It read,

Dear Mr. de Ratour:

I heard from Jack Willis he's one of the guys that checks the monitoring gear in the labs that there was something fishy going on with the mice in the Juvenistol Project. He told me over a beer that the surveillance camera covering the area where the mice are kept has been malfunctioning for some time now. Not only that, but when he reported it to Clara, she's Dr. Fortese's AD, she said it didn't matter and gave him a bunch of make-work recalibrating lab equipment. He didn't say anyone was fiddling with the mice or anything like that to screw up the experiments but he said they could if they wanted to. It may not mean squat, but I'm telling you this because I've heard a bunch of people are pissed off at you for not signing off on the business deal.

Worried

After reading it, Dr. Fortese all but shouted, "Who in the hell is Worried? How can you give any credibility to anonymous slanders like this. Mr. de Ratour, please understand, we are serious people. We..." She quite literally threw her arms in the air with exasperation.

"Carmina has a point, Norman," Winston said to me quietly, the melody gone from his soft Caribbean voice.

"I have found this anonymous person to be highly reliable in the past." I spoke with sudden, painful consciousness of how foolish I appeared in their eyes.

Too late. The hostility had grown all but palpable in the large cheery room with its tall windows giving out onto a bright autumn sky. Though I had received several calls from members of the team over the past couple of weeks and some emails sounding a note of exasperation, I had not experienced the murderous animosity evident as the meeting came to an abrupt, bitter end. Dr. Fortese, in particular had grown inarticulate with rage. But not quite. She managed, as she collected her things, to say, "You know, Mr. de Ratour, it's small wonder that someone's trying to murder you. You're a dinosaur. You belong in the fossil collections."

Felix shook his head mournfully after the others had left. "If you had shown me those... documents before the meeting, I could have told you how to play them better. I mean, Norman, you should have led with the e-mail. And while they're berating you, as they should have, you spring the SEC stuff on them." He made a face. "Not that it would have made any difference."

Felix left and I sat there musing. Perhaps he and the others intuited my reluctance as based on misgivings beyond those that I stated. Because in fact, I have been operating under false pretenses. Not that all pretenses are not false.

In the privacy of this account, I can confess the deep and abiding antipathy I have for this whole project. When it began a couple of years ago, I signed off on it as basic research, never dreaming that it would progress as far as it has. The problem is that I cannot articulate to myself much less anyone else why the realization of an anti-aging agent so appalls me. There are practical and moral objections, to be sure. If the therapy succeeds and it is expensive, it would become just one more prerogative of the rich. If cheap and readily available, it would mean a demographic crisis of Malthusian proportions.

It's more than that. More than benightedly conservative, my feeling are downright atavistic. Who are we to mess with the order of the universe? More immediately, I have a premonition of a slow, grotesque debacle in which increasing hosts of wealthy, ageless people live endless aimless lives simply because they can afford it.

It occurred to me as I gathered up my folder and the handouts that no one had taken, that if one of these researchers had not hired Blackie Burker to murder me, they would be tempted now to find someone to do the job.

9

When you live in a state of chronic apprehension, seemingly trivial things can take on sudden, daunting proportions. Last night, as I left the museum shortly after six, I noticed a small truck with what might have been the logo of the Wainscott grounds department idling a few spaces behind where I had parked my Renault. Which didn't strike me as out of the ordinary inasmuch as our lot abuts that of the Center for Criminal Justice, which is part of the university.

But when I glanced in the direction of the truck, I recognized the man who had been watching me with particular attention at the theater during intermission. When he noticed me looking at him, he averted his head and drove off abruptly.

The incident left me in such a stew, I broke a promise to myself and called Lieutenant Tracy.

"Interesting," he said, in tone I took to be that of a neutral observer. Then he added, "Norman, I'm overwhelmed at the moment as you know, but I'll see what I can do."

"Any progress with the kidnappings?" I asked.

He said that an organization called the Union of Concerned Bankers had posted a ten-million-dollar reward for information leading to the recovery of the three kidnapped men. I also gathered from the lieutenant that the investigation had hit a dead end. Or, as he put it, "several dead ends." Indeed, he told me that there's a consensus building among the tangle of law enforcement and national security agencies working on the case that there remains little hope of finding the victims either dead or alive. "We haven't turned up a trace. Nada. More than likely they were executed and their bodies weighted and dumped out to sea."

"Really?" I said. "Nothing at all to work on?"

"That and the fact that there's been no kind of ransom note. Of course, that could all change with a phone call."

After a pause, he mentioned the poetry reading again. "It's Commander Adam Morgliesh of Scotland Yard. He's a fellow this fall at the Center for Criminal Justice and I think he may be able to help us with your case."

"But poetry…?"

"In some circles he's better known for his poetry than for his police work. I hear he likes his whiskey and I thought we might get together with him afterwards."

"When's the reading?" I checked my calendar, its numbered days implying a future I no longer took for granted.

"In a week or so. I don't have the time or date, but I'll get back to you with it."

I took the opportunity to thank him for assigning an undercover officer to watch me during the night at the theater.

"What officer? I didn't assign any officer. We don't have anyone to spare right now. We are flat out."

"Sam Bennington. He works undercover for the SPD."

"Ah, yes, Sam. I detect the hand of Chief Murphy in this."

I took the opportunity to talk to the lieutenant on another matter altogether. The university's Oversight Committee has scheduled a meeting on the Byles fiasco. And Constance Brattle, the committee chair, had asked me to act as "liaison" with the Seaboard Police Department.

The lieutenant responded with what sounded to me like a verbal yawn. "I'll let the chief know, Norman, but as I've said, we are flat out."

As too many people know by now, some weeks back, on a warm, sunny day, Wainscott Distinguished University Professor of Aksumite Art and Architecture, Chauncy Byles, Jr., *emeritus*, had a run-in with the Seaboard Police that has flared into a veritable *cause célèbre*.

The elements of the story are simple enough. On the morning in question, Gladys Timble, a staff member working in a nearby university office, happened to glance out the window and see the professor, whom she didn't recognize, indulging in what to her seemed like suspicious behavior around the bicycle stand outside of Champers Hall, the newly founded, female-only residence in the undergraduate division. (Named for Marigold Champers, 1839-1941, abolitionist, suffragette, prohibitionist, eugenicist, feminist, Wainscott benefactress and a distant relation on my mother's side.) It turned out that Ms. Timble is one of those sensitive souls who suffer trauma in the wake of near-life experiences. She dialed 911. When asked to describe what she called suspicious behavior, she said the person in question appeared to be sniffing the seats of the bicycles parked there.

According to the SPD report, Sergeant Norma Jones and Patrolman Tom Albinon, already in the vicinity in a cruiser, responded immediately. Upon arrival, they observed that the professor, a tall, elderly but still spry individual, did in fact appear to be bending over the bicycles in a manner described by the 911 caller.

When asked by Sergeant Jones what he was doing, the professor turned to the police and said in an arch tone, "That, sir, is none of your business."

(The exchange between the sergeant and the professor was not only witnessed by Officer Albinon, but caught in detail by a small video camera affixed to the upper part of his uniform.)

Officer Jones, in a polite manner, said, "I'm sorry, sir, but I will need to see some identification."

The video makes it clear at this point that the professor had become visibly disconcerted, to put it mildly.

"Identification? You want me to identify myself?"

"Yes, sir."

His fists clenched in evident indignation, Professor Byles contains himself for a moment and then bawls out, "You don't know who you're messing with."

"Yes, sir, that's why I'm asking for identification."

The professor, however, continues to vent his rage, insulting the officer in no uncertain terms until Sergeant Jones takes out handcuffs and informs the cursing, gesticulating man that he is under arrest.

In asking for my intercession with the SPD, Professor Brattle, the hard-bottomed chair of the committee and an expert on blame, told me, "It may be necessary to convene a special meeting of university officials and appropriate leadership figures among the local police to see what steps can be taken to keep this kind of incident from occurring again."

I agreed, of course, but counseled that feelings and ruffled feathers be allowed to subside first.

In the meanwhile, the professor has brought suit against the police department. Through a lawyer, he maintains that he is far-sighted and has difficulty telling from the markings on a bicycle seat which of them was his without his glasses, which he had left in his office. An attorney representing the attorney for Miss Timble stated that all inquiries must be directed to the Office of the University Counsel, which, in the wake of budget cuts has been described as "malfunctional."

There has been one calm and bright spot in this sea of troubles. On Sunday, Diantha and I attended an exquisite little gathering in the "tree house" where Alphus lives with Boyd Ridley, a graduate student who, as noted previously, serves sporadically as his "keeper."

Diantha, currently walking on air after several very favorable reviews of her performance in *Triad in Silence* (admittedly on obscure websites devoted to avant-garde theater), agreed to accompany me, although I know she is still not quite comfortable around my chimpanzee friend.

Alphus had greatly enhanced his habitation since I was last there. Set on a hillock amidst and just surmounting maples and oaks, his aerie is reminiscent of those manned towers that used to dot the forested landscape and served to locate fires in remote places through triangulation. It is, however, a good deal larger and, in place of a framework of steel girders, a web of sturdy wooden beams support the twenty-by-thirty-foot structure on top. A riveted pipe about eighteen inches in diameter rises through the center of the bolted timbers and serves both as a conduit for water, power, and sewage and as the post for a spiral staircase. Fast grow-ing vines and creepers have climbed and covered a good deal of the structure and give it a fairyland aura.

We met on an enclosed deck that opens on the seaward side and affords marvelous views of the harbor, the bay, and the islands. Alphus was at his courtly best, especially in his attentions to Dian-tha. It may be instinctive among primates, including ourselves, to try to win over those who feel ambivalent about us.

For the occasion, he wore a green gray jacket of sum-mer-weight wool he had tailored for him in Jaipur. It went well with his chino Bermudas and button-down white oxford shirt in the open collar of which he sported a cravat of black silk. But he had done something to his appearance which took me a moment to figure out: A professional, I would guess, had shampooed and fluffed out the hair on the top of his head and combed it such a way as to cover his protuberant ears, about which he is very sensitive. He had also trimmed his side whiskers and beard.

It is gratifying when a national celebrity welcomes you like a special guest to his home. Thus it was with Alphus, showing us in and employing that affecting signage that goes with introduc-tions. I was very pleased to see Millicent Mulally again. She was the former resident of Sign House who had rescued Alphus as he sought uncertain refuge in Thornton Arboretum after escaping from the museum. Evidently pregnant, she was there with her husband Gregory, a tall, dark-featured attractive man who could talk well enough but is apparently totally deaf. Like all of us, he signed.

I was also pleased to see Boyd Ridley again. He shook my hand and gave me a hug. Lucille, his lady friend, also went out of her way to make us feel welcome. On the small side, with green eyes, raven hair, and a pale Botticellian face, Lucille is one of those women in whose presence good men suffer.

We settled into the comfortable wicker chairs furnishing the deck for a convivial time with tea and delicate sandwiches. The conversation centered around the kidnapping of the three men and various theories appertaining thereto. No one held out much hope. Nor did anyone venture to mention what so many people think: it was a rough form of justice, but justice nonetheless.

"And what about you, Norman?" Alphus asked, his hand motions eloquent as he referred to the apparent attempts on my life. "Has your situation improved?" Alphus explained my circumstances to the others, most of whom already knew about it. Indeed, I could feel that they regarded me as something of a celebrity. Or, perhaps, just a curiosity.

I replied that I was hanging on as best I could.

The talk was wonderfully quiet but vibrant with motion as people chatted, interrupted, and made asides, producing what can only be described as a kind of visual noise. I joined in from time to time as the topics shifted around from Alphus' upcoming book about the environment, the warming climate, and the cooling economy.

In the midst of this animated chat in voice and sign language, Alphus beckoned me to follow him up to his own retreat -- a small room perched atop the center of the main structure and scarcely visible from below. We went up a vertical ladder and through a trap door into a space about ten feet by ten feet and surrounded on all sides by windows. "Leopard proof" Alphus signed in all seriousness, closing the small trap door after I had emerged through it.

"Wonderful," I said, glancing around and then out at a kestrel skimming over the tree tops.

He followed it closely. "Great birds here," he signed. He picked up a bird book and leafed through it, showing me the scarlet tanager, Baltimore oriole, indigo bunting, and several less striking members of the class of Aves. I noticed a pair of specially adapted binoculars and a chart for sightings.

"My favorite," he gestured, turning to the appropriate page, "is this." He indicated a rose breasted grosbeak. "Saw an early arrival in the snow. Human art will never come close to that kind of beauty."

I nodded in easy agreement.

He gave me his version of a smile and signed "home." He invited me to sit down at a desk-like counter facing west toward the Hayes Mountains and a great red sun melting through clouds lit lilac and crimson. From a drawer, he produced a reasonably priced single malt and two glasses.

"I keep it up here," he signed. "Ridley has joined AA and I'm trying to help him."

We toasted each other, sniffed the fumes of the whiskey, and sipped.

From another drawer he took a three-ring binder containing a manuscript titled *A Voice of Nature* that had red stick-ons marking a number of pages. As I already knew, it was a work dealing with climate change, pollution, species extinction, and the ravages wrought by human kind.

"When you have time," he signed after he had handed it to me, "I want you to go over the whole thing, but right now, could you glance at the places I've marked?"

"Certainly," I said aloud and wondered at the request.

"It includes my general take on mankind," he signed by way of explanation. "And though I have to be honest with myself, I don't want to appear to be prejudiced about any particular group."

I nodded and glanced at some of the chapter headings: The Varieties of Human Excreta; The Promise of Climate Change; Humankind as Terminal EcoCancer; The Larger Morality of Democide; Human No-Go Zones.

I then perused the pertinent passages. There was a preamble of sorts that castigated *Homo sapiens sapiens* as a group and urged that the binomial designation be changed to *Homo ecocidens*. It read in part, "Not all human groups are equal in their destruction of the biosphere, but all of them make significant contributions each in its own way to the ecocide that is devastating the planet." Which set the general tone of the chapter.

Another place marked with a sticker dealt with broad groupings of the species under discussion. He began with what he termed "my fellow Africans." These pose "an immediate and growing threat" to his own genus. "Their population grows in direct proportion to their food supply, much of which is augmented by shipments from the west.

"They appear unable or unwilling to practice any control over their population numbers. Western NGOs would do well to pay women who have more than two children to have themselves fixed if they want to forestall a demographic catastrophe that will afflict both human and non-human life forms."

Citing statistics and data from satellite imagery, he went on, "The human populations of Africa are not merely encroaching on the habitats of *Pan troglodytes* and *P. paniscus* and all other non-human species, but they murder chimpanzees in large numbers as 'bush meat.' Given that we share ninety-eight percent of our DNA, this is nothing less than a form of cannibalism. Not to mention the indignity of being reduced literally and figuratively to a tasteless euphemism."

The text turned to various other groups with a mixture of mild optimism and dire pessimism. But when Alphus came to the Chinese, the tone grew apocalyptic: "The Chinese will complete the destruction of the environment begun in the modern era by the Europeans. They do not have the collective or cultural imagination to be environmentalists except in the sense of keeping the air and the water barely clean enough for themselves to survive. Their relentless drive to 'modernize' and industrialize may signal the end of any hope for the viability of NHS (non-human species) on the planet.

"Unlike the people of India, for instance, who respect other life forms, the Chinese, in their vast and vacuous human vanity, kill and eat anything and everything else that lives. As part of their so-called 'folk medicine' they are killing and eating the dwindling wild tigers of the world to help them with their little erections."

I glanced up to find him watching me. Out loud, I said, "But, Alphus, I thought you didn't care much for big cats."

He sighed and signed, "Big cats are far less a threat to my species than the Chinese and people in general."

"You seem to have a special animus… "

"The Chinese I have met do not like me. I can tell. I, in return, don't like them. They are afraid of me and somewhere, I'm sure, they have a recipe for chimpanzee flesh sautéed with ginger and bean sprouts."

I held up a hand and wagged a finger at him, but good naturedly. It was a bit like talking to my inner ape. I said, "Remember, Alphus, the first corollary of The Golden Rule: You must take people one at a time."

"Even the Chinese?"

"Even the Chinese."

He thought for a moment. "You mean you have to know someone before you can despise them?"

"That's one way of putting it."

He pondered a while longer. "But why? No one takes chimpanzees or porcupines or chimney swifts one at a time."

"Too true." I returned to the text.

"The white race is the worst of all, though I have many white friends. The Caucasians initiated and sustained the on-going ecocide. They invented the modern world with its science, industry, technology and medicine. Without that, there would be far fewer human beings on the planet today and the rest of the living world would not be in danger of mass extinctions.

"In addition, on a per capita basis, the whites are the swine of the planet. They consume individually and collectively far beyond their means. Americans of all stripes lead the way. For all their vaunted leadership, they wax fatter, more ignorant, and more unhealthy every day.

"In this regard, it might be useful to conduct research on the carbon footprint of the extra fat Americans lumber around with. What does it cost the environment to accumulate and maintain these millions of tons of adipose tissue? What is the cost to the biosphere in resources to treat the resulting diseases?

"It is true that most conservation efforts are led by white people. But as it stands, it is far too little and far too late."

"Comments?" he signed as I finished reading.

"A couple," I said. "It's very good, but very dire."

He nodded, watching me closely. Given his capacity to sense anything like insincerity, I was bound to be honest, which I liked to presume I would be anyway. I said, "It's tone is... well, prejudicial."

"But I am prejudiced. People kill and eat my kind. Are you not prejudiced against great white sharks and the AIDS virus? It's the same thing."

As I thought of a response, he went on. "I am thinking of writing a foreword in which I express my deep admiration for the human species. The fact is, my friend, I suffer from what can only be called 'species envy.' Sometimes I console myself with the thought that while you may be the brightest, you are no means the best."

I nodded. "And, of course people are prejudiced, particularly against each other. It's just not voiced in polite society... With a few exceptions."

"Such as?"

"Well, among genteel liberal types, it's perfectly okay to be openly bigoted about Catholics, Mormons, and evangelical Protestants. But generally, open prejudice against racial, ethnic, religious, and other groups is strongly discouraged."

"Isn't that hypocritical?"

"Yes, but even among the pure of heart, a measure of hypocrisy is necessary for civilized life. In this regard, you should read Orwell's essay, 'England Your England.' You should read Orwell, anyway."

He nodded. "What else?"

"I would take the word *little* out of your reference to Chinese erections."

"It sounds like prejudice?" He gave me his version of a laugh.

I smiled. "Yes. But it also demeans the discourse. It weakens your argument by lowering the tone. Besides, I doubt there is any certified data on the size of Chinese erections."

"But, Norman, you forget, I am a chimpanzee. I can say anything I want."

"That may be true. But you will leave yourself vulnerable to questions about the size of chimpanzee erections. I mean do you guys have a whole lot to brag about in that department?"

He pondered that for a moment, then nodded ruefully. He pointed to the bottle. "Another touch before we join the others?"

"Just a touch."

10

In her most irrepressible, beguiling way, Dinatha inveigled me to have Ivor Pavonine out to the cottage for a cookout dinner. "He asked specially, saying he would like to get to know you better. And, really Norman, he has helped me tremendously. Rache Fenwick, she's an L.A. agent, has texted me, asking for my resume or the equivalent. I mean, he has opened some doors that I would never dare knock on."

Of course I agreed, gritting my teeth behind a real smile for her. What would it cost me? An evening of gritting my teeth behind a fake smile, making conversation, making noise.

So, on that Friday evening, the weather being unseasonably warm, we had Mr. Pavonine for dinner out at the cottage. Thank God he didn't accept my somewhat limp invitation to spend the night. Not that he noticed my lack of enthusiasm when he made his entrance, a bouquet of yellow roses in hand that matched his hair.

From the moment of his arrival, the man acted as though he was on stage or in front of a camera, perhaps with a sound track in his ear, something suitably manic from Stravinsky. He also kept reminding me of someone, but any overt resemblance to any other person was so glancing, so maddingly ephemeral, that I could not pin it down. I wasn't even sure what the characteristic was. Perhaps the odd way he smiled or the mobility of his face or even the way he moved. Perhaps it was no one, just a freak of my fervid imagination. I don't like being haunted, especially when I don't know by whom.

Right off he asked me to show him the garden wall where I had been standing when Blackie Burker shot at me. So, I got a flashlight and we went down the path to the old stone foundation where

I had crucified the apple trees, now virtually leafless. He took the light from me and all but exulted looking at the wall. "Right here, yes, you can see where the bullet impacted." He spoke with cheerful malevolence, his voice insistent, his eyes all over everything.

When he asked to see where Burker had shot himself, I demurred. "Too dark to see anything. And I doubt I could find the exact spot. Besides, I have to get cooking."

As I prepped the grill out on the small deck to the left, which has a view of the lake, he hovered, talking to my back. "You know, Norman, I admire the way you're out in the world. A lot of Hollywood types, not that I'm really a Hollywood type, envy people in the real world."

Into my studied silence, he waxed on. "I mean, all we do is make up stuff and act it out. There's a tremendous ache to do something real. To be like you."

I took that with a grain of the salt I was shaking on the steaks in preparation for barbecuing. And when I made scoffing noises, he persisted. "You don't understand, Norman, but I regard you as a man of action. That is to say, you don't just exist, you *act*. You act in the original sense of the word, a word that has been corrupted by theater and film."

"Or the word simply has two meanings," I suggested mildly.

"But it shouldn't. It's too basic. And the meanings are in direct contradiction. When he acts, an actor pretends. It would be more accurate to call actors fakers. Because that's what actors are. They get on stage or in front of a camera and they fake everything. They fake their tears, their joy, their passion, their hatred. And the better they fake something, the more they are rewarded and applauded."

I maintained a studied silence, attending to the meat I was searing on the grill, one of those which, when covered, reminds one of an old-fashioned flying saucer. I noticed he had a bottle of beer and was holding it by the neck with his fingers the way it's done these days.

He then plunged into one of those off-the-cuff philosophical expatiations I dread. "But, Norman, that doesn't mean it's not an art. Because isn't all art a kind of faking." In the glow of the porch light, his viridescent eyes took on the passive intensity of a stalking feline. "I mean when you read a novel, isn't it just a story made up in someone's head? Or when someone paints a picture. It's a contrived likeness. How many Christs on the cross are there? All of them imaginary!"

"Except music," I put in. "What does music imitate?"

That stumped him. But only momentarily. He was agile of thought if nothing else. "Music is the exception that proves the rule. Among the arts, it is *sui generis*. You could say that music imitates itself, which is the purest sort of imitation."

I disagreed with a studied silence. I turned the steaks over, slipped a few more oak chips onto the coals, and covered them. We had been drinking, he especially. But he showed no effects beyond what might be called his usual self-intoxication.

My silence did not deter him in the least. "The fact is, Norman, we have not progressed one iota beyond the aesthetics of Aristotle. We are still slaves to imitation..."

"Except for abstraction in whatever form."

"Abstraction is a cop-out. It is a response to the limitations of imitation. It presumes that we have exhausted every possible form of copying from nature or from previous art. It is a headlong plunge into the seductive pit of the technological fallacy."

"Which is?" I said, as much out of politeness as curiosity. I had reached the critical part of grilling the steaks -- deploying the cover long enough for the hot, spiced smoke to suffuse the meat but not so long as to overdo it.

"The technological fallacy is the notion that art advances and improves with time and innovation. Ships have certainly improved since Elizabethan times, but are the plays, say, of Harold Pinter, any better than those of William Shakespeare? Are Henry Moore's excremental leavings any better than Michelangelo's *David*? Are the dodecaphonic offerings of Schoenberg an improvement on the suites of Bach?" As though to reward himself he took another bottle of beer for himself from the cooler and opened it.

I protested that I admired Moore's sculpture, but conceded the point even though I had absolutely no idea where the man was heading with his dissertation.

He did not leave me in suspense. "We need a whole new aesthetic. It is imperative, even urgent, Norman, not merely to imitate life but to fuse art with existence in such a way that they are inseparable."

"I don't see how that's possible." I took the lid off to a great cloud of smoke, put it to one side, and cut into one of the steaks. Still on the rare side.

"But you and a few other select, lucky individuals have already done it. You have made your life a work of art."

I laughed. "It wouldn't bring much at auction I'm afraid."

"No, no, Norman. Your life is beyond valuations. Might as well put a price on the Sistine Chapel. Look at yourself -- a distinguished museum director, an accomplished writer, virile husband and doting father, sleuth extraordinaire, nemesis of evil incarnate, and quite an excellent chef to judge from… " He had his nose up and poised, taking in the fumes.

"You flatter me," I protested. I was starting to feel that acute discomfit that descends when someone presumes to define you, even when the definition is laudatory. In this instance I sensed as well subtle mockery.

"But, Norman, you of all people are worthy of flattery." He took a long swallow of beer. Then, without missing a beat, he changed course, coming at me with, "So what was it like to take down the great Freddie Bain?"

"I've already written about that."

"I know, but those are only words on paper. I want them warm and living from your mouth."

I cringed, not altogether inwardly. "Well, to begin with, I didn't 'take down' anyone. I was defending myself and Diantha from a grotesque monster in his lair."

"The Eigermount."

"Of course…"

"You came up through the snow after reconnoitering the place."

"I did."

"You poisoned his German shepherd with morphine-laced hamburger."

"You know it well."

"And all the time Freddie and his associates had been watching it on a television hooked up to the security cameras."

"Yes, and apparently enjoying it very much." As I spoke, Pavonine's smile recalled in some hideous way the moment I blundered into the Frankenstein castle and found Bain and his henchmen waiting for me.

"So then, the confrontation."

"Yes."

"He wanted that tape one of your professors took of a cannibal ceremony in South America."

"You know more than I remember."

"Yes, yes, but those are incidentals. You refused to give up the tape."

"Of course."

"So he threatened you and Diantha."

"He did."

"At which point you took out your Smith & Wesson 38-caliber revolver..."

"You know it well." It was all coming back to me, not just the details but the aura of the thing, that distinct and yet vague feeling about specific memories of places, people, and events, and that is all but indescribable.

"I read everything about it I could get my hands on."

"So why are you asking me? You know more about it than I remember."

"I want to know what you were feeling as you murdered another man."

"But I didn't murder him. I shot a criminal in self-defense."

"Yes. Yes! You wounded him with the first shot after he taunted you."

"Yes."

"How did that feel? I mean aiming and squeezing the trigger?"

"I don't remember. I had done it before I knew I had done it."

"Then…"

"He drew a pistol. I shot him again, this time in the shoulder, making him drop his weapon."

"Did he cry out?"

"I don't remember."

"Then what happened?"

"He reached for the gun on the floor and I shot him in the heart, at least according to the autopsy report."

"Yes, yes, the heart. Was it hard to do?"

"In retrospect, I think it bothered me more to poison the dog."

"Oh, I like that! So, so, there must have been a touch of *jouissance* in pointing your gun at his heart and bang! The joy of murder!"

"It wasn't murder. I shot the monster in defense of myself and the woman I love."

"Even better. Righteous murder. Like burning a heretic."

I looked into his mad face and what I didn't want to reveal to the man or even to myself was the bone-deep, atavistic flash of malignant power edged with glee I experienced in aiming the gun at Freddie Bain's heart and pulling the trigger and hearing the blast of the discharged bullet echoing the doom I was delivering.

"Come on, Norman, 'fess up. For that one moment, that split second, you felt like a god, didn't you?"

"Yes," I said after a moment of hesitation, half realizing that I was confessing to this man, whom I despised, something I had avoided admitting to myself for years. Avoided and yet, in odd moments of recollection, titillating myself with reenactments, fantasizing about things I might have said as, with revolver cocked, I stood over the man, who had no real chance of reaching his weapon.

I and the steaks were saved by Diantha coming out to tell us we were to come indoors as everything was ready.

Pavonine's assault did not let up during the meal and he scarcely noticed that the steaks were overdone. He questioned me relentlessly about the cases I had worked on even though he knew about them in detail. He said he would love nothing better to join me in investigating any new murders.

I found being around the man for any length of time not just irksome but exhausting. There was no repose or off-hand small talk during which one might get to know the man behind the character or the character of the man. He certainly gave the impression of being a little mad, not so much with the madness of genius -- which is one of those banal clichés about creativity -- but with obsession and the license it grants itself.

Nor was I gratified by the way his overblown appreciation of Norman de Ratour, the man of action, appeared to augment Diantha's esteem. I wanted no refraction of myself through his warped lens, I almost told her later when we prepared for bed. But, as though excited by the man's vision of me, the dear woman had grown forward in her amorous intentions, and I am only human.

11

I knew we were in for an interesting day with the Augusteins when I saw their yacht, *The Wandering Jewel*, tied up at the same dock that is used by the Shag Bay ferry. A gleaming white fiberglass thing with all the usual nautical accouterments, it was a lubber's boat and longer at the waterline than *The Islander*, the sizable ferry that plies between the larger islands dotting the bay.

On the drive to the dock, Felix had told me that Maurice likes to be addressed as "Captain" when aboard his yacht. "Captain it shall be," I said with an inner wince.

But I made the appropriately appreciative noises as Felix led me and Theresa, his charming and lovely Filipino wife, up the clanking gangway. At the top, we were greeted by the captain, who stood rigged out in boating attire -- Greek fishing cap, navy blue windbreaker, tan turtleneck, a pair of white duck trousers and, of course, deck shoes. Not that he quite looked the part, perhaps because of his rather short stature and round beaming face.

"Norman, my good friend, welcome aboard. And you, Felix. And this must be Theresa. Be still my heart. Come this way. Simone, my first mate, ha ha, is below arranging a small bite to have." The Mittle-european aspect of the man's accent sounded stronger than I remembered it.

And below was Simone, who stood a good three inches taller than her husband, was perhaps twenty years his junior, and acted ten years his senior, being stiff and unsmiling as she greeted us with minimal civility. Indeed, she struck me as mannish, with a carapace of short black hair like a textured helmet framing a disgruntled face perhaps once pretty. She spoke briefly and harshly to her husband in what sounded like garbled French. He answered her in what sounded like garbled German. Then she resumed her ordering of the cabin boy in setting out a light meal.

They were the kind of couple that makes you wonder if they actually live together. That is, do they share a bed, at least occasionally? Have they reproduced? And if so, to what effect?

As we moved on, Captain Augustein said to us in a stage whisper, "Simone does not like boats. She does not like New England. She does not like giving money away." Then he laughed, his face reddening with self-amusement. "And I don't think she much likes me."

We managed some chitchat, thanks mostly to Felix, who appeared uncharacteristically protective of his young wife. Theresa struck me as exotically beautiful even in our increasingly multicultural world. She had dressed fetchingly in turtleneck, windbreaker, and form-fitting pale jeans. She smiled easily enough, but held herself back as sounds of casting off reached us from outside. With mugs of coffee in hand, we began a tour of the boat, which was gently rolling in a gentle swell.

I have been aboard these kinds of floating palaces before, but never one on this scale. We spent some time on the bridge looking at and hearing about the control and navigation systems, the blinking and oscillating display screens in the muted brilliance of LED illumination, all of which could take the boat around the world without mishap. Theoretically. We met the real captain and his mates, who appeared part of the bland, polished woodwork. That was as nautical as it got. The rest was like inspecting a luxury lodge beginning with the grand master cabin with ensuite bath, sauna, hot tub, and rub room, complete with an array of appurtenances that made the eyes and then the mind glaze over. Then the guest suites, the bar, the dining room, the lounge, the small pool with a retractable cover. All the while I yearned to be up on deck, taking in the salt-tanged air, the sun-spangled sea, and the pine-clad islands with names like Dog, Deer, Whale, Bone, Cutler's, Hanks, Hope, Despair, Little Hog and Big Hog.

"So where's the ogress?" Felix whispered to me as we made our way along a passageway to appreciate yet another feature. "Down in the bilge chained to a bulkhead?"

"You got us into this, Felix," I whispered back.

"I call this the master's den," said our host, clicking on fiber optic lights to show us his den, a cranny in dark cherry paneling and all the usual stuff, including a secured collection of expensive single malts.

"Your boat has an interesting name," I ventured, having visually appreciated a 1939 bottle of Macallan before handing it carefully back to its owner.

"Ten thousand American," the owner told me. "And I don't even like the stuff that much." He frowned, then smiled. "Maybe we have a dram later. Ah, yes, the *Wandering Jewel*. I changed the name just a little. In case I wanted to take it through the Suez Canal, ha, ha." I bought it from Manny Schlosser. To help him out. Poor Manny was up to here with Bernie..."

"Bernie?"

"Madoff. Look, I warned him. I told him something's rotten in the state of Denmark. He wouldn't listen. Then it was all gone. In a phone call. Now he's got lawyers hanging all over him like a wet suit that doesn't fit. No offense, Felix."

"I'm used to it."

"What is your nation?" I asked our host. "If you don't mind my asking."

"My nation? We are Alsatian. Simone is French Alsatian and I am German Alsatian." He laughed. "Oil and water. But I went to school in America off and on. When someone called me a Yank, I said, yeah, yeah, more like yanked, you know, back and forth, back and forth." He laughed his brimming laugh.

At one point, lagging behind the others, the happy man turned to me and whispered, "Theresa has a nice ass, don't you think?"

"Admirable," I said with an inward cringe at being caught. More than once that morning I had availed myself of the opportunity to appreciate, surreptitiously, I had thought, the pert roundness of Mrs. Skinnerman's buttocks.

When we finally got on deck, we were on the seaward side of the island in the cove directly in front of Hobbes Landing, perhaps a hundred yards offshore, and dropping anchor amidst an escort of raucous gulls.

At the sight of the place -- a large handsome three-story clapboarded pile, white with green shutters and dormers spacing the mansard roof -- I was drenched by a wave of nostalgia that broke out of the past and left my eyes moist. On summer Saturday afternoons, I would go on the old ferry with my mother and father and Aunt Eudoxia to dinner at what was known as the Hobbes Landing Hotel. I was left to roam around the place while the adults sat on the balustraded veranda that adorns all four sides and had a drink or two.

Auntie, as I called her, was a spinster who spoke her mind freely, more than once wondering aloud why life had to be so damn biological. In one of the vegetarian tracts she produced, she wrote, "It's not what you are eating but who you eating, you should ask yourself." She didn't hold her liquor very well and would get flirtatious with the waiters as we went into the Edwardian dining room where we sat in chairs of dark crimson plush around a table draped with heavy linen. It had a simple menu of seafood and steak that sentiment makes utterly memorable. Along with the piquant taste of fried clams smeared with tartar sauce and my mother telling me not to put so much ketchup on my french fries, I remember the lounge with its high ceiling, great stone fireplace and pine-paneling that looked like it had caramelized over the decades. I have heard the style described as "genteel woodsy."

I was recalled to the sunny present by Captain Augustein's voice. "We would go in and tie up, but the dock's in bad shape. We'll put down a launch to go in. But first, let me show you something."

We went back inside and, with Felix, squeezed into a small elevator and ascended to the "crow's nest." It was an enclosed lookout that afforded a three-hundred-and-sixty degree view that took in the heaving Atlantic, the distant city, the rugged shoreline, and the islands scattered around us as though by some coherent geologic process.

Resorting to his role as a businessman, Mr. Augustein declared, "You know, this part of the country is really undeveloped.

Look at these islands. Empty. What, a couple of landings. The shacks of lobstermen. A few summer homes. Have you ever seen so much waste of space in your life?"

"You mean it should be developed?" I asked.

He caught the derision in my voice and looked up sharply. "Of course. But tastefully."

"There's no taste good enough to improve this scene," I said absently. Then, "What kind of good taste have you planned?"

"You be the judge." He produced a sheaf of architectural renderings and laid them flat on the small chart table. I watched in dismay as he unrolled the future -- a four-story modern thing with curving balconies reminiscent of those gigantic cruise ships, which are the ultimate in nautical kitsch and themselves the des-tination wherever they may sail. The renditions showed appliqué shingling here and there of the kind you adorn the squat buildings of shopping centers to comply with local codes. A planned marina had yachts and large sailboats tied up in orderly rows. The out-buildings included a tier of cottages and a sprawling clubhouse for a new golf course.

The god of all this rapped the sheaf with his meaty knuckles. "But guess what? The Shag Bay Historical Society will not let me tear down the old place and they will not let me put up any of these new buildings."

"I see."

"And that's where you come in, Norman. You know the shakers and quakers around here, ha, ha. I need you to talk to them for me. I need you to talk sense to them."

"But I agree with them," I said.

"About this?"

"About this." I wrapped my own bony knuckles on the plans. "It's hideous."

"What Norman means…" Felix began to say.

"What Norman says Norman means," I said, suddenly irked.

The developer was puzzled. "But I put up something very like this near Fort Myers and people loved it."

"That's Florida." I calmed down. Then, with sudden inspiration, "Maurice… Captain, people go to Florida for the future. They come up here for the past."

"So…?"

"So why don't you renovate the old place and do the other buildings in the same style. I doubt the historical society would have any problem with that."

The man's small eyes went sharp. They shifted around, first at me, then the plans, and finally at the old hotel. At length he said, "You know, Norman, you may be right." Then he laughed. "And I won't have to build you a parking lot." He put a hand on my shoulder. "Let us have some lunch and then we will go ashore and look this place over with new eyes."

We sat down to a pleasant collation of salad, French bread, cold cuts and cheese with a light dry wine. We ate on deck, the day being sunny and mild with very little breeze.

"What will you call your… project?" I asked when the talk began to lag.

"Hobbes Landing."

"Hobbes Landing on Big Hog?"

"No, no. Hobbes Landing on Grand Cochon. Or Ile de Grand Cochon. Or maybe we'll look up the original Indian name. That always adds a certain cachet."

We had to stop talking as a Coast Guard helicopter clattered toward us, hovered noisily overhead, and finally moved on.

"Didn't the kidnappings make you hesitate about sailing up here?" I asked when conversation was again possible.

He shook his head. "The barn door is always most secure after the horse has fled."

Felix nodded. "Seaboard is crawling with grown men and women talking into their lapels. A regular circus."

"Do you think there's any chance of the three men being alive?" Theresa asked me. She had been exchanging glances with the waiter, who was apparently of her nation.

"Not without a ransom note," our host answered for me, echoing the conventional wisdom. "But who knows. They may be right here. They have a suite already on the second floor of my hotel." At which he again laughed.

We presently went ashore in the launch and climbed up onto the shaky dock without incident. Though a spacious sloping lawn gone to seed, we mounted a wide, gently rising walk of brick, stepped in places and weedy in the cracks. We followed it up to the veranda and the main entrance, two high mahogany doors that had weathered over the years with side windows of figured glass.

But the key, supposedly in a box under a loose board, was not to be found. No matter, we walked the long, veranda, watching out for more loose boards underfoot and stopping to shade our eyes and peer inside. Amazingly intact, I thought, with slipcovers on the armchairs and sofas in the large living room. A wall clock had stopped at three forty-two. The morose, mounted moose over the fireplace had lost an antler and a large, cracked mirror in the dining room reflected the bare tables and the plush chairs tilted against them, as though reserved.

"I think you are right, Norman," Maurice confided in me as we fell behind the others. "Restoration would be expensive, but perhaps not that bad. There are skilled workers around here."

We were on the landward side going slowly along the veranda stopping every once in a while to peer in. At one point, in a sunny spot, I stopped and sniffed. "You'll need to fix the septic system."

The entrepreneur shrugged. "The least of my problems, Norman, the least of my problems."

I gave him a skeptical look. I said, "The bedrock's not that far down."

He waved me off. "Norman, they've got systems today you can put anywhere." He laughed. "And turn the stuff into champagne and caviar."

By then we were on the north side of the old hotel and looking out onto a gently rolling stretch of marsh and pine forest. "That will be the golf course," he said with a strange note of diffidence.

"Absolutely necessary?" I asked.

"Absolutely necessary. It's like a place of worship for a whole tribe of devotees. But I think we'll keep it simple. Maybe a nature trail around the edges." He laughed his laugh. "We'll keep the rough rough."

We stepped off the veranda and looked in the direction of some derelict outbuildings, once used as garages or stables or both. The man began to say something and stopped as another helicopter, this one with different markings, came in from the sea and circled overhead. Finally, after a low, noisy pass, it flew off to the north.

Captain Augustein shook his head. "Felix is right. Americans can't tie their own shoes anymore." Before I could venture an opinion, not that I had one, he went on, "You know, Norman, Simone has taken quite a shine to you. But then I can never tell what is going to make the woman happy."

"I hadn't noticed," I said, wondering what, if anything, was the import of his remark. I didn't mention that she perhaps intuited my reluctance in the whole parking garage matter. As he said, she didn't like giving away money.

We moved onto the veranda and met Felix and Theresa who were on their way back from a cursory look at the outbuildings.

"Anything there?" I asked.

Felix shrugged. "Nothing much. Hotel junk and a neat old car."

At which point a cloud covered the sun, a breeze rippled the cove, and our host said it was time to go back aboard his jewel.

12

It was a Friday afternoon on a crystalline October day, the sky a turquoise dome and the air keen with energy when I decided to bike home early from the office and drive out to the cottage. I tidied my desk, or at least my laptop, enough so that I could return on Monday with a clear conscience. I wanted to get back to the garden to tend the roses for their winter sleep and put up storm windows and storm doors against the coming Atlantic gales. Above all, I wanted to repossess the place where someone had tried to murder me. I wanted to vanquish demons.

To this end I had packed a bolt-action Remington rifle with a ten-power scope that took 220 Swift cartridges that I bought at Chandler's the week before. "Pick off a quarter at three hundred yards," old Mack Chandler told me as he bundled up my purchase after we had done the paperwork. I didn't reply that picking off a human head at three hundred yards would suffice if it came to that. Not that Mack hadn't sniffed out what I was up to, showing me a box of 220 Swift rounds, the slug small but the casing huge. "Do some damage with these babies," his nod as good as a wink.

I glided homewards on my bike through the leaf-blown light as though moving back through time. Because October days like this afflict natives like me with a poignant nostalgia and an inexplicable sense of expectancy. Inexplicable, because what mostly looms in the months ahead is the drear gray and cold of our northern winter.

My mood darkened markedly at the sight of Ivor Pavonine's sleek little convertible parked at the curb in front of our house next to the monster Humvee of the private security firm. I was frankly getting sick and tired of this man's insinuation into the bosom of my family. He is oblivious to what are called boundaries, not to mention the common courtesy of phoning ahead to announce his imminent arrival much less to ask, however indirectly, whether or no his visit would be welcome. The situation has only gotten worse since the success, the very modest success, of *Triad in Silence*.

I will admit that, like any man who loves his lady, I am susceptible to jealousy. Ivor Pavonine is not unattractive and he has a knack for charming others by including them in the golden glow of his abundant self-regard. And Diantha does dote on him. She brightens visibly in his presence. Her eyes grow more animated, her enunciation sounds younger, more professional, her very posture improves as though she is on stage performing.

But what can I do? When you love someone, you want that cherished someone to be fulfilled and happy. Or, at least at some default minimum, not to be unhappy. In this regard, it is extraordinary what one will suffer to foster the happiness of one's spouse, children, friends. Indeed, that happiness is most often intricately entwined with one's own happiness. Wherein lies the rub. Because, to keep Diantha happy, I find I must accommodate, with at least a pretense of goodwill, not only a person I take to be a certifiable charlatan but a person I dislike. I am, moreover, alone in this predicament. Good friends, out of consideration for Diantha -- with the exception of Izzy, who can read my heart -- will not indulge me in any sign, a roll of the eyes, say, to signal some much needed sympathy. If I am willing to tolerate the man's intrusion, who are they to complain? I sometimes wonder that they take Ivor Pavonine at his own estimation, and that it is only I, through smallness, jealousy, and expectant annoyance, who finds him offensive.

Nor was my annoyance in any way mitigated by what happened the night before. Diantha and I were getting ready for bed. She had put on a particularly fetching nightie, the kind that covers only to reveal. I was standing in my shorts when she gave me a full body hug and said as I felt her against me, "Norman, have you ever considered the possibility of *a ménage à trois* with Ivor?"

"No," I said, taken aback and looking down at her upturned face and marvelous cleavage. Feeling oddly defenseless, I resorted to humor. "With him it would be more like a *ménagerie à trois*.

She pulled away. "Why do you always joke?"

"Good God, Diantha, are we already in one?"

"With whom?"

"With Ivor, of course."

"No."

"Would you tell me if we were?"

"Yes. But it's not at that stage yet."

"Would you like to get to that stage?"

"I thought that we should at least discuss the possibility."

"Why? Diantha, if you want to start an affair with Mr. Pavo-nine, you don't need my permission. That's ultimately your busi-ness, however much it would affect me and the children."

"We... I was thinking of something more involved... with you."

"In one big bed?"

"Whatever."

"Count me out."

The look of puzzlement on her face provoked in me a sliver of incredulous anger laced with jealousy. I said, "You should know me better than that. And even if I were so inclined, it wouldn't work."

"Why not?"

"Frankly, I can't imagine him loving anyone but himself. The man is not real."

"I was being serious."

I was on the point of saying something nasty when, with a sigh of resigned relief, I realized what was behind Diantha's gro-tesque suggestion. "I suppose this is more of his life is art is life nonsense."

"It's not nonsense. It's real. It's making the ultimate leap. It's not just imitation. It's actuality."

I sat on the side of the bed and rubbed my eyes. I said wea-rily, "Exactly. And he asked you to broach this... possibility with me, didn't he?"

Diantha considered for a moment, but, being an honest soul, she is not good at dissembling much less lying. "I suppose he did."

"And you're supposed to report to him how I reacted?"

"More or less."

"Diantha, don't you see, he's just using you."

"But…"

"No buts." I fumed for a moment, standing, walking around, fisting my hands. I said, "You are an adult American. You are free to mess with that character if you want to. What you are not free to do is let that, that fraud worm his way into this family for the sake of his bogus art. If you don't draw that line, I will."

"Meaning?"

And there she had me. Because what could I do? Make him *persona non grata*? Beat him up? Hire someone like Blackie Burker to "take him out." Hardly. It would all be grist for his inane mill. But above all else, I did not want to be small or appear small in these matters. I wanted to be as large as an F. Scott Fitzgerald character. That is, I wanted my love for Diantha to encompass her happiness at whatever cost to me. But in bed with the lights out, I turned away from her knowing I would lie awake, seething inwardly at this alien thing that had crawled into our life.

Now, the sight of his vehicle placed me in something of a dilemma as I straddled my bike, leaning to one side, one foot on the ground. I had no desire to sneak in soundlessly and try to catch them in some compromising situation. Nor did I want to proclaim my arrival with seemingly inadvertent noise so that they would be fore-warned should they need to be. I considered turning around and pedaling back to work simply to avoid the man and this situation.

But, to quote Peter de Vries, I had premises to keep and miles to mow before I sleep. Besides, damn it, it was my home and I was not to be usurped even for a moment. So I did what I always do. I opened the garage door and parked my steel steed in its accustomed place. I then crossed the enclosed breezeway and let myself into the kitchen. All the while I was trying to do that most difficult thing, which is to act normally. Because when you are trying to act normally, you are not acting normally. I paused as was my custom to check the mail on the kitchen table before removing my helmet and trouser clip. From the refrigerator I poured myself a glass of lemon-flavored seltzer and carried it and the mail into the dining room. "Di," I said in as normal a volume and tone as I could muster. Their apparent absence puzzled me. Were they out for a walk? Upstairs in bed? Had I underestimated the man? Were they hiding in the cellar?

It was then that I saw them through the French windows that give out onto the conservatory and thence through another set of windowed doors to the garden. Standing on either side of the wrought iron table in the encircling arms of the rose garden, they appeared to be having a heated exchange. A lovers' quarrel? I wondered, unable to hear their voices. Because they were being most emphatic with each other. I could tell Di was angry from her facial contortions, but the chopping motion of her hand seemed faked to me. Ivor might have been placating her, nodding and holding up a finger to make a point.

Again I considered weaseling out, that is quietly packing what I needed for the weekend and leaving the house. But again it struck me as cowardly. Besides, they were colleagues of a sorts and colleagues argue. Besides in the mail there was an article on repatriation of Native American artifacts in the *Museum Director's Monthly* that I wanted to read. I went back into the kitchen and did just that.

Shortly afterwards, Diantha and her director came into the house in a state of some excitement to judge from the color in their faces.

"Norman, you're home!" She spoke with surprise but with no trace of guilt.

"Norman," Ivor echoed, grasping my hand and putting an arm across my shoulder.

I reciprocated as best I could, chagrined at my own sense of relief.

"There's ice in the fridge," Diantha said to no one in particular. "I'd join you for a drink, but I have to pick up Elsie and Norman, Jr. at Bella's."

"I'm heading out to the cottage," I told her. "I left a message…"

She made a moue. "I didn't get it."

Ivor said to her, as though resuming an interrupted conversation, "I think you're right about Myra's reaction to the disappearance of Toby. He is her husband, after all."

Diantha turned to me. "We were just rehearsing a scene from *Chronicle*."

"What chronicle?"

"*Triad with Voice*... I. P. changed the title."

"To?"

"To *Chronicle of a Murder Foretold*," the author put in.

"So there's to be a murder?" I asked.

The man shook his large blond head. "It's still very much a work in progress."

"I see. I was wondering what you were being so theatrical about."

"You watched us?" The man was suddenly alert.

"I noticed you were out in the garden... talking with emphasis."

"Did you think we were having a quarrel?" His eyes had become malign in their amusement. He had taken out an electronic thing and was thumbing words onto a screen.

"I suppose."

"A lover's quarrel?"

"Well, I might have except... "

"Except what?"

His insistence annoyed me. I said, "Except that you're not a lover."

"Really?"

"I mean of anyone but yourself."

The remark stung Diantha. "Norman! Really!"

"No, no, it's great." The man was positively beamish. "Norman, you should write dialogue."

"I'd rather speak it."

"Better and better."

I shrugged. "Surely candor has a place in this life as art stuff?"

"On stage we're lovers," Diantha chirped with an enthusiasm that made me scowl.

"But this is great," Ivor went on, lost in what could be taken as an artistic reverie. "I can write this whole scene into the play because in the play Lans is writing a play for Gwen also, who, as you know, is the younger wife of Arturo, an older academic. The writer and the woman are rehearsing the play, the husband comes home, sees them, and thinks they are lovers."

"But that isn't what happened, is it?"

He gave me a condescending smile. "But I have poetic license."

"Issued by yourself," I rejoined, knowing that the man, in the vastness of his solipsism, was immune to insult.

"But how does that advance the narrative?" Diantha asked.

The director smiled his indulgent smile. "It is not a linear narrative, remember. It's about levels. Like life. No, not like life, but life."

"Sounds like a gimmick to me," I said, turning back to my article.

"Yes, a gimmick. Yes, that's a good line, too."

"I won't be long," Diantha said, heading out the door, car keys in hand.

I wanted her to stay and for this fool to leave. I wanted to talk about the possibility of her and the children joining me later at the cottage. I wanted to be with her.

But I was stuck with this… pest. I had an urge right then to take out the Glock, hold it against his skull until the supercilious smirk faded from his face, and tell him to leave and not come back. But, of course, the damn fool would be writing it all down.

Instead the phone rang. It was Lieutenant Tracy.

"Norman, that poetry reading by Commander Morgliesh is tonight. I'm sorry I didn't let you know earlier. I've been up to here with that kidnapping thing."

I thanked him and hung up the phone. To go or not to go? That was the question. The cottage beckoned. And of late I have grown socially lazy. Because it is an effort being with other people.

Smiling and making nice when you don't feel like it. Saying the right thing. Saying anything. On the other hand…

On the other hand, I have to confess that the prospect of help from such a distinguished source as Adam Morgliesh of Scotland Yard interested me far more than a poetry reading. Not that I am averse to verse, to pun a little. Indeed, I consider poetry the chamber music of literature, but, like chamber music, the work and the performance of it must be first rate if they are not to grate on the ear and on that part of us alive to aesthetic bliss. A false note may be ignored in the tumult of a symphony or in the unfolding of a novel. But when the poet stands there alone with only his words…

Regarding any engagement with art, I use a simple equation: the pleasure, wonder, or enlightenment derived from a poem, novel, concert, film, etc. must at least equal the effort invested. With great works of art and literature, the exertion of appreciation can result in endless reward. Alas, of late, the production of poets and poetry has reached industrial proportions, a result no doubt of the profusion of creative writing departments. It is an excess based also on the notion that self-expression is good for you whether or not you have anything to express.

I exaggerate, of course. It may simply be that poetry has become such that only fellow practitioners can appreciate the felicities, the problems solved, the ingenious allusivity. Such were my thoughts as I built myself a noble martini, the exact amount of ice melt being crucial, as a distinguished biochemist once told me, all the while ignoring my guest, who hovered and talked, reducing language to noise.

13

A considerable turnout milled around in the spacious library of the Center for Criminal Justice. It was an incongruous mix. Among the word-stricken, bleared-eyed, unkempt types who frequent poetry readings, were a good sprinkling of cops, some still in uniform, as well as lawyers and other worthies from Seaboard's criminal justice establishment. I also noticed a lot of women. Perhaps they were confusing Morgliesh with a character in the crime novels of a well-known British mystery writer.

A crew from Channel Five busied themselves setting up lighting, testing mikes, and arranging two cameras, one stationary and one on a dolly. They were there at the behest of the BBC, though there would no doubt be a snippet about the event on tomorrow's news.

As we stood around before taking our seats, I found myself gratified by the apparent esteem with which many of those in attendance held me. One burly state trooper -- Sam Brown belt, jodhpurs, the whole rig -- sought me out to shake hands. "We're behind you a hundred percent," he said. Marvin Grimsby, the center's director also came over -- I had given the Bernard Lecture here a couple of years back -- and introduced me around.

I already knew Lieutenant Tracy, of course. He was there with his wife Katrina, a petite, dark-haired, pretty woman. We were chatting when Detective Lupien of the state police came over. We shook hands warmly. He asked me how I had been faring. I told him there were longer and longer stretches when I forgot all about being shot at or nearly run over.

"But stay alert," he told me, the warmth of his voice belying his dark stony eyes.

While settling in on a chair at the end of one of the several rows arranged before the lectern, I took his advice and glanced around at the stacks that led off on either side. I began absently thinking that these benign refuges from the clamorous world would soon be gone, along with the books and peace and quiet they harbor. What couldn't you find on-line? The age of Gutenberg, including these temples of reading, were disappearing right before our eyes. What next? A fine wire implanted in the appropriate part of the brain for the direct transmission of organized thought, which is what reading and writing is, after all.

At which point I gave a visible lurch. Watching me intently from the stacks to my right down near the lectern was the tall, dark-haired thirty something man who had been watching me at the theater and in the parking lot. He also bore a resemblance to the driver of the Humvee that nearly ran me over. He held my gaze for several seconds before turning and pretending interest in a book he had in hand.

A moment later there was movement around the lectern. Marvin Grimsby in company with Wendell Brothers of the Wainscott English Department and Commander Adam Morgliesh of Scotland Yard emerged from a side door. The latter two sat on chairs provided and Grimsby began his words of welcome. I glanced again at the stacks to find my stalker had disappeared. But surely, I thought, touching the Glock in its belt holster, he wouldn't try anything with all these cops around. If I wasn't safe here, where would I be safe? But his presence began to gnaw at me.

Brothers, a pale, shaggy man who, like so many literary academics, appeared bereft of words, introduced the poet in halting phrases before hitting his stride. Brothers spoke of the new territory Adam Morgliesh had opened up for the searching light of poetry. "If his verse to date has been unflinching in its collision with life, the commander's new collection, *Rigor Mortis*, is unsparing in its confrontation with final things. These poems, with their sparseness of language, with their subtle, honed wit, and with their fateful cadences, compel the reader to shake hands with his own mortality. But not alone. As the 'Bard of the Yard' -- as the commander is known in some quarters -- so plangently depicts, we are all standing in our own tumbrel as it creaks its way to our own particular and personal gallows."

The Scotland Yarder acknowledged the scattering of applause with a downcast nod as he arranged his material on the lectern.

There was more of the Oxford don about Commander Morgliesh than of an intrepid public detective. His large, saturnine face with its strong nose and pouched eyes wore an expression of tolerant, subdued humor. It was of a piece with a tall, sturdy frame, abundant, graying hair, a neat blue button-down shirt, club tie, and an old but by no means shabby corduroy jacket.

I had not taken time to retrieve any of his poetry from the library or even to peruse samples on-line. So, except for Brothers' introduction, I was quite ignorant of the man's work.

He took a moment to thank the Center and those who had organized the reading. Clearing his throat and speaking in a rich, Oxbridge accent, he said, "I won't spend a lot of time explaining my poems as I trust they speak for themselves." In an aside, he added, "If a poem cannot speak for itself, then what can?" He smiled and went on. "I will be reading from this new volume the title of which, *Rigor Mortis*, alludes to the rigor of both death and poetry and to their simple and absolute strictures. By that I mean there is no poetry without words and there is no death without finality. At least for now."

I tried to listen. But seeing X, as I called him on the wanted poster in my mind, I had walked back into the nightmare of terror. That is to say, I was in the grip of a fear that feeds and festers in the imagination while in no way being imaginary.

The commander was saying, "I have been asked why, as a law enforcement officer, I write poetry. I think the question is a polite way of insinuating that something as squalid as crime and as pedestrian as police work is antithetical to poetry and to those Olympian realms to which it aspires. Or once did, at any rate. I have no coherent answer to the assumptions in that question. I can only tell you that we must look within ourselves to find that larger world into which to escape the quotidien banalities of existence.

And, as we all know, police work too often involves that ultimate banality of which Hannah Arendt wrote so eloquently."

As he went on, I glanced around again. My stalker was nowhere to be seen. Or was that he, behind me and to my left, sitting in one of the lounge chairs that surrounded a low table strewn with periodicals? I thought of discreetly taking the Glock from its belt holster and making it handier in my side pocket.

Or was I just being melodramatic? Perhaps the fellow was one of those shy but devoted fans who fixate on someone for God knows what reason. Or was he a kind of spotter, keeping an eye on me and communicating my movements to a trigger man whose silenced pistol already rested on the bindings of some law book as he took careful aim?

Behind the lectern, the commander peered down at his text and intoned the title, "Troping the Light Fantastic" and began, reciting from memory:

Time is the fire
We burn in,
D. Schwartz told us.
He's right.
A few of us
Blaze brightly
In our hours
And leave an afterglow.
More of us
Smolder dimly
Waiting for a spark
Before we burn out.
Most of us
Are grateful
Simply
For the light.

"Speaking of light," the commander said, turning to the technician in charge of the filming, "could you angle that light just a bit. It's right in my face."

He waited. He cleared his throat. He read "*Circ de la Vie.*"

> We all balance
> Above the abyss.
> There is no safety net
> To ease the drama
> Not of who falls
> Or of who hangs on
> But of when.

I eased from my chair and stepped into the nearest opening in the stacks. The commander was saying something about the influence of Philip Larkin on his work. I shifted the Glock from its holster to my side pocket where I encircled its butt with my right hand. The commander began reading "After Larkin."

> Between death
> And decrepitude
> We usually choose
> The latter.
> It's not just
> Fear of that
> Undiscovered country.
> It's that we think
> We'll get better,
> The way we have
> Gotten better
> All our lives,
> As though there's
> A cure for time,
> As though life itself
> Were not fatal.

He said, "Working out a poem has been likened to solving a crime. But too much should not be made of the comparison. Words are both more available than the bad guys, but also just as intractable if not more so. It might be better to say that they are both, justice and poetry, compelling in that they each satisfy a craving for order."

In the twilit world of the stacks, I found myself in a section devoted to the philosophy of law to judge from the titles about Leviticus, the Code of Hammurabi, and the like. I paused as the poet recited "Again."

> The murdered body
> Of the young woman
> Lay dumped
> Like so much rubbish
> In a roadside ditch
> Beyond the verge.
> Futile anger gives way
> To pity
> And to a yearning
> For the pale Galilean
> To come again
> To teach us again
> About doing unto others.

The phrase "murdered body" resonated as I moved toward the light at the end of the row I was in. I did not want to be a murdered body, I told myself. Anything but a murdered body. I came to a line of carrels, those modest chair-and-desk cubicles where apprentice scholars practice their trade. These were spaced against the wall and facing off to my right. They were empty.

I paused to listen as the commander read a poem about what he called the bogus art of murder.

> Murder for some
> May be a form of art
> With its own rules,
> Its masterpieces and duds,
> And a tradition going back

And back and back and back
To our ape ancestors.
Murder may be just.
Murder may be necessary.
Murder may be clever.
But murder is never art
Because murder has no claim
To beauty.

Still trying to listen, I was attracted to a carrel where the chair was pushed back as though recently vacated. A book lay open on the desk. I paused, hearing the commander's voice but not his words. Overcoming scruples about invading the privacy of another, I glanced down at the book. Then I turned it enough to glimpse the title and author: *The History of Murder* by Colin Wilson.

Paranoia came over me in waves of muddled fear and self-doubt. Had someone known I was coming to the reading and deliberately left a book open, one that I would see as a portent? Of course not. I was being silly. Or was I? Cat and mouse games are all very well as long as you are not the mouse. Touching my Glock again, I moved along the carrels on high alert.

I paused then because I wanted to listen to the poetry. I reached a spot along the row of cubicles from where I could hear the recital quite clearly. The commander intoned the title "Knowing," and began.

The price
Of knowing
Is knowing
That you
Will know
And know
Until the day
You know
No more.

I was contemplating knowing no more when the back of a head belonging to a tall, dark-haired man came into view in the last carrel. Had he been dozing, bent forward, head in arms. Was it he? And if so, what was I to do? Creep up to him and poke the barrel of my gun into his upper vertebrae for a hotly whispered interrogation? Just who are you? Why are you stalking me? The object of my gaze, perhaps sensing it, turned and gave me a puzzled look. It was not he.

It was then, with a heady sense of empowerment, that I knew I was not to be the victim of terror this time. I would systematically track this guy down and confront him, with the Glock if necessary, and make him tell me who he was and why he was stalking me.

The poet sipped water from a glass and indulged in a manly clearing of his throat before talking about how he had selected and arranged the verse in his new volume. "I came up with three general categories: crime, death, and miscellany. I like to think that time is the theme linking all of them. But, of course, there may have been a bit of shoe-horning here and there. 'Oh, To Be in England' expresses what might be called perverse nostalgia." He read,

> When in some grand place
> Listed on the National Trust
> Or in some idyll green,
> I yearn for the banality
> Of the real Britain,
> Of pebble-dashed blocks
> And treeless car parks
> And motorways that lead
> From nowhere to nowhere.

I kept moving. I went past the carrels toward the back of the hall along the stacks, checking into each as I went. No one. I came out where the lounge chairs were set around the table. Not there, either. I returned to where the stacks opened into the rows of chairs and kept out of sight while still able to see and listen.

The commander was peering around at his audience. The mobile camera dollied to his left. After another sip of water, he said, "Poetry is a funny business. The fact is, if you read the ingredients on a tin of curried lamb with just the right cadence and tone of sententiousness, you can make it sound like poetry. Bad poetry, perhaps, but poetry nevertheless."

He turned a page. "Ghosts," he intoned.

> You don't have to die
> To be a ghost.
> A lot of us already
> Haunt this sphere
> As much with
> Our presence
> As we ever will
> With our absence.

Like a ghost, a determined ghost, I melted into the stacks that walled off the back of the hall. The titles here ran more to popular fare. I might have browsed *Criminality and Creativity* or *Criminals I Have Known* or *Who's Who in Organized Crime* or *The Gravity of Law* or *The Midnight Court* had I not been otherwise occupied. I moved with uncommon stealth behind the first column of books and peered out at the ranks of attentive listeners. X was sitting in the back row of chairs over to the right. But he had changed from a windbreaker and chino trousers to a brown turtleneck and jacket of dark green tweed. As I pondered, quite seriously, how and where he had changed his clothes, it occurred to me that I had entered a shadowy area of my own mind. Because suddenly my stalker was everywhere. All of the tall, dark-haired men of a certain age could have been he.

This may have resulted from a mild psychopathological condition unique to myself. I remember once, during a visit to Innsbruck in Austria when, while waiting in the train station, everyone I looked at resembled Mozart to a remarkable degree -- or at least his likeness as rendered in the della Croce oil. At first I found it amusing and somewhat incredible. I considered asking them if I could take their pictures. Then, as the episode persisted and deepened, it grew alarming. The spell didn't break until I came upon a short, heavy woman sitting with her back to me. When, trying not to seem nosy, I positioned myself for a glance at her round, scowling face, she turned out to be the very likeness of Beethoven.

I paused to calm myself. I closed my eyes, took several deep breaths, and slowly counted to ten. I have found that the unassailable logic of numbers is an effective antidote to impending mental chaos. It worked. When I opened my eyes, the taller men with dark hair of a certain age had all returned to being themselves. Which did not mean, of course, that someone was no longer stalking me. I reminded myself that someone had paid Dennis "Blackie" Burker to kill me. That wasn't imaginary unless all of life is imaginary, a kind of dream we consent to.

The poet paused without apparent annoyance as several latecomers entered and found seats. I took the opportunity to cross over to the stacks lining the other side of the hall. The carrels here, all empty as far as I could tell, followed a line of windows that gave out onto the parking lot between the Center and the Museum.

I again positioned myself where I could see the commander, however narrowly, and hear his recital. He was saying, "I write poems about crime as a category and about crimes as something that happens to people. I think it a bit of moral kitsch to assert, as someone has, that all poetry after the Holocaust is obscene. One could say, though, that anything convincingly *noir* after the mass murders of the Twentieth Century is at best problematic and at times inadvertently laughable. I would argue that poetry is not only possible, but necessary in that poetry has as much to do with truth as it does with beauty. Or, better, what might be called the beauty of truth." He bent his head and read "Time."

> They say
> You can
> Save time,
> Find time,

Lose time,
Make time,
Keep time,
Waste time,
Do time,
Buy time,
Sell time,
Borrow time,
Kill time.
I say
    Time is
A bomb
Ticking away.

Without thinking, I looked my watch. And sure enough, there was time ticking away. I checked the stacks and the carrels. No one. I sat down and listened as the commander read several poems without pausing, starting with "Don't Worry."

Getting older
You tend to think
More about death.
You wonder when and how.
Will you go to bed
And not wake up?
Will you see it coming?
How will you react?
Then the ceremonies.
Who will show up?
What will they say?
Most poignantly,
You don't want
To be forgotten.
Though eventually you will
Unless you've done
The unforgettable,

Such as write
A great symphony,
Or the unforgivable,
Such as murder
A lot of people.
Until you realize that,
Being dead,
It won't make
Any difference,
Certainly not to
The no longer you.

"Green Gold"

Nothing gold can stay
Says the New England bard.
I would say
Gold would not be gold
If it could but stay.

"Sex"

If sex is nature's way
To get us to do
Our Darwinian duty,
Then what is love
But a kind of luck,
Not just finding it,
But knowing
You've found it.

"Keeping"

A murderer can
Take your life.
But he cannot

Keep it,
Anymore than
He can
Keep his own.

"The Moral"

Crime doesn't pay
Unless you have
A business plan.

It was right then that serendipity befell me. I turned on the hard chair that went with the carrel and happened to glance out the window. There he was, jacket, chinos, and all, striding across the Center's parking lot and then into the museum's, disappearing into the dark amidst the fringe of trees on the other side. It was he, I was sure. I considered easing my way out of the library and going after him. But I satisfied myself with a cautious sense of triumph. I had flushed the S.O.B.

I felt like I had vanquished danger if not death, at least for the time being. Perhaps it was this small exultation that made me susceptible to the series of poems the commander had launched into. I caught the end of a poem about the relief of death.

...
The end of everything,
It's true.
But it should be a relief
To let others
Worry about others
And about the world,
Which will continue
To go to hell
The way it
Always has.

"Soul Addressed"

> Don't be too proud
> Of your fine brain
> Or of your wonderful body.
> They're only rentals.
> You're not even
> A tenant at will.
> If it's any consolation,
> They'll be torn down
> Shortly after you vacate.

The commander paused as though mulling over what he was to say next. He said finally, "Death might well be called life's dirty little secret. We don't really want to think about it much less wax poetic on its behalf. And yet our mortality remains at the core of our existence and is the driving force of our individual and collective creativity. How else explain religion and how it has inspired everything from the literature of the Hebrews to the Gothic cathedrals to the music of J. S. Bach? The question is: would each life be the miracle it is if it never ended?"

"Been There, Done That"

> Death is only
> The non-existence
> That existed
> For an eternity
> Before you existed
> And will return
> For another eternity
> When you renew
> Your non-existence

"To Cease"

> Think of it as
> An act of charity
> In which you
> Cede your place
> At the feast of life,
> Where, more than likely,
> You've had more than
> Your fair share

As I listened to these poems and others in that vein, my enthusiasm waxed into something more profound than enthusiasm. I experienced the kind of assent that happens when one hears one's convictions trenchantly articulated. He made me feel justified in my resistance to the project to prolong human life.

"Proud Death"

> Death be not proud?
> Nonsense, John Donne.
> Without proud Death
> To sort things out,
> We would still be
> Archaea
> Oozing gas
> In the ooze.

"Presumption"

> Life is
> The presumption
> Of the living
> So that when
> Someone dies
> We say

He passed
Or he passed away
Or he went to heaven
Or he went to hell.
Would it not be
More honest
To simply say
He ended?
Or would that, too,
Be presumption?

"I'll finish with a poem that's my favorite in the collection, though I'm not sure why. It's titled "You Would Think."

You would think
That the rich
Suffer more
When they die
Than do the poor,
The rich having
So much more
To lose.
Or is it the poor
When they die,
Who suffer more,
Life being most
Of what they have?

The commander arranged his papers and said "Thank you very much."

I was surprised at the applause, which was loud and sustained. There was a scattering of questions. When did he know he was a poet? Who was his favorite poet? At the question, "Commander, where do you find your poems?" he smiled and thought for a moment. He said, "Some poems come to you. Some you have to track down. Others, ghost poems, I call them, flit around in the shadows just out of reach."

I stood aside as the commander patiently signed books. Presently, there was only Grimsby, myself, the commander, Detective Lupien and Lieutenant Tracy and his wife. I turned to Morgliesh and introduced myself. "I enjoyed your reading very much," I said with the pleasure and enthusiasm of honesty.

"And I have taken much pleasure in your work," he replied. We shook hands cordially.

Lieutenant Tracy said, "Norman, Commander Morgliesh has asked to be assigned to your case, on an unofficial basis, of course."

"I see."

"But I thought, out of courtesy, we should ask you first," the commander explained.

"I would be more than honored," I said. "And, we can use all the help we can get."

Lieutenant Tracy politely excused himself. "Another meeting with the federals," he said, glancing at his watch. "Otherwise I would love to join you for a drink."

Detective Lupien nodded ruefully, but didn't put the matter quite so politely. "The Feebs love meetings. They don't really accomplish anything, but they do provide the illusion of doing something."

When the others had left, the commander turned to me. "I feel like a good whiskey, a beer, and some bar food. Fish and chips. How about you?"

"Sounds good," I said. "There's the Pink Shamrock, not far from here. It's a gay pub, but with a mixed clientele, if that matters. More to the point, it has decent food."

He laughed. "We might get taken for a couple of old poufs. No, altogether the best. Lead on. Food is food."

14

Behind the polished bar of the Pink Shamrock a formidable array of bottled spirits doubled themselves in a framed mirror reaching nearly to the ceiling. In the same mirror, as in a glass darkly and extending back into semi-darkness, sat older men glancing around and away. Through a door beyond them was the snug, a small room for private parties. In the better lighted precincts of the place sat junior faculty, a few noisy undergraduates, and the odd solitary drinker absently looking at the large screen perched high in a corner and tuned to an athletic event with the sound off.

Commander Morgliesh and I were led to a table in a well-lighted area not far from the snug. I took reassurance from the ambience, furtive and defiant at the same time, and, of course, from the presence of the commander. I also had my back to the wall and my Glock in a new shoulder holster from which I had rehearsed drawing in front of a mirror. Presently a waiter, an attractive black woman of college age, brought us menus and asked what we would like to drink.

The poet took her in with his seemingly mild eyes. "I would like a double Bushmills single malt, no ice, and a glass of soda on the side, no ice." He smiled at her with confiding friendliness. "Poetry makes one thirsty."

She gave the commander a second glance and then a sly smile.

He asked, "Would you recommend the fish and chips?"

"They're very good."

She didn't give me much notice as she took my order. "Same drink," I said, "but with ice in the soda water."

"And the fish and chips?"

"And the fish and chips."

"You know, Norman," the commander said after she had left, "I think Americans are better looking than the British."

"Perhaps it's our dentists."

"Of course, of course." He glanced around. "The Pink Shamrock. Only in America, I swear. But, you know, it works. There a great word you have... *funky*. I must bring Winifred here"

"Your wife?"

"Yes. She would appreciate this place." To an unvoiced question, he went on, "Winifred teaches Medieval Welsh literature at Jesus College, Oxford."

"Jesus... I spent a year there. Marvelous memory. And Medieval Welsh?"

"Poetry mostly. Winnifred is drawn to all things counter, spare... "

"Yes, Hopkins."

"She's become an authority on the origins of *La Morte d'Arthur*. You know, delving into the legend as recorded by the Welsh cleric Geoffrey of Monmouth, who wrote more in Latin than Brynnic Gaelic. Of late she's been researching Gwerful Lechain, a feminist poet of the fifteen century whose erotic poetry sounds quite modern."

With that, an unpleasant bell sounded in my psyche. Arturo, Gwen, Lans. But, surely, I was no monarch and most of our tables are rectangular. "We'd love to have you over. I think Diantha and Winifred would get along nicely."

The drinks arrived. The commander raised his small tumbler and inhaled.

"Cheers."

"Cheers."

We lapsed into easy silence as the commander looked around the place like a tourist might. Or a poet. He said presently, "You know, I get more on edge before a reading than I do arriving at a murder scene."

"You do it very well," I offered.

"Yes. But as I remarked, if you read this menu with the right intonations, you could make it sound like verse."

"So," I ventured at length, the Bushmills loosening my tongue, "how does it feel to have a fictional character modeled on yourself?"

He smiled, his face sardonic. "I'm not sure were not all fictional characters based on ourselves. But, to answer your question, I like to think I'm a bit more human than my imaginary counterpart. I mean I do love to visit old churches, but there's more to it than that. I mean why make so much of his being private when he has so little to be private about? But I quibble. She's actually done a very good job in many respects. Portraits, written or painted, tend to exalt or debase the subject. Or both."

"But she never really describes you, does she?"

"In one of her early works she states I bear a likeness to Durer's *Portrait of an Unknown Man*. But in life I believe I look a lot more like Signorelli's *Unknown Man*."

It made me remember that someone had said I bore a resemblance to the minister skating on Duddingston Loch in Raeburn's celebrated painting. I said, "I am familiar with neither work. But 'unknown man' is something of a misnomer, don't you think? I mean no one is completely unknown. Their mothers must have known them."

He shrugged. "Well, in relative terms, we are all more or less unknown."

"And, like this imagined character, you're a poet."

"I am."

"Strange that I never saw any examples of your poetry in the fictional version."

"Yes, it is rather strange. You know, I offered to write some for her, just for that character. But she turned me down. Or never really got back to me."

"But your work is… first rate… "

He shrugged. "One critic dismissed it as 'death-affirming,' and labeled me, libeled me I should say, as a 'poetaster.'" He paused to sniff and sip his whiskey. "The problem with attempting verse, Norman, is the inevitable comparison with the best. Take that Seamus Heaney poem 'Oysters.'" He bent toward me. "I mean, listen, 'In the clear light, like poetry or freedom/Leaning in from the sea. I ate the day/Deliberately, that its tang/Might quicken me all into verb, pure verb.'"

"Beautiful," I murmured, leaning back as though to avoid the salt spray.

"Or take the opening of Frost's 'To Earthward.' It goes, 'Love at the lips was touch/As sweet as I could bear;/And once that seemed too much;/I lived on air...' That is the real thing, Norman. That is the word made flesh. That is reality transfigured into language such that the language itself is the reality and not just referential, not just 'about' other things."

He paused and a frown canceled the mildness of his expression. He said, his tone dismissive, "By comparison, there are times when I think that what I write is a lot of Larkinesque muck about death. People believe death is profound when it's merely inevitable and final."

"You underestimate yourself," I said, producing a copy of *Rigor Mortis* for him to sign.

"You're too kind." He took out a pen, thought for a moment, and then inscribed it.

"The fact is," I went on, "with what's been happening to me lately, not just the attempts on my life but a very pointed conflict at work, I find I have a new appreciation both of life and the dimensions of death."

He closed the book, handed it back. "And..." he said, pausing to catch the waiter's eye and gesturing for another round. "I want to hear what you have to say."

For a moment I was tongue-tied, all but mute, without even sign language. Then it came to me, couched in words that seemed to have composed themselves. I said, "Life is beautiful, precious, and sweet precisely because it is transient. As you say so well, it is death, without which there would have been no evolution and no human life, that drives the world. It's also the great leveler. The richest, the poorest, the famous, the obscure, the mighty and the powerless all come to dust."

He smiled. "Too true, too true."

We drank slowly and well. The food arrived and the Englishman pronounced the fish and chips up to snuff. We also talked shop. He complained that high tech forensics has taken the art and craft out of murder investigation. "In the past, Norman, it took a certain amount of experience, intuition, and intelligence to find the perpetrator. Nowadays, a veritable laboratory on wheels shows up at the scene of crime. And if the criminal broke wind in the course of his crime, well you can probably get enough DNA to nail him. And then there are surveillance gadgets everywhere. Who needs a detective when breaking the law is like a film production with lights, camera, action."

He paused, voiced his appreciation of the tartar sauce, and went on. "The fact is, most of the time we have a pretty good idea of who did the deed. The challenge is proving it. By that I mean building a case strong enough to take before a jury and against a battery of sniffy barristers. Most mystery fiction, you know, where they have three or four suspects to pick from and a lot of carry-on about when the garden gate got locked and what time the dog barked. I mean, really, that's pure poppycock, pure fantasy. Real detective work…" He trailed off. "The fact is, Norman, I'm no longer in the game. They sent me over here as a 'fellow', but I'm really being put out to pasture. People of my rank are all administrators, we schedule meetings and look after the paper trail."

We both worked on our plates of food. He said, "When I was a lad, we bought fish and chips from a little shop run by an Italian. You got the whole thing in a cone of old newspaper, with vinegar and salt. I'm still looking for that taste."

I mentioned how much better fried clams seemed when I was younger.

Then, abruptly, he said, as though continuing a topic from before, "I believe in evil. I believe there is a willful, gratuitous element in a lot of crime. People do have a choice. Of course, there are those who cannot help what they do. But I think they are few and far between. Simply because you lack the imagination to put yourself in the place of the person you are harming is not an excuse. Evil can be complex but it is still evil."

I gave a nod to my Irish friend behind the bar as the commander went on. "My own moral dilemma is that I enjoy going after criminals. I enjoy tracking them down, cornering them, and bringing them to justice. So in a way, I welcome evil. Evil is my necessary evil. Without evil I would be like an antibody with no disease to fight."

"And what's happening to me right now is your necessary evil?" I smiled to blunt any possible offense.

"Too true, too true." He took a small sip of his third whiskey, savored it and held the glass up to the light. "You know, I think of good whiskey as Celtic wine. By that, I mean that it has a seemingly endless capacity to improve. Though perhaps it is my age." He smiled. "There may be a poem in that. Something about the vintage of the drink and the vintage of the drinker."

"But we don't all improve with age."

"Yes. I may steal that from you." Then, picking up another thread, he said, "You know, the paradox of crime is our collective and individual fascination with it, despite its too evident banality, not to mention the pain and suffering of its victims. I mean that evil, in its manifestation as crime, particularly murder, is usually grotesque, commonplace, glamorous as dirt, and ineffably sad."

With a prompt from me, he admitted, "It's probably in our genes, the dark crucible in which humankind evolved. 'Man hands on misery to man…' and all that."

After a silence of eating, he launched into a disquisition on murder that he had obviously been thinking a lot about. "What amazes me is how little actual discussion, research, and writing there is about murder quite aside from statistics and its entertainment possibilities. It needs a good, critical analysis."

"I'm not sure I follow you."

"Well, for a start, murder comes in as many forms as there are people. Think of all the ways you can commit murder. Gunshot, of course, strangling, poisoning, stabbing, starving and endless variations thereof. And motives are even more various. Greed, jealousy, revenge, rage, pride, envy, and madness."

"How do you define murder?"

"What an excellent question. The answer is not as obvious as one might think. Murder of course is the deliberate ending of the life of one human being by another human being. A lion killing a stray jogger on safari in Africa is not murder. But Christians killed by lions in the Colosseum for the enjoyment of the populace is murder."

"What about the killing that goes on in warfare?"

"Another good question. I would say that in actual combat that killing is not murder whereas killing captured, unarmed soldiers is murder. The key element is defenselessness on the part of the victim."

"So someone killed in duel is not murdered?"

"No. Choice is involved and it assumes that both parties are equally armed."

"What about an execution?"

He pondered a moment. "Depends, doesn't it? When the state of Florida executed Ted Bundy, I would call that a legal execution. When Stalin deliberately starved to death upwards of six million Ukrainians in the terror famines of the early thirties, that was murder, mass murder."

"And there are degrees of murder."

"Exactly. The distraught wife who gives her long-suffering terminally ill husband an overdose of sleeping pills is only technically a murderer and, in my opinion, far less guilty than the drunken sod who slams his vehicle into another car and kills people."

After a pause, I asked, "Tell me, do you have children?"

"Oh, yes, we have children and grandchildren. My love life has not been tortured, as it may appear in the fictional version of my existence. Not, mind you, that I want to complain overly about how I've been depicted. And, speaking of unknown men, let's not forget that we have our own unknown man to find."

"You mean the person or persons who arranged to have the late Mr. Burker shoot at me."

"Indeed."

And to my surprise, he took up his brief case, rootled through it and came up with a file. "Let's get down to it, shall we?"

Over coffee and complementary biscuits, we began by going over possible suspects from my past. The brothers Snyder were still in legal captivity. Mr. Damon Drex appears to have disappeared.

He turned pages. He said, "I'm quite intrigued, frankly, with what's happening at the Genetics Lab."

I nodded. "I suppose we have to look at that."

"To be sure. Let me ask you, has Professor Fortese been among those pressing to go onto the next stage on that anti-aging treatment?"

"As a matter of fact, she has. She has been particularly adamant."

"And while everyone stands to benefit from this marriage of pure research and commercial exploitation, Carmina Fortese would benefit most?"

"Right. But Professor Fortese is one of Wainscott's leading scientists. She may have a pecuniary and professional interest but…"

Commander Morgliesh, now very much the investigating officer, smiled with an indulgent wryness. "You are undoubtedly right. But let me acquaint you with some realities of which you may not be aware."

"I am listening."

"Professor Fortese has some not-so-distant relatives in Rhode Island, notably the half brothers Dominic Fortese and Patrick Fortese. They are the tail-end of a crime family that prospered in the thirties and then all but died out… as far as that business went. There's also another branch of the family involved in Pyrapharm, the Naples-based pharmaceutical firm, a director of which just happens to own a significant share of Rechronnex."

"How did you get all this?" I asked, not trying to dissemble my surprise.

"Off the record, way off the record… "

"Of course."

"Detective Lupien of the state police and your good friend Lieutenant Tracy have both briefed me and shared the results of their own low-keyed investigations. And, you can't keep an old bloodhound from sniffing around."

"I see. You were saying, about Rechronnex ... ?"

"As you are aware, Rechronnex is currently under investigation by the Securities and Exchange Commission."

"Yes, but I'm not up on the details."

"They've been running a scam in which they profit whether their projects succeed or not."

"Yes, the hairless mice."

"Right, but enough of the projects pay off. Otherwise no one would invest. But sometimes, because there's so much money sloshing around the system these days -- or used to be, anyway -- people are desperate to find a place to put it. Rechronnex floats a proposal about an anti-aging drug, and the fund managers and the other rich guys line up begging for a piece of the action. In some cases, there's probably a kick-back. And if it doesn't work, the investors are out a few tens of millions they can write off against gains. You spread the risk wide enough, a million here, a couple of million there, and pretty soon..."

It was in that context that we discussed the email I had received from Worried. I explained Worried's significant involvement in earlier cases. He was considering that when the check arrived. I took it with eagerness and fished out a credit card. "Sorry, Commander, your money's no good here. In fact, I should probably arrange something of a budget if you're going to be working on this thing."

He nodded, but was clearly thinking about something else. "If and when the occasion arises. Also, send over a copy of the email. It may prove quite significant."

I had signed the chit and was about to rise when he beckoned to hold a moment. "Let's not forget Victor Karnivossky. We have to consider any possible involvement on his part."

"Yes," I agreed, "but how?"

"I've already spoken with him and he's agreed to meet with us."

"You astonish me. How did you manage that?"

"Through friends. They gave me his private number and I called him up. I'll check with you tomorrow and we can set up a meeting."

We got up and made our way outside. The commander stopped and inhaled the cool fresh air. He said, "We have to keep you alive, Norman. Unless you're half in love with easeful death."

"Not quite yet," I said, taking in a deep draught of my own.

"Winifred will be coming over in a week or so. We'll plan to get together with you and with your wife."

"We'll do it," I said as we shook hands.

I walked back down Belmont Avenue and into the museum's parking lot aware of the darkness and possible danger around me. But there was comfort in the touch of the Glock and knowledge that another competent professional was also working on my case.

15

The university's Oversight Committee met this afternoon at the behest of Professor Ébène, Chair of the Victim Studies Department. We were summoned to address what she calls "The bicycle seat incident outside Champers Hall."

As many people know, Ébène, a mononymous female of color, began life as Deville Pruitt, who, to judge from photos of him as a youth, was very much a male, indeed, a rather pale male. About a year ago, Professor Ébène "came out" with considerable fanfare, as a "trans-gender, trans-conscious, trans-temporal human being" and was greeted with much acclaim. She often will begin a pronouncement with, "As a former male…" She wears her hair in cornrows each secured with a bead of ethnic origin. Her blue eyes and high cheekbones give her a strangely Nordic look. That, and her broad shoulders and hips noticeably slender even in the full skirts she wears with knee-high riding boots have given rise to rumors that she began life as a white male.

Her memoir, *From Black Brother to Black Sister: Odyssey of an American Soul*, provoked any number of think pieces in serious journals and made several of her fellow academics envious with its attendant notoriety. Not that the response was all positive. One critic, an African American woman -- presumably from birth -- contended that "Professor Ébène represents a typical example gender imperialism on the part of males." Another critic accused her of "elbowing for space on the over-crowded moral high ground and making a mockery of black culture by lapsing into homeboy argot when the occasion suited." Yet another lumped her with men "cashing in on the hard-fought gains women of all colors have struggled for since time immemorial."

More recently, she created wavelets with a foray into the murky depths of race polemics in the form of an essay titled, "The Racism of Snow." To quote, "Although snow is white and cold and hostile to life, it is not, by itself, inherently racist. What makes snow racist is its elevation by white people to a normative good within the context of a common discursive nexus that has become the unconscious standard."

She goes on to ask, "Would white people flock to ski resorts to repeatedly slide down steep hills if snow were black? Would they urge their children to make snow men and snow women if snow were black or brown?" It then goes on to discuss "tropes" like "Snow White" and dreaming of a "white Christmas."

She ran into some flak from environmentalists when she claimed that the alarm over melting icecaps at the poles was generated by the white race who "came from snow and thrive in snow" and fear "losing their global identifying patrimony."

Heard more than once to exclaim that "Punctuation is racist!" Professor Ébène is known for uncovering "whiteness" in many aspects of daily life. Among these is dental hygiene ("Why all the emphasis on white teeth?"); punctuality ("the worship of white time"); Christianity ("worshipping the white son of a white god"); grading for courses ("the white quantification of learning"); and the Gregorian calendar ("with all its naming of days and months after white gods or white emperors").

To quote my friend Izzy Landes, "What's next as racist? Clean water and fresh air?" It's hard to believe, he says, but this kind of nonsense is now taken seriously by what he calls "the idiocracy."

At present, Ébène occupies a named chair on comparative victimization. In that capacity she was recently widely quoted as saying "Victimhood is not for everyone," apparently in response to the increasing number of people of all stripes claiming victim status. She speaks perfectly fluent, academic English, crossing her t's and dotting her i's and keeping who and whom where they belong. Her occasional resort to "Blackish" as she calls it, is deliberately "performative" and deployed to remind her listeners that she speaks from a moral realm that includes the linguistic.

Most of the unusual suspects, as Izzy calls them, showed up for the meeting. Izzy, of course, is the author of *The Nature of Nature* and its companion book, *The Science of Science*. He is a good and close friend and like me casts a baleful if amused eye on the proceedings of the committee.

Father S. J. O'Gould, S.J., an authority on Teilhard de Chardin and author of the forthcoming *The Future of Eternal Life*, arrived wearing his collar, a courageous gesture at a time when so many of the Catholic clergy are pilloried in public whether they deserve to be or not.

The Reverend Randall Athol of the Wainscott Divinity School, who personifies just how far the Protestant ethic has declined, came late and made his apologies. He was accompanied by Professor J.J. McNull, an eminent member of the many committees on which he has spent a considerable part of his career.

I was glad to see Berthe Schank, now positively svelte, her long dark hair piled up in back like a proper Boston lady of old. Marriage -- to a woman -- has done wonders for her, though she can still wield a sharp tongue when the occasion demands.

I noticed that Ariel Dearth, the much maligned and very busy professor and practitioner of law, was sitting next to an attractive addition to the committee. It turns out that a young woman named Tyler has been hired to take the minutes of the meetings and, with the advice and consent of the chair, deal with the media. I don't doubt that, before long, Tyler, who has a degree in something, will need an assistant with a degree in something.

The chair graciously introduced Tyler to the committee members along with Muriel Gaskins, as assistant professor of English at the university. Professor Gaskins, in her thirties and fetching in a slender, fresh, freckled-faced way, she made no effort to dissemble a certain impatience with being among us. I adduced that she was filling in for an older, more established colleague, a favor that would no doubt help her reach the promised land of tenure.

On this occasion I should note that it is with real regret that I report the passing of John Murdleston. He apparently had been in ill-health for some time. My regret is both professional and personal. I liked John very much. He was a voice of common sense on the Oversight Committee. As curator of the museum's extensive collection of Paleolithic coprolites, he typified the kind of cooperation that once thrived between the Museum of Man and Wainscott University, where he was a professor and noted scholar. His monumental *The Origin of Feces: What Coprolites Tell Us About Evolution* still remains the standard work in the field.

I understand that there is some sentiment to have the museum's extensive collection of coprolites named in his honor. I have no objections whatsoever. Indeed, I must talk to Edwards, who is in charge of exhibits, to mount a special one as a tribute.

Chair Constance Brattle, the well-known expert on blame, after some preliminary remarks, ceded the floor to Professor Ébène. The professor stood, cleared her throat. This time she eschewed her caricature of black speech in saying that "I hear from some of the sisters black and white say they mount their bikes now with a feeling of violation. You know what I'm saying? Some of them are carrying a can of spray cleaner that they put down on their seats after they park their bikes on the campus or in the town."

I glanced at the others, but except for Izzy, who caught my eye, the faces were blank or portentous. Knowing nods went around the table. It was like being in the presence of a holy fool whose every utterance is tolerated if not applauded.

"Perhaps," someone ventured, "we should ask President Morin to make a statement declaring that the university will spare no effort to make sure the bicycle seats of all students, faculty, and staff will be kept inviolate."

The professor of victimization frowned skeptically at this offering. "What we be needing…" She paused and began again, "What we need is action, real action."

I raised my hand. "Aren't we jumping the gun here. I mean we are not at all certain that Professor Byles was acting inappropriately. He may well have thought he had parked his bike there and was trying to find it without the aid of his glasses. I've forgotten at times where I parked my own bike. And he is far-sighted."

I tried to sound a reasonable note, but in fact I was on edge. That morning, Commander Morgliesh phoned to tell me that we were to meet Victor Karnivossky the day after tomorrow at Freddie Bain's old place out in the country. It was not something I looked forward to. Mr. Karnivossky was not called "Dead Meat" for nothing.

Someone was saying, "Isn't the appearance of bicycle-seat sniffing as bad as the thing itself?"

Ignoring this, Professor Ébène, who makes no effort to hide her personal and professional dislike of me (she considers the MOM a bastion of white-male triumphalism and refers to the collections as a "trophy hoard"), eyed me with cool malevolence. "The fact is that through my network of sister colleagues, there be, there are reports of incidents at other institutions."

"You mean bicycle-seat sniffing is more widespread than we think?' someone asked.

The interrupted professor nodded. "In many ways, it doesn't matter what Professor Byles was doing outside of Champers Hall on the day in question. The very fact that the students..." She paused and began jabbing her hands as though about to speak Blackish. "...that the sisters are afraid of being violated speaks volumes to the kind of society we be having here in Wainscott, in Seaboard, and in the United States of America, the richest country in the world."

"Not for long," someone murmured.

In a lower register, Professor Ébène added, "These are real people with real names and real feelings and... "

"And real bicycle seats," Izzy put in.

Professor Athol, matching Professor Ébène's righteousness, though on a lower key, commented, "I think it is incumbent upon the committee to make sure that the Wainscott health services have made appropriate counseling available to those at Champers Hall who need it."

"What about enforcing the law?" someone asked, turning to Arial Dearth, whose full handle is the Von Beaut Professor of Ethics and Litigation Development. The committee relies on him for legal advice.

"I doubt there are any statutes on the books specifically prohibiting the sniffing of bicycle seats," he sniffed. "A judge might regard it as lewd and indecent behavior, but it would have more weight if the state legislature or at least the city council passed a law."

"So, there are no statutes dealing with what might be called olfactory trespass?" Professor Athol asked.

That launched Izzy Landes and Father O'Gould into a bit of badinage about being nosy. Counselor Dearth reminded them that voyeurism in some circumstances was against the law and that olfactory trespass might be considered a form of voyeurism.

I ventured that olfactory trespass could go both ways.

"In what way?" someone asked.

"In the sense that *smell* is both a transitive and intransitive verb."

To evident puzzlement around the table, Izzy said, "Norman means that one can smell a dead fish that smells."

Ms. Gaskins, who had been surreptitiously reading something on her open laptop perked up. "The fact is, bicycles are far more than just a vehicle for getting around with relative ease. The Irish satirist Flann O'Brien cited instances in his native land where man and bicycle had virtually melded together to become one creature."

"And to what is this pertinent?"

"Well, you could say that bicycles, like people, have private parts. I mean that's why we're so sensitive about this."

"Yes, but other than the seat, what parts of the bicycle might be vulnerable to molestation?"

"Certainly not the wheels."

"Except to dogs."

"I think we should get back to bicycle seats," Chair Brattle said. "The question is, given the urgency of the situation as outlined by Professor Ébène, what are we going to do about it?"

At that point in the proceedings, having little to add to the discussion, I took a leaf out of Professor Gaskins book, though I did feign attention, glancing up few minutes to frown or look puzzled, while reading over *A Voice of Nature*, the manuscript Alphus had given me for editing and suggestions. I opened to the chapter titled, "The Varieties of Human Excreta."

He begins quite dispassionately with an overview of excrement as it is generally conceived. He alludes to its rich tradition as a metaphor down through the ages and across all cultures, particularly in reference to speech and ideas. He then changes gear into what can only be described as a muck-raking mode. "The only way to look at pollution of whatever kind is as a form of human excrement. Over the centuries and particularly in the last hundred years people have allowed themselves to defecate anywhere and at any time with waste far more toxic than mere excrement. Humankind, in short, has treated the biosphere as an open sewer. As a consequence, all of creation gags on the waste of God's chosen species."

Alphus goes on to explain how, "In the world at large, excrement is part of the natural cycle. One organism's waste is another's nutrition. The byproducts of metabolism, perspiration, respiration, and ultimately, our very bodies, recycle endlessly through the biosphere. Thus, as Hamlet tells us, 'a King may go a progress through the guts of a beggar.'"

He then declares that ordinary human excrement, "though the product of a grossly swollen population and though laden with heavy metals and other impurities, poses no great problem for the environment."

I raised my head at this point to hear someone suggest that bicycle seats "could be covered when left in a public place."

"Wouldn't the sniffers simply remove them?"

"The covers could be made lockable."

This provoked a discussion very much in the subjunctive mode as to who would provide said covers should they be available. Was it the responsibility of the individual to protect his or her bicycle seat from olfactory molestation or did this fall within the purview of the university in providing security for its students and scholars?

I dipped back into the manuscript. "In the larger sense, however, the varieties of human excrement are all but endless and far more toxic to the living world than any amount of plain old shit." I was about to put a question mark next to the last word, but decided it was apposite in the context.

There follows a long and frankly depressing section devoted to the various kinds and amounts of poisons spewed into the air, discharged in water, and spread on the land. He asserts, "Research shows that human waste in one form or another can be found fouling the earth's atmosphere, suffusing the oceans of the world, and lacing the soil and subsoil of every part of the planet. It even infects the ice of the melting glaciers."

I heard the Reverend Athol say, "Perhaps those who are worried about their bicycle seats could remove them and carry them with them after they park their bikes."

Another member suggested, "We could place the bicycle racks in locked enclosures to which only those who park their bikes there would have a key."

Another countered with, "Yes, but isn't it possible that there could be sniffers among those with keys?"

I went back to the manuscript. "Among the most malignant forms of human excrement is that spewed out in what are called persistent organic pollutants or POPs. The original 'dirty dozen' in this category included aldrin, chlordane, DDT, polychlorinated biphenyls, and toxaphene, just to name a few."

Then, "Nor do these toxins excreted by human activity simply persist in the environment. These same POPs are also classed as PBTs, that is, persistent, bio-accumulative, and toxic. The lipid solubility of POPs allows them to pass through biological membranes and accumulate in the fatty tissues. Ironically, our bodies, be we fish, flesh, or fowl, cannot excrete these poisons that human beings have so carelessly dumped into the environment."

I confess I did not want to peruse the paragraphs that followed. These were devoted to radioactive contamination from power plants, bomb tests, and medical devices, what Alphus labeled, "permanent pollution."

"Horseshit," said Berthe Schank. "I've never heard such horseshit in my whole life. If some old guy wants to sniff bicycle seats, who in God's name is he hurting? Surely this committee has more important matters to discuss." She stopped, exacerbated. "You know what we are? We are now the little old ladies in tennis shoes."

Izzy said, "I agree with Berthe. Though it may be unseemly, Professor Byles has every right to sniff bicycle seats outside of Champers Hall on a sunny day. Under English Common Law, what is not expressively forbidden is allowed, is that not right Professor Dearth?"

"Well, the activity to which you refer may not be expressly prohibited by law or regulation, but may come under the provisions outlawing obscene and indecent behavior, as I said." He went on in his awful voice, "the university, at the very least, could pass a regulation expressly forbidding the molestation of bicycles on its property."

"Sniffing the seat of a bicycle scarcely seems like molestation."

"If you were the injured party, you would feel differently."

I went back to the manuscript, to a section labeled, "Practical Steps." Alphus begins by questioning the concept of a "carbon footprint." He writes, "The phrase is metaphorically deficient inasmuch as footprints are, by their very nature, ephemeral; they are easily erased by wind, water, and human agency. Nor is the devastation of the biosphere limited to an excess of carbon in the air. As noted earlier, the range of noxious effluvia caused by human existence ranges from carbon to toxic chemicals to radioactive waste. The effects of human activity go from the extinction of species to the destruction of forests to the poisoning of the planet's waters.

"A more accurate measurement of this biospheric destruction might better be termed the Excrement Index or EI. In this figuration, an individual's total despoliation of the environment would be calculated and given in a sliding scale. This would range from 1 (for, say, a celibate Bhutanese monk living in a cave on donated rice husks) to a Wall Street banker with penthouse apartments, multiple mansions, yachts, private jets, etc., whose IE might be 10,000 on an open-ended range."

In a note to me neatly typed and attached with tape, he asks "Does the word *excrement* in this context have too much of a positive connotation? Should I consider calling it Long Term Toxicity Index (LTTI) or Poison Quotient (PQ) or something of that sort?"

I wrote on the same note, "I think PQ would answer nicely as a kind of negative IQ."

In the manuscript proper, Alphus comes out strongly against any trading in "Excrement Index credits." Instead, he suggests that one's IE be taxed on a graduated scale and the revenues dedicated strictly to "environmental healing and preservation." The number of children "spawned" by an individual would also be included in the calculation of one's EI. Thus, the African chieftain living in a compound with four wives and thirty offspring would be an object of censure even if living too wretchedly for anything like taxation.

Professor J. J. McNull, who had been glowering through his beard during most of the meeting, asked for and was granted the floor. He said, "I think this is all well and good, but we are forgetting a vital aspect of this whole business. This committee must get to the bottom of how and why two members of the Seaboard Police Department were allowed to question and frankly harass a distinguished member of the Wainscott faculty."

I lifted my head from Alphus' text to hear my name being bandied about, something to the effect, "Norman has agreed to contact the Seaboard Police and arrange for them to attend our next meeting." When I didn't object, it was moved and passed that I approach my connections in the SPD to see if personnel of "decision-making capacity" might be induced to attend a meeting of the committee to discuss steps that might be taken to avoid such incidents in the future.

I said I would make inquiries but that, given the kidnapping at Hooker's Point and the resources devoted to finding and rescuing the victims, it might be some time before anyone was free to attend. But I added that I would do what I could do and went back to what I had been perusing.

Alphus concludes the chapter on what I can only take as a facetious note: He suggests that there be a coat of arms for the human race, which he describes thusly:

Arms: Per fess argent (sale) and vert (mal) in chief a dead martlet, wings askew and eyes closed and in base water gules barry semy dead fish.

Crest: Out of masoned gules chimney stack sable thick plumes of smoke and pellets.

Supporters: On the dexter side, barry sable and argent, obese in Wyvern aspect, neck gorged with sausage links purpure, bezanty. On sinister side, barry sable and argent, obese crowned king sejant at stool.

Motto: In Latin -- *Terra est nostra cloaca*. In English -- The world is our sewer.

16

That descriptions of dreams in literature or over coffee in the morning usually fall flat, I will not dispute. But that will not deter me from recounting what has suffused my day with an aura of horror and fascination. The word nightmare does not do it justice. I swear it consumed my sleeping night, but in all likelihood flashed though my sleeping brain in seconds. Or not. Because it persisted, came back and then back again as though the dream director wanted different versions. Of what, you may ask, and I will tell you, though by now the remembered sequence is a scrambled mess of piquant fear and febrile loathing.

The recurring core of the thing has Ivor Pavonine hanging in the tree instead of Blackie Burker. He does not shoot at me but he does taunt me to shoot him, telling me to aim at his heart and pull the trigger and enjoy it. Taunt me? More like tempt me. Of course, being a dream, it took liberties with reality. Diantha shows up with Bella and the children and begins to spread a picnic *sur l'herbe*. She has stopped at Abe's Seed and Supplies for a wedge of country cheese, and I plead with them to keep back, under cover, because it's not really Blackie Burker or Ivor Pavonine up in the tree with a rifle, but Freddie Bain, AKA, Manfred Bannerhoff, AKA you name it.

They ignore me, spread a blanket and bring out devilled eggs, Abe's cheese, magnums of champagne, fresh French baguettes. The moose from the Hobbes Landing Hotel, his antler restored, comes smiling out of the woods to tell us all is forgiven. All the while I hold a cocked revolver, even when I am pouring the champagne into fragile flutes for any number of guests, including my Aunt Eudoxia and others from the beyond. All the while, again, the figure in the tree, who goes from foul-mouthed Blackie

Burker to Ivor Pavonine cum Freddie Bain to Christ on the cross as rendered by Michelangelo, presides like a target I long to shoot and kill.

The problem is (Sigmund, are you listening?) that every time I raise the gun to fire, its barrel goes soft and uncertain, a bit like Abe's cheese, and the guests at the party laugh and tell me to cover myself. They will not listen when I tell them that the thing hanging from the tree, even if it is just a porcupine, is dangerous. They don't mock me as it is my property and my picnic, but, almost worse, they tolerate me as a likeable, even interesting fellow who owns an old museum in town.

I admit to what might be called liberated jealousy when Diantha, dressed in what might be called epidermal tights, takes a glass of wine over to the tree and hands it to Ivor Pavonine, obviously tumescent in revealing tights. Aunt Eudoxia, a spinster, is not subtle in her encouragement. I raise my gun again, but it is only my hand, index finger pointing, my thumb the hammer of my make-believe revolver which is firing impotent bullets at the thing hanging from the tree.

For me it is the lingering aura rather than the fading specifics of a dream or dream sequence that haunts the morning after, the day after, the year after. A glow of righteousness surrounded my frustrated desire to shoot and kill the thing hanging from the tree. Though dreams grant permission to dream, I resisted the daydream of having Ivor Pavonine, in whatever incarnation, helpless on a tree while I, with dark pleasure, riddle him with bullets. I resisted and indulged that dark fantasy at odd moments of normal, everyday consciousness as I went about my routines as husband, father, museum director, and reasonably ordinary human being. In those re-creations -- not unalloyed to recreations -- my better self would inevitably intervene: it may be human but it is wrong to take pleasure in dreams of evil.

The dream and its persisting aura left me in a quandary that nagged at the corners of my mind while conscious: Was I playing the complacent cuckold? Was my wife and this other man hiding an affair in plain sight? I would not be the first husband to be deceived by an ambitious spouse dreaming of bigger, brighter worlds. I forget that Diantha is a trained actress. Could she not be playing the role of my wife with all the finesse of her art? Actors routinely inhabit two worlds at the same time -- the real and the imagined, often, one assumes, confusing the two. Could it be, I ask myself in the hollows and holdings of my heart, that her life as my wife constitutes the imaginary and her acting with Ivor Pavonine on and off the stage the real?

But here, my imagination fails me. I can suspect, halfway envision, but not really picture them in the throes of passionate love-making. But then the chemistry between two people can have an unsuspected volatility. Men and women can change utterly once the bedroom door is closed and the clothes come off. The modestly dressed bookish librarian can turn into a tigress on the mattress, etc., etc.

The strange thing is that I can imagine Diantha committing adultery, but not with Ivor Pavonine. She is a vital, large living being while there is something self-cancelling about that man such that what is left over he would need keep for himself.

I am not proud of these half suspicions. I want my love to be absolute and without conditions. Meaning I am even less proud, indeed embarrassed, by meaner calculations. To wit: Surely Diantha wouldn't squander herself on someone as incidental as Ivor Pavonine. There have to be standards in such matters. Not that I wouldn't be wounded were she to cavort with some glib, glossy office-holding politician or a muscular, famous athlete or a wealthy banker. But Ivor Pavonine? What does that make me? At which point in my musings I have to resist fantasies of gaudy, vengeful murder, one inflicted with equal doses of pain, humiliation, and terror.

A final, curious observation. The thought of Diantha committing adultery with Ivor Pavonine with all that it would entail -- the kisses and endearments culminating in a naked, writhing juncture -- makes her very real to me. In that torrid light, I could see her as an individual with a life, an identity, an existence quite apart from my own. I love her the more for it even as the demons of jealousy rattle their manacles in the cage where I restrain them and even as the thought of removing her would-be lover from this world flares darkly in my heart. It takes an effort to resist that lightless flame, to eschew the dim glow of its details. For murder is all about details, especially the foretaste of the terror one would wreak on the one who would supplant one's love.

17

For the drive to visit Victor Karnivossky with Commander Adam Morgliesh, I borrowed Diantha's car -- a powerful sports utility vehicle with an instrument panel worthy of a jetliner. Under my shirt I put on the lightweight bulletproof vest the SPD had sent me and carried the Glock snug in its shoulder holster under my jacket. The fact is, I needed all the props I could get to muster the courage for the meeting, the confrontation, the showdown or the shoot-out -- whatever it was we faced on that blustery autumn day.

"The rap sheet on Victor 'Dead Meat' Karnivossky goes back decades," Lieutenant Tracy told me when I called to tell him that the commander and I planned to meet with the man. "But he never spent a day inside."

"Do you think it's risky?" I asked, hoping I didn't sound as nervous as I felt.

"Hard to say. I doubt it, but you never know. He has a reputation for efficiency. When he said someone was dead meat, they were just as often disappeared meat."

So even with the Glock, the vest, and with one of the preeminent law enforcement officers in the world sitting next to me as we drove northwest out of Seaboard towards the Eigermount, trepidation clutched at my vitals. Besides, it was an inauspicious day, the sky baleful with scudding clouds and the air hectic with erratic winds. I sank into Poesque gloom as we drove though the quaint village of Tinkerton, a virtual ghost town in this season. Then Crystal Lake, its somber waters dark as the dank tarn of Auber. Then up through stands of pine and hemlock into the ghoul-haunted woodland of Weir. I exaggerate, of course, but there are days when the very air smacks of the tomb.

We missed the turnoff, backtracked, and presently came to the drive. Around a bend past a stand of birches there it was, Freddie Bain's former redoubt, high, wide and round, a sinister gothic folly of cut granite crouching against the forested hillside, the slits of its vertical windows gazing out, blank and pitiless.

I very nearly lost heart. For it was here, in the calm wake of a wracking winter storm several years ago now, that I bungled my way into the place, shot Bain in the heart, and rescued Diantha. I never relive that horrendous event without a vivid sense of how close we came to being murdered.

But Commander Morgliesh showed a determined cast of face as I parked the SUV and as we trod the faux bridge across the faux moat and were sounding the knocker dully on the great oaken doors.

To my amazement, which I politely dissembled, the same Babushka who had served the previous occupant opened one of the studded portals and showed us in and took our coats. Very little had changed. The hollow heart of the absurd place rose four stories to an octagonal skylight, the same antlered heads, gazing out with cervid placidity, festooned the massive fieldstone fireplace and the same sofas and chairs remained upholstered in black leather. Oddly enough, Bains' Nazi art had been replaced with oils of Queen Elizabeth and Prince Philip, which hung alongside a Union Jack.

The Babushka withdrew with a gummy smile and we stood in front of the fireplace where birch logs crackled merrily.

Presently a side door opened, and a stout, dignified man, old but not elderly, was pushed in seated in a wheelchair. He was carefully attired in a tweed hunting jacket, gun patch and all, white shirt, lilac cravat, gray slacks, and shining black loafers, "Gentlemen," he said without preamble, extending his hand, "you honor me with your presence."

We shook hands, gave our names, and settled ourselves around a coffee table on which stood a bottle of sherry and three small glasses of the kind you might find in an Oxbridge common room. His assistant, a look-alike for Vladimir Putin except for his hair, which covered his head like a cap of brushed fur, kept one fist behind his back in a waiterly fashion as he poured wine into the three glasses.

"*Shalom*," our host said, lifting his glass and sipping thoughtfully.

We drank to his health. I began to relax. One doesn't wish peace upon someone in Hebrew and then have him shot. Unless one is being maliciously ironic.

Mr. Karnivossky regarded us with benign curiosity. He bore a striking resemblance the British actor who played Gandhi in the film of that name. Bald and white as a white egg, he looked down a great beak of a nose which was of a piece with the pleated back of his Prussian neck, shrewd dark eyes, and strong mouth, gone just a bit tremulous with age.

"Now, gentlemen, what can I do for you?" he asked, his accent Russian but with more than an edge of the King's English.

The Scotland Yarder, his eyes and voice deceptively mild, leaned forward and said, "You may be able to help us with a problem."

"Please. I am at your service."

"As you have surely heard by now, someone hired Blackie Burker of South Boston to travel all the way up to Mr. de Ratour's cottage to take shots at him with a sniper rifle."

"As I've been told."

Our host looked at me with consideration. "You are lucky to be alive, Mr. de Ratour. Among other things, Mr. Burker was known as 'Sure Shot Burker.'" Then, "Yuri," making a circling motion with his finger.

The assistant recharged our glasses. We lifted them and sipped again.

"And you want to know if I had anything to do with it?"

"Or if you could help us out with anything you might know or have heard about it," I put in to soften any implied accusation.

He held up his hands, palms out. "*Da, da*, I have heard the stories. Victor Karnivossky is moving into the Seaboard area and taking over where Manfred Bannerhoff left off. You know, until this mad business up the coast, I had FBI officers working over-time to keep me company. The fact is I am retired. But I trust you gentlemen not to trust me when I say that. In my business, retirement can be perilous."

"And you have no idea… ?" the commander ventured.

He shook his impressive head. "Neither I nor any of my colleagues had anything to do with the assault upon Mr. de Ratour. Indeed, I am indebted to you, sir, for dispatching that… that storm trooper. I let him have this territory for his business operations. I exacted only token tribute. But he wasn't satisfied. No, he wanted to interfere with my business elsewhere. I do not take kindly to people who lack a sense of due gratitude."

He paused, nodding, getting back on the track of his original thought. "I do not know who hired Mr. Burker to shoot at you, my friend. To tell you the truth, as I said before, I am surprised that you are still among the living. Mr. Burker was known not to miss."

"He didn't miss himself," the commander put in.

Mr. Karnivossky's head went back in silent mirth showing strong, even teeth. He signaled for another splash of the excellent sherry. We paused and sipped again. They were small glasses and, I realized, we were drinking it like shots of vodka.

He inhaled audibly and his expression turned shrewd, the impressive dome of his forehead furrowing as though to match the back of his neck. "I may be able to help you," he allowed. He paused to muse or pretend to muse. "But I must ask something in return."

The commander and I both nodded in a provisional sort of way. "Tell us," my colleague said.

Mr. Karnivossky cleared his throat. He said, "I am having some difficulty in obtaining a visa to visit your country, Commander Morgliesh."

"What kind of visa?"

"A resident visa would be ideal. But I would settle for something less. I thought you might have some influence with the Home Office. I know my reputation is not all that savory, but I am, as I told you, retired, and there are no outstanding warrants or that sort of thing. I mean it's not as though I am some kind of terrorist…" He trailed off and smiled.

"I know a few chaps in the Home Office," the commander allowed. "I'll see what I can do."

"You should know, Commander, in your efforts on my behalf, that my legal name is now Victor Carnovan."

The commander noted that down, spelling it out. "It might take a while."

"Anything would be much appreciated." He paused, "In return, I will make inquiries among… persons I still know in Boston. If nothing else, I will point you to persons you can talk to."

At some unseen signal, Yuri cleared away the wine and glasses and indicated to the Babushka where to place a silver tray with matching tea service on the table before us. Cups and saucers, small plates, and a platter with crumpets, which we call English muffins.

"Are those crumpets?" the commander asked with amused surprise.

"The very thing," said our host. "And Earl Gray tea, of the stronger kind." As Yuri hovered, waiting to pour, he went on with an awkward casualness, asking, "Do you get down to Kent very often, Commander?"

"I did when I was a boy. My uncle was Rector at Saint Bothenwith's near Margate."

"Yes," our host said. "You know Austen Abbey?"

"In fact, I do. Lord Marlgrove's old place. My Uncle Albert knew the family quite well. His wife and Lady Marlgrove were cousins. We visited one Christmas when I was a boy. An impressive old pile, but not very comfortable. Drafty, you know. I believe the west tower is Norman. Why do you ask?"

"I have acquired it."

"Have you really?"

"Yes, some while ago now."

"Is it in good nick?"

Our host hesitated and the sharp eyes grew momentarily puzzled. Recovering, he said, "Quite. The holdings are much reduced, but it has a good trout stream and excellent grouse shooting. It's not far from Chartwell, where Churchill…"

"Of course."

"Do you get there often yourself?" I asked, even as I sensed something askew.

He shook his impressive head. "To tell you the truth, Mr. de Ratour, I've never been."

"To Kent?" the commander asked.

"To England."

After an embarrassed silence of tea pouring, sorting out sugar and milk, the commander said, "You know, Mr. Carnovan… "

"I would esteem it if you would call me Victor."

"I was going to say, Victor, that you speak English very well. Even, I might say, with an English accent."

"Yes. We all of us in the Soviet Motherland listened to BBC. We did it furtively, of course. Under Stalin it would have meant a bullet in the back of the head, lower down, you know, near the neck."

He took a deep breath and again his eyes lost their focus. "God, what a gray, endless desolation we survived. Those British voices were like hearing echoes of a bygone mythical civilization. We thought of it as a godlike realm of order, law, decency. We scarcely believed it existed but dared not disbelieve lest we gave up hope altogether. Do you remember William Hardcastle? *The World at One*. I still listen to the BBC. In the middle of the night. It makes my insomnia bearable."

We buttered and jammed our crumpets and sipped our tea appreciatively.

Our host brightened again. "Commander, did you ever listen to *The Archers*? We listened all the time. We would gather to practice our English and drink tea with English pastries. Or our version of them. Someone had a recipe for plum pudding, but you know…"

"The Archers are still on," the commander said.

"Yes, but it's not the same."

In the midst of this very English moment, the commander asked, "Victor, does the name Fortese mean anything to you?"

"Rhode Island. Once they were big time. Got too smart for the business."

"What do you mean?"

"They all went to college. They became doctors, lawyers, professors, legitimate businessmen."

"What about Patrick and Dominic Fortese."

"They're the remnants. Small time."

"And have you ever heard of Rechronnex?"

His eyes took on a shrewd look. "I have heard of it. Associates tell me it is the future of the business. It works both sides of the street."

"What do you mean?"

"I mean it has a legitimate and profitable side. Behind that front, I do not know. Money laundering of the higher sort more than likely. Of the high volume and half-legal kind, you know, for corporations and executives. Gambling in the form of high risk investment. Insider trading. Kickbacks to fund managers. Why do you ask?"

I explained the situation at the lab, telling him how Rechronnex had made a generous offer to form a joint venture and how I was under considerable pressure to sign off on the deal.

"And you haven't?" our host asked.

"Not so far."

The commander said, "The point is this, Mr... Victor, the Fortese brothers are distantly related to Dr. Carmina Fortese who is the chief researcher on the Juvenistol project..."

"Juvenistol?"

"It's an anti-aging medicine or will be if successful," I explained. "It's under development in the museum's Genetics Lab."

He again gave his silent, mirthless laugh. "It's something I could use. But, please, continue, Commander."

"Well, in your considered opinion, would it be far-fetched for someone at Rechronnex to have hired Blackie Burker to take a shot at Norman. Perhaps as a warning?"

"Why only a warning? As our great leader Marshall Stalin taught us, 'no man, no problem.' Gentlemen, when a lot of money is at stake, murder is always an option. An organization like Re-chronnex would have many... how do you say, tentacles. And, a nod's as good as a wink. I will make inquiries, of course"

Our host appeared to drowse for a moment, as though the wine, though in modest amounts, had had an effect. But in fact, it had made him garrulous and philosophical. He looked at us each in turn. He said, "I think you do not appreciate just what it means to be respected and respectable. I mean, here you are, Commander Morgliesh, eminent in your field and a poet, I am told, and now a fellow at the Center for Criminal Justice. Curious word that, fellow. Hale fellows well met and all that. Very British. Some of the fellows I deal with..."

He closed his eyes and appeared again to nod off. And again his voice held sway. "What Communism prepares you for, if you have even a scrap of ambition, is a life of crime. It does that by reducing the individual to a scheming rodent looking for any kind of margin, any kind of advantage. I have always wanted to make those western intellectuals with a soft spot for Marxism to spend a month, just a month, mind you, living under Communism the way millions were forced to do for decades. So look at me. A criminal. But I make no excuses. If I have been a thief I have been an honest thief. I never harmed an innocent, not directly, anyway. I was in a rough business. But let me say this, when I loaned someone money, I did it on terms that were more just than those made by American banks and those other corporate gangsters. They make people like me look like honest businessmen. They have the politicians all sewed up, especially the liberal Democrats who make so much noise about the little man. They don't have to buy the Republicans because they're already on the side of money. They make you yearn for Stalin to come back and shoot them all in the back of the head."

He glanced at each of us. "I will tell you, this kidnapping up the coast is not good. No ransom. It is a sign of what is to come. If the gnomes of Wall Street do not relent, there will be blood. They are the ones that create the Hitlers and Stalins of the world. They leave people no other choice. The Romanovs and their kind would not relent. It was the assassination of the Tsar's family that began the mass murders that culminated in the destruction of the Jews. Americans think it cannot happen here. But Americans, like the Communists and the Nazis, are human beings and our species, gentlemen, has shown again and again how ready it is to..."

In the course of this monologue, a door on the side opened and a tall, muscular man in his thirties entered and stood beside our host. Dark haired and wearing a black turtleneck, he had cold eyes that took in mine with impassive hostility and then turned away. With an unpleasant jolt of surprise, I realized he looked very like the man who had been driving the Humvee that tried to run me down. I mentally adorned him with a baseball cap and affixed sunglasses to his closed, averted face. It's the guy, I almost said aloud to the commander.

"Excuse me, gentlemen," our host said and wheeled away a couple of paces. The newcomer bent over the white dome of his master and said something in Russian in a low voice.

I didn't know what to do. Should I stand up and accost the man? Say something like, "Excuse me, sir, but I believe you tried to kill me the other day." But I wasn't a hundred percent sure it was the same man. I had only glimpsed him for a few seconds in the uncertain mirror on my speeding bike.

The man left abruptly and at a signal I had not noticed, Yuri approached us bearing our coats. We stood up. Mr. Karnivoss-ky-Carnovan wheeled himself back and kept talking. "And you, Mr. de Ratour, you dispatched Freddie Bain in this very room." He glanced around, his gaze wandering. "You would be surprised by the way you are admired in certain quarters." His eyes kept moving. "Monstrous place, isn't it? Like a nightmare come to life. Only, you know, I like it. If I cannot get to Kent I will stay here. The Italians go to Florida when they retire. Me, I've got cold in my veins. Russian cold. The kind that stopped the French and the Germans."

I did manage the wherewithal to ask, "Excuse me, Victor, that gentleman that just came in, is he in your employ?"

"Ivan… Yes. He is my nephew. But I am afraid Ivan is rather dim at times and unruly. I am trying to teach him the business and some manners. I tell him that computers are the future… in whatever business. But I think he watches too many gangster movies…." His voice drifted off.

We had donned our coats but were prevented from making our goodbyes as our host, reinvigorated, kept talking. "Yes, a ridiculous place. The university should buy it and make it into a conference center."

"Perhaps," I said, pondering the idea, "you could donate it to Wainscott. Take a big write-off. It has land with it, I believe."

"Nearly four hundred hectares."

"About a thousand acres," the commander put in. "Significant."

"Do you think they would accept it from me?" Mr. Karnivossky-Carnovan asked.

I thought for a moment, dissembling a smile. What a nice problem it would make for Malachy Morin and his administrative satraps. "I don't see why not," I allowed. "But they might ask for an endowment to go with it."

"Really?"

"For maintenance. And you should insist on a non-de-acquisition clause."

"Which is?"

"They would not be allowed to sell it for, say, a hundred years."

"Interesting, interesting."

"And you could have it named after yourself. Say, Carnovan Hall."

"Yes, yes, I like that. I will look into the matter. Perhaps I will leave it to your admirable institution. The only thing I would ask in return is to visit your museum and have you personally escort me around it."

"It would be a pleasure," I returned, shaking his hand.

"I would delight to join in, if I may," the commander said.

My uncertainty about Ivan as the man who tried to run me down vanished the minute we crossed back over the fake drawbridge. For there, parked next to Diantha's SUV, was a big black Humvee. I strode up to it and bent over the right front fender. It was scuffed all right, but not enough to be conclusive evidence of a hit-and-run incident.

"Commander," I said, straightening up. "I am positive that the young man we just met tried to run me down in this vehicle."

"Really?"

"Yes, really," I repeated, amazed and somewhat annoyed at his sang-froid. "In fact, I'm going back in right now and demand an explanation."

"I wouldn't do that."

"And why in hell not?"

"Norman, let's get in the car and talk about it."

Which we did, he buckling his seatbelt, me grasping the steering wheel and staring fixedly ahead, fuming.

"First," he began in what I took to be his 'good cop' voice, "the man will simply deny it. Second, I will call Victor myself to thank him for his hospitality and, third, ask him about Ivan and, if necessary, to rein him in, if that is necessary. I will not need to be blunt for him to get the message."

I buckled up and began driving. But I still wanted in some way to confront the thug. At the same time, I was relieved not to have to do just that. I said, "Is it possible that what we just participated in was so much theater."

"Not necessarily."

"I don't follow you."

"Our Anglophilic friend is old and growing infirm, at least in body if not in mind. It wouldn't surprise me in the least if Ivan didn't take it upon himself to have you eliminated. Especially if, in his ignorance, he thought you, of all people, posed a threat to an expansion of their operations in the area."

"Do you think he hired Burker?"

"That's what I am going to find out."

18

I woke to full consciousness from a dream of apple mash and fresh cider, voicing to the darkness the words, "Where there's excrement, there's life."

Diantha sighed beside me. "What did you say?"

I said," speaking as realization prickled through me, "where there's excrement there's life."

"Oh, Norman, you're having one of your nightmares. Try to go back to sleep."

"No, no, you don't understand. It never made sense."

"What never made sense?"

"Even if it had been a broken septic system, which it wasn't."

"I don't follow you."

"At the hotel… Hobbes Landing."

"Jesus, Norman, what time is it?"

"Quarter past four."

"Please, please go back to sleep."

But I couldn't. I knew all too well the smell of an enclosed jakes. The round smell of shit, Patrick White called it in one of his excellent novels. In my youth, I had gone with my father to visit a distant cousin of his who had apple orchards and a cider-making operation well inland. The only facilities had been little more than a large enclosed box set upright over a hole with an old Sears catalogue for toilet paper and a swarm of well-fed flies for company.

I made coffee and paced until around seven. Diantha came down yawning in her bathrobe and we talked about things coacal.

She played devil's advocate with persuasive logic. "Kids break in there all the time, Norman. Other than carving their initials on the paneling, what else have they got to leave behind?"

That did deflate my swelling enthusiasm. But only for a few minutes. Though no expert on the subject of ordure, I could not get out of my mind the memory of that week with Uncle Paul and the distinctive odor associated with what my father referred to as the privy.

At seven thirty I rang Detective Edmund Lupien of the state police. I would have called Lieutenant Tracy, but the islands were out of his jurisdiction. I explained what had happened while we were looking over the old hotel on Big Hog Island. I told him how it took me a while to realize what was bothering me and how I woke in the middle of the night remembering the exact same odor on my uncle's farm so many years before.

The detective told me in his calm way to get on some warm clothes and stand by. He called me back twenty minutes later. It seems the Coasties and the FBI had done a room-to-room of the old place two weeks before with dogs and had turned up nothing.

"But," I began.

"I know. Meet me at Spindler's Wharf as soon as you can. I'll arrange for one of our patrol boats to pick us up there."

The state police boat, a modified Zodiac with windshield and wheel, was just adequate for the swells running across the strong incoming tide. But no one minded, certainly not Brewster, the young man at the helm who looked like a lobsterman with his sunburned, open face. He stood at the wheel and cut across the swells ignoring the drenching spray, turning the boat to face and ride up the larger ones.

Then the calm, early morning sunshine as we entered the cove and tied up at the old dock in front of the hotel. Except for the crying of gulls, the lap of water, and a scolding jay, the place was silent.

Brewster tagged along as we mounted the front steps onto the magnificent old veranda. Strangely enough, we quickly found the key in a box under a loose board where it was supposed to be. The big door creaked open, and I swear there was a whoosh of escaping ghosts as we went in. I led the way across the large hall with its great fieldstone fireplace and old stuffed furniture still covered with winter slipcovers. Time seemed not to have stood still but to have moved sideways into some alternate realm.

We went across to the west-facing side. I stopped to get my bearings. Augustein and I had been just outside taking in the landward view when we had remarked the smell. I opened one of the massive French windows and stepped outside. "Here," I said, "Just about here."

The three of us stood and walked around the spot and sniffed, our noses in the air, next to the wall, down near the dry rotting flooring of the veranda.

"No do-do here," Brewster said, giving me a glance of amused dismissal. And in truth, all we could smell was the cold, clean salt air of the North Atlantic.

The detective gave no sign of agreeing with his colleague. His face remained set in a thoughtful, attentive expression. "Let's check the cellar," he said, taking a flashlight off of his belt.

It was the stuff, superficially at any rate, of Gothic novels. We went into the dining room, where the polished, woodsy pine paneling of the reception hall had given way to peeling wallpaper of a fox hunting theme and beaded wainscoting. The one-antlered moose still gazed down with glassy indifference from over the mantle and a modest crystal chandelier still hung from the ceiling. The tables with chairs tilted against them still waited for diners to come and order the lobster special. We went through swinging padded doors into an antechamber of the dining room. Here a capacious dumbwaiter and a wide staircase led to the cellar and a large, well-equipped, out-of-date kitchen. Several stoves with overhead ducted fans ranged along one wall. There were floor-to-ceiling cupboards, a giant old fridge, a trough of soapstone sinks and a long work table of thick, well-worn and nicked maple. Over the stoves, rusting pans hung in descending order of size like some kind of musical notation. All those meals, I thought to myself. All those lobster dinners.

A doorway, its door gone, led into the rest of the cellar, a cavernous place cobwebbed like the kitchen and windowless with walls of stone, some of them cut to fit. An ancient furnace and a row of hot water tanks stood rusting amid a tangle of pipes.

"Coal-fired" Detective Lupien said, playing the beam of his flashlight over the scene. The stab of light came to rest on a heavy oaken door secured with a large bolt rusted shut. On the lintel was a barely discernible sign reading "ROOT CELLAR."

"No sign of anything here," I said quietly, disappointment in my voice.

But again, Detective Lupien did not betray anything like agreement with me. "Let's go outside," he said as we climbed the broad stairs in the light of the first floor.

By now I feared we were going through the motions. We stepped again through the French doors on the landward side. The detective stood for a moment to get his bearing. Not far away a brick chimney stack rose unobtrusively through the veranda floor and went up through the ceiling. He then went down the steps and poked around the dilapidated lattice skirting the bottom of the veranda.

"There's nothing here," Brewster said with barely disguised impatience. "The Feds went over with dogs, metal detectors, you name it."

"I know," his superior answered. "But let's check around, just in case." He turned to me. "Norman, what's that over there?" He pointed to what to me looked like stables converted to garages. It was about a hundred yards off the northwest corner and linked to the back of the hotel with an overgrown drive of crumbling asphalt.

We walked over to it and then around it, checking doors, which were all secured. We looked through dirt-encrusted windows. Amid the odds and ends of hotel furnishings was a 1939 Packard with running boards, just like the one my grandfather had owned.

We were about to call it a day, or at least a morning, when the detective pointed to a protuberance from the ground about thirty feet from the main building. "What's that?" he asked and we walked towards it.

"Looks like a cold frame to me," I said.

At first, it didn't look like much at all, a bulkhead perhaps, its top doors rotted away, the resulting rectangular cavity half filled with leaves and other natural debris.

Detective Lupen leaned and then knelt down. He scooped up a handful of the litter and examined it. "Any pine trees right around here?" he asked.

"The whole state's covered with them," Brewster said. And gave a derisive laugh.

"No, I mean right here."

"There," said Brewster, pointing to a stand of evergreens not far from the garage.

"Those are hemlock," I said. "The only pine is that big old thing on the other side of the hotel."

Detective Lupien's noncommittal face showed a quizzical smile. He held up a twig with several cones attached to it and looked at me.

"Could have blown over here in a gale," I said.

"Yeah, but look at all these other needles?"

I shrugged. "I suppose."

He stood and walked around inspecting the ground. "No other pine needles around here..." He trailed off as though speaking to himself before kneeling again. "Let's clean this out."

"With what?" Brewster asked.

"Our hands." He had already started, using both of his to lift bunches of the stuff out onto the surrounding ground.

More than a foot down, we came across a set of slanting wooden doors. On a rusted hasp was a new Yale padlock.

Detective Lupien turned to Brewster. "No radio contact and bring my bag from the boat. And hurry."

"Shouldn't we call this in?"

No. The bad guys might have scanners and I don't trust our frequencies."

We waited wordlessly for the young man to sprint down to the boat and return.

From his bag, a kind of briefcase, the detective took a key-ring hung with various fine, wire-like probes. Patiently, working one and then another, he succeeded in springing the lock. By now we were all tense with expectation and ready to be both shocked and disappointed.

The doors creaked open revealing a stairwell of wooden steps leading down into utter darkness. The lieutenant turned on his flashlight. "Brewster, you stay here. I'll call you on the walkie-talkie if it's all clear. If you don't hear from us, call for backup."

"But… "

"No buts. Norman, get your Glock ready. Wait till I'm down to give you the all-clear."

A moment later he was at the bottom of the ladder and signaling for me to follow him. Which I did, gingerly, too excited for anything like fear.

We were in a tunnel about six feet high buttressed with eight-by-eight timbers like a mine shaft. In one direction it led toward the garage and in the other direction toward the hotel. We followed the floor of flagged stone toward the latter. Sooner than we expected we came upon a heavy steel door held shut with thick bolts, one of them recently installed.

"Keep your weapon ready but down," the detective whispered. "And brace yourself. This may not be very pleasant."

Leaning against the door, he prized the new bolt back. Then, with more effort, he worked the other one loose. Slowly, carefully, he pulled at the door. It swung open almost decorously with a creak like time. In the beam of his flashlight were three pale, bearded faces, hands shading their eyes.

"I'm Detective Edmund Lupien of the state police."

One of them said, "What took you so long?"

Another one said, "What's the market doing?"

The third said, "I have to call my wife."

"We have to move quickly," the detective said in an oddly formal voice. He turned to me. "Norman, go back to the top of the bulkhead opening and wait there to help these gentlemen out." He then spoke into his walkie-talkie. "Brewster, scoot up to the hotel and get as many of those dustcovers as you can and bring them to the boat. And absolute radio silence."

As I was going up the tunnel, I heard one of the rescued men ask, "What's the hurry?"

"Your kidnappers might be watching us and we don't have that much firepower."

It went as expected. I stood at the top helping the captives, who were weak to the point of trembling, up into the bright day. Upon emerging, one of them got on his knees and said a prayer. Another opened his arms to the sky. The third asked if he could borrow my cell phone.

I shook my head and said, "Sorry, radio silence."

"I insist."

"I'm sure you do."

Detective Lupien closed the entrance and scuffled some of the debris back into the cavity. We went down to the dock in a line, hands to shoulder as in the Bruegel painting. We helped them into life jackets and settled them on the bottom of the boat.

The detective was on his radio. "Ambulances and heavy security," I heard him say. "Local and state police only. You might send out a helicopter to cover us."

Just then Brewster came at a brisk walk, his arms filled with tattered and dusty dust covers. The detective and I put these over the shoulders of the three men as Brewster fired up, untied, and headed out of the cove into the wind and swells.

As we plowed our way back to the modest skyline of Seaboard with its spires and office blocks, I moved to sit next to the detective. "Edmund," I said, keeping my voice just loud enough to be heard, "I don't want my name associated with any of this."

He looked at me puzzled for a moment. Then nodded as I said, "I've already got someone taking potshots at me. I don't want to be on any more hit lists."

"Gotcha. I'll tell Brewster. He's not the sharpest knife in the drawer, but he'll keep quiet."

A state police helicopter flew out to cover us for the last several hundred yards into the wharf. Ambulances and patrol cars made a light show with their pulsating blue and red strobes.

I managed to slip away unnoticed just as reporters and news trucks began showing up. I walked home, at least two and a half miles, breathing in the cool autumn air as deeply as though I had been entombed with the three men. I was also pondering what to do with the ten million dollars, tax free, that had been posted as the reward. I had a fleeting fantasy of taking it and moving away, beginning a new life in a different, perhaps warmer part of the country. More realistically, I considered giving at least half of it to the museum, anonymously, of course, something for the Little Theater, a million to Detective Lupien with the suggestion that he give, say, $50,000 of that to Brewster. And keeping the remainder for my own family. None of which I would be investing in bank stocks.

19

Lawyers representing the Union of Concerned Bankers have told the lawyer representing the state police that there will be difficulties in handing over the reward of ten million dollars. My request to remain anonymous apparently has nothing to do with the difficulty. Detective Lupien, who has become my unofficial conduit to those negotiations, tells me the conditions of the reward are worded "leading to the recovery of the three men alive and/or to the capture and conviction of those responsible for the kidnapping."

According to the lawyers for the bankers, since the *and* precedes the slash in the wording cited above, it governs what follows in such a way as to make it a necessary part of the conditions. That means that, in order to qualify for the reward by this construal, I will have to find out who kidnapped the banker and the lawyer and their legislative lackey and I will have to make sure they are convicted.

After some thought, not to mention chagrin, I brought the matter up with Felix on a hypothetical basis, telling him I had heard from a friend at the state police that there had been a complication in the granting of the reward.

At first he shrugged. "What did they expect? That bankers would act ethically?"

"You would think…"

"Nah, bankers have trouble giving away money to anyone but themselves and politicians."

"But what about the bad publicity?"

"What, over a measly ten million? They give themselves tens of billions every year in bonuses, Norman. The banking industry is immune to bad publicity. It lives in a state of bad publicity. It doesn't care. It doesn't have to care."

He stopped and stared at me, amazed pleasure lighting his scarred face. "Norman, it's not you? You didn't... ?"

"Of course not... " But I am not good at lying, certainly not to someone like Felix, whom I trust like a brother.

"Norman... You amaze me. Yet again."

"I am officially denying any involvement with this matter."

"Why?"

"Someone is already trying to do me grievous bodily harm. I don't need the Ad Hoc Committee for Economic Justice Now to add me to their list of enemies. Felix, seriously, this has to stay top, top secret."

"My lips are sealed. I understand your position. But you sniffed it out. The day we went out there?"

I laughed. "Quite literally. I caught a whiff of their latrine when we were making the tour."

"On the porch. The landward side?"

"Exactly."

"Damn it, I did, too. I remarked it to Theresa. She said she didn't smell anything. How did you... ?"

I explained how it came to me in a dream, my uncle's orchard and cider making. As I spoke, Felix listened, head bowed, but somewhat distractedly.

"You know what? I think we should sue the bastards. Breach of contract, plus damages. Pain and suffering. Legal costs. My clock's already running. Not for you but for them."

"But I don't want to reveal my part... "

"You may not have to. There's lots of precedence for that. My God, Norman, what are you going to do with ten million?"

I explained that, after distributions to my family, to Detective Lupien and to Officer Brewster, and to the Seaboard Players, I planned to give more than half of the ten million dollars to the museum.

"That's very generous. Very generous, indeed." He rose and headed for the door. "I'll try not to think of that when I make out my bill." Then, seriously, "You'll be hearing from me."

Generous, perhaps, I mused after he had gone. But in fact, I find myself greedy for more -- for the museum, not for myself. Of course, one could say they are one and the same, such is the immersion of my identity with this marvelous old place.

As a consequence, I have been in contact with Mr. Augustein and plan to follow up on his offer to support the museum -- in whatever form. In fact, it was Mr. Augustein who called, reminding me how he had jokingly said the kidnapped men had a suite in his hotel.

"You know, Norman," he said, "that smell you picked up on the porch, I bet that was from them. Too bad we didn't put two and two together. We would be ten million dollars richer. Ha, ha."

Not that you need it, I kept myself from saying. Instead, giving my voice a collegial note, I said, "You know, Maurice, I would like to discuss further your ideas for a parking lot..."

Ya, ya. And I want to have you go over some plans my planners have planned. You know, for Ile de Grand Cochon."

The secrecy surrounding my own role in the matter has held as far as I can tell, though I am sure it will get out later. In the voluminous media accounts of the kidnapping, captivity, and rescue, my name has yet to emerge. The story has legs, as they say in journalism. Perhaps because above all else, the public loves what one commentator called "a good resurrection story." Not that any of those resurrected remotely bear any resemblance to Jesus Christ.

It turns out that the arrangements at the Hobbes place did involve a suite of sorts. One follow-up television feature showed that the tunnel we had used connected a crawl space under the garages to the cellar of the hotel, where it opened through the bolted, blast-proof door into a bomb shelter.

It seems that the three men had been left only with the clothes on their backs, a hunting knife each, and a small pinch light one of them happened to be carrying. Using that light, they found a strong oak door behind a pile of miscellaneous hotel junk leading they knew not where. Hacking with their knives, they managed to carve a hole in the door large enough for them to slip through. On the other side, they found they were in the root cellar. It had been walled off from the hotel kitchen area with cinder blocks.

Inside the root cellar they discovered a shelf of pickled rhubarb in Ball jars, a tin of maple syrup still good, more or less, a forty pound bag of greenish flour in a sealed metal container, and a round of cheese so hard they had to use their knives and a loose brick as a hammer to break off chips. (I doubt they'll be publishing a book of recipes, but who knows?)

They moved the food back into their original quarters and used a corner of the root cellar as a toilet. Not far from where I had caught their smell on the porch, a pipe led from a catchment cistern on the roof. It supplied them with water on an intermittent basis. Once that froze as winter came on, they would probably have died of thirst if not exposure.

It didn't take Homeland Security and the FBI long to come lurching in and try to claim the case. But it was too late. Shortly after we landed on that memorable day, Detective Lupien gave the press a terse and factual statement. He said it was the state police, working with a local citizen, who had found the three kidnapped men. That made the national and international news before the Director of Homeland Security and an FBI suit (marvelous bit of slang, that) held a joint press conference.

Director Janet Fousset told the press that "the system worked." In the follow-up questioning, it was clear that neither she nor the suit next to her had a clue as to what had happened. "Those details are still coming in," they said more than once when asked basic questions.

An elderly lobsterman living on Little Hog told a television crew, "Hell, the FBI was here half a dozen times." Standing in a plaid shirt, blue trousers, and high boots turned down low, the old salt said, "I told them I didn't hear anything on the night those fellas got taken. But I told them that there was tunnels and bunkers over in the old Hobbes place. Back in the fifties, Stanton Hobbes, the grandson, he had a few extra cards in his deck, if you follow my meaning. Anyway, he blasted a bomb shelter right out of the granite and put in all kinds of stuff down there. I told the Federales more than once that if I wanted to hide someone, that's where I'd go. But they already knew more than I did."

Whether I can claim the reward or not, it has provoked in me this vicarious greed that is quite as pertinacious as plain old selfishness. What's not apparent to myself is whether the avarice I speak of had anything to do with my change of heart regarding the Juvenistol project. Because I find I am seriously considering signing off on the proposed joint venture between the Genetics Lab and Rechronnex.

20

At the same time, I was still hesitant about the arrangement with Rechronnex when I went to lunch with the director of the Genetics Lab, my good friend and colleague Winston Maroun. We met at the Creole Lounge on one of those storm-racked days when the onshore wind blows right through clothes and flesh to the very marrow of the bone.

"I do miss my Barbadian homeland, Norman," he told me as we touched together our pina coladas with their slices of pineapple wedged onto the rims of the glasses next to the tiny umbrellas. "It's paradise and sometimes hell down there, whereas up here I feel like I'm spending my life in a cold purgatory."

I wondered if I were hearing the prelude to a threat -- that he might resign and go elsewhere were I not to sign off on the Rechronnex arrangement. He had been urging me with increasing force to do just that, and his was not the kind of advice I was inclined to ignore.

"As you know, Norman, I have been delegated by the team to bring you around." He spoke in soft Caribbean intonations with a mixture of candor and charm that was well nigh irresistible. At the same time, I remarked an edge of exasperation in his voice that I had not heard before. Even without that, I felt the moral force of this very persuasive man, a free thinker who never indulges in the cant phrases and stale wisdoms so beloved by the liberal left and the illiberal right.

"The lab has done its job," he went on after we had sipped from our extravagant drinks and indulged in museum small talk. "The basic research is finished. We have shown the way. Now it is the role of entities like Rechronnex and big pharma to take it to the next step."

I nodded, more to show that I understood him rather than that I agreed with him. "As you know, Winston, I have personal and professional doubts about the whole enterprise. I mean, Aging and death..."

He held up his hand like a traffic cop. "Norman, I don't think you quite grasp that this is not a decision you can put off. If you delay signing much longer, the word will get around, and, at the very least, I will have enormous difficulty recruiting top-flight researchers from Wainscott and elsewhere to replace those already planning to jump ship. The lab's endowment, as you well know, has suffered grievously and the name itself will only carry us so far."

We paused to order from an array of Creole dishes on the menu. He had the shrimp gumbo and I the calamari with a salad on the side. The waiter, a winsome, either very tanned or naturally brown woman of twenty-something, went with the sense of the place -- the bamboo decor and potted palmettos and pungent food.

Winston leaned back, his long handsome face in seeming repose as he regarded me closely with pale, penetrating eyes. "It's not only staffing, Norman," he resumed, "but this particular cat is out of the bag. You know as well I do that somewhere, sometime, and more likely sooner than later, someone will come up with an elixir that will significantly prolong life whether derived from our research or not. Or one or more of our people will take what we've developed, tinker with it a bit, and cash in. And, let's face it, greed for life will never be seen as a sin."

I trusted him implicitly even if, as a leading member of the research team, he stood to benefit handsomely -- several millions now and the prospect of royalties.

I mentioned the email from Worried.

He sipped from his drink and glanced up smiling. "All the more reason to let Rechronnex do the heavy lifting." Then, "Seriously, whatever the merits of that ... communication, I have utter faith in Carmina. The very fact that she had some tainted antecedents and distant family members who are on the shady side has, in my opinion, made her more than scrupulous, especially when it comes to research. Let's face it, Norman, how many of us have relatives or ancestors who are less than Simon pure. I am myself descended from both slaves and slavers."

"Too true. The Normans, my people on my father's side, started out as little more than plundering marauders, gangsters, if you will."

"And still are, fictionally, at least."

"Really?"

"The Sicilian Corleones are more than likely descendants of Coeur de Lion, Richard the Lion-Heart. He was King of England and Lord of Ireland and Count of Maine and ... "

I smiled and sipped and brought us back to the issue. "If there's any substance to this email, there could be both ethical and legal problems. I mean Rechronnex could sue us for misrepresentation..."

"Did you read the offer? They agree to accept the project as it is unconditionally. Norman, consider this. The museum's financial woes would be alleviated, at least for a while."

After a moment of silence, he gazed at me thoughtfully. "But that's not really what bothers you, is it?"

I nodded. "It's this, Winston. Along with everything else, we are now pathologizing old age and death. We're becoming a fat, timid nation, giving big names to ordinary woes, and wallowing in institutionalized self-pity, all the while treating the miracle of life as though it were nothing but a progression of diseases. Shyness, one of the more endearing traits among some of us, is now listed as 'social anxiety disorder.'"

He nodded as I had, smiled, and then frowned. "Norman, that may well be true, but it's your personal opinion, not a fact." He bore in, "What is a fact is that you have left me in an untenable position. You hired me to make these kinds of decisions. And now, just on the verge of success, you pull the rug out from under me and the team."

I winced, perhaps visibly. To be criticized with cause by someone one admires, respects, and even envies cuts deep. I said what I had said before. "The whole enterprise presumes that death, even a timely death, is the worst thing that can happen to someone."

"But isn't it?"

"I don't think so. I think that the death of one's child is the worst thing that can happen to someone. Losing someone you love to another person can, I think, be worse than death. How many lovelorn people have committed suicide, that is chosen death over living without the person they love?"

"Okay."

"Or death may be preferable to certain kinds of humiliation. And why should a man or woman of eighty or eighty-five want to keep hanging on? A great scientist still unraveling the secrets of nature or a great artist or an indispensable statesman or woman, perhaps. But how many of them are there? A handful."

Face down, he slowly moved his head from side to side. Then, directly, "Norman, I am far more interested in giving a doting grandmother a few more years to spoil her grandchildren."

Of a sudden, he had me. I felt I was in the presence of greatness, not of mind or professional accomplishments but of spirit. I resisted saying touché. I almost said, I'll sign this afternoon. Instead, I prevaricated. "I need another day or two."

"I'm sorry, Norman. I need an answer right now. I need to go to the team this afternoon and tell them the deal is on."

In the awkward silence that ensued, he came at me from another direction altogether. "Tell me, Norman, how does it feel to be hunted?"

I smiled, more to myself than to the world. I was about to say that mere words do not suffice, but checked myself. If anyone had an ear for the strained note, it was Winston. I sipped my savory drink. I said, "One never feels normal. You become keenly observant, not to mention wary and, frankly, suspicious of everyone and everything. No rolling out the garbage bin in the dark, though, when I think about it, that might be the best time to do it."

He leaned forward, as though to let me confide in him. He said, "Perhaps a return to our state of nature. I mean when we were as much prey as predators."

In a gesture I later thought of as jejune, I pulled aside my tweed jacket to reveal the gleaming Glock in its shoulder holster. "I am prepared to prey on anyone who would prey on me."

He gestured back, hands up, then leaned forward, obviously impressed. "The real thing. But could you bring yourself to use it on another human being?"

"I'm afraid I could. And, embarrassed to say, with pleasure if my own life or that of anyone I care about was threatened."

His pale eyes grew paler and seemingly larger. "Yes, of course. You shot that gangster." Something akin to horror tinged with pleasure showed on his good-natured face. Then he laughed. "I want to assure you Norman that, however much you get cursed among the professionals at the lab, no one there, certainly no one to my knowledge, has had anything to do with the assaults on you." He paused to smile. "Despite what they take to be incomprehensible provocation."

Before I could respond, a loud, almost jovial "Winston!" interrupted our back and forth. Looming out of the palm fronds, beads rattling, and smile in high beam was Professor Ébène. She clutched a briefcase against her chest and proclaimed, "You are just the person..."

Winston rose as did I. But she utterly ignored my presence as she effused something about an upcoming meeting of a committee on which they were both members. She ended with "We need to lunch," and swept away, an important, busy somebody.

Winston kept his expression neutral, but he knew what I was thinking. He said presently, "She used to make me wince, but she does persevere. And she wants my name on her board, you know the credibility of scientific credentials. Of course, I deplore the kind of race hustling she does and, to be frank, the way she assumes I'm one of them and therefore, on certain matters, scarcely possessed of a mind of my own."

"When you say, 'one of them,' do you mean...?"

"A person of color, a nice way of saying non-white as whites are now the chosen people to despise."

"And you see yourself as..."

He laughed. "*Homo sapiens sapiens*, if I am to be precise in the way Linnaeus would have us. Everyone thinks I am African

American when I am not that at all. I am Barbadian and my DNA profile looks like a pie chart of genes."

The waiter came by with two fresh pina coladas. "Courtesy of Professor Ebony," she said and put them down.

I admit to being mollified by being included in the gesture. "You were saying," I said, touching his glass with mine. "Your pie chart."

"To your health ... and survival. Yes. A fairly big wedge of English, slavers, no doubt, another of Lebanese, a sliver of Carib, apparently, and, yes, a generous helping of black Africa, slaves, no doubt, of which I am neither proud nor ashamed as, personally, I had nothing to do with the exertions that created me. If anything, I consider myself the future of humankind in more ways than one. In the advanced countries, particularly in the west, we will all soon be happy mongrels."

Our food arrived. We sampled each other's and then tucked in for a few minutes. Left hanging, as we both, I think sensed, was the crucial question of our meeting -- would or would I not sign off on the Rechronnex deal.

Not that Winston seemed anxious to push me on the matter as we ate and drank. He told me how he had studied under Allen Counter at Harvard Medical School. "Allen, God love him, is a marvelous specimen of the species or subspecies of which the professor thinks I am a member. Allen went around the globe finding places where black Africans and African Americans had left their mark, including, Greenland. He was black and proud of it and when he sounded the racial note it was telling and relevant."

"Greenland?"

Winston related how Matthew Henson, an African American, had accompanied and been instrumental in getting Robert Peary to the North Pole in the early part of the twentieth century. Along the way they wintered over with Greenland Eskimos, a hospitable people who provided each man with a young woman for company on those long cold nights. As a consequence, each had fathered a son. Decades later Counter tracked down the two sons, octogenarians Anaukaq Henson and Kali Peary in their village in the far north. He arranged to have them come to the United States to meet their kinfolk and visit Cambridge, where they were enthralled by the sycamores along the Charles.

"What I want to do is talk Professor Ébène around to Allen's way of thinking. As it stands, she personifies the problem in America."

"What problem?" I asked, feigning puzzlement, though I knew what Winston thought of the chair of Wainscott's Department of Victim Studies.

"She, Professor Ébène, and thousands of her ilk have a vested interest in maintaining the victim status of African Americans. Indeed, Norman, that status has all but been institutionalized and it is the most destructive thing that has happened to American blacks since slavery. It's nothing but a form of bondage."

"Aren't you exaggerating just a touch?"

"To the contrary. It's a thriving industry and getting bigger. It involves jobs, careers, and, above all, moral gratification. Black America provides the white do-gooder class with an endless, unquestioned opportunity for virtue."

"But, Winston, come on, slavery was an ugly, a very ugly chapter in our history." I meant what I said, but I also wanted to keep him diverted as I scrambled in my mind for what to say when he got back to me.

"Good God, man, the history of humankind is one long ugly chapter when it comes to that. What group hasn't suffered atrocities? Think of native Americans. And the Jews. And the Irish. You don't hear them bleating on and on... with a few exceptions. Look, I know it is only decades since some of my ancestors were bought and sold like chattel. I know that blacks are still vulnerable, that they don't have the margins of other groups. But they will never fully emerge until they throw off the shackles of victimhood. He paused. "Tell me to shut up."

I laughed. "Winston, I will never tell you to shut up."

We ate well and with appetite for a spell, chewing our food and our thoughts. Until Winston put his fork down, then picked it up, holding it erect as to conduct with it. "And, something you might find interesting."

I waited as he frowned to himself. Then, "I am trying to convince the good professor that there's more to victim studies than moral blackmail. A lot more."

I indicated with a nod that I was interested in what he had to say.

"I mean, she's obviously something of a fraud, but I think I have convinced her that victimology, for want of a better word, ought to be studied as the vast phenomenon it has been in history. Think of all the battles, wars, persecutions, purges, genocides, democides in human history. All of them created victims. And, beyond that, where does victimization fit into the evolutionary scheme? Winners and losers. And, very often, the winners lose and the losers win, given time. The Normans conquered but the Saxons prevailed."

"Does she listen to you?"

"Not at first, but she perked up when I told her that in the human realm the subject was still in its infancy except for fodder for editorial writers and elegiac books like Wounded Knee. Who, exactly is a victim? Were the Japanese victims of American terror bombing in World War II? And if so, were the Germans as well? All kinds of questions begging out there. Does being a victim confer a moral advantage? Or is victim just a polite word for loser? Ébène flits around these questions, but I think I've intrigued her. Whether she has the scholarly or moral muscle to follow through is another question."

I was loath to interrupt what was turning into a soliloquy on Winston's part as I wanted to avoid the question of signing or not signing the contract with Rechronnex. When we settled into our coffee, he continued, "Every time I hear that cant phrase 'systemic racism' I want to reach for a gun. The word 'systemic' has a fake, technical gloss to it, as though to establish it as a scientific reality. And you can't argue with science say the educated ignoranti who have no notion that all that science is one long, intricately involved, disputatious search for truth."

"But there has been racism."

"Of course, the whole bloody world is racist and tribal beyond imagination. But, in the United States, particularly, there has been systemic anti-racism, beginning with the four hundred thousand men, mostly young white men, who died on the Union side during the Civil War to free the slaves. Think of all the civil rights legislation. Think of the affirmative action programs, of which I am a beneficiary. Half of black Africa wants to come here because they know African Americans are treated far better in this white society than they are in their black-ruled countries. I've been there. Poverty, squalor, corruption, violent regimes. But, of course, none of it is their fault. It's the legacy of colonialism."

He paused to check my reaction but was on a roll and kept going. "Nice white liberals have higher expectations of their dogs and cats than they do of black folk. In fact, African Americans of all stripes are the moral pets of the virtue class. I can't tell you how many white liberals I've seen positively swoon at their own virtue when it comes to people of color."

I found myself saying with more conviction than guile, "Okay, Winston, but there was discrimination. And if it wasn't enshrined in law, it was in our hearts. And, even now, there's a kind of inner dismissal on the part of a lot of whites when some issue regarding black America arises. I'm guilty of it myself at times."

"No doubt. No doubt. But white people are no longer the problem. It's what African Americans think of themselves that's crucial. They've all been issued a victim-status card. They can and do play it any time they want. They are above blame and criticism. And it is precisely this low expectation of themselves that is destructive. Black men are not even expected to care for their children. Seventy percent of black kids grow up without a father. Think of that. All of the do-goodery in the world, all of the programs and hand-outs, all of the professional pity cannot make up that neglect."

I was nodding, ever more in thrall to his articulated indignation than out of any ulterior motive. Though I had reservations, he made sense. At another level I was thinking, I'll beg for a couple of more days to make up my mind. I'll try to reassure him without committing myself. I'll stall without seeming to stall.

I tuned back in to hear him say, "As far as I'm concerned, America needs another MLK, this time as an apostle to black people. He should tell his people, now is the time to man up, to stay home and take care of the kids. Now is the time to shun rappers who glamorize violence and degrade women. Now is the time to renounce the cult of drugs and the criminality that comes with it. Black men and women need to free themselves to get a handle on their own genius. And where better to do that in America, this open-handed and open-hearted nation where anyone, and I mean anyone, can make it. Plug black energy into that outlet and stand back. But it will take discipline and patience and persistence and, most important, the shedding of grievances. I mean how we all love to cling to our hurts in our personal and public lives. But the world, ultimately, doesn't care. It grinds on and on, pausing, every once in a while to recognize and pay lip service to man's inhumanity to man."

"You sound like you could be the second MLK," I ventured in all seriousness.

"Nah, I lack the charisma, the ambition. I'm a scientist, Norman. Of course, I would cherish the fame and fortune that would derive from increasing our longevity, but I could never be King reincarnated. I care, but not enough. My calling puts me in a lab coat, protective covering behind which I can tell myself that I am working to prolong human life whether that human is white, black, brown, yellow or some combination thereof. Enough. Thank you for listening, Norman. It means a lot to me."

I shrugged with my hands. "You make eminent sense, Winston," I said as I thought to myself that being with this man reminded me that with time the least interesting and relevant aspect of any human being is their race, their ethnicity, their gender, or their sexual preferences. Character and personality and intelligence count for so much more and, of course, whether or not they have anything interesting to say.

He was saying, "I'm sorry dear friend. Here I am, once again presuming on your empathy and understanding."

"You have both," I said, "for what they're worth."

Winston laughed his rich Caribbean laugh. And then abruptly became serious. "Norman, you have to decide. I'll be honest, I am being recruited. And, frankly, you can find someone to replace me, but a lot of the others are already gathering up their marbles to go elsewhere. You won't be able to replace them."

I didn't hesitate. "I'll sign."

He nodded slowly, appreciatively, taking me in. "Just like that?"

"Just like that."

"Why?"

"Because I trust you."

For what it's worth, I now have a modicum of protection. Late that afternoon an SPD cruiser pulled up in front of our house and parked there. When I went to work the next day, there was an undercover officer waiting for me in the form of a smartly dressed black woman. She introduced herself, showed me her badge, and escorted me to my office.

"I'll be around," she said. "Off and on. And if not me, then someone who'll identify themselves."

I have almost but not quite begun to relax.

21

I have seldom seen Diantha in such a happy flutter. Between the aromatic kitchen, where she tended a pan of lamb shanks baking under sprigs of rosemary in a sauce of finely diced tomatoes and shallots, and the resplendent dining room, where she fussed over a table set for eight with my mother's flower-patterned Royal Doulton, she gave orders to me with beseeching charm. I attended in turn to the wine glasses, ice for the drinks table, un-pitted olives should anyone want a martini, and other sundries. I had already banished Decker to his cellar quarters. And Bella had the children well in hand up in their playroom, where I could faintly hear the television.

We had a small spat as to when to start the new potatoes. I maintained that we could parboil them and cut down on their baking time as they were small. Diantha said they should be boiled and served on the side with unsalted butter. She also wanted everything ready when people showed up at seven thirty. She could then socialize without having to think about the potatoes, tossing the salad and warming the gravy boat for the sauce, along with the myriad other details that go into a dinner party.

I understood her anxiety. The party was to include Ivor Pavonine and Joanna Beck, the latter a widow of means bent on tidying up her late husband's reputation by good works, including significant support for the Seaboard Players. Commander Adam Morgliesh and his wife Winifred were coming. And finally, the Talty-Clydes, Alice and Edwin, a wealthy, socially prominent couple, friends, or at least acquaintances, of Joanna's, who were being courted as potential supporters for the theater.

Diantha had dithered over what to wear, settling finally on a high-waisted, short gown of indigo silk in the Empire style that came just below her knees and opened above to an expanse of creamy cleavage. Her dark abundant hair, swept up in the most fetching manner, showed to advantage her regal neck around which she wore a pearl choker.

Inasmuch as the invitation called for "festive dress," I decided on my grey brown suit of light tweed over a black turtleneck made in Italy. Which is about as rakish as I get.

I paled in comparison to Ivor, who, bedecked in a scarlet dinner jacket and peacock bowtie, arrived first, coming through the door with a welter of words and a bouquet of dahlias. "Di darling, you look like a vision. Where did you get that naughty dress? You'll have all the men slavvering over you. Isn't that a nice word. *Slavver.* I think I just made it up."

"Do you think it's *de trop*?" Diantha asked, taking the bouquet and a kiss on the lips.

"*De trop*? Sweet girl, it's got 'do me standing up' written all over it." He whinnied just a bit.

Diantha gave me a quick don't-tell-me-I-told-you-so glance. Because earlier, in planning the party, I had inveighed against inviting Ivor. I used phrases like "loose cannon" and "a bull, or at least a steer, in a China shop."

Right then, I shrugged with my eyes. It was her show.

"And you, Norman. It's good to see you're still among the quick." The man laughed, then patted my back, and pumped my hand with firm enthusiasm, the way you might ruffle the ears of a dog you know won't bite.

I made some welcoming noises while noticing that Diantha was in fact having some second thoughts. The verbal liberties of cutting-edge artists like Ivor Pavonine don't always mesh smoothly with well-heeled respectability. And, for all her defense of Ivor and his proclivities, she had acknowledged that she and Joanna faced a formidable problem: it would be difficult to avoid the recent rescue of the three kidnapped men as a topic of conversation given that the whole planet appeared to be talking about it. Especially the inevitable question: did these three men, a Wall Street banker, a corporate lawyer, and a U.S. Senator, deserve being rescued? Insofar as Edwin Clydes had made a fortune devising and peddling intricate financial instruments so removed from anything of tangible value as to be all but non-existent except, when things went wrong, as "toxic assets" and insofar as Di and Joanna wanted him to fork over some of his ill-gotten gains to the Little Theater's shrinking endowment, they needed to avoid the whole issue of retribution. Which is why Diantha asked me in that endearing way of hers to help redirect the conversation should Ivor take it into those treacherous waters.

"But he's writer in residence," I protested. "Surely he knows that the interests of your organization and his own coincide."

Diantha let out her signature sigh -- breath through pursed lips, eyes rolling up. "Norman, darling, I.P. wants living theater, not contrived plots. He's an artist."

Then let him starve, I nearly said. Aloud, I murmured "Let's hope you don't end up with the former."

On the other hand, Ivor did possess the capacity to make people laugh or at least smile. And Joanna had told Diantha who had told me that if we got Edwin Clydes to smile it was a good sign and that if we got him to laugh it was practically a done deal.

Ivor and Diantha went off by themselves to arrange the flowers. A forecasted rain began to fall. I started a fire in the living room. It had begun to crackle when the doorbell rang.

Joanna came in smiling and holding two Bean bags full of goodies. And goodies they were. I helped her unload and set out the canapés. These included a platter of Irish smoked salmon with thinly sliced soda bread, several cheeses with long names, and caviar with capers. The bags also contained three bottles of Lafite Rothschild Pauillac.

An attractive woman of the black-haired, pale-complected kind now going just a bit thick in the middle, Joanna had covered herself with a flowery number that reminded me of a shower curtain. Ivor came in and gushed that she looked like spring had arrived early.

Damp from the rain and also bearing wine, a modest Bordeaux, the Talty-Clydes, Alice and Edwin, joined the party around the fire. I played bartender, bringing her a glass of chilled white and him a diet Coke.

After introductions and the smallest of small talk, the conversation immediately flagged. I heard myself ludicrously referring to the weather, something about "a real nor'easter."

Alice ventured an appreciation of the house, saying her family had owned one similar to it outside of Boston. When her husband frowned, as though to correct her, she said she was talking about the one in Newton her family had owned when she was a little girl.

Though the couple were well into their fifties, Alice Talty might have passed for thirty something. For this occasion she had dressed in a black sheath number with a white Eton collar and held herself in a way that used to be called poise. Joanna told Diantha who told me that Alice kept several specialists in Mercedes with the amount of work done on various parts of her anatomy.

Her husband, tall and on the gaunt side, wore what might be called a sports suit, bespoke obviously, in the fine tartan tweed of some obscure clan. His carefully groomed reddish hair had begun to fade, and his gray eyes gave nothing away. He evinced a tolerance that went from feigned interest to puzzled skepticism about what was being said. He added little himself, but listened at a remove, as though thinking about something else. I had noticed before that the very rich often keep their own counsel, a result perhaps of knowing their wealth already speaks volumes.

Diantha excused herself to check something in the kitchen and Joanna asked Ivor how his new play was going.

"It goes," Ivor said brightly, turning on the Talty-Clydes all his facetious charm. "But of course dinner parties like this one are theater *par excellence*."

"In what way?" Joanna prompted him.

"Well, think about it. The table gets set the way the stage is set." He was standing, gesticulating. "And we, the diners, are both the actors and the audience. There's a beginning, a middle, and an end. There's lots of dialogue and always, always, the possibility of comedy and even tragedy. It's life is art is life at its most spontaneous."

Edwin Clydes nodded but did not smile.

I breathed a sigh of relief at the arrival of the Morglieshes. They came in out of a downpour with all the aplomb of the British, shaking their umbrellas and unbuttoning their mackintoshes. From the pocket of his, the commander produced a bottle of Irish single malt.

Then it was introductions and what can we get you for a drink. "I'll wait" said Winifred, whose presence immediately filled the room as she entered it. A woman of about sixty, I would guess, she was tall, almost willowy, with thick silver grey hair platted and curled up on either side of her pleasant if beaky face.

Drinks and hors d'oeuvres passed around, and the party resumed. The rescue of the kidnapped men came quickly to the fore as a topic given that the commander was a law enforcement officer of international eminence. Joanna asked him what, as a professional, did he think of the operation.

"Oh, well done, well done, indeed. But you know, it shows that the locals usually know more than the big guys, as you might say." He had in hand a glass of whiskey neat and his voice, oddly reassuring, went with the paisley cravat in the white shirt beneath his corduroy jacket.

"But who is the private citizen who led the local constabulary to the old hotel?" Winifred wanted to know. In a shift of grey linen with a wide leather belt and a torc of beaten gold worked in a Celtic knot, she exerted a natural, low-key attraction.

No one but Diantha and I knew, of course, but I found it gratifying as I played host with the trays of canapés to hear the guesses. I also stood ready to intervene should Ivor start talking about the rescue as a miscarriage of justice.

Which he did, but indirectly. Squatting next to the fire like a large troll, he expatiated about the kidnapping as an art form, saying, "I mean talk about dark, dark theater. Not their rescue, which was a bit trite, like all happy endings, but their capture and confinement."

"What do you mean?" asked Alice, like a good student.

I noticed that her husband's face remained impassive and wondered if I should steer the conversation into subjects with more comic potential and thereby unleash a torrent of beneficence. But what?

"The sheer hellishness of it," Ivor was saying. "Set the opening scene. The door to their tomb closes. They are left to their own devices. They each have a hunting knife... "

"Yes, but where's the audience?" Winifred asked. "Surely you can't have theater without an audience."

The ever glib Ivor smiled, the firelight catching his dandelion hair. He said, "Oh, but you are the audience, the theater of the mind and the imagination being the most extravagant theater possible."

"Ivor, what's your favorite comedy?" I asked abruptly, my question sounding like the redirection it was.

Ivor furrowed his brow in a rare frown. "Comedy doesn't interest me, Norman. Stage comedies are hollow fantasies... "

"Even those of Oscar Wilde?" asked Winifred. She wasn't one to let large statements go unchallenged.

"Especially Oscar Wilde. No one talks like that. No one in life is that witty."

"Apparently he was."

Edwin Clydes was nodding vaguely and his thin lips appeared on the verge of a faint smile.

"But, Ivor," I said with a false chuckle, "I know you laugh. I've heard you." I smiled around at the group and took in Mr. Clydes, the sides of whose mouth appeared to be about to dimple. "You certainly know how to amuse yourself."

The commander and his wife laughed. Joanna laughed. Alice laughed. And her husband's eyes had narrowed ever so slightly in response to the skin of his cheeks rising above the bowing of his lips. I beamed my encouragement at him, trying to remind him that it is impolite not to at least smile when others are laughing. It seemed to work. The sides of his mouth twitched a little once or twice. Silently, I implored him. Just a smile, damn you. Just a little hiccup of laughter.

There might have been a fleeting grimace. Then Ivor killed the moment, saying with affected archness, "I laugh at life, not at rehearsed jokes."

The rain came in gusts against the windows making cozy the primordial fire, which snapped and danced in the grate. The salmon and caviar proved popular. I refilled drinks. Ivor began again, like a wound-up doll, directing much of his chat toward the commander and his consort with whom he was obviously impressed. "I've always wanted to write a murder mystery for the stage," he said to Winifred, who was putting pieces of salmon on the soda bread.

"Really?" she spoke with feigned interest. Then to me, "Norman, I would adore a touch of what the commander's having."

Ivor, oblivious, burbled on. "Yes, the curtain would open on an Edwardian living room with a corpse in the middle of it. Then the five surviving characters would appear each in a monologue to the audience declaring their innocence. Then, one by one they would be murdered, all save one, who, of course, would be presumed to be the murderer."

Joanna led the applause, though the commander looked dubious. "An easy job for the police in that case," he said.

"Unless the last one standing merely murdered the murderer," Ivor said and glanced around with his awful smirk.

"Yes, but what do you do with all the bodies?" Alice wanted to know.

"Oh, for them we have a stage crew," Joanna put in and got a good laugh.

Except for Edwin Clydes. He wore a mask of mildness behind which he might have been conjuring another ingenious way of scooping millions from the ocean of dollars still sloshing around the world after the crash.

Diantha gave me a tap on the shoulder. Kitchen duty beckoned.

"We've got to do better," she said in a lowered voice as we bustled about in the kitchen, she with the salad, I with the shanks, which I set out on a warmed platter along with the rosemary.

"I had him right on the edge and your friend Ivor killed it."

"You're sure he didn't smile?"

"I really don't know. Maybe it was a pre-smile. I mean I don't even know what his smile looks like."

She said, "Why don't you tell a joke?"

"I'm not good at jokes."

"The one about the Pope and M&Ms."

"This Pope isn't Polish. And they might be Catholic."

"Norman, I'm counting on you."

A touch exasperated, I sighed and said, "Diantha, really, I don't know how to make small talk with the wealthy. I mean, what do you say, 'Congratulations on all your money. I'm appropriately envious. How's your new private jet?'"

"You're being snide."

We were saved by the abrupt appearance of Joanna. "What can I do to help?" she said brightly.

"Get moneybags to smile," I muttered.

"Oh, but I think it's going very well," she gushed. "There's still dinner, and I don't think he'll resist the Lafite."

The impending discussion stopped abruptly at the appearance of Alice in the doorway. She also wanted to know what she could do to help.

"I think we're all set," I said, suddenly liking this quiet and quietly attractive woman. "Perhaps you could take the salad plates. We never did get them set out."

She didn't move. She said, "I just want to say, Joanna and Diantha and Norman, that this is a wonderful party. I mean, really, I've never met such interesting people… "

"Why, thank you," I said, as urbanely as I could. "Is Edwin enjoying himself?"

"Oh, who knows what Edwin's thinking?" She gave a little laugh and took the salad plates. Joanna followed her with the new potatoes, which were done to a turn, their delicate skins about to burst. I remembered the bread I had sliced earlier. We were just arranging things on the table and the sideboard in the dining room when the doorbell rang. "Who could that be?" Diantha asked, taking off her apron and rubbing her hands on it.

I shook my head. "Whoever it is, let Joanna get it."

We bustled about and were on the point of calling our guests to dinner, when we heard the unmistakable voice of Sixpak Maldoon, the lead vocalist of the Redneck Rappers and a former swain of Diantha's. "Dig the threads, man," he was saying to Ivor, who had brought him to the double doors of the living room like a prize he had just caught.

Diantha looked at me horror-struck. "Oh, no," she said, "Oh, please God no."

"Di, an old friend of yours… " Ivor Pavonine was in full, malevolent beam. "I've invited him to dinner. Sixpak says he would love to join us."

As the others, standing now, looked on with something like shock and awe, Sixpak came in as though from behind the curtains. "Di, baby! Man, are you a sight for sore eyes."

Dripping wet, guitar case in hand, patched duffel on the floor, his shaved head needing a shave along with his face, his clothes sad in their shabbiness, the man glanced around with the heavy lidded gaze of someone permanently drugged. "Love this crib, baby, always loved this crib."

"Norman, do something," Diantha hissed at me under her breath.

"What?" I stammered.

"Give him some money and call him a cab," she said in a stage whisper. Then, louder, "Sixy… I'm afraid… "

"No bother, man. I'm cool with it. I'd appreciate the grub. Ain't eaten in I don't know how long."

"But…"

"Di, it's cool," Ivor said, holding Sixy's arm.

"Ivor, please, please," Diantha begged. "Really, we only have settings for eight."

Which wasn't strictly true in terms of tableware. And we had cooked at least ten shanks.

"We'll just set another place." Ivor could scarcely contain the mad glee in his voice. "Remember, Di, life is art is life, especially dinner parties."

In the midst of all this, I noticed Commander Morgliesh regarding Ivor with a deliberate, assessing gaze.

So, introductions of a sort were made and we settled ourselves at the table as Diantha, fuming, set up another place, hissing again at me about how Sixy's arrival had messed up her carefully planned seating arrangements. Sixy ended up in the middle of one side flanked by Ivor and Joanna and directly across from Winifred, who regarded him with amused expectation.

I went around serving out the shanks. The potatoes and sauce followed. Salad if you wanted it now. Joanna poured the Paulliac. We were all ready. From my end of the table, I raised my glass. "To the Seaboard Players and the Little Theater."

"To life is art is life," Ivor added.

There were murmurs of appreciation around as people tasted the wine. I watched Edwin Clydes for signs of approval. He might have been amused in a disdainful way.

Sixy quaffed his in one go and put his glass down like it was a sturdy beer tankard. People turned to look at him. Into their waiting silence, he declared, "Man, that is some smooth shit."

"You're a connoisseur," Winifred said with mocking alacrity.

"Yeah, you could say that."

"It is excellent," I put in. "And thanks to Joanna."

"Here, here," the commander said, helping me out.

Edwin Clydes had resumed his frown.

Diantha looked ready to weep.

Ivor turned to the new guest. "So, Sixpak, what brings you to Seaboard?"

Sixy, already eating greedily, raised his head. His dazed gaze had deepened. At the same time he sounded quite lucid, saying, "The band broke up. D'you know that, Di? The Redneck Rappers are no more."

"So what happened to the Redneck Rappers?" Winifred asked, leaning across the table towards him.

"Like kaput, man. Danko's like in permanent rehab." He tapped his ill-shaved skull. "No one answers the door. And Raunche, he's off with some chick in New Mexico who eats soil or some shit like that." At which point, he leaned back, closed his eyes, and appeared to go to sleep.

In a transparent attempt to change the conversation, noticing that Edwin Clydes's frown had begun to deepen, I said to the table at large but through Winifred, "Ivor is writing a play for the Seaboard Players."

"And Diantha's going to play the lead," Joanna said brightly.

"What's the play to be called?" asked the commander, apparently an old hand at contriving conversation.

Ivor preened. "Well, it started out as *Triad with Voice*. But, given developments, I'm calling it *Chronicle of a Murder Foretold*."

"Man, that sounds heavy," said a reviving Sixpak, reaching for the Lafite and eating again with great relish, wiping up the juice on his plate with torn-off pieces of bread.

"So you will have your murder mystery on stage," Winifred said.

"Not so much a mystery, as..."

"As?"

"An exercise in reality."

Then another deadly lull. Winifred again leaned across the table toward Sixy. "And what will you do now, now that your band has disbanded?"

The lead vocalist of the disbanded Redneck Rappers put down his lamb shank on which he had been gnawing as though it were a drumstick. His eyes didn't quite focus. "Doing... Man, I don't know. I'm just trying to get my shit together..."

"Really?"

"Yeah." He looked at her with puzzlement, slowly focusing again. "It's a way of saying... you know I'm saying...?"

"Well, yes, it's just that the image it conjures is a bit unfortunate."

"Yeah, it ain't all roses. Not like the old days. Di, remember that night when we smoked some of that Nepalese weed and you and Danko's chick did the whole band?"

Into the silence that followed, Ivor, eyes aglitter, asked, "You mean slept with the band?"

"Yeah, but there wasn't much sleeping. Man, it was intense. Hottest night of my life. I got the *Orifice Rex* cut out of that, my one real hit."

"Dear me, Diantha," said Winifred with evident admiration, "most of us only dream about such a romp."

"So how many were in the band?" Ivor, who had scarcely touched his food, egged on the rapper.

"Well, there was me and Danko and Raunche, Stump, Redman, and what, a techie named Bigger, a real jerk. Yeah, I mean talk about a cluster fuck..."

"Yes, but there were some controlled substances involved," I offered lamely, indirectly coming to Diantha's defense. She sat there in pale, silent horror.

"Man, it was more like out of control substances. Danko had this Nepalese shit that was like, man, like being on Everest... " He mumbled off to himself.

I noticed that Alice, who sat next to Winifred, had grown big-eyed with interest. I helped her to more wine. Her husband's frown had become a scowl.

Ivor said, "Man, Sixy, you are out in front of us all."

"Yeah. Out in front and out behind. Ha, ha. Those were the days. And the nights. We were doing this gig in Bakersfield and I ended up with these four chicks..."

"You were alone?" Winifred asked.

"Yeah, except for the chicks."

"Dear me, how did you manage?"

"Don't ask me. It was like getting eaten alive. Sucked dry. Next morning I got a piece of paper and wrote down..." But he was drifting again and couldn't remember what he had written down.

Winifred, her torc catching the candle light, said brightly, "So I take it you are quite the lady's man?"

Sixy seemed to have gone into his fuzzy mode again. But he straightened and said distinctly, "A lady's man?" He might have taken it as a put-down. "Lady, you happen to be looking at a dude who's had more pussy than a toilet seat."

"Really?"

"Really."

The table had grown silent and still again.

Winifred gave a little, facetious sniff. "Well, I suppose that would depend, rather, on the toilet seat."

Sixpak gathered his scattering wits. "What are you talking about?"

Winifred leaned in for the kill. "Well, if the toilet seat in question were in the men's room of a men's club in, say, Riyadh, then there might well be a dearth of what you call pussy."

Alice Talty, who had been drinking well, was the first to laugh, which she did with a clap of her hands. Then everyone joined in, except her husband, whose frown had become a glower.

At the height of the hilarity, Sixpak pointed a finger at Winifred, the way celebrities point at people, and said in mock black talk, "The white bitch be messin' with ma hayd!"

More laughter, even Diantha, who couldn't believe that her evening might still be a success, perhaps *de scandale*, but a success nonetheless.

The doorbell rang. "Saved by the bell," someone said.

With puzzlement and relief, I rose and went to see who it was. And there under the small portico stood Alphus and Boyd Ridley both a little damp from the rain.

"We were in the neighborhood," signed Alphus. "But if we're interrupting anything…"

Ridley, as he liked to be called, looked sheepishly at the welcome mat. They had been drinking. Alphus had on a shirt, tie, and his lemon yellow jacket, but the tie, his flashy blue one, hung badly askew. Ridley had the collar of his biker jacket turned up against the rain.

What could I say? Go away, we're having a dinner party with respectable people? The wine, my better nature, and a sense of mischief spoke. "Come in, come in. You're just in time to meet some nice people."

For dinner as theater, it fell like a stroke of genius, at least to Ivor whose pale eyes brightened and whose hands came together in a resounding clap. Introductions were made, mostly by me, Diantha being mute with relief or consternation or both. I sketched in Alphus' provenance, his ability to sign and my role as a translator if anyone wanted to talk to my good friend.

"Some supper?" Diantha offered not quite convincingly.

"We've eaten, thank you," Ridley said. "But a glass of wine looks good."

Sixpak, coming out of a wine and substance stupor, looked up with wild surmise, startled, even fearful. "Gorillas in the mist," he muttered aloud. Then, as though to himself. "It's getting worse. I need to..." And bowed his head and closed his eyes.

Chairs were found. Alphus sat next to me at the head of the table and thanked Diantha for a glass of the Lafitte.

For once Ivor was tongue-tied, even face-tied. The arrival of the new guests had taken him beyond the theater of the absurd. He leaned forward, his amazement growing as Alphus sniffed his glass of wine, held it up to the light, sipped, and worked his mouth. Everyone there watched, pretending not to be dumbfounded.

Putting his glass down with deliberation, Alphus began signing, but slowly as though still meditating. I translated. "He says it has an equivocating, even shy nose that belies the prominent cassis fruit overtones and rich shades of cedar of its tongue. He also loves the lingering complexity of its finish."

Though his fug, Sixpak said, "I'm not feeling well."

Ivor held his hands apart, brought them together, and loudly, "Print it!"

Sixpak stood unsteadily to his feet. "I need the facilities."

I rose immediately and went around to make sure he didn't spew on the table. As we were leaving the room, Winifred said, "Be sure and lift the toilet seat."

Sixpak did spew copiously into the still water of the toilet bowl, retching until he heaved drily over the contents of his stomach. Strange, I thought, how food, so delightful and enticing on the plate, becomes a disgusting mess once swallowed and regurgitated, not to mention when it's been fully digested. But I found, standing there, that my annoyance with the man had mellowed to pity, heart felt however close it was to contempt. I even helped him wash his face with a cloth before leading him back, more or less presentable, to the party at the table.

It seemed the cue for Edwin Clydes to stand. "Alice, we must go."

"Now?"

"Now."

The table fell silent again except for these two. The sound of the gusting rain could be heard. Alice, her lips trembling, began to rise. Then stopped. Then sat down. "No."

"Alice…"

"No. I'm staying."

"Alice…" With a hiss now, his face in full scowl.

"No, damn it, Edwin. I'm having fun for once in my life. I like these people. They do things. They say things."

"One last time, Alice…"

"One last time, Edwin, no."

Her husband turned and strode from the room. I went after him. "I'll get your coat," I said, trying to keep my relief from being too obvious. I led him down to the closet near the front door. Ivor was exulting, "Brilliant, bravo, absolutely brilliant!"

I didn't apologize to Edwin Clydes. I scarcely said good-bye. What was the point? I doubted I would ever see him again.

The evening did fizzle a bit after that. When Sixy collapsed gently on the sofa, the commander and I helped him upstairs to a bed in a spare room. Alice had a cry in the kitchen with Joanna and Di, who told her not to worry, that she had done the right thing. We had desert, French silk chocolate pie, and coffee. Ivor kept taking verbal bows until the commander took him aside and said they were all leaving and that a taxi had arrived for him and Joanna and Alice.

Then the party after the party. I let Decker out of his dungeon in the cellar and checked on the children. Bella had left with a sweet wave not long before. I availed myself of the Irish malt, half remembering someone saying there was no such thing as a large whiskey, before joining the others. The six of us unwound with amicable chat, signage and voice, around the dying fire. Winifred stifled a polite yawn. "Augie, we should let these good people go to bed."

They graciously offered to give Alphus and Ridley a lift home, an offer accepted with much evident appreciation as Ridley didn't drive and cabbies often refused to take Alphus. He gave me and then Diantha one of his big hairy hugs in parting.

Then it was just Diantha and I in the kitchen sobering up and clearing up.

"We didn't get Edwin to really smile much less laugh. But a great success nonetheless," I ventured, stacking the hand-rinsed plates in the washer.

"Easy for you to say," she spoke with an edge of bitterness. "You weren't humiliated in front of everyone. Yeah, a great laugh. At my expense."

I very nearly said, "Life is art is life," but instead put my arms around her and murmured in her ear, "If people judge you for that, it's only a form of envy."

She cried in my arms. "And poor Alice…"

"Alice will be fine. It's poor Edwin who's in for a rough time. He doesn't know it. He just fell from power."

"And Sixy. I want him out of here. First thing in the morning."

"I'll give him some money and call a cab."

She looked up into my eyes with a teary face. "Oh, Norman, only you beneath the moon and under the sun…"

"But it's still raining."

Which made her laugh.

22

On Sunday I went with Diantha to services in Swift Chapel. She remained troubled in the aftermath of our dinner party and was contending for the first time with the possibility that Ivor Pavonine is not only a charlatan, but a villain. And if not an out-and-out fraud, then certainly not the friend she took him for. I resisted the temptation to preach but did murmur something to the effect that art's license does not include cruelty except in those special cases when it is justified by wit.

When she mentioned, all too casually, that she had been thinking of giving the Reverend Alfie Lopes a call, I suggested that we attend services and, at the coffee afterwards, she could ask to see him privately. Because, in fact, Diantha has, over the past few years, sought that good man's counsel from time to time.

Alfie is what you might call a black Brahmin of the Boston kind, very much in the old Groton and Harvard mold. He refers to himself as an Afro-Saxon, but in origins he is Afro-Portuguese by way of Cape Verde.

"So much better than a shrink," Diantha told me more than once after having had a chat with him over tea. "As much as anything, it is the way he listens that helps. You can almost hear him doing it and you sense his sympathy and the deep inner peace that puts almost anything in the perspective of something far greater and more profound than any passing angst."

Indeed, the Reverend Lopes has that gift of finding a large context for almost any subject however excruciatingly exacting he can be delineating it in the King's English. (He is on occasion referred to as the parsing parson.) On this Sunday, after ascending the pulpit and arranging his Geneva tabs, he told us he would speak on town-gown relations and how that essential harmony had of late been disturbed in a way that cast little credit on either party.

"I refer, of course, to the unfortunate confrontation between Professor Byles and Officer Jones of the Seaboard Police Department." He avowed that he would not take sides in the dispute whatever his institutional sympathies as he had infinite respect for the local constabulary and its role in maintaining the orderly basis of civilized life.

"In all such altercations, the decorum of language -- the governance of the tongue, to quote the poet Heaney -- is of paramount importance. And in this instance, I was struck in a close reading of the event by what might be called role reversal. It is Officer Jones who sounds the polite, the inquiring, one might even say, the gownish note when he states, 'I am sorry, sir, but I will need to see some identification.'

"Professor Byles, on the other hand, speaks in what can only be called the argot of the street when he tells the officers, 'You don't know who you're messing with.'

"It is understandable given the circumstances that Professor Byles would suffer a lapse in grammar and syntax not to mention temper. To have been technically correct, and these things do matter, he should have said, 'You don't know with whom you are messing.' Not that there's any real requirement that sentences should not a preposition end with. So, at the very least, he should have said 'You don't know whom you're messing with.' Of course, had Professor Byles been in the British Army and spoken neutrally to a comrade, the sentence could be construed as a question in the form of an affirmative and would have had reference to dining arrangements.

"But in fact, Professor Byles' words are freighted with far more significance than that. To return to the syntax. Note that the critical pronoun *who* in both of these utterances takes the objective form not because it is the object of *know* but of the preposition *with*. As such, it is relegated to a modifying phrase in a subordinate noun clause. Or is it?

"It deserves better. Because what Professor Byles has uttered far transcends the sum of its rather meager parts and its expressive banality. However inadvertently, this scholar of things Aksumitic has struck a note that resonates with remarkable force. Beyond any grammatical parsing, his assertion constitutes nothing less than the *cri de coeur* of modern mankind.

"To make the matter clearer, I will take the liberty to recast this portentous declaration of the professor in a more normative syntax. As such it becomes, simply, 'You don't know who I am.' More significantly, the *who* here becomes the predicative nominative of the noun clause that serves as the direct object of the verb *know*.

"In this reconfiguration -- which magnifies its import without doing violence to its meaning -- the assertion attains a fluidity of meaning staggering in its implications. Meaning that this is no longer the plaint of yet another self-important academician venting his self-indulgent indignation to representatives of the law; this is the wisdom of an inadvertent philosopher. *You don't know who I am.* Nothing better encapsulates the existential plight of beleaguered, alienated western man who, at the very apotheosis of his power and achievement, finds himself estranged from the world he largely fashioned. Is it not we, writ large, who no longer know with whom we are messing?

"In short, we find ourselves confronted with nothing less than a crisis of identity. To take just one example, as the natural world shrinks and shrivels around us, the old question about man's place in nature is answered by another question, 'What nature?' Beyond that, I refer you to Father O'Gould's excellent *The Future of Eternal Life* for an exhilarating and disturbing vision of what is to come."

The preacher took a moment to let that sink in and to marshal his thoughts. He continued, "The reverberations of the professor's seemingly simple and pointed taunt to an officer of the law goes deeper than what might be called our cosmological plight. It touches and disturbs the very tectonics of our ontological bedrock. Because, how many times in our daily intercourse with others have we said to them, however silently and however unconsciously, 'You don't know who I am.' Indeed, we all live under the sway of the necessary illusion of thinking we know who our friends and loved ones are, not just by name or personality traits, but by character, by spirit, by soul. More to the point, we assume they know who we are at that same profound level. Alas, so often we don't and they don't. And hence the near curse of Professor Byles' assertion even when our nearest and dearest are involved."

Diantha took my hand and squeezed it. She whispered, "I don't know who Ivor Pavonine is."

I whispered back, "I'm not sure he does, either."

The Reverend Lopes, his round *café-au-lait* countenance magisterial above his old-fashioned clerical garb, had paused again as though to commune, not with any notes he might have on the lectern before him, but with a higher power.

He continued, "In short, I have come to believe that what we are dealing with is far more than the utterance of another professor with enough titles hanging off his name to make a tin pot dictator blush. No, this singular asseveration has, when reduced to its elemental force, implications no less than cosmic. Because, in this secular age, when assailed by the slings and arrows of ordinary fortune and with nowhere else to go, do we not, if only unconsciously, turn to the God of our Fathers and say, more in sorrow than in anger, 'Lord, you don't know who I am.'

"There are those who, in the wake of this unfortunate incident between town and gown, have characterized it as a 'teaching moment.' The question begged, of course, is who is to teach and who is to be taught? I maintain that the ramifications of Professor Byles' statement make all of us both teachers and taught.

"I say that because, finally, the statement we have been mulling over touches all of us to our very core. Is it not what we think to ourselves when, alone, sometimes naked, either literally or figuratively, we peer into a mirror? Too often it seems that we are looking at a stranger and too often, that stranger is looking back and saying, 'You don't know who I am.'"

He brought his hands together. "May God bless and keep you all."

216

I swear there would have been applause if not a standing ovation had Alfie not banned such outbursts in the chapel as a matter of policy. At the gatherings after the service, Diantha and I, paper cup of church coffee in hand, both congratulated the minister. And when Diantha told him she would like to drop by some time for a chat, he was graciousness itself. "Come at four tomorrow for tea. We need to catch up, anyway."

At home, a small roast in the oven, just the two of us with Elsie, Norman, Jr., and Decker, our black lab, Diantha turned to me and said, "Alfie is right, you know."

"About?" I asked, checking my watch to see if it were not too early to think about a drink.

"About I.P.. I don't know who he is and he doesn't know who I am."

I nodded but said nothing.

She brushed back a strand of hair in that fetching way she has. "I mean, he didn't need to foist Sixpak on us the way he did. And he knew exactly what he was doing."

"The question, Diantha, is what are you going to do about it?" I had decided on a cup of tea, the black Irish kind, with milk and sugar.

"Mostly, Norman, I am going to keep him away from you."

"Really?" I asked, just slightly puzzled.

"I've already told him not to drop in anymore without calling first. But he's always asking about you. 'What does Norman think of this? What's Norman doing about that?' He is really obsessed with anything to do with Norman de Ratour. I don't know why he's always on about your reactions to the attempts on your life. I swear he's taking notes."

I returned to the museum the next morning with a spring in my step. I walked to work through a cold autumnal drizzle, the collar of my trench coat up, the brim of my trilby down, the weight of the Glock comfortably on my belt. I felt like a private eye out of a Raymond Chandler novel. I felt secure. Assassins tend to avoid inclement weather.

Alas, it did not take long for events at the museum to bring me down to the quotidian realities of running an institution that deals with the public. In this case, a young man had managed to get into the public areas before they were opened to general admission. Old Mort noticed something amiss on one of the monitors. The individual in question, clearly visible in a replay of the incident, was attempting sexual congress with one of the more comely Neanderthal "maidens" that constitute part of the Diorama of Paleolithic Life. He had not only unbuckled, unzipped, and unleashed himself, but he had lifted the maiden's loin cloth up over her realistic and quite attractive buttocks. He then proceeded to produce a tube of ointment with which contents he slathered her inner thighs before grasping her by the waist and proceeding, evidently, to satisfy himself.

At which point, security showed up and quietly led him away. Mort, whose judgment I trust, handled the matter in-house. He told the young man, who goes by the name Chaff, that we had a tape of the whole thing and that if he showed his face or anything else in the museum again, the matter would be turned over to the police. Chaff readily agreed to that. But he also asked for a copy of the footage of himself and the young Neanderthal. He wants, apparently, to put it on Your Tube or one of those outlets for all to see.

"What did you tell him?" I asked.

"I said we'd think about it."

I shook my head. "Out of the question."

Mort looked puzzled.

"If that gets out, we'll have a crowd of needy males in here molesting the models. It wouldn't do."

He nodded. "Yeah, you're right. And, let's face it, we've already got enough problems with security, I mean, with people taking potshots at you."

I had scarcely settled down to a stack of correspondence when Clay Mallard, who is chair of the Curatorial Council, insisted that I call an emergency meeting of that body to discuss the incident among the Neanderthals. I reluctantly agreed, knowing too well what the issue would be.

The council, in fact, is split over two approaches having to do with exhibitions. One faction, which is headed by Nancy Jevons, an assistant professor of anthropology at Wainscott and curator of the Neanderthal diorama, favors "open" exhibits. She and a few others are in favor of please touch, though not, perhaps to the extent of the young man that morning. "The minute you put it behind glass, it becomes dead and the experience second-hand," she said with firm conviction. "What happened this morning, however extreme and unwelcome, demonstrates how realistic and effective the current exhibit is as it stands."

Mallard and his supporters are of the do-not-touch school, even when the objects on display are not irreplaceable treasures.

We met in the Twitchell Room and I played moderator as the curators, all serious, competent professionals, repeated what they had said before and then repeated what they had to say now. I was about to suggest we appoint a subcommittee to explore the matter further, but then realized such an entity already existed. So I asked how their work was coming along and managed to turn the issue back on them as my mind drifted, as it tends to do nowadays.

Speaking of Neanderthals, I was abruptly summoned on Wednesday morning to appear at the local FBI office to answer questions about "my recent activities." And again I was advised to bring along counsel.

Felix and I arrived on time and were shown into the same room and asked to sit at the same table. The same duo, Agent Atkins and Agent Willard, presently came in and, after crisp, dry, law-enforcement handshakes, took chairs opposite us and opened the file folders they had brought with them.

The theatrics involved a spell of studied silence in which both agents frowned at the contents of their folders. Agent Atkins, who was the large, black, and imposing one, started off in the good cop role. "We understand, Mr. Ratour, that you and one Adam Morgliesh visited one Victor Karnivossky not long ago."

"That's right," I replied.

"Both are foreign nationals, is that not true?" said Agent Willard, the small, white, and unimposing one.

"You should know better than I," I replied.

Felix said, "Mr. Morgliesh is British. You know, the mother country, Grand Alliance, special relationship… "

They didn't know. Agent Atkins nodded meaningfully. "Can you tell us what that meeting was about?"

"You don't have to answer that," Felix said.

"I don't mind. We went there to ask him if he had hired Blackie Burker shoot at me."

"And why did you ask him that?"

"To find out if he did or not."

Which appeared to stymie them for a moment. Recovering, Agent Atkins said, "And why do you think he might want to hire someone to shoot at you?"

"Don't answer if you don't want to," Felix said wearily. "They're on a fishing expedition."

"I have no fish to hide. Some years ago, In self-defense I killed one of Mr. Karnivossky's competitors, one Freddie Bain, and there was apparently some theorizing that I might now be his new competitor."

"Are you?"

"You mean in his role as a museum director?" Felix asked.

"And what did Mr. Karnivossky say in response to your question?" Agent Willard asked.

"He said he had nothing to do with any attempt on my life."

"And you believed him?"

"Under the circumstances, we did."

"And what were the circumstances?"

"He served us tea and crumpets."

"Tea and crumpets?"

"Yes. It turns out he's a confirmed Anglophile."

"An Anglophile?" Agent Atkins repeated ominously.

"Yes, but as far as we know, he's never been charged with or convicted of Anglophilia," Felix put in with a sly smile at me.

The agents nodded knowingly and changed the subject. Agent Willard asked, with discernible hostility, "What caused you to visit the old hotel on Big Hog Island in the presence of Maurice and Simone Augustein, both foreign nationals?"

"You don't have to answer that," Felix said again, like a recording.

I shrugged. "Mr. Augustein happens to be in the parking garage business…"

"And he wanted to build a parking lot on Big Hog Island?" Agent Atkins all but sneered.

"No, he wanted to build a time-share resort there."

"And you're an expert on time-share resorts."

"No. But he wanted to show me his plans for the old place."

"And why would he want to do that?"

"I think he wanted to impress me."

"And why would he want to impress you?"

"You don't have to answer that."

"He wanted my support in the community to help pave the way for the development."

"In exchange for what?"

"He had offered to support the museum."

"You expect us to believe that?"

"My expectations regarding you gentlemen are severely limited."

After a long pause of slow nodding, Agent Willard stood up. Like his colleague at the last meeting, he did it with such a flourish, it might have been rehearsed. That is, he pushed back his chair, rose slowly, turned, walked away, pivoted, and came back. He put his hands on the back of the chair and leaned forward. The expression on his face, knowing and cynical, was that of someone who has watched a lot of cop movies. He said, in his large voice, "You want to know what I think?"

"Not particularly."

"I think that you and Victor Karnivossky master-minded the kidnapping at Hooker's Point. You knew the perfect place to stow those guys. Karnivossky supplied the muscle."

Agent Atkins, as though on cue, said, "And here's the smart part. You didn't ask for a ransom. No notes, no nothing."

"Because," said Agent Willard, who had sat down, "You knew the bankers' friends would cough up big time to get them released."

"And when that award was posted, you knew exactly where to take the local authorities to rescue the kidnapped parties."

Felix looked at me. "Sorry, Norman, but I'm speechless." Then, to the two agents, "Do you gentlemen have one tiny shred of evidence to support this… this absurd scenario?"

Agent Willard, as though in reply, shuffled some papers in his folder. "Mr. Ratour, in the course of your first visit to the hotel at Hobbes Landing, you told Mr. Augustein that you thought you smelled a malfunctioning septic system."

"That is right."

"But later you changed your mind."

"Yes, it's all in my statement to the state police."

"And why did you change your mind?"

"I realized later that what I smelled smelled more like an enclosed privy than a malfunctioning septic system."

"And you're telling us you know the difference?"

"Yes."

"Really?"

Felix said, "My client knows his shit." He laughed, more at them than what he had said. In a voice that had turned hard, he said to me, "Norman, that's enough. No more questions. No more answers. This is useless." To them he said, "Let me inform you gentlemen of something. If you want to question Mr. de Ratour again, you will have to subpoena him. For that you will have to show cause. And, in the meanwhile, if you or your colleagues come near my client, I will hit you with enough lawsuits to keep your tiny brains doing paperwork for the next five years."

He smiled and stood up. "Come on, Norman, let's get out of here before I lose my temper. Or my mind."

23

Commander Morgliesh's voice sounded plumier than usual coming over the speaker phone on my desk some days after the dinner party. He asked, "How carefully did the authorities go over the area where Mr. Burker took his shots at you?"

I turned away from the desktop screen where I had been perusing a long message with accompanying pictures. The well-meaning widow of a local antiquarian wanted to give us some items of both questionable provenance and dubious value, including several late Nineteenth century Audubon cromoliths that would end up in storage. But how to say no gracefully?

I frowned. The commander had posed a good question. I said, "I'm not sure, Commander. I believe the FBI asked the state police to do it and they turned it over to the county sheriff's office. You know, passing the buck."

"I think we should take a look around."

"When?"

"No time like the present. Are you busy this afternoon?"

"Let me call you right back. If we go, we should plan on an overnight."

I checked the screen, looked at my calendar. Nothing I couldn't put off for another day. I clicked on the intercom. "Doreen...?"

Her sweet young face, now showing the strains of motherhood, appeared in the doorway. "Yes... ?"

"I'll be out the rest of the afternoon and most of tomorrow morning. Call me on my cell phone if anything important comes up."

"No problem."

"I'll be at the cottage with Commander Morgliesh." I said that casually. There had been difficulty in getting office phone calls transferred to my pocket phone, on which I was growing more and more dependent.

"Got it."

"Oh, and there's a meeting of the Education Outreach Task Force at two. I've typed up my suggestions. You should attend, read them into the record. And take notes."

"I was supposed to leave at three."

"Yes..." I had grown anxious to get away. "Okay. How about take off all of tomorrow... no, better, the day after tomorrow off instead."

"Deal."

At home, packing an overnight bag and putting a few perishables into a cooler, I realized why I was anxious: I wanted to confront what I been avoiding. Despite acquiring a high-powered rifle of my own, I had grown reluctant to visit the cottage since the incident with Blackie Burker.

It was one of those November days when the sky is drear and most of the leaves have been stripped from the trees and are rustling or rotting underfoot. It's a time of year that fills me with a poignant, bittersweet ache in which I find myself full of nebulous expectation and trans-timeness, as though the trees, the wind, the water, and the sky are exactly as they were when I was a boy.

It didn't help that, not long after picking up the commander and leaving the environs of Seaboard, I noticed a few vehicles here and there pulled over to the side of the road. Hunters, I realized, men with scoped hunting rifles. The thought depressed me because I now knew what it was like to be a deer.

We drove through forest and past the occasional farm, many of them, -- white house, red barn, maples, pastures, and stone walls -- worthy of Norman Rockwell's brush. The commander took it all in, enjoying himself. At one point he said, "I've remarked that Americans prefer their weekend places to be in wilderness or at least semi-wilderness. I mean compared to the English."

"Perhaps because there's more wilderness here," I replied. "In much of New England the forests have come back."

"True. But there are lots of wild places in Scotland and Wales. No, I think the tradition began with the nobility and the great country places that were their seats of power."

"I don't quite follow," I said.

"I mean they didn't escape to the country so much as come in to London where they built houses to attend court, Parliament, society balls, and, eventually, business."

I was driving my old Renault and paying attention to the road. I hardly noticed how abruptly he changed conversational gears, asking, "What can you tell me about this person, Ivor Pavo…?"

"Pavonine. Not a whole lot. I'm told he's so cutting edge in the theatrical world that he's scarcely part of the blade. Why do you ask?"

The commander rustled in his new windbreaker as he shifted in the seat. He had paused as though to choose his words carefully. "His behavior at your dinner party struck me as strange, odd."

"He is something of an oddball."

"I mean something more than that. What he did was pernicious. Even cruel."

I nodded. In all of my reviling of the man, I had not considered that.

"What I mean," he went on, "is the way he took unseemly delight in Diantha's acute embarrassment and your sympathetic discomfiture. Winifred, I know, didn't help much. I think she was just trying to distract the poor sod."

I nodded. "Diantha keeps telling me that Ivor's an artist, that he has…"

"Poetic license. Extraordinary how many people assume the license without the poetry."

He took a folded sheaf of papers from the side pocket of his jacket. "I ran a background check on him."

"Really?" I was surprised. "Whatever for?"

"Because in this line of business, Norman, even the most far-fetched of possibilities can turn out… "

"But Ivor…" I laughed. "I mean, really, Commander."

"Can I ask you something personal?"

"Of course."

"Has there been any kind of a dalliance between Diantha and Ivor?"

"Nothing very real. Not as far as I know. He sometimes acts the gallant, but, frankly, it wouldn't surprise me if he plays for the other team."

"Or for no team, perhaps."

"Exactly."

"Well, here we are," I said to the commander with feigned cheer as we turned off the road and pulled up next to the cottage. The sight of the place, the neglected garden, the wind-shivered lake, the pine-topped bluff brought back the shooting with a sharp haunting edged with fear. Which mingled in a disorienting way with the simple joys of being there. It helped to have the commander along as I unlocked the door and walked into the late autumn mustiness of the kitchen.

"Anyone home?" I asked the neglected ghosts, in whom I half believed. No one answered. I turned on the vented gas heater to provide background warmth. I also lit a fire in the main hearth for something for us to come back to. The commander looked around and made appreciative noises.

We decided to put off unpacking until we had reconnoitered as we only had a couple of hours of daylight left. With a thoroughness I should have expected, the Scotland Yarder had me retrace my actions and steps on the day of the shooting as best as I could remember. Thus we walked out to the garden and my two-dimensional apple trees. Several frost-sweetened fruit still hung on the boughs and we each helped ourselves to one. Then, not without some palpitations, I acted myself in restaging the assault, standing where I had stood.

The commander closely inspected the stone wall and the marks left by the bullets. Feeling slightly ridiculous, I re-enacted my crouching scamper as I fled the garden to the safety of oak tree and then the cottage itself. I told him about retrieving the Smith & Wesson from the bedroom. Together we followed my path up the drive and across the road into the hardwood glade. Then the logging road, the car, and finally the tree on which Blackie Burker had been snagged when he dropped the rifle and shot himself.

"This is the exact tree?" he asked, standing under it.

"It is," I said. "I think they would have found anything he dropped or left behind."

He nodded, but skeptically. He picked up a piece of dead stick and began poking with it through the surrounding leaf litter.

"What do you think you'll find?" I asked. I joined in with a stick of my own but with no great hope of turning up anything.

"There was no cell phone in the evidence bag. Which may or may not mean anything. Except that there was a charger. And he didn't have a landline at home and there aren't that many call boxes left."

"We call them pay phones."

"Exactly."

After a while, he stood upright and looked at the other trees nearby. When I glanced at him inquiringly, he said, "It may not have been the only tree he climbed. Not all of these would have given him the same vantage point. And remember, he was a consummate professional according to the state police report."

"And a climber of trees."

"Yes. Hence, 'Birdman.'"

I followed him as he walked slowly along the edge of the bluff peering up into the pines that were large enough to support a man. He stopped under one of the bigger ones and checked the ground. "He climbed this one," he said with a confidence I found surprising. He picked up some pieces of dead branch and showed them to me. "Just a hunch as you Yanks say, but…"

We scoured the nearby ground and came up with nothing. At that point I might have given up. And I thought the commander had called it a day as we retraced our steps to the death tree. But he kept going back to where the bluff began to slope laterally. The ground cover became more brushy and I thought we were more playing at detective than doing anything useful.

He stopped to look closely at another tree right on the edge of the wood that apparently had also been climbed. Here we got down on our hands and knees to search. We had been at it only a minute or so when he said, "*Voilà.*" I looked up to see him holding a cell phone gingerly with the tips of his thumb and finger. He then retrieved a pair of latex gloves from his windbreaker pocket and put them on.

As I stood next to him peering at the thing, he flipped it open and turned it on. It still functioned despite several rainstorms since the day of the attempted murder. "Battery's almost dead, he said. He smiled and put the thing in a small plastic bag. "It will need charging. Let's keep looking."

We didn't find anything else and returned to the warmed cottage. From a locked cabinet I took out a bottle of twelve-year-old Lagavulin and poured us both a straight double. We sipped pensively.

"I think we should examine the phone before we turn it over to the FBI," he said matter-of-factly.

I nodded in agreement. "It might be more useful to turn it over to the state police."

"Yes... Yes, Detective Lupien does know what he's about. My God this is a real island malt, isn't it? I can all but taste the sea air."

24

"But the man was trying to kill me." I was speaking with considerable vehemence, rankled not a little by the expression of nonchalance mixed with puzzlement on the pocked face of Felix Skinnerman.

"That is a mitigating circumstance, to be sure... "

"Besides he shot himself."

"True, but you admitted in your statement to the police that there had been gunfire between you."

"So what? He dropped his rifle while trying to light a cigarette."

"Which you had objected to?"

"Dead pine needles catch fire very quickly."

"Was that part of the exchange?"

"We exchanged words, not bullets, about the matter."

"I don't know, Norman, it doesn't look good."

"Felix, the man was a professional killer. He was on my property with a high-powered rifle taking shots at me."

"That's going to be hard to prove."

Felix had arrived at my office ten minutes earlier with the news that the estate of Blackie Burker was suing me for ten million dollars for wrongful death. He had that look on his face.

I dissembled my chagrin. I said with false calm, "What else could I have done?"

"Call the authorities."

"Felix, I could not find my cell phone. And even if I had, it doesn't always work. And my family was about to arrive at the cottage. At any minute."

"Okay, that's another mitigating circumstance."

"I cannot believe this."

"Norman, I'm only telling you what the law is."

"Then the law doesn't make sense."

"Whoever said it did?"

"Then what's it for?"

My attorney looked at me with frank surprise. "Norman, you don't think the law is there for you?"

"Then who is it for?"

"You poor lamb. Why it's there for the lawyers, of course."

"But…"

"The same way the banks are there for the bankers. The same way the university is there for the faculty and for the administrators. And, deep down, Norman, you know this museum is here for you and the curators."

I sighed in defeat. "So what do we do? Counter-sue his estate?"

"I doubt there's much there. And what will you sue for? The pain and suffering of being sued?"

"I'll sue for attempted murder on his part."

"We only have your word for it."

"There have to be fragments of his bullets on the wall where I was trimming the trees."

"Yeah, it sounds good, but you'd have to prove you were nearby when he fired those shots. Look, your homeowner's insurance probably covers it."

"So let them handle it?"

"Sure. They'll settle out of court. For a pittance. Their lawyer will get most of it. Unless you want to make a stand on principle."

I might have squared my back and lifted my nose and done the right thing. But I was morally enervated at that point. I muttered something about thinking it over and as we turned to museum business, I surreptitiously glanced at my schedule for the day on the computer screen. I faced an Oversight Committee meeting in an hour and then I was to have a "planning" lunch with Commander Morgliesh at the Edge.

"And, Norman," Felix said at the door on his way out, "Please sign off on that Rechronnex deal. You will save yourself a whole lot of bother."

I nodded but without any certainty. Even that decision, as Felix well knows, is becoming difficult to implement. The redoubtable Robert Remick, a member of the Governing Board for decades, says he has found an obscure provision in the Rules of Governance that, he claims, requires the assent of the board on matters dealing with significant financial decisions. And this after complaining I had not been "pro-active."

25

Even though three of Seaboard's finest were present in the Twitchell Room, there at my request, the committee insisted on sticking to its agenda, which led off with a report from the Subcommittee on Lexical Standards. When I began to protest, Chief Murphy, who was in attendance with Lieutenant Tracy and Sergeant Lemure, said it was okay, as long as it didn't take too long. They were there for the third item on the agenda -- "Town-gown relations with special reference to the Seaboard Police Department and senior faculty."

The second item involved a report from the Library Oversight Subcommittee and involved the removal from university libraries "any books, films, and any other material deemed offensive to any members of the greater Wainscott community."

Professor Randall Athol of the Divinity School, chair of the Subcommittee on Lexical Standards, distributed a paper titled "Words and Phrases under Consideration for Proscription."

"*Stupid*," Izzy Landes muttered with a frown, regarding the list. Then, shaking his nimbus of white hair, he declared, "But stupidity exists. It's all around us. This list is stupid."

"Really, Professor Landes," said Chair Constance Brattle, "you will have an opportunity to comment."

"Okay, I understand. But what do we use instead of stupid? Differently intelligent?"

"We can't," I said. The word *intelligent* is also on the proscribed list."

"Gentlemen, gentlemen," tutted the chair.

"The word *gentleman* is also on the list," someone said.

"Along with the word *lady*," Professor Athol pointed out.

"No more ladies and gentlemen? What instead, men and women?"

"Women and men."

Father S.J. O'Gould, S.J., a moderating voice on the committee, ventured, "Really, Randy, I don't see why the words *achievement* and *excellence* are included as well."

Professor Athol cleared his throat. "We put those words on the list as well as *intelligent* because they are essentially invidious inasmuch as their usage implies their opposites."

"So what?" Izzy demanded. "Their opposites exist."

"Research has shown that these particular words foster an ethos of white privilege and elitism that is detrimental to members of vulnerable groups."

"That's like saying we shouldn't use the word *joyous* because it implies its opposite."

"Yes, we should consider that."

"And what's wrong with the term *personal responsibility*?" I asked.

Professor Ébène took my question. Rattling her cornrows, she said, "A professor at Princeton has found that the term *personal responsibility* is a racially charged code phrase aimed at people of color."

"That's absurd," I said with some heat. "The very notion that the term could be considered racist is in itself racist."

"And it shows precisely why the word *stupid* is so useful," Izzy put in.

The chair held up a hand. "Can we move on with the next item on the agenda, please. She glanced at her laptop screen then up. "Mx Schultz?"

Mx Schultz, the assistant librarian for community standards, a person of no discernible gender or age, hair cropped short and teeth to match, spoke in a voice that could have been generated by the slate it held in its many ringed fingers. "Per directives from the subcommittee on book and media content in Wainscott's libraries, the following books have been eliminated…" It paused to clear its throat and then, "*The Old Testament* and the *New Testament*. The novels *Robinson Crusoe* and *Moby Dick*. The following plays of William Shakespeare: *Macbeth*, *Othello*, *Hamlet*, and

Lear. Mr. Shakespeare's other words are currently under review. We have also eliminated *The Adventures of Huckleberry Finn and Tom Sawyer* by Mark Twain and *Lolita* by Vladimir Nabokov. The other works of both of these authors are also currently under review. *The Great Gatsby* by F. Scott Fitzgerald has been eliminated as have most of the works of William Faulkner..."

Izzy shook his head and threw up his hands and recited: "*Dort, wo man Bücher verbrennt, verbrennt man am Ende auch Menschen*"

"Please speak English," ordered the chair.

"I am quoting Heinrich Heine, a German Jewish poet of the early nineteenth century who was later banned by the Nazis. To translate, "Where they burn books, they will ultimately burn people also."

"We're not talking about burning books," interposed a person who appeared to be the librarian's assistant. "We're not allowed to."

"I see," said Izzy, glancing around at the other members as though gauging their wonderment, if any. "And just how do you plan to eliminate the books in question?"

"We pulp them, of course," said Mx Schultz.

"Pulp them?"

"In accordance with the university's goal of becoming carbon neutral by 2030... It's in the directive."

"Recycled, in other words."

"Yes."

"As?"

"We're not sure."

"Toilet paper, perhaps?"

"Perhaps."

"And, of course, Wainscott would never burn people it finds objectionable as the Nazis did."

"Of course not."

"You'll just pulp them, right, in accordance with the directive."

"We don't have the authority to pulp people."

"And we don't have the facilities," added the assistant.

Izzy raised both hands. "I rest my case."

"Can we move on to the case involving the Seaboard Police Department?" Chair Brattle asked, and did the equivalent of shuffling papers with her laptop.

Across the table, Sergeant Lemure caught my eye, screwed up his heavy florid face, and said "This what you people do?"

In the silence that followed, I mentioned that we did have three members of the SPD who were there at our request. I motioned that we table further discussion about what books to burn or pulp and proceed to the issue of police-university relations. After some discussion, the motion was seconded and carried.

Professor McNull, who is a career committee member and the embodiment of professorial rectitude to the tips of his trimmed whiskers, cleared his throat portentously and said he would like to make an opening statement. The chair acceded to his request. With that he stood and speaking with the authority of a committee veteran, he said, "I have to say that I find it more than credible that a member of the faculty of Professor Byles' eminence can be all but assaulted on Wainscott property by a Seaboard... cop." He paused, perhaps sensing that the word "cop" struck a wrong note. Then, "What I would like to know in the first place is what the Seaboard police were doing on Wainscott property without express permission."

Faces clouded with indignation and some confusion around the table. Izzy Landes ventured, "Pilgrim Street is a public thoroughfare. And the 911 call came from a university employee."

Professor McNull gathered on his whiskered face one of his formidable frowns. "The fact remains that a most distinguished professor was accosted by Seaboard police on university property."

Chair Brattle, clearly contending, along with other committee members, with competing pieties, said, "But there have been several reports lately of young males loitering around the residence and the bicycle racks."

Professor McNull scarcely acknowledged her. "Let me read from the record." He picked up a folder in front of him. He went through what everyone by now had heard any number of times:

"Professor Byles: 'You're asking me for identification?'

"*Officer Jones: 'Yes, sir.'*

"*Professor Byles: 'Let me repeat, you want me to identify myself?'*

"*Officer Jones: 'Yes sir.'*

"*Professor Byles, 'Young man, you don't know who you're messing with.'*

"'*Yes, sir, that's why I'm asking for identification.'*"

Professor McNull looked up. "Here, I think we have the crux of the problem."

"Which is?" I asked.

"Officer Jones should have recognized Professor Byles as a Wainscott faculty member."

Izzy put his hands up. "Not only that, but let's face it, if a professor as eminent as Chauncy Byles is not allowed to pull rank on a mere cop, what's the point of all of our status?"

"I take exception to that remark, Professor Landes," Professor McNull sniffed. "You must be aware that among his many other distinctions, Professor Byles is an honorary citizen of Ethiopia."

Izzy feigned amazement. "Had I but known… "

"Gentlemen, gentlemen."

Professor Athol raised his hand. "Excuse me, Chair Brattle, but the word *gentleman* is on the proscribed list."

Chair Brattle sighed. "But we have yet to vote on the list." She turned to Professor McNull, "So what are you suggesting?"

"I think that, in cooperation with appropriate staff from the university, the Seaboard Police Department should train their officers to recognize senior faculty or, certainly, the most distinguished among the senior faculty, so that this kind of situation does not happen again."

Captain Murphy looked doubtful. "The officers are already busy with a lot of community outreach… duties."

Lieutenant Tracy said, "Well, we could open a registry if the university would furnish us the names and the mug… head and shoulder shots."

Sergeant Lemure nodded his agreement. "We've already got a registry of Level One sex offenders. There's probably some overlap."

Captain Murphy cleared his throat. "That raises a question. Does the university really want a list of its personnel in the police department files? I mean with all that implies."

Professor McNull was undeterred. "I think it incumbent upon the Seaboard Police Department to take measures so that this kind of thing never happens again."

"With all due respect, Professor," the chief said with some acerbity, "if a member of the Wainscott faculty breaks the law or is suspected of breaking the law, he or she will be treated like any other citizen."

On my suggestion, the committee agreed to appoint a sub-committee to look into the matter. The police officers were thanked and excused.

As I was showing them out, I took Lieutenant Tracy aside for a moment. "I think you should know that we found Blackie Burker's cell phone at the crime scene. Or, I should say, the commander found it."

"Anything on it?"

"I don't know. I'm meeting the commander for lunch today to go over it."

The lieutenant gave me one of his looks. "He should turn it over to the FBI, you know. Tampering with evidence and all that. Not that they'll do anything with it. They're still chasing their tails looking for the kidnappers."

"Oh, I think he's already done that."

"Keep me in the loop." Then, jerking his head in the direction of the Twitchell Room, "You can't make that stuff up, can you?"

26

Commander Morgliesh glanced out of the north facing window of my office in the museum. "You have a marvelous view from here, Norman."

"Yes," I said, it's usually dotted with sails, especially on weekends during the summer."

"I can't remember whether my fictional incarnation sails or not. It never had much charm for me."

"I believe your waters are a good deal rougher than ours."

"Depends on the season."

The commander had dropped by to take me to lunch at the Edge where we might, "discuss your case." When I reached for my overcoat, he said, "You won't need it. It's quite warm out."

It was indeed a warm, sun-spangled day. We decided to walk, which gave me an opportunity to point out some of the interesting parts of the old city and its waterfront.

"We call this Indian Summer," I explained to him, as we walked along Belmont Avenue. "It's a time, usually in October, but now it's coming later, when autumn loosens its chilly grip and gives us a welcome aftertaste of summer. The term is no doubt considered inappropriate these days by the lexical police. But Native American summer or First Peoples summer doesn't have the same ring."

"Yes, the word police. We have them, too. And, Of course your Indians are different from our Indians." We were waiting to be shown to a waterside table.

"But I imagine *Indian* is still a perfectly respectable word in England. I mean they are Indians from India, at least originally."

He laughed. "It depends on whom you are speaking to."

"Well, yes. Hereabouts, if you say colored person you will be excoriated as an out-and-out racist. If, however, you say 'person of color' or, better yet, 'people of color,' you will be considered in the vanguard of the struggle for racial justice or non-racial justice, I'm not sure which."

"But aren't we all people of color when you get right down to it? Except for some of the corpses I've seen. That is if gray is no more of a color than white."

Simon, of Simon and David, the co-proprietors of the Edge, led us to a pleasant waterside table under a shading umbrella such was the warmth of the day. I noticed a couple sitting at the table next to us. The man was of my vintage while his wife looked younger, but not as young as Diantha. I could tell from the way they sat restive with their drink glasses all but empty that they had been there a while. And, in truth, the place was busy.

It didn't take long, however, for Marlen, one of their better waiters, to stop by and take our orders for drinks and appetizers. The commander asked for a pint of ale and a dozen oysters on the half shell. I also ordered a pint of ale and the crab cakes, which the Edge does as well as anyone along the coast, especially with mustard and capers sauce.

"I rather think the Americans do seafood as well as anyone," Morgliesh said as we looked out over the old harbor. "I especially like the way they do their fish and chips."

I glanced at the menu and read from it. "You mean the medallions of scrod in a light batter with *pommes de terre frites de maison*? I doubt they'll taste anything like the ones you got in a cone of newsprint back when."

"Indeed, but I think I'll have the codfish cakes and baked beans. When in Rome… " Which is what he ordered along with a dozen oysters for a starter when Marlen returned with our ales.

I asked for the crab cakes to start with and a Caesar salad with croutons on the side for my main course.

We got down to business. The commander said he had charged the cell phone we found up on the bluff, but the results were disappointing. "Calls to and from a callbox in South Boston at a pub called Tir na Sean. Another couple of calls to and from a call box outside a pub in Somerville, that's near Boston, by the name of The Thirst."

"So what do we do now?" I asked.

"I think it's time we paid a visit to the Athens of America."

"Boston?"

"Where else? I have a friend on the Boston Police... actually he's retired, but he may be able to point us in the right direction."

Marta, the lady at the next table squirmed some more and tried, index finger pointing skyward, to get Marlen's attention.

At which point Marlen appeared and began busily setting down a plate of oysters and the crab cake order on a serving table between us and the annoyed couple.

When it became apparent that the food was meant for us, the gentleman at the neighboring table, his face flushing, rose and, holding his napkin in one hand, said to Marlen, "Excuse me, but we arrived here and ordered a good twenty minutes before this party. And yet they are being served before us."

Marlen looked at his order book. "You're having?"

"The crab cakes and lobster bisque."

Because it was precisely the kind of thing that would have gotten under my nails, I stood up as well. "Marlen," I said, "Please let the gentleman have the crab cakes. We have more than enough oysters to hold us."

"Certainly," said the commander. "And there's more where those come from."

When the gentleman protesting seemed dubious, the woman said, "That's very kind of you. We have been waiting an awfully long time."

So Marlen took the crab cakes and placed them on the other table along with two small plates. The man thanked me graciously, mollified to all appearances.

"Well done, Norman," the commander murmured as he slid half a dozen oysters onto a side dish for me. "The world can always use more civility."

I squeezed lemon juice on a forked oyster and put it in my mouth. My dining companion did the same. He chewed, swallowed, and smiled. "'My tongue was a filling estuary...'"

"Precisely. Is that yours?"

"Hardly. The Irish bard."

We talked about Victor Karnivossky, and the commander described his efforts to help him with a resident alien visa. At one point he stopped to laugh. "I was having difficulty until I happened to mention in one of my communications that I thought Mr. Carnovan would make a perfect English gentleman."

"And that helped?"

"Remarkably. Something did. He's not out of the woods yet, but I trust he'll shortly be shivering in Austen Abbey."

We chatted about our upcoming trip to Boston. I told him that Lieutenant Tracy wanted to be kept in the loop.

"Of course. I would have told him about the cell phone, but I wanted some time with it before turning it over to the Feebs, as they're called. I fudged the day of our finding it. Not that it matters."

I nodded, distracted by the gentleman at the neighboring table who was saying to his companion, "Really, Marta, you should try this. Best I've ever had."

"I know, dear, but it's been cooked in the same kitchen as lobsters. You know what Doctor Kearns said."

It was a few minutes later that that I caught that nearly premonitory flash of disturbance that immediately precedes a crisis. Perhaps it was the audible gasp of Marta followed by an exclamatory "Stanley!" I turned to see the object of her concern slouch forward into his plate, tilt sideways, and nearly fall off his chair.

The usual commotion ensued. People scraped away from tables and stood up. There were calls to "give him air" despite a sudden onshore breeze. Was there a doctor in the house? I went over to the stricken man and asked him what I could do.

"I'm fine," he gasped. "I'm fine."

It was then that I realized that the man had been eating food meant for me. Were we at the scene of an attempted murder? The same thought had occurred to Commander Morgliesh, who murmured to me, "We might want to call the authorities."

But Marta was assuring all of us. "It's a mild anaphylactic shock. It's happened before, folks. He knows better."

Simon, with David in tow, arrived from the reception area. Simon, distraught, immediately began to swear that lobsters were cooked in a separate part of the kitchen. The stricken customer and his wife reassured him that he nor the restaurant was at fault even as they prepared to head for the door. We all went back to our meals.

The commander looked at me with that grimace of his. "This may not be here nor there, Norman, but I think we need to get to Boston sooner rather than later."

27

Diantha announced and I listened dutifully when she informed me that she was inviting Ivor Pavonine, or, I.P. as she calls him, over for cocktails so that I can get to know him better. All this despite his malevolence at the Talty-Clydes party. ("I.P. being I.P." she had said, shrugging it off.) And, I did not have the heart to tell her that I would like to get to know him less. Because I was takenby her evident sincerity and by the thought that a wife usually doesn't want her husband to get to know her lover better. Unless, of course, it was an effort to hide matters in plain sight, something Diantha is not capable of.

Then it occurred to me that she was doing it for her career. And why not? If she believed that creature could help her, could I not put up with him for a couple of hours if that would help? So, with as much grace as I could muster, keeping my groan inward, I acquiesced. For which I got a bouncing smile, a hug, and a kiss and the gratification of making her happy. But expectation cuts both ways and in this case the thought of having to converse with this creature had me wondering if there were enough whiskey in the house to see me through the ordeal. It was another little cloud to add to the thunderheads building all around me.

When I ventured that we might add another couple or two to this little party, Diantha said no as she no doubt intuited correctly that I wanted to dilute Mr. Pavonine's presence with the presence of others. With, say Izzy and Lotte and perhaps Winston Maroun there, I could, with a sufficiency of hard spirits, contrive a conviviality with the grotesque incubus the man had become in my mind. I could smile and smile and be a villain of hypocrisy and triple talk. I could survive the encounter with my psyche and good humor intact.

Alas, Diantha was having none of it. She wanted me to know, "what a truly interesting man he is. He's full of ideas. And you've said that you love ideas. Besides, he thinks the world of you. He dotes on you, Norman. He wants to know what you're thinking and what you're doing. I swear he knows more about you than I do. So do this, just this once, just for me, please."

Which I did the following afternoon, a Saturday, with as good a grace as I could manage, helped along with one or two quick shots of bourbon which helped me fix the simulacrum of a smile on my face and a contrived note of urbanity in my voice.

Little good it did me. Ivor, as I now called him aloud, was far more drunk -- on himself -- than anything I could manage out of a bottle. The day being unseasonably warm, we sat on the patio deck in the garden, man-to-man and armed with drinks, as Diantha bustled about with canapes. I noticed he wore a yellow linen shirt that matched his goldilocks. I noticed a feral, manic glint in his eyes. Immediately he asked me about the threats to my life, but, I sensed, more out of an avid curiosity than any sympathy he might have.

"They have several leads," I said, echoing the dialogue you hear in detective dramas. "But the authorities are very tight lipped about it."

"Yes, of course, that would be expected. But what I mean, Norman, is how are *you* taking it? Does it crowd out other thoughts during the day, not mention the wee hours?"

"Not really."

I was lying, of course. I wanted to disappoint the eagerness I heard in his voice. It is only in horror films that one should enjoy the fear that others feel. But I kept that to myself along with so much else, working diligently on a generous triple of one of those single-barrel bourbons I keep for special occasions. I found myself in a delicious haze in which, as the Irish Bard wrote, when you have to say something, say nothing.

Until, with a start, I realized that the man had gotten onto the subject of art and was cueing me to make responses beyond good-natured noises of assent. I tuned in just as he was saying something about the human propensity to make art of the most ordinary of things.

"Such as?" I asked, my voice encouraging, talk about art being better than talk about my state of fear.

"Noise," he said, and lifted the glass of beer half of which he had already quaffed.

"Noise?"

"At its most basic, Norman. Are not the sonatas of Beethoven a species of noise? Vibrations in the air to which our ears are sensitive."

"Something of a stretch," I said even as I bit on the large kernel of truth in his assertion.

"Not just noise, Norm… Norman, my friend," he went on, leaning into me, his tone touched with an unctuousness I'd not heard before. But then he was a man of many manifestations.

I waited. Where was Diantha with the food and her presence, which might distract the man into the ease of frivolities?

"Think of Versailles, a work of consummate art, is it not?"

"Not to my taste."

"Yes, yes, but we are not speaking about taste, are we, Norman? Tell me, what is Versailles?"

I shrugged. "A building. A group of them. A compound. A palace."

"A building for what? It's a house! It's a place where people lived!"

I could not keep up with his sudden exultation. "Okay, a house."

"Okay? Come on. My point is that Versailles is shelter, one of the necessities of life that over time has taken on thousands of forms from Zulu huts to Manhattan penthouses. Habitations. As common as the rain they're meant to keep out. And in the case of Versailles and Buckingham Palace, etc., elaborated into high art. The same for food. For basic nutritional needs, a burger and fries at Huncan Dines suffices, but people pay extravagantly at Tour D'Argent for the *foie gras ravioli*. Which I highly recommend by the way…"

"Meaning?" I asked, if only to show that I was listening.

"Meaning that food, another basic necessity, has been raised to the level of art."

I nodded my acquiescence because, despite my antipathy of the man, his eyes and voice like grappling hooks, I had to concede he was onto something basic -- the human impulse to elaborate basics into art or the artful. "You have a point," I conceded, but weakly.

"A point! No, Norman, a whole philosophy. If nothing else, life is the raw material of art. Life itself... Think, we reproduce it on the stage and in movies and novels. We love to dramatize. We make artful everything. The Art of War by... you know, the Chinese guy. The art of love and by that I do not mean pornography, which is the mere coupling of couples. Unless, of course, it's done artfully."

I almost said, speaking of couples, but I did not want to go there. Instead, "I should see if Diantha needs help."

"Not just basics," he carried on, oblivious to my attempt to escape him, "but the intangibles that we take for basics."

"Such as?"

"Justice!"

I was out of my depth, which, as the alcohol took effect, had grown shallow enough to see the bottom. "I see," I said, seeing nothing.

"Think of courtroom dramas, Norman. They are the very essence of living theater. I love the robed judge with his gavel. The witnesses duly sworn in. The attentive jurors, a humble, orary peerage. Raise your right hand. Do you swear? I mean *all* the tropes. The surprise witness. Objection your honor! Objection overruled. Will counsel please approach the bench. The jury will ignore those last remarks. The expert witness. These fibers match those... The damning evidence. The shrewd cross examination."

He paused, adjusted his cravat. He feigned thoughtfulness, a finger raised to hold my attention. Then, as though inspired, "In the best, the most dramatic cases, life can quite literally hang in the balance."

"I'm not sure I follow you," I said, encouraging him when I should have been edging away.

"My apologies. What I mean, of course is that trials for capital offenses are, with any luck, but the preludes to the intense drama of the execution chamber. That is a whole genre all of its own, in which the lead is the star of his own legal murder. It's ritual turned real, the ritual supplying the necessary grace, the dark sanctification for the necessary outward show of gravitas. How the heart beats and the mind quakes when the tumbrel, in whatever form, is heard bringing the condemned to the gallows with the rope already around his neck. Think of the priest with draped stole and open prayer book walking with the tough guy into the room where old sparky waits, its unbuckled straps ready for his arms and legs, the headpiece poised like a metallic skull cap. Or the up-to-date, air-tight gas chamber. Or the good old firing squad with one bullet a blank to ease the conscience of the sharp shooters. Any last words. Last words! After millions of words, millions, not just the condemned but all of us come to our last words. That would be a book! Then the hush before the signal. Then the signal. A pause. The trap door opens with a crash. Or the switch gets pulled. Or the cyanide pills drop into the pan of acid behind the chair and the fumes rise. Or the voice rings out "fire!" That, Norman, is the ultimate moment of drama."

I was half listening and half adding up the moral toll of what Diantha owed me for putting me through this torture. "I'm not sure I get your point." Saying nothing to say something.

"My point! My point, Norman, is that death can be as artful as life. Its approach fills us with dark, dark wonder. It is the ultimate act of imagination but futile in that we cannot imagine it, we cannot imagine nothingness because, very simply, there is nothing to imagine. Poets, priests, philosophers, savants high and low, learned doctors, and condemned criminals have knocked on that door only to find it locked... for all eternity. Let's face it, death, actual death, is the least interesting part of murder and being murdered. Death is the end of life and as such the end of murder. A corpse cannot feel and cannot suffer. To paraphrase one H. Humbert, death is but the ancilla of art."

Through the defensive fog of my very good bourbon, it occurred to me, however reluctantly, that the man was on to something. Not that he wasn't an utter charlatan, but charlatans can be fascinating in the way, as someone once noted, that the bad taste of Philistines can be exhilarating.

"Think of it," said our guest, "think of the greatest execution in history. And by execution I mean murder because executions are merely murders sanctioned by law or done with style, as in execution style. But I digress. I speak of course of the crucifixion of Christ. That remains the most famous and consequential murder in all of history. And it is with Christ's grotesque death that murder reaches its apotheosis as art. It is rich beyond imagination. And when I speak about the art of murder, Norman, I speak about the act itself, not depictions of the act in words or images, though in the aesthetic of art as life and life as art, the two ideally merge in one transcendent reality."

I murmured something, but in fact my presence was superfluous. A nodding dummy would have sufficed for his rapturous self-absorption in his own words and the sound of his own voice. It ran on.

"Think of the millions, more like billions, of crosses out there in the world, some tiny, some gigantic. And these are but the symbol of countless depictions, a lot of them grotesquely graphic, of the godman hanging in agony with only death to deliver him. It has been depicted over and over again by great artists, by Raphael, Velazquez, Rembrandt, Durer, Rubens, Bellini. I am of course drawn to that of Domeniko Theotokopoulas, the Greek. Oh, you know, with his mannerism of elongating forms, stretching poor Christ to show the agony of a man being slowly and gruesomely murdered. But even the Greek's crucifixion pales next to Michelangelo's. That is an image to haunt even a confirmed pagan like myself. His nailed Christ is both an ordinary man and a tortured god. You can feel the strain in the marvelously rendered musculature and in the face, the beseeching eyes raised to heaven, the expression gauzy with pain and dying hope. It is horrific and beautiful, but then, Michelangelo could not resist beauty, however dark.

The final agony is that shard of hope in the face of Christ beseeching heaven amidst darkening despair."

He finished his proration with a look of gloating triumph he did nothing to dissemble.

To puncture this balloon, I had enough wits left to say, "So you're an aficionado of Auschwitz and the mass starvations and shootings of Stalin and company?"

He looked genuinely aghast. "Good God, Norman, you miss my whole point. I deplore anything smacking of genocide or democide. Mass murder is mass vulgarity, it is industrial death, a matter of organization and engineering. It is a form of kitsch. Art, like life, is above all things individual."

I was saved by Diantha, who, like an angel of deliverance, pushed through the door, a tray of comestibles in her hands.

28

Izzy Landes dropped by my office this morning, bringing me an excellent cup of coffee from Dell's Deli along with a small bag of deadly pastries. He had called ahead to tell me he needed to talk to someone sane. I braced myself for a gripe session. I say "braced" because Izzy does not bitch and moan about trivial matters.

It didn't take long after pleasantries and sipping of coffees and opening the bag of goodies, for him to get to the issues at hand. "I tell you, Norman, tell you, I no longer recognize my beloved Wainscott. I don't mind that we now have more foreign students than ever. You know they pay full freight and with the administration adding layers of new administrators by the day, the costs keep going up. But what a bunch of grade grinders foreigners are. They parrot back with deadly precision what I tell them and what I give them to read. They question nothing. If I told them that Newton also came up with the law of gravy and gave them the recipe, they would write it down, word for word."

I laughed and resisted a large, fruity blueberry scone. "Perhaps you should try that as an experiment."

He acknowledged with one of his wry smiles. Then, continuing, taking comfort, I could tell, from my sympathy, he said, "That's the least of it, frankly. Grade grubbing is a long and hallowed tradition. The fact is, Norman, Wainscott is on its way to becoming the academic equivalent of a police state. The old days of the Oversight Committee are nothing to the diversity regime ruled over by Dean Whatsitsname who now has assistant deans for race, gender, sexual orientation, language, and morphology." He neatly tore a glossy Danish in half and took a bite.

"Morphology."

"Meaning fat in the old days. One cannot discriminate on the basis of weight. The word 'obese' is no longer allowed as being invidious."

"People think they can change reality by changing the language."

"Fair enough, but now we have to sign off on 'attestations' that we will not use our power differential, whatever that means, to discriminate against students or staff on the basis of race, gender, etc., nor to use our position of power to seduce, harass, etc. or, and I quote, 'make any member of the university feel uncomfortable or unsafe.'"

"Yes," I agreed. "It's getting beyond parody."

"Way beyond parody. It's a kind of institutionalized witch hunt. The political correctness police must be kept busy. They need infractions. They need to 'take action' and show results, regardless. And they need to file monthly reports, reports that no one with half a brain or half a grain of common sense would read or take seriously."

After a silence, he continued. "And you know, Norman, as a professor of the history of science and technology, my courses get scrutinized monthly by the PC police for 'diversity content.' The problem, as even those dullards know, is that most of the scientific and technological advances over the past four centuries and more have been made by white males. It matters not. The committee on course content diversity formally requested that I be more inclusive in the content of my courses."

I succumbed to the scone.

Izzy went on. "You can imagine the uproar when I emailed back that I would gladly include any credible research about, say, a Tajikistani lesbian of the nineteenth century who discovered an unknown element or built the prototype of a flying machine."

"And…?"

"I was called in for a meeting. I repeated my challenge. One of them looks at me with fatuous disdain and says, 'That, Professor Landes is your job.'"

He looked away and then went on. "I responded, facetiously I thought, 'You mean make it up?' And she looks me straight in the face and says, 'If that's what it takes.'"

I signaled my incredulity with a shake of the head.

"If that's what it takes," Izzy repeated. "One certified idiot on the panel who made a great deal of being referred to by its pronoun *it*, asked me how I could be so sure that a Tajikistani lesbian did not discover a new 'thing' in the nineteenth century. I said in reply that there is no evidence that such a person made such a discovery. It then said, 'So it's possible?' I replied "It's possible but not very probable that there are little green men on the other side of the moon who make cheese they sell at the farmers' market.'"

"Did anyone laugh?"

"Are you kidding? And when I added that there was such a thing as historical accuracy, objective proof, another fool told me with a straight face that terms like historical accuracy and objective proof were just racist devices to keep white males in power. Talk about going down the rabbit hole."

I might have laughed, but there was something akin to despair in my friend's face and voice. Humor, is no defense against the absurdities of those in power. And there was worse to come.

"And then it got personal."

"Personal?"

"Personal. Another member of the panel, some teaching assistant in social sciences, the only white male there besides me… Christ, I'm starting to think like them… said to me, 'How do you explain that your introduction to the history of science contains so many references to Jews?' The other fools on the panel sat there nodding. There it was, right out in the open. I thought I was in Nazi Germany."

"What did you say?"

"I held my temper. I said, 'Because, sir, despite real barriers and discrimination, Jews have played a significant role in the development of modern science starting with Einstein.'"

Again, despair showed on my friend's face and I felt helpless to say or do anything to assuage his misery. He went on, looking away as though talking to himself. "I now see their strategy, Norman. In the name of justice or what someone called 'retroactive equity,' they are legitimizing the hatred of white males. And once that's established, they'll come after the Jews as Jews. They won't use the fig leaf of being anti-Zionist, they won't need it. Open Jew-baiting and what that leads to will be seen as racial justice, social justice, economic justice, you name it."

That can't happen here, I wanted to say, but common sense told me it could. "So, what was the response?"

"There was none. I was dismissed like a naughty school boy. It looked around at its colleagues and said I was free to go…"

"And?"

"I got up and left. That afternoon I received the following." He paused to take a folded piece of paper from his vest pocket. He read, "'You are hereby required to appear before the adjudication subcommittee of the course content committee regarding comments made by you in a meeting dated…' etc. etc."

"What did you do?"

He took a bite of the Danish, chewed, swallowed, wiped his mouth with his napkin, and smiled. "I told them with much satisfying sarcasm that I would under no circumstances appear before their absurd committee, that I was tenured, and that tenure could only be revoked for good cause. I also told them if they wanted to proceed against me or in any way impugned my reputation, I would take the matter to a court of law and sue them for half of Wainscott's endowment."

I laughed. Vintage Izzy. "What then?"

"I got an unsigned note that the subcommittee was only acting according to regulations."

"And you responded?"

"I wrote back that the leaders of Nazi Germany responded in a like manner when questioned at Nuremberg. I know, I know, I shouldn't throw around references to that unspeakable tragedy in what's a piddling dispute in academia."

"I'm not so sure it's piddling," I said. "Let's face it, if tenure is meaningless, then the university as an arena of unfettered free thought and discussion is at an end."

"Too true, alas, too true. But Norman, how do you handle this at the museum. Surely the forces of political correctness are rampant there as well."

I smiled and with a twinge of dietary guilt, finished the remainder of my scone. "Oh, they are, they are. The museum has been accused of being nothing less than a repository of white male looting going back centuries."

"And how do you handle that?"

"I bring out correspondence from various groups and societies all over the world stating that they are honored that the Museum of Man is preserving and providing such a prestigious setting for displaying their cultural heritage. A lot of time they write that they don't have the facilities to curate and preserve the objects involved."

"You're a smart one, Norman. They should make you president of Wainscott."

"I wouldn't dream of it."

"Too bad. We need someone with principles. Malachy Morin -- I keeping spelling his name Moron – talks about academic freedom and doesn't have a clue."

I nodded and I was pondering my existential state when, as though with from a telepathic prompt, Izzy asked, "Any more incidents?"

"I'm not sure. I think someone tried to run me down on Belmont Avenue with one of those army jeep things when I was on my bike. It could have just been road bullying, but ... who knows?"

"Yes, I imagine that's the worst of it. I mean the state of fear. How do you do it?"

I resisted a shrug. "I've developed a sense of fatalism, which is different from courage."

"I'm not sure I follow you?"

"Unless I make myself absent at your summer place or some other hideaway, which I am loath to do, whoever is trying to kill me will, with any bad luck, kill me."

"Are you armed?"

I reached under my coat and pulled out the Glock 19. I shoved it gently over to his side of the table.

The professor of the history of science picked it up with a certain prudence of movement. "It's loaded?"

"Yes, but the safety's on."

He held it the way an aesthete would hold an objet of great value. "How well we engineer instruments of death. I can feel the love and precision that went into it." He slid it back to me. "I hope you never have to use it."

"I hope none of us do. But I'm starting to think that it may come to that." Izzy nodded. "The nightmare of history repeating itself."

29

Commander Morgliesh and I flew from Seaboard to Boston on a pellucidly clear day. The flight took us down the stern and rock-bound coast, the sea blue and the land brown in its late autumnal mantling. "Those brave Puritans," the Englishman said, as though to himself. He sat in the window seat of the turbo-prop, utterly enthralled by the scene unfolding below. We had been airborne and companionably silent for a half hour, when he said, "You know, Norman, I've always been a great admirer of New England and its culture."

"It's a deal richer than a lot of people realize," I rejoined.

"Yes, it has a restrained and refined opulence in its arts and letters." He then extolled the writers, the blossoming in Concord of Thoreau, Emerson, the Alcotts and others. He was especially taken with Emily Dickinson. "It's frightful how many of the educated English are not aware of Dickinson and her diamond-like verse. I mean, we all know, 'Hope is the thing with feathers/That perches in the soul...' But there's 'Frequently the woods are pink,/Frequently are brown/Frequently the hills undress/Behind my native town.' Several of her best are among the furniture of my mind, to sound a grandiloquent note." He went on to talk about Hawthorne, Melville, and Henry James. "I've always thought Melville overrated. How that whale tale churns on."

"Melville was born in New York," I said.

"As was James, but I've always thought of him as a New England writer, even, at times, a British writer."

Which launched him into that enduring topic -- the difference between the Americans and the British. "You know, when I first came to these shores, I expected to find a subspecies of the English. You know, like the Australians, the New Zealanders, and even the Canadians. It was something of shock to find instead a unique, distinctive culture. Not, mind you, that we didn't grow up on a diet of cowboys and gangsters, not to mention private detectives."

We hit turbulence just about then, with one severe bounce. The commander scarcely seemed to notice it, fastening his seatbelt and going on about America and Americans until we landed.

The traffic was snarly as we made our way in a cab from the airport to the hotel in Boston's Kenmore Square. It was late afternoon when we settled into our rooms and I had time for a brief doze before we met for a drink with Mike Callahan in the hotel bar. A large friendly man, Mike had retired from the Boston Police some years before. He and the commander worked together when IRA sympathizers were shipping arms to Ulster out of Boston and other ports along the east coast.

We sat in one of those rounded corner booths with comfortable seats and ordered drinks and then some bar fare. There was talk of the old days between the two lawmen in which I was generously included.

"Cloak and dagger stuff?" I asked.

The captain grimaced. "Mostly someone dropping a dime. Or a quarter. Whatever it was in those days." He toyed with his drink like someone trying to watch what he drank. "You'd be surprised how routine it so often is. Vengeance among the bad guys is a wonderful tool of law enforcement."

Which launched us into a belittling of cop shows. Captain Callahan, now working for a private security firm, declared, as a waiter placed plates of food in front of us, "It's the ones that present themselves as the most realistic that are the most far-fetched. It's like those hospital shows. Pure fantasy. Cops, especially detectives, do talk about their cases, that's true. But if you listen carefully, cops mostly talk about their details, who made detective, over-time, retirement, the bitching amount of paperwork, and the house they're fixing up on the Cape."

We got down to business. The captain looked over the phone numbers and the names of the bars the commander had gleaned from Burker's dropped phone. "I don't know anything about this place in Somerville. But in Southie, at this place called The Camel, you could ask for Kevin Fitzhugh. He might be able to steer you to the party at, what's it called, in Cambridge… The Widening Gyre?"

We finished our drinks with a toast. "To lady luck," the captain said.

The commander sighed a world weary sigh. "Dame Fortune… she certainly is a strumpet."

The Camel turned out to be an unprepossessing place lodged snugly in a neighborhood that had from all appearances escaped improvement.

A long-coated denizen glanced up from his empty glass as we entered and then quickly dropped his gaze. He was of a piece with the place -- little more than standard bar with television and some booths, several of which were occupied, one with a young man and two rather loud, rather drunk women.

We took stools at the bar and waited for the barwoman, who was what a southerner might have described as a honky-tonk angel -- of a certain age, with hair and face carefully in place and her ample charms a trifle more ample than charming.

"What can I get you gentlemen?" she said with practiced ease and a discernible curiosity, her expression asking who the hell are you guys?

"I'll take a pint of Guinness," the commander said.

"A glass of Bass," I put in, half British myself in the wake of the commander's intonations.

"And some information perhaps," the Scotland Yarder added as she, after the ceremony of pouring his black creamy brew, placed our drinks in front of us.

"Information?" she repeated.

"Right. We're looking for Mr. Kevin Fitzhugh." The commander raised his glass to her. "Cheers."

"Kevin Fitzhugh?"

"Kevin Fitzhugh," I repeated.

She put up a finger to indicate she would take a minute. Another customer had come in and needed a double whiskey and soda, easy on the soda. She served him and went through a curtained doorway behind the bar.

Not long afterwards, a man of our age with blunt features on a large, round balding head emerged through the curtain and leaned into us from across the bar. Without preamble, or perhaps this was his preamble, he said, "I need to know who I'm talking to before I say anything."

"I'm Adam Morgliesh of London."

"And I'm Norman de Ratour."

"What do you do, Mr. Ratour?"

"I'm director of a museum up in Seaboard."

A glint of respect showed in the subdued cunning of his pale eyes. "So you're the guy that took out Blackie."

I said, "He took himself out."

"That ain't the word on the street."

The commander asked, "Indeed, and tell us, what is the word on the street?"

The man caught the whiff of hauteur in the commander's repeat of the phrase *on the street.* His face went sour for a moment. "Let's take that booth in the back where we can talk."

We moved to a booth in the back next to the restrooms and a bank of payphones no longer in use to judge from the loose wiring. The commander said, "What are you having?" as the barwoman hovered with a lip-sticked smile.

"The usual, Ellie," our host said and turned to us, sitting side by side across from him. "Okay, the word is this. D. M. wants to move in on Freddie Bain's operation or what's left of it."

"Whose D. M.?"

"Dead Meat. Victor Karnivossky. Anyway, since it's no secret that you whacked Freddie, D. M. figured he'd send a signal by whacking you. So he calls up Blackie and arranges things."

"Do you believe that?" the commander asked.

"No."

"Why not?"

"Because the guy that came in here looking to hook up with Blackie Burker was in no way someone Dead Meat would be caught dead with."

"Do you know who that person was?" I asked, resisting the subdued thrill a sleuth feels when a case shows its first faint cracks.

"I've got a name, but I don't think it means much."

We waited as Ellie served Mr. Fitzhugh what looked like a double or triple whiskey with a beer on the side. He raised the whiskey, said "*Sláinte*" and drank off about half of it. He took a deep breath and a sip of beer. "He gave his name as Stan Magee."

"Magee?"

"M. A. G. E. E."

"Could you describe him for us?" I asked.

He nodded. "He was medium built, weird eyes. He had black hair in a ponytail and about a four-day beard. To me he sounded like one of those guys that have gone to college but end up a biker wannabe. Except that he had a funny accent. I'm not sure how real it was. He told me he was a free-lance journalist trying to do a story about how you arrange a hit." He looked thoughtfully at his whiskey. "You know, the usual stuff. Who do you see, how much does it cost, how do you make sure the guy making the hit doesn't try to shake you down. All that kind of stuff."

"Were you not afraid that he might have been an undercover police officer?" the commander ventured.

"Nah, the guy wasn't a cop. I can smell cops." He looked directly at Morgliesh. "You're a cop. Not one of ours, but definitely a cop."

The commander bowed his head. "Very good. Very good, indeed."

"So you told him how to contact Blackie Burker?" I asked.

"Not on your life. I told him go see someone I know over at The Connemara."

"Where's that?"

"Just up the street. First left. Can't miss it."

"What's his name?"

"Jerry Clark. You can tell him I sent you."

"Mr. Fitzhugh, do you know who we might contact at The Widening Gyre? Directly?" The commander had bent towards him, holding his eyes.

Kevin Fitzhugh looked directly back and shook his large head. "I wouldn't tell you if I knew. Pretty soon word gets around that you've got a big mouth. It's unhealthy."

"So why did Blackie Burker call you?" I asked.

"Who said Blackie called me?"

The commander leaned forward. "The late Mr. Burker dropped his cell phone near the scene of his demise."

"What does that have to do with me?"

"You were the last person he called."

"How come I haven't heard from the Feds then?"

"Because they haven't had it very long and, frankly, they're not very efficient."

"You could be charged with tampering."

"With evidence?"

"With evidence."

"Evidence of what?"

"That the deceased called me."

"What did he call you about?"

He signaled to the waitress. "Let's get another drink."

On the television over the bar a football game had begun, a blur of motion along with sound effects that I always thought would puzzle a Martian.

As we waited for another round, he said, "The Burkers often called me. I sometimes came into possession of used Mercedes. They have a shop not far from here. They fix Mercedes. Sometimes they take them apart as well."

"Isn't that what you Yanks call a chop shop?" the commander said.

"You know, you're right. That's what we are, Yanks. Easy to forget these days. Yeah, you could call it a chop shop."

"And if Mr. Burker had called you about this Stan Magee, what might you have told him?"

"I would have said that I didn't think the guy was undercover."

"Tell me, Mr. Fitzhugh, do you think you could identify this Stan Magee if you saw him again. Or a picture of him?"

"I probably could but I won't."

"Would money talk?"

"Money never shuts up."

"But not where you're concerned? In this instance?"

"I don't rat out people for love nor money. I've got to live and work around here."

"Is there any way we can get in touch with you... directly?" I asked.

He smiled. "You already have my number. It's the one Blackie called."

We got up to leave, our fresh drinks barely touched. "You've been very helpful," the commander said, but didn't shake his hand.

The man shrugged. "No big deal. I owe Mike Callahan a favor, a couple of favors comes to that."

But Fitzhugh's lead, if it could be called that, turned into a pub crawl, however abbreviated, such that I wished I could, in movie fashion, reduce it to those quick, in-and-out fades as we visited several depressing bars in our search for the name of the elusive contact. Alas, we were obliged to go through the motions in real time. "A species of desolation," the commander remarked, quoting his favorite Irish poet as the night wore into a dreary sameness: the same television showing the same game; the same sour reek; the same hunched figures; the same suspicion. And in each case, the same answer -- so and so in such and such a pub might help you.

In a place called The Kinch, on the advice of a gentleman named Seamus Joyce, we escaped the orbit of South Boston and journeyed to Cambridge and The Widening Gyre near Harvard Square to find a man named Rory Gallagher.

On the cab ride over, I said, "Commander, I don't know how much more of this I can take."

He smiled. "Welcome to real police work."

"But why the run-around?" I asked.

He nodded. "I think they've made the trail of references long and complicated enough so that it would be difficult to nail any one of them for conspiracy or aiding and abetting."

At my suggestion, the driver took us across the Charles and then up Memorial Drive. The water gleamed darkly in the reflected light of Back Bay on the other shore. We drove by the river houses of Harvard and up Kennedy Street into Harvard Square.

"A lot of redbrick," the commander said, rubber necking like any tourist.

"Cheaper than stone," I said. "The place was built by Yankees after all."

We found The Gyre easily enough and sat at a long bar and near a large television on which played the same game we had seen before.

"The amazing thing about sporting events," the commander said, as he joined me in a distracted gaze at the screen, "is their irrelevance. I mean to everyday life."

"Unless you put money on them," I remarked and watched as referees gathered in the middle of the field to confer like a panel of judges about some infraction of the rules.

"Right," the commander agreed. "But unless you've wagered something, whether your local football team, the Patriots, I believe, wins or loses has little or no impact on the important aspects of one's life. By that I mean your work, your finances, your family, your love life or lack thereof."

"Yet people are passionate about who wins and how."

"That's the mystery."

"Perhaps," I ventured, "it's an outlet for tribalism. A relatively harmless one."

He nodded. "Yes… I hadn't thought of that."

Just then a thick-set, red-haired man with a boxer's broken nose and skeptical blue eyes stopped in front of us. "'Ou's lookin' for Rory Gallagher?" he asked in an accent the commander later told me was that of Ulster.

"We are," the commander said evenly.

"And 'ou's we?" the man persisted.

263

"I'm Adam Morgliesh and this is my colleague Norman de Ratour."

"*Sasannach?*" the man said, his eyes on the Englishman.

"*Tá sé. Ach, ba i an Ghaeilge mo seanmháthair...*"

The man's eyes widened at that. "*On áit?*"

"*Gaillimhe... Contae na Gaillimhe.*"

"*Cad baile?*"

"*Béal Átha na Sluaighe.*"

The barman nodded appreciatively. Then, "What will ye have to drink?"

"Bushmills," said the commander.

"Ye want the black or the cooking Bush?"

"You don't have the malt?"

"For this crowd?"

"A little seltzer on the side then."

"The same," I said.

"As for Mr. Gallagher..." the commander began.

"I'm at your service." He turned his back to pour the drinks.

"Mr. Joyce at The Kinch said you might be able to help us," I said.

"Indeed. And how is Seamus keeping these days?"

"He looked well enough," the commander said. He pointed to his drink. "Will you join us?"

"I will and thanks."

The barman gave himself a tot. "*Sláinte*," he said, lifting his glass.

"*Sláinte mhaith*," rejoined the commander.

"And what did Seamus say I might help ye with?"

"He said you might be able to tell us about a gentleman who knew the late Mr. Burker."

"Ach, that business." He gave us a look of disgust and knocked back his drink. "I want nothing to do with it." And walked off.

I had begun to repeat myself about simply going to the place and asking around when Mr. Gallagher came back. "The man ye want is O.P. Finn."

"O.P.?"

"Oliver Plunkett. Everyone calls him The Professor. You'll find him in Somerville at The Thirst. You didn't hear it here. I want nothing to do with this business." He turned and walked off again.

We finished our drinks. The commander paid, leaving a hundred dollar bill on the bar.

Out in the bracing air, walking up towards the Square to find a cab, I asked, "What was all that about... the Irish I think?"

"He asked me if I was English. I told him I was, but that my grandmother was Irish."

"She was?"

"Anglo-Irish. She was a Trench from Galway, Ballinasloe, the Earls of Clancarty. They were very good landlords but staunchly anti-Catholic."

We found a cab and asked to be taken to The Thirst. After a journey through the back streets and thoroughfares of Cambridge and then Somerville we arrived at the pub. Entering, we were enveloped in an aromatic fug of smoke from a turf fire and a blaze of fiddle music against the lowered murmuring of a full house.

Luck would have it that a couple were abandoning a booth about half way up the room. No one objected when, after inquiring glances around, we took it, sliding in on either side of the table and then turning to watch the fiddlers to the left of the bar on an improvised stage.

It ended with terrific energy and art, and I joined with the commander in the applause.

As the applause abated, a young man with knowing eyes appeared next to our booth. "What can I get for you officers?" he asked, glancing away at nothing in particular.

"Officers?" said the commander in his best Oxbridge voice. "Of what, pray tell."

"The law," the waiter said, caught off balance, his smile forced.

"Indeed," said the Englishman. He smiled in return, his face confiding and conspiratorial, "you are very astute. And, as for getting something... Norman?"

"A glass of Bass."

"We only have Harp."

"Close enough."

"A double Bushmills malt, seltzer on the side, no ice." The commander smiled again.

The waiter pivoted and left.

"Flattery seldom fails, the commander said easily.

"But you have to keep it subtle, as you did."

The drinks arrived quickly. The waiter, young eyes wary but intrigued, set them out and said, "Can I get you anything else, gentlemen?"

The commander put up a finger. He lifted his whiskey, sniffed and sipped. "Marvelous…" Then, "We'd like a word with The Professor."

The waiter gave a superior laugh. "The Professor? What do you want him for?"

"My Mercedes needs fixing," I said.

"The poor bastard couldn't fix a broken shoelace."

"But he might know where to get it fixed," I offered.

"You could try the Yellow Pages."

"But this is a special job."

The waiter shrugged. "The Professor's the little guy at the end of the bar. I'll send him over."

"And bring him a glass of what he's having," the commander said after him.

The Professor was what you might call a dry drunk. A leprechaun of a man with bandy legs and an upturned, eager nose, he wore an old suit of muted tweed, a white shirt, and a silken bowtie slightly ajar. His small bright eyes waxed friendly, shrewd and suspicious in rapid succession as he hovered.

The commander, sliding over to accommodate him, said, "Thank you, sir, "You're very good to join us."

"Professor Finn at your service," he announced in what I took to be an upper-class Irish accent. "What can I do for you gentlemen."

We said our own names and shook hands around.

"Morgliesh," the professor said. "From the Gaelic. Large stream or something close to that."

"Quite," said the commander, intrigued.

"You're not from the old country so?" the little man said, getting in next to the commander and giving me a knowing look.

"Not your old country." The commander spoke with particular emphasis.

"You're not of *Clann na hÉirann* then?"

"*Au contraire.*"

Our guest clapped his hands. "As Beckett said in Paris when asked if he were English. "Marvelous." Then, mock serious, "Tell me, what is it you do?"

"I'm a poet."

"Ah, a priest of the invisible."

"You read Stevens?"

"I'm acquainted with his work. I understand you are making inquiries regarding a motor car of German manufacture."

The waiter put a drink down in front of The Professor. "VSOP and ginger," he announced, his distaste evident.

"Thank you, Brent. That will be all for now." He sipped. "Yes, yes, I know, a miserable concoction. But wasn't I weaned on it." He lifted his foreshortened face, sniffed the air and said, "This automobile..."

"Actually," I put in, "we're looking for a gentleman who wanted the Burker brothers to fix his car."

"Are you now?"

"We are."

"I believe there are any number of people who take their custom to the brothers Burker, now, sadly, only one."

The commander nodded encouragingly. "We were looking for one in particular."

The Professor lifted his drink to the waiter who was passing. "Would you put some brandy in it, Brent, for Jesus sake."

To us, he asked, "And what would be the nature of this particular gentleman, may I ask?"

I found myself cringing inwardly at the professor's display. Except for his physical stature and a pronounced fetalism of physiognomy, he could have been a parody of myself at my worst. Perhaps it was the bowtie, which I used to wear more than I do now, or the resort to stilted language, or the knack he had for looking down his imperious if red-bloomed nose, all the marks of a lifelong academic *manqué*.

"We have information that he is of medium build, ill-shaven, with dark hair tied in a ponytail," the commander said.

"One of them."

"One of them."

"And at what date, approximately, would this gentleman have been soliciting my services?"

"Around the middle of August," I put in.

He tasted the refreshed glass that Brent put before him. "Better. Many thanks, dear boy. Well, gentlemen, you are in luck. I recall the person you mention with considerable clarity and some distaste. I'm not sure, however, that I remember his name… "

"Stan Magee," I prompted.

"The very man."

"Can you tell us what Mr. Magee wanted with the brothers Burker?" the commander asked.

"He told me that he wanted his motor car fixed."

"Permanently?" I asked.

The little man turned appraising eyes on me. He said, "I saw your likeness in the newspaper. You're the one who shot Blackie."

"He shot himself," I said.

"Nice cover story that," he said, expecting, I think, that I would wink back some acknowledgment.

Instead, I said, "Tell me, Professor, what is it that you profess?"

He smiled like an actor cued to a favorite line. "To paraphrase the great Oscar Fingal O'Flahertie Wills Wilde, sir, I have nothing to profess but my genius."

"And to what do you apply this genius?" I persisted.

"My area of expertise is toponymy. More specifically as it applies to the Celtic realm."

"Toponymy?" I said.

"The study of place names. From the Greek, of course."

"Interesting," said the commander.

"Indeed. The word Briton is itself of Celtic origin. But, of course, the realm of the Celts reached far beyond Britain being as it is historically vast. The tribes left their names all over Europe, the Near East, and beyond."

I could tell the commander was anxious to continue his questioning, but our guest had picked up a head of steam. He went on, "There were, just to name a few, the Vatici, the Parisii, the Belgae, Gallipoli, Albini, Vandali, Linguini, Scoti, Itali, Venetti, Atlantici, not to mention the Remi. It goes on and on. Galatia straddled the Anatolian plateau in what is now Turkey. In fact, anywhere you come across the prefix *gal* or its many variants, *cal*, *kel*, *gael*, you are in the Celtic realm. Think of it, now. There's a Galicia in Poland and one in Spain. There's Gaul, even Portugal, though Kolkata might be a stretch."

"Kolkata?" I asked.

"Calcutta," the commander said.

The Professor drank from his glass and leaned in between us and his voice dropped. "A place name of some dispute is Galilee. Israeli scholars claim it's from the Hebrew for province, perhaps of Aramaic origin. But I ask, the province of what?"

"Really?"

"Indeed." He glanced around and leaned across the table. His voice dropped close to the inaudible and his small eyes glittered. "I fully expect my current research to bear fruit that will reshape our view of the world as we have known it."

"Please go on," the commander said.

"I have found evidence of an ancient Celtic tribe of the near east called the Semitii."

I exchanged glances with the commander. Like myself, he had an expression of dissembled incredulity.

"In other words, gentlemen, I am going to prove that the Israelites were nothing less than a lost tribe of Ireland."

"Amazing," the commander said, not altogether seriously. "I wasn't aware the Irish had lost a tribe."

"Sir, everyone has a lost tribe. But please, not a word. Not a whisper. This must remain, strictly, *entre nous.*"

"*Entre nous,* it is," said the commander.

"Back to Mr. Magee," I said, stifling a yawn. It had been a long and boozy day.

"Ah, yes, our mysterious motorist. Well, most people in his position want their automobiles fixed permanently. He did not convey anything to me to the contrary. But then, I was not privy to his subsequent intercourse with the brothers."

The commander pivoted towards him on the bench. "Do you get a fee for your services, Professor Finn?"

"I have been helped from time to time with my own mode of transportation." He lifted his glass. "Of a spirituous nature."

"Do you know where we could contact Mr. Magee?" I asked.

"Strange you should ask. I was going through my wallet this morning when I came across a piece of paper with a phone number on it. I believe it's the one Mr. Magee left me to call him should I need more information about his… needs. I'm not sure where I put it."

I took out my own wallet and produced a sheaf of bills. "Would this help your memory, Professor?"

"Indeed, that kind of paper does help focus the mind."

We bargained in a gentlemanly sort of way. After I handed over five fifties, he gave me a scrap of paper.

Glancing at it, I could see that an attempt had been made to disguise the script. The numerals were in block form, that is, the eight had been made by placing one square on top of another. The five looked like a truncated swastika, and the three a backward capital E.

I pushed it over to the commander. "Clever," I said.

"Perhaps too clever." He turned to our informant. "And you saw Mr. Magee write this down?"

"I saw him with my own eyes." His own darkened with realization. "You know, I should have charged you more, come to think of it."

The commander nodded sagely. He said, "And your coordinates, Professor, if you would oblige us."

We got a frown and then a reluctant scribble on a napkin. I picked it up and repeated it.

"We'll be in touch," the commander said as we rose and excused ourselves. To one side the exhilarating, frenzied music had begun again and the Professor was bowing, his smile like a fixed mask.

30

The phone number turned out to be "no longer in use," according to a mechanical voice when we tried it out the next morning, calling from one of the last standing phone booths in the Boston area. The commander did some tracking through a private eye he knows in the area. By mid-morning the PI, a vivacious young woman and an expert at this sort of thing, reported back that the number had belonged ten years before to Jenssen's Swedish Pizza of Racine, WI, no longer in business.

The commander did some creative fuming and finally came up with an imaginative way to ferret out the party who approached The Professor for the purpose of having me shot. "We will hold a kind of audition for the part, a touch of what might be called informal interrogation. 'The play's the thing/Wherein I'll catch the conscience of the king!' Or the conscience of the culprit, if he has one."

The day after our return from Boston, he dropped by the museum to make arrangements. No longer the imperturbable investigator, he paced my office with pent-up energy as he outlined his plans.

"First, Norman, we'll need a public place, but one with some privacy, the snug in a pub would work.

"The Pink Shamrock has what you could call a snug."

"Excellent. Having alcohol available should help. How many might it seat?"

"About ten, I think."

"That should suffice."

"For?"

"For what you might call the usual suspects and their accomplices."

"How are you going to get the professor to cooperate?"

He smiled. "If monetary inducements prove insufficient to make him play his part, I believe we can bring to bear some investigative pressure."

"But what about the… suspects? Why will they show up?"

"I'm not sure. Leave that part to me." He mused a moment, sensing my feeling of rebuff. "All right, let's start with Ivan, Ivan Samka, an AKA, obviously. He's in Mr. Karn… Carnovan's employ…"

"And was driving the Humvee that tried to… "

"Exactly."

"But why would he cooperate?"

"He'll do what Victor tells him to do."

"And you have that gentleman in your debt?"

"He thinks so."

"The visa came through?"

"It's on its way."

"And the other suspects… ?"

"As we may have discussed, one Patrick Fortese is currently resident in Seaboard, living in an in-law apartment that is part of the house of Professor Fortese and her husband."

"Why would he cooperate?"

"He'll do what his sister tells him to do. She wears the trousers in that family."

"Good," I said. "Excellent. And I'll ask Alphus to join the… interviews."

"Your chimpanzee friend? The wine connoisseur?"

"Yes. He has an uncanny ability to tell whether someone is lying or not."

The commander smiled. "He would be the perfect touch."

I had some misgivings about the whole proceedings, but decided to leave the matter in the hands of this consummate professional. I have other pressing matters to attend to. This morning I signed the agreement regarding the joint venture between the lab and Rechronnex to further develop the anti-aging treatment Juvenistol. There are members of the Governing Board who will object, but the power of such boards is largely negative. They theoretically can veto things, but rarely try to reverse an action already taken mostly because the bureaucratic machinery to do so is not in place.

It proved the most difficult decision I have had to make since taking over direction of the museum. I found myself ensnared in what might be called the alembics of choice. To be perfectly frank, I will admit that financial considerations were involved. I might be more high-minded about the matter if I could be sure of the reward money that is due to me. Nor have I much faith in any support the Augusteins may give the museum until I have a signed check in hand.

But in fact, my main considerations remained philosophical. And here I am still deeply conflicted, torn between my own misgivings and the views of Alphus on the one hand and the urgings of Winston Maroun and the others at the lab on the other. I was in the midst of these second and third thoughts, when Alphus texted to see if I could drop off those parts of his manuscript he had given me to look over. I said of course.

31

I drove to his eyrie to which I find myself attracted despite the long climb. We took a small pot of coffee and some biscuits up the ladder to his study and to a fine view of the trees under a sky turning dramatic as a storm moved in from the sea.

We fixed our coffees and made ourselves comfortable. I mentioned that I would like his presence at the meeting in the snug involving individuals suspected of trying to kill me or, at the very least, intimidate me.

Alphus agreed with alacrity and patted my back reassuringly with his paw.

Then, together, we went over my suggestions and emendations to his manuscript.

I agreed with him that something like a LTTI, or Long Term Toxicity Index, while something of a mouthful, would make a good substitute for "carbon footprint," the inadequacy of which he so succinctly describes. I took the opportunity to endorse his idea that there be a tax on an individual's LTTI beyond some acceptable minimum. All the while, he nodded appreciatively and took notes on a laptop.

We ended on the coat of arms for the human species as noted before. I suggested he consult a reputable heraldist to make sure it complied with all the strictures of that arcane activity.

As we were finishing up, he looked at me with an inquiring expression. "Something's troubling you," he said. "It's nothing in the book, I hope."

I shook my head. "The book's fine. It's just that I find myself full of doubts about having signed off on the Rechronnex arrangement." It wasn't the kind of thing I could explain easily even using ordinary words in speech.

He considered for a while and then shook his head. Signing elegantly with his hairy hands and fingers, he said, "If we are going to radically prolong the life of the average human being, then we must also radically control population growth. Else the world will be swamped worse than it already is with people. There will simply be even less room for other species."

I said in response, "But, at least for a good while any new treatment for aging will only be available to those who can afford it."

Alphus shook his head and signed emphatically. "There are hundreds, even thousands of labs out there. Once the pharmaceutical is released, they will back-engineer the molecular structure and then start producing knock-offs. It's too big. It's about youth, Norman. People would rather die than grow old. And when that happens, there will be more and more people. And that translates into more pollution and fewer and fewer other life forms."

I had no answer to that. I stood and looked out to sea, but for once its seeming infinitude did not re-assure me.

32

I was in an unsettled frame of mind two days later when I attended a lecture at Margaret Mead Auditorium at which Father S. J. O'Gould, S.J., reprised his recently published book *The Future of Eternal Life*.

Tall, courtly, and growing older in a dignified way, the Jesuit began with *Genesis* and with that seminal proposition that man was created "in the image and likeness of God."

A highly regarded disciple and scholar of the evolutionary theorist Teilhard de Chardin, the Jesuit developed an idea he had touched on before. "If we are to take this central truth of Genesis literally," he said in his soft Cork accent, "then its obverse must also apply: God in turn is very much in the image and likeness of man. That means that God, like *Homo sapiens* is a creature/creator in the throes of evolution. This makes eminent, even poetic sense insofar as the whole universe is evolving, including, it now seems from the evidence, the speed of light. The only constant is change."

He drew some audible gasps when he said that if Darwin was the avatar of this new covenant, then, among his many apostles, the remarkable Ray Kurzweil had particular relevance today. "Because it is through computation and, more directly, through cybernetics that human life, that is to say, self-comprehending consciousness, will grow and evolve. Kurzweil has predicted that there will be 'artificial' intelligence by 2040. I predict that it will happen sooner. And, as revolutionary as it will be to have a beeping R2D2 device successfully passing the Turing Test, the radical departure from human life as we have known it will occur through replication of the consciousness of an individual mind, an intelligence, that is, which already exists."

The priest had a considerable audience spellbound as he continued to expatiate on his thesis. "How we get from here to there remains to be seen. Considerable progress has been made in BCI, or brain-computer interface, particularly in the field of prosthetic management for the handicapped. The Brazilian Eduardo Miranda has used visually stimulated brain waves to compose music. In other words, I see human intelligence both being created in and transferred to a non-hydrocarbon life form. I see a capability to do nothing less than download, upload, or offload our minds. I see the advent of what has been called *Homo cyber*."

I must confess that I began my inner rebuttal long before Father O'Gould finished his disquisition. More like *Homo cipher*, I groused in denial even as what he said gained my reluctant credence. At the same time, I'm not sure I grasped just how proximate and credible the Jesuit's prognostications were until he began to outline what he called the "necessary circumstances" for on-line consciousness.

At the lectern, letting what he had said sink in, he continued, "What has gone unnoticed, though little seems to go unnoticed these days, has been the spontaneous development of a counter-world where a disembodied human mind might not only survive but thrive. I am referring, of course, to the internet. Indeed, the internet, cyberspace, whatever we call it, already exists to the point that the word *virtual* no longer means something less than real.

"I will come back to the internet as a medium for human consciousness in a moment. First, I would like to underscore just how much human activity already crowds into cyberspace. Think of how many of the lives of young people and people not so young that are now grounded in Facebook and other social media. There they indulge, sometimes quite passionately, in what can only be called virtual living. Increasingly, these pages proclaim, 'This is I, this is the real me,' as though the living, breathing person is little more than an adjunct, a pretext, for the creature alive on the screen."

He also recounted how, not long ago, the son of a friend died after a bout with cancer. Remarkably, the friends of the young man continued to send messages to his Facebook page, many of them written as though the deceased were still alive and many of them with pictures of themselves.

"In real terms, the internet already accounts for a good deal of non-virtual life. Today's economy is unimaginable without the internet. Aside from commerce, a good deal of our wealth resides in binary form. If you invest in gold, a truck doesn't back up to your door and unload carefully packed ingots of the stuff. Indeed, you won't even get paper certificates unless you ask for them.

"Key parts of our infrastructure would collapse if the internet were to suddenly cease. Our power grids, communications networks, and defense systems would no longer function. As such, nations are gearing up, not to fight with guns and other weapons, but in cyberspace. Because to shut down a nation's internet is to shut down that nation."

He paused, gave us one of his shy smiles and continued. "The question begged, of course, is whether the internet would be a suitable home for the human mind, not to mention the human heart and the human soul. Well, for starters, there would be much to do in this semi-ethereal state. You could listen to music, watch old movies, play games, travel, and even make money. Indeed, I would argue that there would be wealth, perhaps even social and economic classes in this new virtual state. People with sufficient resources will be able to have themselves beamed up to the moon to the Mars Rover for a ride around. In terms of space exploration, we will not need to find water or oxygen. All we will need to find is energy and the universe pulsates with energy. We will be able to study endlessly at virtual universities. On-line gambling already exists. But how about getting a little tipsy on virtual whiskey? How will we see, how will we hear, you ask. But consider the billions of video lenses and microphones already in existence and more and more of them linked in.

"We will look back upon this crude, hydrocarbon existence from the distance and proximity of cyberspace with awe and horror. Imagine having to breathe constantly. Not to mention ingestion, elimination, disease, and death. How could people have lived like that?

"On the dark side, there will be crime. As long as free will exists, there will be evil. Disease will persist as well. After all, viruses already abound in this new sphere. There will be hacking, harassment, theft, and perhaps even murder. But only perhaps. While it is difficult to imagine human life without murder, we may be able to transcend that as there will be plenty of provision to make back-up copies of ourselves. Which would not rule out death. Suicide would still be available.

"What will happen to the family? What will happen to love? What will happen to procreation? All good questions and I won't pretend to have answers for them. Curiosity will persist. And there will remain, deep down, the search for God and the sacred. And, surely there will be governance, which means there will be politics. There will be parties, votes. Who knows, perhaps someone will set up a monarchy. There will be taxes. You may escape death but you will never escape taxes. Will there be achievement, striving, pleasure, athletic contests, heartache? More than likely. Will everybody be the same? I doubt it. Cultural values and perhaps prejudice will still play a role.

"It won't happen overnight. It may start out as a kind of game. Plug in, turn on, and drop out. I imagine that at first individuals will switch back and forth between their flesh-and-blood selves and their cybernetic selves. More and more of us will opt in, will choose the relative eternity of a solar-powered internet over the certain decay and death of our hydro-carbon existence. If there is a widespread conversion, a kind of cyber rapture might well ensue."

Again, the shy, Irish smile. "I can envision a scene where ordinary mortals come across a body kept in animated suspension inside a special maintenance bag. Whose body is this? Jack Jackson's. He's gone on line. When's he coming back? Don't know. His maintenance contract ran out two weeks ago. I've been trying to contact him. Well, keep trying."

I wasn't amused. I was suddenly conscious of a vast, growing alien life form of our own creation right in our midst. At our fingertips. At our voice command. As so often happens, the aliens we fear turn out to be ourselves. Suddenly it seemed we were destined to become electronic ghosts, wisps, sprites that you could hear whirring in the air of the old, fading world. What would happen to those of us who will not want to "convert" to the cyber form of life? You try it and don't want it. What happens to them? They simply die out? I know there are too many of us. I know we are messing up the planet, that we are making it inhospitable for other life forms. But I did not want to let go.

As though reading my thoughts, Father O'Gould went on, "Depending on how quickly the "conversion" takes place, the natural world should benefit greatly with a much reduced human population still in hydrocarbon form.

"Over time, these on-line beings will no doubt be obsessed with their roots, the fleshy chrysalis from which they evolved. And while they may denigrate those obsolete, doomed, crude entities known as human beings, they will be fascinated by us. They will exclaim to one another about the conditions under which we live."

But, Father O'Gould, I wanted to protest, isn't that exactly what makes life precious? The fact that we cannot take it for granted. That we have to struggle, but that there is joy and fulfillment in that struggle.

The good father was saying, "Before any of this happens, of course, technology and philosophy will have to solve the bottomless conundrum of exactly what it is that constitutes consciousness as the basis of every individual human life and identity.

"Where, finally, does God fit into all of this? May I risk heresy and venture that we, through those divine sparks of intelligence and consciousness, of curiosity and creativity, are destined to inhabit the known and unknown universe? That we will become God."

Or will we be a form of pollution? I wondered.

He concluded by saying that "It is through technology that God, which is the evolving universe and everything in it, will create the immortal soul, giving everlasting life, virtually, to an ancient belief. And whether one spends this new eternity in heaven or in hell will depend, as it always has, on how one acts towards others because there will be, perhaps more than ever, free will."

At the reception afterwards, sipping wine from a plastic glass, I found myself amazed and then increasing appalled by the good father's vision. I felt a deep, atavistic threat. This too, too solid flesh no longer seemed very solid. Even so, I approached the author, my friend, and gave him a copy of the book to sign. At the same time, I said, "But, Steve, What about achievement, striving, pleasure, sadness, madness, love, hate, envy, despair?"

He looked up at me thoughtfully, his pen poised. "I know what you're thinking, Norman. Remember, I am not advocating so much as reporting. I can only hope that, despite everything, we will remain human in that deep, existential sense, at least to the extent we wish."

His response did little to mollify my angst. Driving home, I remained filled with a subtle, pervasive, creeping horror. I could hear all the arguments. Consciousness is consciousness. Who cares whether you, that thing inside your head, exists in cyber-space or fastened to a dying animal?

Would you even be safe in death? Or will they, whoever they are, with a bit of DNA and whatever record of your consciousness you left behind, these words, for instance, be able to reconstitute your mind and soul? And thereby imprison you forever in their cyber vortex?

I was conflicted as well. Because, from a conservationist's point of view, fewer actual people would relieve the pressure on the biosphere. There would be a good deal less of the planet devoted to farming, for instance, not to mention mining and manufacturing. As Alphus so eloquently puts it, we are messing up our blue-green home; we are making it inhospitable for other life forms. But... There was so many buts.

Above all, the Jesuit's prognostications left me aching for that most piquant and palpable expression of our physicality. I wanted to achieve that culmination of sensation that I know no consciousness blinking inside a gadget could ever experience. My desire sprang not only from love and hormones, but from an impulse I can only describe as metaphysical. I drove homeward, in other words, with every intention of seducing my young wife.

It was still not too late. I pulled into a shopping mall and bought a dozen red roses at a supermarket. I pictured a glass of wine as we sat on the couch together murmuring the kind of sweet nothings that are everything to the purpose.

I came into the house as noiselessly as I could. I quietly uncorked a bottle of decent Merlot and left it to breathe. I set the flowers in a vase. I contemplated starting a fire in the fireplace. All the while I gloated just a bit that no on-line wise guy could ever do this. Upstairs, I could hear voices coming from the small room in the turret that Alphus had occupied. Diantha had reclaimed it as a study and yoga space. Having set the scene below, I softly mounted the stairs.

At the threshold, I stopped and peered through the half-open door. Diantha, in black leotard and hooded sweatshirt, earphones and hand mike, sat in front of her opened laptop gazing intently at the screen. I heard her say, "But Jason hasn't been told yet." Then, "He said he is the message." Then, "I don't think the parallel will work." A moment later she took a deep breath, turned, and noticed me in the doorway.

"Norman…"

"Diantha…"

"I've only got a minute. I'm live again in two minutes."

"What are you doing?"

"It's an on-line play, but in real time. I'm doing a read-through audition sort of."

"What's it called?"

"*Binaries*. I think I've got a real chance. But I'll be a while. Could you check the kids?"

I nodded and watched as she turned back to the glowing screen, her face intent and quite, quite beautiful. With a silent sigh, I retreated down the stairs. I recorked the Merlot. I contemplated the making of a martini. But then gin under these circumstances is more of a dead-end than an escape.

33

I confess to second thoughts about asking Alphus to accompany me to the Pink Shamrock for the meeting with the investigating authorities, with Professor Finn, and with the two suspects. Commander Morgliesh was to arrange to have Patrick Fortese and Ivan Samka there to question them about any involvement by them in the attempts on my life. I hesitated about including Alphus as I feared he would be a distracting presence. On the other hand, my primate friend has an infallible nose for mendacity, a faculty that could prove very helpful in determining who had hired Blackie Burker to shoot at me on that memorable afternoon.

My doubts soon vanished. I had scarcely pulled up in my coughing Renault when Alphus, comfortably attired in windbreaker and Bermuda jeans, came down from his eyrie on the outside, swinging with simian grace from specially designed bars protruding from the timbered frame. He gave me his grimace of a smile along with a pawshake, got in, and dutifully fastened his seatbelt. On the drive to the Shamrock, I instructed him on what to watch for. The procedure would be fairly straight-forward according to the commander, I told him, but I remained in the dark as to details.

The snug at the Pink Shamrock is a room set off from the rest of the pub where, judging from its size, a small group could get away from the noise of the bar and restaurant to make noise of their own. I remember it as being cozy and roomy at the same time, its woodwork darkened with age, a sizable table with padded banquettes on two sides, and comfortable chairs pulled up or set against the wainscoting. A serving hatch with a tray-sized shelf connected to the back bar and a framed lithograph of a horse and jockey from long ago at Longchamp hung on the wall between it and the door from the main bar. The shades on the two windows behind the banquettes were usually drawn as the view, the parking lot of a nearby supermarket, did not inspire.

So, thither did Alphus and I proceed, my having reserved it earlier and at the same time received permission to bring my friend along as an emotional support animal. It is a ruse I have used before in securing him access to restricted venues, but valid enough on this occasion as I was in a state of some agitation. My mood was echoed by an afternoon chill that had set in under an uncertain sky with the promise of snow. I parked the car, and Alphus and I walked in the direction of St. Patrick's symbol of the Trinity -- the shamrock -- pulsating in luminous pink on a hanging sign outside the pub.

We were the first to arrive. I sat on the end of one of the banquettes while Alphus, kitty corner to me, took a chair, his hairy lower legs and prehensile feet, clad in special shoes, not quite reaching the floor. Through the serving hatch, a Dutch door with a shelf into the back bar, I ordered a pale ale while Alphus had a small glass of sherry.

"Cheers," I said, lifting my ale when it arrived. He gave me a thumbs up and sipped from his glass.

Shortly afterwards, we were joined by Lieutenant Tracy and Detective Lupien, both of whom I had briefed as to the proceedings, including Alphus' attendance. To judge from their wry looks, I'm not sure how seriously they took the meeting but, significantly, they ordered non-alcoholic drinks. It didn't take long for the state police detective to warm to Alphus who signed small talk congenially while I translated. I alerted them to Alphus' role as a breathing and very reliable lie-detector machine.

We were thus occupied when Commander Morgliesh arrived with Professor Finn in tow. Introductions all around, everyone easy enough, though the professor, tugging at the lapels of his thread-worn coat, gaped at Alphus. He availed himself of a brandy and ginger ale. The commander, urbane in a hacking jacket, white shirt and club tie, asked for a scotch and soda, no ice, from the aproned barman who had come in to take orders.

At this point, I should explain the seating arrangement as it has a bearing on what was to transpire. Picture a room perhaps fifteen by twelve feet. The table, approximately five by eight feet, sets in the corner diagonally across from the door opening into the bar proper. Once we had introduced ourselves and shuffled around, Lieutenant Tracy ended up on the banquette next to me with Detective Lupien kitty corner under the picture of the horse and jockey. Commander Morgliesh sat on a chair near the open area next to the door. Professor Finn, clearly distressed, sat beside him.

"Shall I call this meeting to order?" asked the commander, placing a box and a folder on the table in front of him and glancing around at us.

"Where are our two suspects?" I asked. "I was under the impression that messieurs Fortese and Samka were to join us."

"Indeed," The commander smiled enigmatically. "But I don't think that will be necessary. I've been digging around and come up with some answers concerning those gentlemen."

The other two officers looked at him with surprise. "So let us in on what you've found," said Lieutenant Tracy.

The commander sipped his whiskey. "I still miss not having a smoke when I drink. But, to business." He took us in with a glance both intense and benign. "As we may have discussed, one Patrick Fortese is currently resident in Seaboard, living in an in-law apartment that is part of the house of Dr. Fortese and her family."

He slid a glossy black and white photo from his file across to me. I heard him say that the man was out on parole, one condition of which stipulates that he remains under the supervision of his cousin.

I started with amazement. "This is the guy who's been stalking me." I spoke with unabashed indignation. "He was at your reading. I flushed him out. He was at the theater the night that... He was in the parking lot... "

"He's employed by the buildings and grounds department at Wainscott."

"But how did you... track him down."

"Old-fashioned police work, dear Watson."

"But surely Carmina Fortese has nothing to do with this."

She doesn't. I don't think Patrick's activities necessarily implicate the professor."

"And why not?"

"Consider. Patrick drops in for dinner with his attractive cousin and her husband. In the course of the evening she complains bitterly about you and how you're holding up a critical step in her path to fame and fortune. Patrick listens attentively and sympathetically. How can I help? he asks himself. He reverts to his old ways. He knows people who know people. Though not the brightest bulb on the tree, he harkens to the American ethos to think for himself. He takes the initiative."

"Amazing," I muttered, handing the photo back.

"But he didn't hire Blackie Burker to take pot shots at you."

We all looked at him quizzically.

"Consider again," the commander went on, a touch impatient, as though a cigarette would help. "Patrick works for buildings and grounds. Where would he get the ten thousand down payment to hire Blackie Burker? More like twenty thousand all told. And, remember that Mr. Burker was not one to neglect collecting what was owed him"

"So...?" I began.

The commander smiled. "Patrick wanted to intimidate you by stalking you, especially when he learned you had been shot at. In the dim reaches of his mind, he connected the shooting and your refusal to sign off on the Rechronnex contract. He wanted to up the ante, as Americans say."

"I'll be damned," I allowed myself. Then, "Okay, but what about Ivan Samka?"

"You were right, Norman, in identifying him as the person who nearly ran you over in a Humvee. But, again, it had nothing to do with the shooting at the lake."

"Then what was that about?" Lieutenant Tracy looked and sounded skeptical.

The commander lifted his drink and considered. "I brought it up with Victor. It was indeed Ivan Samka that nearly ran Norman over. But Victor assured me that it was purely coincidental.

He told me that Ivan bullies cyclists on the road when he's driving, especially when they get in the way. He's from the old country where bicycles are not esteemed."

As I listened, it occurred to me that this was like one of those crime novels in which the canny sleuth, in this case Commander Morgliesh of Scotland Yard, lists and dismisses the suspects one by one until, with ingenious logic, in the best Sherlockian manner, the culprit is revealed. But in this case, the good Scotland Yarder had only two suspects and I found it more disturbing than gratifying that he could discount both of them so readily.

"Then who?" I asked with an edge of annoyance.

"I agree, what is this meeting all about?" The imperturbable Detective Lupien showed signs of impatience.

"Patience, gentlemen, patience." The commander glanced at his watch. "Any minute now unless all my instincts are wrong."

A moment later, as though on cue, the door from the bar opened and, as the alert reader has no doubt surmised by now, Ivor Pavonine made his entrance. He did it with a flourish, a pale scarf looped around his neck Oscar Wilde fashion and his trench coat draped over his shoulders like a cloak. He paused to take in the scene or, more likely, to his shining eyes, the *mise en scène.*

With great aplomb, he said, "Commander, good to see you again. And how is your charming wife? Please give her my regards."

"She's fine, thank you."

"My, my, but this is quite a convocation you've arranged," He remained standing, creating around himself a stage of sorts, however small. He took us in turn. "I know the good Alphus from that memorable party. And Norman, of course. And…"

"I think you know Professor Finn," the commander more stated than suggested.

"Of course, our little professor *manqué.* No offense meant, Professor. We are all impostors in the end. And the other two gentlemen. They strike me as members of the constabulary, plain clothes detectives perhaps?

Detective Lupien nodded and spoke his name and rank. Lieutenant Tracy did the same.

"Nice to meet you both. And I mean no disparagement mentioning your plain clothes. Lots of policemen dress very well." He gave his little whinny. "So what do we do now, Commander? Are you going to interrogate me? Grill me? Good cop, bad cop? A whole subgenre of the theatrical, all but Socratic."

"You might think of it as an audition."

"Oh, but I love auditions! Talk about *cinéma vérité*. He twirled a bit and a malign smile lit his face. "I mean the people who are too real always get rejected."

"Would you like to sit down?"

"Oh, do let me have my hour upon the stage."

"Ten minutes should do it," said Lieutenant Tracy.

The commander nodded at Ivor. "You're on."

"I am indeed. And such a very select audience in what, a theater in the square."

"Or a courtroom," Detective Lupien offered.

Ivor Pavonine beamed with delight. "Yes, yes. This is a courtroom drama, is it not? And, as I've remarked before, courtrooms are a living stage filled with real life drama."

Mildly, the commander said, "We won't take much more of your time, Mr. Pavonine."

"*Mr.* Pavonine? *Mr...* ? No, it's exactly the right note. Don't change a thing. Please ignore me. I am used to directing."

The commander bowed. "Mr. Pavonine, would you be so good as to exchange a few lines with Professor Finn?" He produced a wig from the box he had placed on the table. "And would you be so kind as to wear this for us?"

"A prop! Oh, but I love props. We all need them, do we not, whether on stage or in life. They come in all sizes and shapes. Think of the furniture and furnishing in the living rooms and bedrooms and offices where we stage our lives, all filled with props. The doubtful Picasso sketch in the living room is but a prop, propping us up, so to speak. But, of course, the most important props for you are each other as right now. And, all of you gathered here are my props."

He clapped his hands and with a gesture a bit overdone, he took the wig and held it as though it were Yorick's skull. "Oh, this is too rich, too rich."

"And your lines, sir." The commander held out a clipboard.

"My lines?"

"Just read them," I said.

He turned to me. "I admit nothing, Norman, only that I am an artist of the real and that the world is my stage." He put the wig on. He stooped and picked up the clipboard and walked back and forth, reading silently as he went. Then, "Brilliant, Commander, brilliant."

"Will it be necessary, Mr. Pavonine, to proceed?"

"But of course. We all know how *Othello* ends, but we stay to the curtain, do we not? And why spoil what is nothing less than a coup *de théatre formidable*? No, the show must go on."

"As you wish."

Detective Lupien leaned over to me and whispered, "That's our man."

The lieutenant nodded his agreement. "But let's let him strut and fret for a while."

I was amazed. Ivor? I knew he was a borderline nut case, perhaps one of the mentally walking wounded. But someone who would arrange to have me shot?

The professor said, "This gentleman fits the role exactly."

"Even without a run through?" The commander did not appear surprised.

The prime suspect shook his head. "No, I insist. We must speak our lines." He paused and then he began, "'Mind if I sit down?'"

The Professor merely scowled at him. Then, lamely, "'Not at all. What can I do for you?'"

The bewigged actor checked his audience. "'I was told you knew someone who could fix my Porsche.'"

"'And what's wrong with your car?'"

"'The clutch. But it could use a complete overhaul.'"

"'I see.'"

"'I was told you would know just the man I need.'"

The Professor pushed his chair back and stood up abruptly. "This is the guy. I refuse to participate any further. I want to go home."

Ivor Pavonine laughed without mirth. "Oh, this is good. Always loved improv. The very essence of life, is it not, improvising from hour to hour, day to day. Most people improvise their whole lives. What to say next? So let me applaud. Such spontaneity. Clap, clap."

"Hold on, sir" said Detective Lupien to Professor Finn, who was heading for the door. "I think the FBI will have some questions to ask you."

The professor looked accusingly at the commander. "You promised me, you…"

"But, Professor, I was in no position to promise you anything."

The professor visibly fumed. "Christ, never trust an Englishman."

Ivor Pavonine, taking it all it, said, "This is wonderful, wonderful. Norman, how can I ever thank you… This is the very pinnacle of my life's work. Theater has never been this real."

My right hand fisted, I snarled, "You hired that man to kill me?"

"Not to kill you, Norman. On my honor, I told Mr. Burker only to wing you, to wound you superficially… He agreed and charged me extra for it."

"You fool, he shot at my head." I was angry enough for violence. "He tried to kill me."

"Yes, and death is such a trite device. Much too over used."

"But why, why?" I asked, thinking there might be an answer even from this demented creature.

With another dramatic gesture, he turned with thespian deliberation and, facing his sparse audience, spoke as in a soliloquy. "Because, Norman, you are the leading man, the star of your own life, the very exemplar of life is art is life. I was merely toying with the script, helping to direct. You were at a point in the drama of your existence when you needed a challenge."

He smiled, he preened, he went on. "I'm glad he missed you, Norman. He didn't realize that he was in the service of art. Oh, and this dénouement, on however modest a stage... it's too right, too right. The Bard said it best as always, it's a tale told by an idiot full of..."

"Then you admit it," Detective Lupien said, interrupting him.

"Admit? Nay, I proclaim, I claim... I was the author of it all."

"Easy, Norman, Lieutenant Tracy said, putting a reassuring and restraining hand on my shoulder.

"Of course, I did. As a work of art, your life needed touching up a bit, Norman. We cannot be products just of ourselves. Every life is a collaborative effort."

"You're mad... "

"With the madness of genius."

I had no words to damn him with. I sat there fuming, half ready to take out the Glock and shoot him in the heart. He kept talking like some wound-up, life-sized, malignant doll.

"Oh, come, come, Norman, I never meant to have you murdered. It would have been premature. No, I am an artist, one whose whole life has been a work of art. I am my own most exquisite creation and everything I do is artistic, especially your murder which I have orchestrated like the maestro I am. Most of all, I wanted you to experience the essence of murder. Which, of course, is the dread anticipation that it inspires, the terror of feeling that violent death could be around the next corner. How few people these days ever get that privilege? Even terminal cancer patients drowse out their last days in a drug-induced stupor. But you, you, the great, the renowned Norman de Ratour would know and know keenly what it was to live your life second to second."

I admit we all sat there just a bit spellbound. What he said made a kind of savage sense even as it bordered on lunacy. And then, of a sudden, it crossed the line into actual madness that only in retrospect appeared inevitable. Because, in a matter of fact way, the way someone might move a chair or pick up the phone, he produced a revolver from under his sweater and pointed it at me. "The drama isn't over, Norman. Not by a long shot. Or a short shot."

"Put the gun down, Mr. Pavonine." Lieutenant Tracy had his own weapon out and pointing at the man.

"Wonderful, wonderful," Ivor Pavonine said, his eyes ablaze with demonic glee. "Oh, to be shot on stage. To die on stage." He gave his laugh. "Life is one long audition, is it not, for the role of corpse? Ha, that's the part we all get to play. I think that's rather good, as your perceptive wife would say, Commander."

"I will shoot," the lieutenant said.

"Not yet, not yet," the mad man pleaded. Let me have my few words." And with that fished out of his pocket a sheaf of crumbled paper. "To wit... Ah, here we are. Attend! The pleasure of murder..." He paused to see if we were all listening. Then, "The pleasure of murder derives from the keen, atavistic pleasure of power, of having the ultimate power over another human being, human beings being the most real thing in the world. Are they not? I almost want to be the victim. I would like to tell those against whose temple I held the barrel of a cocked pistol to savor the moment yourself, in this case you, Norman, as billions have done so vicariously over the centuries. Savor the moment before the stupendous reality of nothingness. Murder. Murder! It's in our genes, is it not, hunting and being hunted. It's what makes us uniquely human. No other species spends so much time and ingenuity relentlessly killing its own. Men especially love war. They love killing, else why would they do so much of it? But I am speaking of individual murder now. And the perfect murder, aesthetically speaking, occurs when the murderer and murdered collaborate, even change roles so that the hunter becomes the hunted and vice versa. Because never is life so keen as when you are about to kill or be killed."

At those words, with a swift, subtle movement, Alphus stood and interposed himself between me and Ivor Pavonine.

"Marvelous! Best yet!" the demented man said with a wild look around him. "And he's signing at me. Oh, oh, the silent screen. Please, sir, give us Hamlet's to be or not to be in dumb show."

Then, directly to me, "Have you noticed my weapon? It's as close as I could get to your own Smith & Wesson. It's no stage prop, Norman, it's real." Then, "Oh, come on, Norman, hiding behind an ape. It doesn't become you."

In fact, he had a clear shot at my head and my upper chest. Not that I was going to remind him of it.

As he raved on, Alphus edged imperceptibly closer to him.

"Don't come any closer," Ivor Pavonine said, his voice ecstatic. "Remember, animals are a lot easier to shoot than people."

For what seemed like a long moment, we were all still, as though part of a tableau, as in a film, when the frame freezes. Then Alphus was moving, toward me, not toward Pavonine, and the lieutenant was saying something loudly. Then came the noise of the gun and a thumping blow to the upper left part of my chest. With a shock of amazed credulity I knew that I had been shot. Amidst the scuffle and shouts, I began to lose consciousness and could think only of Diantha and the children with the most tender love and regret while in a sidereal thought as to a distant star, I faced the coming of that good night with a wistful, darkening haze of poignant gratitude for what life I had been granted. Then nothing.

34

So I died, but on the third day... I blaspheme. Of course, I didn't die as the dead do not get to tell how they died. It was the next morning when Diantha's face hovered above mine as, through a clearing haze, she came into focus.

"Norman, oh, Norman, you're back, you're going to be okay." And stopped to dab at her tears, one of which fell like a blessing on my nose.

"What happened?" I asked in a kind of a croak, my voice like the rest of me emerging from the depths of a bad dream in which the fragments of memory were jumbled together with pieces missing or dropped on the floor. "In the snug," I said, at sea but canny enough to dissemble my confusion. The real pain of madness, as someone once told me, is knowing that you are mad.

"You were shot," she said, the reality in words making her catch her breath.

"In the snug," I managed again, the nightmare resolving into the reality of memory, the pieces, or some of them, fitting into place as in a jigsaw puzzle, the borders easier with the amoeba shapes having a straight-edge.

"Don't try to talk." Diantha had composed herself and in that I found reassurance and the courage to remember, that is re-live, the attempt on my life. No more puzzle but a painfully detailed cinematic re-run. Ivor Pavonine on the pathetic stage of his life soliloquizing about the art of murder. Quite good some of it. Then the gun. I flinched inwardly at the memory of that sequence. I turned away from it.

"Was anyone else hurt?"

Diantha was holding my hand. She kept her face brave. She said, "Alphus tried to shield you." She laughed with an edge of hysteria, the laughing kind. "The bullet went through his ear, you know, the part that protrudes."

I nearly wanted to cry with gratitude. What a guy. "But he's okay?"

"He's fine."

"And the children?" With that word the pain and relief of normalization began.

"They're fine. They send their love. Norman, you have to rest."

"I need to get my clothes and book myself out of here."

"No, you're not. That bullet missed your heart by inches."

She sniffled again with retrospective horror. Then got wife-ly, God bless her. "No, you need to get better. You need to rest and let them take care of you."

And, truth be told, it did hurt in a creaking way when I tried to sit up.

"Please," she murmured and stifled tears. Then bent to kiss me on the lips. "I love you and I need you to get better. We have a lot of living to do."

As in a movie, a nurse, as though cued and evincing the starched authority of her uniform, came in and stood next to Diantha, her smile of a piece with her perky cap. "Well, Mr. Detour," she chirped with that professional cheeriness people use for children, the old, the sick and the dying, "how are we feeling today?"

"We are feeling much better, thank you," I royaled her back.

But better than what I didn't know. I managed a grimace of a smile. I did not have the energy for annoyance. The nurse looked at various dials and adjusted the tubes and medical gear attached to me. Diantha stood, blew me a kiss, and left. Then I was alone, hazing and dazing until, as on an outgoing tide, I drifted off.

The problem with having a retentive memory is that you can retain too much. Thus, upon awakening later and sipping what passed for tea, the billions of dormant synapses in my brain began firing again. The bits of the puzzle not only snapped into place but brightened into three-dimensional life with lights, camera, action. All I needed was background music, perhaps something somber

296

by Shostakovich. But none of the events returned in order, more like vivid highlights, especially the gun pointing at my heart and the gooseberry green of the madman's eyes as he sentenced me to death, an artful death to be sure, in which (he was right!) the despair of imminent doom is deepened by the pain of hope.

I suffered the expected impatience of being a patient, patience being one of those virtues that is not its own reward. But, I told myself, I was alive, I was getting better, stronger by the day, besides which fact the indignities of the bedpan and the awful baby gruel giving way to the farce of hospital fare was of little if any consequence. I had too many blessings to count. Diantha came every day of the ten days before I was released on parole. Commander Morgliesh somehow contrived to get Alphus in for a visit. My hairy friend appeared happy despite having to wear a mask and the bandages over his ear.

Then I was free, walking with Diantha, my dignity restored by comfortable slacks, turtleneck, sneakers, and my old windbreaker. My precious, intact heart beat with joy. The very air breathed like an elixir of life and the light, oh, the light, the day being sunny, spangled my eyes. Take it easy, the various good doctors had advised. Easy. I had all eternity to take it easy. I wanted, as the Irish bard has it in one of his poems, to eat the day. But of course, I lay down when we got home and after I had been with the children.

35

One's body is a wonderful miracle of life when one thinks about it. I mean the way, when it is torn or sliced or broken, it patiently knits itself back together -- with luck and help from the medical arts, of course. So that the puncture wound just below my left clavicle healed itself to wholeness once the bullet had been removed, the blood stanched, and the remarkably small hole in my skin stitched up. Gingerly but after only two weeks, I regained use of my left arm and the palpitations above and in tune with my heart eased to a reasonable throb.

It was, however, still in a sling when I met with Commander Morgliesh in my corner office with the view over Shag Harbor, a view he stood taking in for a few moments with a wistfulness I think was a longing to be back in England. Then, Doreen having brought in coffee and the door closed, we settled down to what the Scotland Yarder called a recap.

I'm not sure I've adequately described the prepossessing air that the man has about him. It combines cordiality and a manifestation of competence that is all but irresistible. After we had finished a few minutes of small talk about people we knew and immediate plans, I asked him straight out, "How did you know?"

"The night of your dinner party," he said at length. "It didn't register at first, but I thought it more than strange the way he went out of his way to cause you and Diantha pain. He positively reveled in it. Of course, he didn't see it as that. The man is seriously deficient in what might be called the moral faculty. He saw it as living theater meaning, that in his twisted mind, reality and make-believe are one and the same. It was then that I realized he was among the barking mad. He simply had no idea of the distress he was causing Diantha and, through her, you."

"Still..."

"Exactly. A long shot until..."

I tried not to show that I was on the edge of my seat the way his "until" lingered in the air as he sipped his coffee. Then, "I might have missed his direct involvement were it not for an idea that came to me as I was going over my notes a week or so before the meeting in the snug. I kept coming back to the name Stan Magee, you know, the character pretending to want his car repaired. An alias, no doubt. But it or something quite like it had been nagging at me. Then, in a stroke it came to me. Stan Magee is an anagram for 'stage name.'"

"That's still kind of thin," I said.

"Exactly. I kept digging. Do you remember the phone number the professor gave us in the bar?"

"Of course. It was no longer in use."

"Indeed. But no longer in use by whom?"

I was impressed mostly, I think, because I hadn't thought to ask that basic question. "And?" I prompted.

"It turns out that some cancelled numbers all but disappear. They enter a great cyber wastebasket and become difficult to retrieve. I was, of course, in over my head, so I turned to Nigel."

"Nigel?"

"Nigel's my thirteen-year-old grandson. He's forgotten more about computers than I'll ever know. Anyway, he set to work, off and on, on and off. The number, of course, was one of trillions out there in the cybersphere. But Nigel is a persistent lad. He came up with a reference to it on a discontinued Facebook site of one Susanna Richards. Nigel e-mailed me that it looked like a dead-end. But he persisted and was able to dig out a reference to a group calling itself The Living Proscenium."

I gave an involuntarily "Oh, Christ."

"You've heard of it?"

"Yes, yes, they did all kinds of theatrical things on line."

"Well, I told Nigel to keep plugging. He didn't come up with much else except that one of the founders goes or went by the name of the White Peacock."

Under my breath, like a curse, I said, "Ivor Pavonine."

"Exactly. And there's more. "Lieutenant Tracy was kind enough to take me along when they searched Pavonine's apartment on Harbor Point. We found a thick file on one N. A. Ratour...

"Norman Abbot de Ratour."

"The very man. And I would say he perhaps knew more about you than you know or remember about yourself. He appears particularly impressed about how you killed the notorious Freddie Bain. And not just newspaper clippings, but downloads of news broadcasts and interviews you gave."

"A kind of demented fan, you might say?"

"I'm afraid that was a pose." He paused, glanced out at the view. "Are you ready for this?"

"That depends on what this is."

The commander leaned into me. He had the expression of someone resisting a grin. "It turns out, Norman, that Ivor's real name is Dimitri Bannerhoff. He is Freddie Bain's illegitimate son."

I slapped my forehead with the palm of my hand and left it there. "Of course! Of course. The damn fool kept reminding me every time I met him of someone I had known. But the irritation of being around him was such I couldn't make the connection."

Now the commander let his smile out, but kept it just a bit sardonic. "It seems that Freddie not only recognized Dimitri as his son but set up a sizable off-shore trust for him on the stipulation that he keep his surname. Strange for someone who had so many names."

"Shades of Hamlet," I murmured, still chagrined at myself for not making the connection.

"Only shades. Let's be brutally honest, Norman, the man let hate pervert his mind and character and whatever talents he had. Evil genius may be too grand a term, but he did use his exceptional mind and talents to make your murder into what might be loosely called performance art. In doing so, he fused the silly notion that artists are free to do anything as long as, as in this case, it has the trapping of art. Not that the word in these circumstances has any meaning. Add to that delusions of grandeur as an artist and the license granted therein and you have…"

"A nut case."

He laughed, paused and went on, "It's a notional cliché that creativity and madness are closely intertwined. Nonsense, of course. Shakespeare and many other great artists were astute businessmen. But in his jumbled mind, Ivor confused art with reality…"

"And art, however intense or transporting, is but a part of reality," I said, interrupting him.

"Yes," he answered, musing. "In Ivor's case, he confused people with puppets. If Punch punches Judy, it's of no great consequence, but if Punch, a real bloke, punches Judy, a real lady, the reality of the law comes into play. He never made that connection. But enough of this psychobabble. Show me around your marvelous museum and then I'll take you to lunch if you're free."

36

It is spring at last and I have come to the cottage to vanquish the demons still lurking here and to finish trimming the apple trees, a job I was doing when so rudely interrupted by the late Mr. Burker. I would have ventured out earlier, but in the wake of these dark happenings, I had been afflicted by a low-grade depression that persisted through a dark, cold winter.

But things of late have been going well. Indeed, I have enjoyed such a spate of good fortune that I suffer from a form of anxiety that the psychiatric industry might well label anxiety-deficit disorder. I jest, of course, but not entirely. With each passing day, the sun grows brighter and ever warmer. And when I get glimpses between distant clouds of a pale blue-green sky, my heart lurches with an ache I cannot fathom. I await with trepidation the beauty of spring, too conscious of how ephemeral it is, of how the lilacs, cherries, forsythia, laurels, jonquils and tulips blossom, dazzle the eye, touch the heart, and then are gone, as though forever. It's a reminder that they will be gone forever one of these days, at least where I'm concerned.

Some good has come out of the events of last summer and autumn. As a result of all the publicity, Diantha has not only been taken on by a diligent agent, but has landed a part in a gritty crime thriller set in blue-collar Boston. It has lots of terse, meaningful dialogue and a plot that, involving heists, drugs, and several varieties of homicide, explores the dark side of human nature. Or that's what she tells me. I have no objections. Indeed, I like to think that I encourage her. My only real objection is to the occasional mouth-sucking kisses so favored by Hollywood that she must indulge with her "love interest," a brawny type with a lot of hair and the jawbone of a horse.

Diantha has maintained her connection with the Little Theater. It continues to thrive, due in part to the fact that Alice Talty has had some luck with an effective divorce lawyer.

The author of much of this recent mayhem, Dimitri Banner-off, AKA Ivor Pavonine, has been confined, perhaps indefinitely, at an institution for the criminally insane or the insanely criminal, I'm not sure which. Despite valiant efforts by his defense counsel, Dimitri persisted in turning his court appearances into what he called "living theater," standing to cue the judge, the attorneys and even the various kinds of officers who shuffled in and out with documents. "But, your honor, this is real. You are the director. I am the star, of course, but we all have our roles to play." On another occasion, he told the judge that this was life as art as life par excellence and that if she would but listen to him, she would know that daily her life and those of the characters around her constitute living theater.

Subsequent institutionalization in his present quarters where evaluation is on-going appears to suit him to a tee. He writes regularly to Diantha. It seems he has formed an acting troop among his fellow inmates. "We are all writing and staging our own plays," he said in one missive. "This is where it's happening. This is the future of theater because here, minute to minute, day to day, life is drama. The characters/people cannot be imagined. One of the guests claims to be a stallion that won the Kentucky Derby. He had been going around accosting women and asking a lot of money for stud fees. He has a wonderful, convincing whinny. We've improvised a training paddock for him in the exercise yard, but there are no mares around for him to cover."

On a more positive note, the Union of Concerned Bankers has finally come through with the award money they posted for the rescue of the three kidnapped men. Felix, God bless him, sent their lawyers a letter mentioning the possibility of a $100 million damage suit for breach of contract, emotional agony, and the like. When they tried to bargain, he upped the amount of the suit to two hundred and fifty million. "You see, Norman," he told me with his sly smile, "these guys are used to numbers like that.

To them it's real. And after a while, ten million starts to look like a pittance."

I am now an unofficial consultant to Augustein Enterprises as it moves forward with development of Hobbes Landing on Ile de Grand Cochon. It's been scaled back to the point where much of the island will be set aside as a nature preserve. There has been some talk about preserving the bunker where the kidnapped men were entombed -- as a tourist destination. And, of course, rumors abound about making a movie based on the incident -- the kidnapping itself, the imprisonment, the families, and then the rescue.

The Maurice and Simone Augustein Foundation is in negotiations with both the museum and the Center for Criminal Justice to build an underground parking garage that will have spaces reserved for the general public -- at a price. A modest plaque of granite or marble over the entrance will simply have "Augustein" incised on it. Closer to my heart, the couple has generously agreed to endow the museum's extensive collection of Paleolithic coprolites. The bequest includes a senior curatorship in John Murdleston's name.

In short, the largesse has continued to pour in, perhaps more than I might wish, at least where one particular property is concerned. Through his attorneys, I have been informed that Victor Carnovan, AKA Karnivossky, has left the Eigermount and its considerable land to the museum along with a generous endowment and a non-de-acquisition clause of a hundred years. I have, as they say, been hoisted on my own petard. To be blunt about it, what am I to do with the place? Lease it out to mobsters?

Once again Commander Morgliesh came to my rescue with a quite marvelous suggestion: why not make it into a museum of murder? Still, I sighed at the thought. It is one thing to run a museum, it is quite another to start one from scratch. On the other hand, there should be no shortage of material for exhibits. I am told that police departments all over the world have repositories of the sad detritus of homicide -- the knives, guns, bludgeons, as well as the confessions, the crime scene stuff, photographs. We could have a section titled "The Evidence Locker."

I will, of course, form a committee to investigate all possibilities. When I related the commander's suggestion to Felix, he grew quite excited in his enthusiasm. "I mean, think about it, Norman. We could find an old electric chair and set it up in a special display. For an extra fee, visitors could be strapped in and given a little tingle. We'd have to be careful, of course, with the wiring and with all of those attorneys out there looking for work."

It appears that Mr. Carnovan has taken up residence at Austen Abbey in Kent. I recently received a note from him, typed by a secretary, no doubt. He tells me that he is thoroughly enjoying life as an English squire. Commander Morgliesh, through whose good offices the Russian was able to take up residence in England, tells me that he has been subscribing generously to various charities and lobbying quietly for a knighthood. Sir Victor. Wonders never cease.

Alphus has finished his book on the environment. I must say that the endorsements he has received for the cover are quite extraordinary. One eminent conservationist wrote, "At long last we have heard from a species other than our own about what people are doing to a world we all must share. Cogently argued, convincing in its passion, this call to action pulls no punches in demanding of humankind that it do nothing less than clean up its act." I must admit, with not a little envy, that it has best-seller written all over it.

I am glad now to have signed off on the joint venture between the lab and Rechronnex to proceed with the development of Juvenistol. In the final analysis, Father O'Gould's book, *The Future of Eternal Life*, describes a situation more dire than what I gathered from his lecture. What he has explored is nothing less than the next campaign in the on-going cultural wars. It won't be about polygamy or allowing women to play professional football. It won't be about the rise of China and the decline of the West or about radical Islam and everyone else. It will center on the choice between ordinary, hydro-carbon life and a rapidly evolving cybernetic consciousness. For any number of reasons, I am on the side of flesh and blood, mostly, I suppose, because I lack the imagination to conceive of any other way of living.

With some prodding from Alphus, who has become my furry environmental conscience, I was able to secure from the Rechronnex deal considerable support for a human-no-go area in Gabon, a west African nation that has already set aside considerable land for national parks. Alphus has been adamant as to the guarantees and conditions in the initial planning. No overflights. No researchers. No trespass of any kind. A sophisticated armed security system and provisions for expansion in the future. We both see it as a bright spot in the struggle to keep the biosphere from being utterly overrun and degraded by people.

Finally, Diantha and I have seldom been more in love. We are unabashedly smitten with one another and at the same time mindful of the challenges her acting career will present, especially as she prepares to fly back and forth to locations in Boston for "shoots."

As I pen this, we are all out at the cottage together, a crimson bulb of sugared water hangs on the porch as we await the first ruby throat of spring. In the meanwhile, I have much to do in the garden, especially with the espaliered apple trees. As their buds swell preparatory to leafing and blossoming, I find I must clip and prune, push and pull and tie back an exuberance of branching boughs with new twigs if I am to keep things up against the wall.

Made in United States
Orlando, FL
10 February 2022

14671261R00173